S0-AHH-247

Dead Ringer

A RON SHADE AND ALEX ST. JAMES MYSTERY

DEAD RINGER

MICHAEL A. BLACK
& JULIE HYZY

FIVE STAR
A part of Gale, Cengage Learning

Detroit • New York • San Francisco • New Haven, Conn • Waterville, Maine • London

Set in 11 pt. Plantin.

Printed on permanent paper.

LIBRARY OF CONGRESS CATALOGING-IN-PUBLICATION DATA

Black, Michael A., 1949–
Dead ringer : a Ron Shade and Alex St. James mystery / Michael A. Black & Julie Hyzy. — 1st ed.
p. cm.
ISBN-13: 978-1-59414-713-5 (alk. paper)
ISBN-10: 1-59414-713-2 (alk. paper)
1. Shade, Ron (Fictitious character)—Fiction. 2. Private investigators—Illinois—Chicago—Fiction. 3. Chicago (Ill.)—Fiction. I. Hyzy, Julie A. II. Title.
PS3602.L325D43 2008
813′.6—dc22 2008031903

First Edition. First Printing: November 2008.
Published in 2008 in conjunction with Tekno Books and Ed Gorman.

Printed in the United States of America
1 2 3 4 5 6 7 12 11 10 09 08

To the writers who inspire us:
Ray Bradbury
Sue Grafton
John D. MacDonald
Stephen Marlowe
Richard S. Prather
Ken Rand

Chapter 1

Ron Shade

I was back to driving the Beater. The red Pontiac Firebird, with all its bad memories, was history. I only hoped that the guy who'd bought it had better luck with it than I did. It had originally belonged to my first love—who'd been murdered—and given to me as payment for finding her killer. I'd barely driven it a few months when someone, thinking it was me, shot a friend of mine through the window. While all the damage had been repaired, the mental scars remained, and I was happy, finally, to let it go even if it was for much less than it was worth.

Still, for me, things had turned around. Mostly. For a change, my bank account wasn't resting just above empty, and I'd won the World's Heavyweight Kickboxing Championship in the roughest fight of my career a few months back. I was hoping that a nice, lucrative case would come my way to sort of round out my good fortunes. So when a blast from the past, Dick MacKenzie, called me, I figured easy street was going to continue a bit longer. Big Dick, as I loved to call him, worked for Midwestern Olympia Insurance, one of the huge companies that kept me on retainer as an investigator.

And after all, I thought, what could be easier than a routine insurance investigation?

Midwestern Olympia had gone through some problems of its own back a year or so ago, riding the crest of the wave to barely avoid bankruptcy, but now they were back in the black. I'd heard that they'd cut a lot of claims from people in disaster areas and hoped that wasn't the kind of investigation they wanted this time. Dick had worked his way up the corporate ladder and had a nice office in the huge brick building. His secretary wasn't bad, either. She smiled and told me to sit in one of the chairs while she purred into the telephone. When she hung up, she looked up at me and said, "Mr. MacKenzie says he'll be with you in a moment, Mr. Shade."

I nodded and spent the time taking in the scenery. The walls were papered with some kind of design that was supposed to resemble wood. Large pictures, reproductions actually, hung on the opposite wall. Early Norman Rockwell from the looks of them, one depicting an insurance adjustor inspecting a smashed-up car while a young couple stares on anxiously. The guy in the painting didn't remind me of Dick, though. In the painting it looked like the insurance guy really gave a shit.

After about five minutes the phone on the secretary's desk rang, and she picked it up. I figured the Great One was now ready to see me.

I walked into his office. His large figure was slumped forward, elbows on the desktop, a thick file in the center. I expected to see the overhead fluorescent lighting reflected off his bald head, but didn't. Instead he'd acquired a full crop of new hair. Whose, I wasn't so sure. I had to give him one thing. His desk was well organized. It looked as neat as a chessboard. As I approached, he rose to his feet with the ponderous grace of an elephant and extended a big hand with a natural salesman's practiced smile.

"Ron, glad you could come over."

I shook his hand and grinned. "Always a pleasure to see you."

Dick's smile was about as genuine as a politician's campaign promise. He indicated the chair in front of his desk, and I sat down, studying his new hairpiece. I could see the fine netting along the front of his hairline. After exchanging a few amenities, he got right to the point.

"We've got a problem," he said. "A big one, and we need someone reliable to check it out. Discreetly, of course, but quickly."

I looked at him. "That's a lot of adverbs."

His brow furrowed. I could see I'd thrown him off his game.

"What's the case?" I asked.

Dick raised his big fingers and rubbed them over his chin, like he was checking to see if his whiskers were sprouting.

"We paid out a cool twelve million a few months ago on an accidental death case," he said. "A guy named Robert Bayless was killed in a traffic accident downstate."

I tried to look encouraging. "And?"

"And the damn thing nearly sent us back into bankruptcy," he said. "It was scrambling time." He shook his head. "That last hurricane season hurt us bad. If we hadn't been able to save on a few claims, it would have been nightmare city around here. Thank God for loopholes."

I thought about the nightmares those people down in the flood zones were having after finding out their insurance carrier denied their claim because they didn't have the right insurance. "Getting back to the case you wanted me to investigate . . ."

"Yeah," he said, taking a deep breath. "One of our agents was at a convention in Las Vegas last month." He paused again.

"And?"

Dick exhaled through his nostrils, his mouth twisting to the side as he stared at me. "And, he saw somebody that was a dead ringer for Robert Bayless in one of the casinos there." I could tell he was gauging my reaction, so I didn't want to disappoint him.

"Well," I said, "was Elvis with him?"

ALEX ST. JAMES

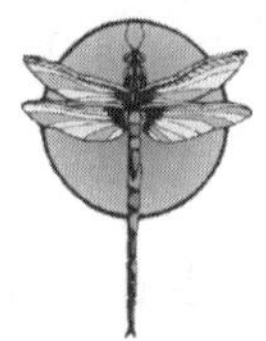

We stood in the underground garage while Bass pranced around the red Firebird like a thirteen-year-old showing off his first copy of *Playboy* magazine. I wondered if he'd adjusted the car's seat forward. The guy who'd sold it to him was a lot taller, and Bass would have a hard time reaching the pedals.

"Okay, girls." His voice had a conspiratorial sound to it. "Tell me the truth. Do the ladies dig a guy with wheels like this, or what?"

Next to me, my assistant Jordan stifled a snort. It was all I could do to keep from laughing myself.

"Bass," I said, "you'll be a certified chick magnet."

He smiled and looked at the car. "I still can't believe it. What I paid for it, I mean." Leaning toward me, he winked. "Got it for a song and a dance, thanks to you."

"I just passed along the info, that's all."

"But still, I owe you."

I let this one pass. Having your boss feeling like he owed you wasn't such a bad thing. Maybe now he'd toss a decent story my way, instead of the fluff pieces he'd been giving me lately.

"It was quite a steal, all right," I said.

His lips drew together and he nodded slowly, assessing the car again.

"I wonder why the guy let it go so cheap?" he muttered.

Leave it to Bass to always find the zipper to the silver lining. Once he started thinking negatively about the car, it wouldn't take long for him to transfer that attitude toward me. Jordan, seeming to sense my concern, spoke up.

"So what's your lady friend say about it?" she asked.

Bass shrugged. "I haven't shown it to her yet. I was thinking maybe I'd drive this baby over and watch the expression on her face."

Knowing Mona, that would be a real Kodak moment. But I wasn't about to let this opportunity slip by. "So, tell me, what's the story you wanted to talk to me about?"

"Oh, that," he said, leaning forward and using his handkerchief to swipe away a speck of dirt from the sleek fender. "It's that piece on the homeless."

"What? But I thought you said you had something really special for me."

"I do." He straightened up and slipped the handkerchief back into his pants pocket. "The piece on the homeless."

"Bass."

He sighed and tried to affect an earnest look. Sincerity wasn't one of Bass's strong suits.

"I have no choice, Alex," he said. "The powers that be ordered it, and Gabriela refuses."

"I'm getting tired of playing Cinderella to Gabriela's evil stepsister. All I ever get are her cast-offs. And the grungy ones, at that."

I'd said it half jokingly, but there was a kernel of truth to my words. Since my recent promotion from researcher to on-air personality at *Midwest Focus NewsMagazine,* I'd been delighted to take it slow—to learn the ropes, as it were, by covering the second-rate stories, while our primary anchor, Gabriela Van Doren, covered the hot stuff.

But the homeless story promised to be an arduous, unpleasant, and ultimately unsuccessful venture. In the past, our station tried to explore the plight of the homeless. I'd gone out countless times to interview people who made their living by panhandling or picking garbage. But by and large, the homeless didn't appreciate intrusion. No matter how many times we attempted to interview society's victims of poverty, we'd been rebuffed, again and again.

Bass shook his head, ignoring me as he made his way around the car for the dozenth time, his gaze locked on the vehicle. "I can't get over it." He ran his hand over the curve of the shiny red fender—not quite touching it. "When I drive her, she purrs," he said quietly, as though talking to himself, "just like a satisfied woman."

Jordan, her coffee-colored face darkening with mirth, gripped my arm. I pulled my lips tight to keep from laughing. I wondered what Mona would say if she could hear him now. But, knowing the cheery little lady, she would probably just give his arm a playful slap and remind him not to tell stories out of school.

Still, I'd had enough car-adoration to hold me over for the rest of the year. "I need to get some work done, Bass. When you can drag your tongue up from off the floor, I'll be in my office."

Jordan fell into step with me as I headed toward the tiny elevator that would take us upstairs. "Remember, you've got a lunch date in forty-five minutes."

Was it that late? My stomach did a little flip-flop when I realized how soon I'd be face-to-face with a very important man from my past.

I threw a glance over my shoulder as the elevator dinged its arrival. "Bass will never even know I'm gone."

Ron Shade

Dick had been prepared for my visit. He gave me a copy of the entire case file, which included a copy of Robert Bayless's death certificate, a traffic accident report, a couple of follow-up police reports, a coroner's report from Furman County, and a detailed report indicating that Robert Bayless had been positively identified through dental records. The body had been badly burned in the crash.

"This seems pretty complete," I said.

"You're damn right it is." His voice had that familiar condescending little lilt to it. "And like I said, watch those expenses. I'll be going over everything with a fine-tooth comb."

"I guess you can do that now that you have a lot more hair to comb."

He snorted. "Always the smart-ass, ain't ya?"

"Where's the guy who supposedly saw him?"

"Herb Winthrope. He's off today. Be back tomorrow."

"I'll need to talk to him."

He nodded absently, as if his mind was a million miles away. Or maybe a couple thousand. "Nine o'clock?"

I nodded as I continued to page through the thick file. "This a record of the payments?"

Dick grunted and winced. "Yeah. Like I said, two mil to his family, and ten to the corporation he worked for. There was a double indemnity clause."

"For which one?"

He snorted. "Both. Why do you think we paid out the ass on this one?"

I rearranged the papers neatly in the manila file and stood up. "Well, I guess there's nothing much I can do until tomorrow then."

"Hey, wait just a goddamn minute." Dick's tone was hot. "I thought I explained to you just how important this case is to the company."

I was always leery of someone who expressed such absolute loyalty to something as abstract as "the company." Like some essential part of their humanity was missing. After all, when I'd been in the army I'd put it all on the line for my country, my flag, the guys in my unit . . . But, for *the company?*

"You did an admirable job of explaining," I said. "Now, if there's nothing else, I'll leave until I can talk to your witness tomorrow."

He started to say something, but then the bluster seemed to leak out of him, like some big balloon deflating. Even his rotund face looked deflated. His eyes went down to the top of his desk, and when he looked up I saw something in them that wasn't usually there. A hint of desperation. He swallowed hard and said, "Ron." His voice was hesitant and I waited for him to continue. "This case is really a big one for us. Really important. MWO might not be able to weather it if we have another bad disaster season."

I resisted the temptation to ask if more people had made sure they had flood insurance.

He licked his lips. "So I'm going to need you to do a good job. A real good job, okay?"

I smiled before I answered. "Dick, I always do a real good job." Then mentally added: even for assholes like you and Midwestern Olympia.

I contemplated Big Dick's plaintive request as I drove home

fighting the always-heavy traffic on the Tri-State Tollway. I'd start in earnest on the investigation tomorrow, with talking to Herb being first on the agenda. But this afternoon, I figured I owed myself a good workout. So I got off at 95th Street and headed toward the Beverly Gym. My manager and trainer, Chappie Oliver owned it, and thanks to the big money he'd won betting on our last fight, he'd been able to buy out the beauty shop next door and substantially expand the gym. The sign in the front window now proudly advertised that Ron Shade, World Heavyweight Kickboxing Champion, trained there.

Sergei Seleznyov, the big Russian I'd taken the title from, was screaming for a rematch. He'd been scheduled to fight another opponent, and I'd been a last-minute replacement. Sometimes, when you've spent the whole preparation time expecting one fighter, and another one comes in at the last minute, you get shaken. Sergei hadn't anticipated my speed, and although he'd caught me with more blows than I would have liked, I knocked him out in the eighth round. But it didn't come easy, and now it was taking me longer than I'd anticipated to fully recover. Part of the problem when you take a fight on short notice. Another problem was that this fight had been under international rules, which allowed leg kicks. Most of my fights used the PKBA rules, which kept all kicks above the belt. Afterward, my legs had been so sore that I felt like ordering a wheelchair to get back to my dressing room.

And now the promoters were trying to sucker me into the rematch, but training, like the recovery, was going more slowly than we'd hoped. Plus, I had nothing to gain by fighting the Mad Russian again. I'd already knocked him out. The bigger money would be calling if I fought somebody else, like my old nemesis, Elijah Day. But I'd knocked him out, too, in a non-title match. With nobody left to beat, I almost felt like retiring. Going out when I was on top. But I finally was beginning to get a taste of the big money, and I didn't want to waste it.

Which meant I had to keep in fighting shape. That had saved me last time. If I hadn't been ready when opportunity knocked with Sergei, I would have gotten beaten into the ground. Hence, my trip to the gym was more than recreational. It was tempered with necessity. Just like my need to keep the money coming in, and a nice, easy investigative case for Midwestern Insurance, or MWO as Dick called it, would keep me occupied and hopefully out of trouble. After all, I reasoned, how many problems could checking up on a dead guy give me?

Alex St. James

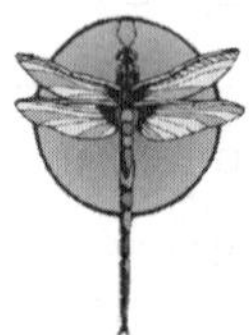

Larry Farnsworth was a lot shorter than I remembered him. Of course, the last time I'd seen him, I'd been about eight years old, when every adult towered over me. Despite the fact that he was still a half block down, and his hair had gone completely silver, I recognized him right away.

As he strode east on Randolph from the direction of his law office on Wells, I had a sudden memory of calling him Uncle Larry. I smiled at that. He wasn't related to my family at all, but at the time it had been more comfortable than calling him Mr. Farnsworth.

Larry kept up a good clip for someone his age and size. We'd agreed to meet at a restaurant on the north side of Randolph. Owned by a Greek man who managed his customers as efficiently as his staff, the restaurant's sea of aqua tables turned over at a rate that kept the lunch crowd moving in and out at lightning speed.

For the first time, I noticed that Larry wasn't alone. He turned to address the man walking next to him. Taller, with chestnut brown hair, and a soft jawline, the other man was closer to my age. I assumed he was one of the up-and-coming attorneys from his firm. Both wore business suits despite the day's warmth. The younger guy's suit was solid black. Geez, he had to be hot. I wondered why in the world Larry brought him along. I'd been very specific about my reasons for meeting, and there's no way this other guy could possess any of the information I needed.

I plastered on a smile as they drew up.

"Alexandrine," Larry said, grabbing me into a bear hug. He planted a huge kiss on the side of my head, then stepped back, tilting his head as he assessed me. "I'm so pleased that you called. Look at you. It does this old man's heart good to see you. Who would have ever imagined that scrawny little girl turning into such a beautiful young lady?"

Young lady? Of all people outside my own family, Larry should know my age. "Young lady" conjured up images of a lithe teenager—fresh, bold, and a little less cynical than someone who'd crossed into her third decade. I'd been about to make a cute quip to that effect, but Larry had already started introductions.

"You remember Nicky, don't you Alex?"

My mouth dropped open. Nicky Farnsworth? Little Nicky? I might've been short and scrawny as a kid, but Nicky had been shorter and scrawnier. Two years older than I was, he'd worn braces before the rest of us got them. They gave him a pronounced lisp and turned his breath rancid. That powerful memory raced up and instinctively I took a step backward.

"Nicky's grown up some, huh?" Larry said, slapping his son

on the shoulder. "How long has it been since you two have seen each other?"

My mouth went utterly useless on me. I'd forgotten him. But it all came back in a rush.

"Alex," Nicky said, extending his hand. "It's nice to see you again."

"Nicky," I said, shaking my head in continued disbelief and catching a whiff of pungent after-shave. Resisting the urge to step back again, I couldn't think of one single thing to break the ice of conversation. Nicky and I hadn't ever had much in common, and the shock of this unexpected reunion kept my tongue tied.

Nicky had been a creepy wallflower. At all those adult gatherings where the parents decided "the kids can just go in the basement and play together," the first ones to the lower level usually commandeered the video games. The rest played *Clue,* or *Monopoly,* or if we were feeling particularly exuberant, *Win, Lose or Draw.* Nicky usually slumped in a chair and stared at everyone else from behind stringy bangs. I'd been the kid who sat near the top of the basement stairs and listened in on adult conversations.

"I mostly go by Nick these days," he said. "But you can call me Nicky if you want. My father can't seem to get out of the habit."

The lisp was gone. As was the greasy hair. Nicky here had grown up. He now bested me by at least four inches, and he'd picked up extra poundage along the way. While I certainly couldn't label him as fat, he didn't wear the extra weight well. Despite only being in his mid-thirties, this guy had developed middle-aged paunch.

"Of course," I said. Then, jumping in with an assumption, I smiled at Larry. "I didn't realize Nicky—" I grimaced, and corrected myself—"Nick . . . worked with you."

That elicited a laugh I didn't understand. Larry guided me

into the restaurant's revolving door. "We have lots of catching up to do," he began, but the circling glass swallowed the rest of whatever he said.

I'd been afraid of this. That Larry might try to avoid the subject. When I first called him, after the requisite pleasantries, I'd offered to come to his office—to treat my request for information like a client/attorney arrangement, rather than a kid/friend-of-family arrangement. But he'd insisted on this luncheon. I thought I'd prepared for every contingency, every argument against his helping me with my quest. But I hadn't counted on him bringing Nicky.

Larry had been the attorney who represented my parents when they adopted me over thirty years ago, a fact I only recently uncovered. Memories of my early years included Larry and Nicky, but they stopped abruptly. There'd been a falling out between Larry and my parents, and he'd disappeared from my life. Until I called him yesterday.

As soon as my aunt accidentally let it slip that he'd handled my adoption, I knew Larry and I were overdue for a reunion.

Seated at a table for four, I had Larry across from me and Nicky to my left. I ordered a salad, both to compensate for the bag of dark chocolate almond clusters tucked into my desk drawer that I planned to enjoy in celebration if this lunch went well, and because a salad, cut into nice bite-size pieces, makes it easier to converse than if I'd had to work my mouth around a double cheeseburger. But I would have much preferred the double cheeseburger.

Twice I attempted to guide the conversation toward Larry's facilitation of my adoption. Twice he winked, patted my hand, and said we needed to catch up first. That we'd discuss that matter over coffee and dessert.

That "matter." Oh, didn't I feel special?

"I looked you up online," Larry said, patting his still-chewing lips with a paper napkin. "Nicky here set up my home computer about five years ago. I've become quite the Internet junkie."

I speared a piece of lettuce. Smiled.

"You're all over the Internet," he continued. "When I saw your picture, I knew he'd never forgive me if I didn't invite him along." He turned to his son. "Isn't that right, Nicky?"

"Dad, it's 'Nick.' Remember?"

Larry ignored him.

There were a hundred questions I wanted answers for. Most of which dealt with my personal adoption quest. But there was no tactful way to shift the conversation. Not yet.

I turned to Nick. "Your dad started to say something outside, but I didn't catch it. You're an attorney, too, I take it?"

Nick, mouth full of a particularly oozy patty melt sandwich, shook his head.

Larry answered for him. "No," he said, with a wide smile. "Nicky—ah, Nick—has got his own business. That's the way to do it these days. Nobody can lay you off. You're your own boss and you have no one to answer to but your own good conscience."

"What do you do?" I asked.

Nicky licked a smear of cheese off his finger. "I'm a funeral director."

There are times that—just when I feel as though I've gained control of a situation—my feet are yanked out from under me. This was one of those times.

"Really?" was about all I could come up with. "That's fascinating."

He shrugged one shoulder. "You should come out and visit sometime. I'll show you around."

Larry beamed as I felt another loss-of-control bomb hit.

"Thanks, but I've been to enough funerals to last me for a while."

"Seriously," Nick said. "There's nothing frightening about preparing the dead for burial."

"I'm not afraid."

He shot me an indulgent look. "Well," he said. "Sometimes people are uncomfortable being in the same room with a body's remains. The first time is especially hard. It's understandable."

"Listen." I cocked an eyebrow at him. "I've watched autopsies."

He had the good grace to look abashed. "Then maybe you'll just come out sometime to visit. We could do lunch."

I gathered a forkful of salad, and held it aloft for just a moment. Although Nicky had conquered that gangly uncertainty that plagues teenagers everywhere, he'd not made the complete transformation from Ugly Duckling to swan. Not that he was bad-looking—I'd have termed him average—but he had a stodgy air about him. And the burgeoning jowls didn't help. His greasy bangs were gone, but the wary stare was still there.

"What a wonderful idea," Larry said. "Nicky, give Alex one of your cards."

I decided I was wrong about Nicky having grown up if he still needed Daddy to coach him on dating rituals.

Jammed into the uncomfortable position of keeping Larry happy so that he'd cooperate when we discussed my adoption, and not wanting to lead Nicky on, I accepted the proffered card. *Sunset Manor Funeral Home—We treat the dead with the dignity they deserve.*

I mustered a smile and reciprocated with one of my cards.

Larry grinned with the cherubic joy of an over-the-hill Cupid.

While there was nothing specific about Nicky that turned me off, his appearance at this luncheon and his father's almost frantic attention to keeping the two of us talking, led me to believe that Nicky hadn't been especially lucky in the love department. And I was beginning to see why. He had a professional, if dowdy, appearance. That could be overlooked—or fixed with a couple of good shopping trips. But his lack of confidence was something any woman anywhere could smell a mile away.

But then again, who was I to judge? I was "single," and had been for longer than I cared to admit.

The waitress finished clearing the dishes away. "So, Uncle Larry," I said, using the affectionate nickname and broaching the subject in as nonthreatening a way as I could, "how long does it usually take to facilitate an adoption?"

"Well, that depends." Larry stretched backward to allow the waitress to fill his coffee cup. "I imagine every case is different."

"You imagine?"

"You understand," he said, "I handled this for your parents as a favor to them."

I couldn't understand what that had to do with anything, but he sighed deeply, then continued, "To be honest, yours was the only adoption I ever handled. I did it as a favor to your folks, and I couldn't see charging them for my time when most of the paperwork was handled through Catholic Charities."

"I tried working through them," I said. "In fact—"

Nicky interrupted to ask why it'd taken me this long to start my search.

I didn't want to get into a long-winded explanation, so I kept it to the barest of minimums. I told him that I knew that this particular quest of mine bothered my mom. There was little doubt that it bothered my dad, too. Now that they'd moved out of state, I felt a certain freedom. I could start this and move forward without their realizing it. What they didn't know wouldn't hurt them.

I looked to Larry. "I'd be willing to bet that at least one of my biological parents was Irish, weren't they?" I hadn't planned to phrase it as a question, but now I stared at him, hoping he'd answer, straight-on, or inadvertently—a wink, a nod—something. But he gave no reaction whatsoever. He simply stared back and patted his lips with his napkin.

"I mean," I added, flipping my dark hair and gesturing toward my freckles, "look at me."

Larry sat there—mute, unreadable—and I wondered if this talent came from dealing with recalcitrant witnesses on the stand until I remembered that he was a tax attorney and probably didn't have a whole lot of court experience. What a waste. The man was a veritable statue when he wanted to be. Finally, he leaned forward.

I thought for sure he would finally answer me, but he turned to Nicky instead. "There are a lot of Irish in your neighborhood, aren't there?"

"Polish, too. Just like you, Alex."

I bit my bottom lip. Literally. Walking that tightrope between politeness and indignation, I made myself smile to soften the clipped tone I knew was coming. "Well, Nicky, that's the big question, isn't it? I don't know if I'm Polish or not." I faced Larry. "Why don't *you* tell *me?*"

Larry patted my hand. I pulled both hands into my lap so he couldn't do it again. "In good time, honey." As though they'd rehearsed it, he then cocked his head toward Nick who licked his lips and sat up straighter. "Did you know that my son is a member of the Chicago Chamber of Commerce?"

Whoop-de-doo. Half my acquaintances were members of the Chamber, but Larry here made it sound like I should curtsey in the presence of royalty.

"He was *invited* to join," he said, "because of all the *pro bono* work he does for the indigent."

"Dad . . ." Nicky said, shaking his head and smiling. "She doesn't want to hear about that."

These guys were totally scripted. I resisted the urge to turn around to see if there were cue cards hanging on the wall behind me.

"Nicky makes a lot of money," Larry added with a wink. "A *lot* of money. His investment portfolio is probably more impressive than mine. I wish I had his money when I was starting my family. Financially, Nicky's all set to get married and have kids—and make some woman very happy. That is, if he finds the right woman." Larry winked again. "But right now, he concentrates on helping those who are less fortunate. Tell her, Nicky."

Nicky turned to me. My assessment of him as "average but not attractive" was rapidly deteriorating into "annoying buffoon."

"The funeral home business saved my life," he said. "If it weren't for old Ketch taking me in as an intern, I might've been in one of those caskets myself, instead of preparing them for others."

I felt a long story coming on, and my brain screamed at me to get out of there. Except . . . I hadn't gotten any of the information I wanted. Nothing. Nada. At this point in my life, Larry Farnsworth was my best—scratch that, my only—source of information about my adoption. Much as I wanted to run out of this restaurant and away from this un-dynamic duo, I kept my rear end plunked firmly in my chair and tried to look interested.

As I worked out ways to redirect the conversation I caught snippets of Nicky's story. I wondered if he'd rehearsed his speech in front of a mirror, or if this was his typical spiel when wooing women.

If so, I could see why he was still single.

"I learned everything I know from old Ketch," Nicky said. I must've seemed attentive because Nicky added, "Maurice Ketcham. He didn't think his name was good for a funeral home, so he came up with Sunset Manor. I eventually bought him out, and when he passed, I gave him the best goddamn funeral you've ever seen."

"Nicky, watch your language."

Nicky reddened. I decided it had nothing to do with saying "goddamn" but everything to do with having his father correct him.

"That's a great story," I said, shifting in my seat to face Larry. "I know how important it is to have good role models in our lives. That's why I'm so grateful I was adopted by my parents." I was forcing the issue here, but I had to. "At this point now, where I'm happy and successful"—I couldn't resist adding—"on my own, I feel the need to search for my roots. I know you understand," I said, keeping eye contact with Larry. "That's why we're meeting today, right? So that you and I can talk about where I came from."

Larry nodded. "Very true."

I heaved a mental sigh. Finally.

"In fact," he continued, "our roots are so important that when we lose touch with family, there's no telling what will happen. When individuals are cut off from those who have shaped their lives, they are adrift . . . lost."

I opened my mouth, but Larry wasn't done.

"That's why Nicky's work with the homeless is so very noteworthy."

What the hell? What was going on here? Was Larry trying to tell me, in a roundabout way, that my parents were street people?

Nope. This guy wasn't into subtleties. These guys weren't here to talk about me, they were here to talk about themselves.

"Dad," Nicky said, again with that rehearsed-sounding tone of admonishment, "I'm sure she isn't interested in any of this, are you, Alex? I bet you haven't even ever seen a homeless person."

What a stupid thing to say. "I work in the Loop," I replied.

"Of course I see homeless people. Every day. In fact, I'm doing a story on them for *Midwest Focus* right now."

The moment the words escaped my lips, I knew it'd been a major mistake.

"Wonderful!" Larry was back to being the cheerful cherub again. "Maybe you can interview Nicky."

Nicky shook his head. "Dad, I don't think so."

"Don't be bashful, son." He turned to me. "He's still kind of shy, you know."

I held up my hands. "I haven't even figured out my angle on this story yet. And, really, I don't think the station is focusing on their deaths. I think our goal is to illuminate the plight of the homeless—and that means that I'll be working with folks who are still alive."

If either of them caught my sarcastic tone, I couldn't tell.

"In any case," Larry said easily, "I should get back to work. But let's do this again, soon."

With that he dropped his napkin onto the table, smiled and did that lean-forward thing that heralded the end of the meal.

I grabbed his arm. "But wait. Who were they?"

Larry looked at me—his face blank. "Who were who?"

This was a successful attorney I was talking to. I didn't for a minute believe that he didn't understand the question. But, just to avoid any further confusion, I said, "My birth parents. You had to have known who they were."

Larry stopped for a moment, then summoned the waitress again. This girl deserved a great tip. Despite the fact that the restaurant was full to capacity, I felt as though we were her only table. "Dessert," he said, nodding to the two of us. "What do you say?"

Now that we were talking about my adoption—the sole reason I'd requested this meeting—I'd have said yes to anything that would keep the luncheon from ending.

I ordered apple pie, Nicky ordered cheesecake. When it came to Larry's turn, he shook his head and patted his ample gut. "Gotta cut the calories, but you two go ahead."

Then, as though there had been no interruption whatsoever, Larry continued the conversation from where he'd left off. "I know you're searching—searching for yourself, Alex. I understand that. Old Ketch was like a surrogate father to Nicky when I couldn't be there for him. But it was Nicky who made the funeral home into the success that it is today. He really found himself there."

My mind screamed with frustration. Another tangent. Another story that had absolutely nothing to do with my questions. I kept my expression polite, but I wanted to tell Larry that I didn't give a flippin' nickel about Nicky's search for himself.

At that moment the waitress returned with our desserts. Larry shoved some bills in Nicky's direction. "You pay for lunch, son." He smiled at us both and stood. "I'll leave you two to talk about it. It's quite fascinating." And before I could protest, he took off.

Ron Shade

I flicked a double jab at the heavy bag when I heard Chappie's voice behind me.

"Sugar Ray used to be able to hook off that jab."

I grinned. "Which Sugar Ray you talking about?"

"Do it matter?" He raised his hands and tilted his dark,

shaved head backward slightly. "Lemme see them cuts."

I lowered my arms and canted my head, feeling his fingers probe the area above my left eye. He made a few sounds, like he was considering how a pair of new shoes felt.

"What's the verdict?" I asked. "Do I get to make some money soon, or not?"

"Not till them cuts heal more," he said, dropping his hands. "Should give them a while longer yet."

"Chappie, it's been over two months."

He nodded. "Six'd be good. Maybe even seven or eight."

"Come on."

"What, you got nothing else to occupy your time? You need to get yourself a hobby. Like playing the guitar or something."

"I got a hobby," I said. "It's called a job. Being a private investigator, remember?"

"You talking about the job that kept you from fighting for the championship them times?" Now it was his turn to grin. I'd lost two previous opportunities to fight for the title due to on-the-job injuries I'd sustained. As if he could read my mind, Chappie continued, "Un-huh. And I seem to remember you needed my help on your last case, too."

I'd taken him with me, but only at his insistence because I was so busted up after the big fight. But Chappie had evolved over the years into something much more than a trainer and manager. In a lot of ways, he was like a surrogate father.

He sighed. "So what you be working on now?"

"Ever hear of a guy faking his death? Disappearing. Starting over."

He nodded. "Happen all the time in the ghetto. Man starts to feel the weight of the responsibility weighing on him. Pretty soon, it be dragging him down. Like he trying to swim in a quick current. Once he makes it to the other shore, he climb out, shake himself off, and don't look back."

Which is why the state's attorney had a special taskforce to trace down deadbeat dads, I thought. But Bayless's family had a two-million-dollar parachute. A payoff like that could do a lot to assuage a man's guilt.

Chappie stooped and picked up some focus pads from my gear bag. "I'm gonna take Alley through some ring work. You keep on working the bag." He slipped a mitt on each hand and slapped them together making a shot-like sound. "It ain't gonna hit back."

I settled in working the bag again, while he took Alley, our young, Russian-born fighter, through the motions in the ring. I paused to watch them, wishing it was me up there. The bag work was so familiar to me that I felt I could do it without thinking, and when I returned to it, my mind began to wander a bit. I considered Chappie's brief explanation of the disappearing man. It happened in places other than the ghetto, too. In Latin America they even had their own word for it. *Les Desaparicidos*—The Disappeared Ones. Maybe Robert Bayless had felt those heavy weights pulling at him. The file said he'd been married with one son. And he was in his early forties. The beginning of a lot of middle-aged crises. I'd know more once I talked to the witness and evaluated what he said. Maybe he'd just seen someone who looked like Bayless. A lot of people look alike. I'd been told I bore a strong resemblance to the former Buffalo Bills quarterback, Jim Kelly. I couldn't see the resemblance myself, but I always answered that I wished I had his money or his career.

As if he could read my mind once more, Chappie called out from the ring apron, "You looking like a million bucks, champ. All green and wrinkled. You ain't gonna hit that bag any harder than that, you might as well go do some of that private investigating."

I bounced around on my toes and grinned. "I'm saving that for tomorrow."

Chapter 2

Alex St. James

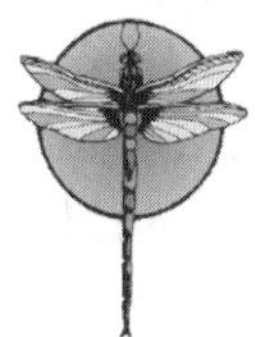

The next morning Bass pulled me into his office. "I have a present for you."

"You're joking." Bass didn't give gifts. He never chipped in for office celebrations, though he always managed to snag a piece of cake. A true miser, Bass skimped wherever possible, though I knew he was well off. I couldn't understand why he didn't live a little. If he wasn't willing to spend money on himself—or his girlfriend Mona—and enjoy life a little, someday he would make the state very rich.

"Nope. Picked it out myself."

With that, he hoisted a large plastic bag onto the desk. Black and bursting at the seams, it landed on his blotter with a solid thunk.

I stared at it for a moment. "You're giving me a bag of garbage?"

"Don't be silly. I'd never give you garbage." Evil grin. "I plan to let you pick out your own."

It took two beats before his meaning became clear. The homeless story.

"No," I said.

Ignoring me, he stood to untie the red drawstring. "You're gonna love this stuff," he said.

"No," I said again.

The first item he tugged out was brown and long and made of itchy-looking wool. "The nights can get cold."

"Bass."

"What size shoes do you wear?" he asked as he pulled out a pair of men's Hush Puppies. The toes were scuffed, the heels were worn to near nonexistence and they had to be at least size eleven. My feet would get lost in those boats.

"I am not going undercover."

His cheer undiminished, he dragged more items out of the never-ending bag, even as I protested.

"I got all this at the thrift store on Halsted," he said with pride. "Can you believe this whole bag cost me only six bucks? I almost feel bad putting in an expense report for such a small amount." He grinned again. "But I will." He came up with assorted pieces of clothing, a purple sleeping bag, and a bright pink floppy hat, which he said would make me more recognizable on television. "It ties under your chin, like this." He indicated the rawhide laces, but didn't put it on his own head. Of course not. He didn't want any part of the cooties that lurked inside.

I sure as hell wasn't about to wear it and I told him so.

Without acknowledging me, he finished his little fashion show. Once the entire bag had been emptied onto his desk, he gave the collection a grimace. In his excitement to display his "find" he'd forgotten himself, and now the junk was leaving second-hand germs all over his pristine office.

Maybe there was some justice in the world. But that still

didn't mean that I'd be taking part in the little adventure he'd envisioned.

"Listen, Bass," I began.

"Wait." He held up a finger, then opened one of his side drawers. "Here you go. The *piéce de resistance.*"

My hand reached out automatically to take the next bag. About a tenth the size of the first one, it was nonetheless weighty. I looked inside. "No way."

"I would've gotten you a smaller version, but the little ones cost twice as much. I figured that you'll have plenty of clothes on, though. You'll be able to find a place to hide it, right?"

The Taser in my hand looked like one of *Star Trek*'s Romulan disruptors. Heavy, gray and with a trigger that itched to be pulled while pointed at Bass, it made me want to scream. He must have sensed my urges, because he pointed to the chair. "Sit."

Even as I prepared arguments in my mind, I knew I was losing this battle. I hefted the weapon in my right hand, shifted it to my left, and then back again. The thought of Bass squirming on the floor in wracking pain gave me something to smile about.

"That," Bass said, pointing to the Taser, "cost me a hell of a lot more than six bucks."

"I'm not doing this."

"You think Gabriela got all the cush assignments when she first started on-air?"

"As a matter of fact, she did."

He fidgeted. "Yeah, well. She's different."

My gaze flicked up to meet his. I knew what he meant. Gabriela was a successful on-air personality not just because of the great stories we covered, but because she was blond perfection. Me, I looked like the obedient girl next-door. The girl who'd go live with the homeless because my boss told me I had to.

I shook my head.

"This is a once-in-a-lifetime opportunity," he said.

"What can you possibly hope to accomplish with me going undercover?" I threw up my hands. "I don't see the angle."

"The angle," he said, wagging his eyebrows Snidely Whiplash–fashion, "is that our station has a heart."

"Since when?"

He held up a finger. "We feel so strongly that the homeless have become invisible in our society that we're willing to risk one of our own," he pointed at me, "to bring the story to life."

"No way," I said when he drew a breath. "First of all, it's been done. Overdone. There are blogs, for crying out loud, written by bored twenty-somethings who treat a weekend of 'playing homeless' as some sort of game. If we intend to exploit the plight of the homeless for ratings, what we should be doing is raising awareness. At the very least, our goal should be to improve their situation."

"And that," Bass said with a knowing smile, "is exactly why we chose you to do this story." He shook his finger at me for emphasis. "You and I may not always agree, but I appreciate the passion you bring to your assignments." Reverting to his customary frown, he added, "But you tell anyone I said that, and I'll take back the gift I got you."

"Some gift."

"Yep. Nothing but the best for my ace reporter."

Ron Shade

I began the northern trek earlier than I had the day before and managed to beat the big back-up before the 95th Street toll plaza. For the most part. Even though I had one of those great I-Pass transponders, the traffic slowed to a monotonous crawl before I reached the Oakbrook exit. Plus, I'd left the special Velcro strips on the windshield of the Firebird, and didn't have any for the Beater. So I had to hold up the transponder whenever I passed through the tolling site, or risk one of those photographic tickets they loved to mail out. Even my Chicago Police buddy, George Grieves, had a fear of them. "Can't get a ticket fixed if you ain't got no Chinaman, and I don't in the ISP."

Neither did I, so I held up the plastic device and crept over toward the exit. I'd factored in enough time to find someplace to eat a good breakfast, while I waited for the minions of MWO to arrive. I found a place not far from the rows of glass-walled buildings and hotels. The area was juxtaposed between O'Hare Airport and the Loop, and built with elegance and style. I wondered what it would be like to be able to afford to live up this way instead of the blue-collar South Side where I had my humble abode.

After ordering my usual scrambled eggs, orange juice, and rye toast, I reviewed the file once more. The traffic crash that had killed Robert Bayless had occurred last November on a winding country road down in Furman County. I wasn't even sure where that was and made a mental note to get a map someplace. I wondered what Bayless had been doing down there. It also mildly piqued my interest that his car had caught on fire and he'd been "burned beyond recognition." Convenient. It had been my experience as a cop that cars in traffic crashes seldom caught on fire. It ain't like the movies, where every vehicle is transformed into a spectacular fireball right after leaving the roadway. Something has to trigger the flames. The crash report gave no indication of what had done this.

The death certificate was signed by the Furman County Coroner's Office three days after the crash. According to the coroner's report, the autopsy was performed by a Dr. K. Boyd. Have to look him up, too. Probably some local GP. It was anybody's guess what Thaddeus Brunger, the coroner, did for a living. It was an elected position, and a lot of them downstate were funeral directors. Toxicology reports showed the presence of a low level of alcohol, Amoxicillan, an antibiotic, and Vicodin ES, a painkiller, in Bayless's bloodstream. The report explained that his dentist had given him the prescription because he'd had two teeth pulled. An aside by the dentist stated that Bayless had been warned not to imbibe. Mixing alcohol with the painkiller could have a synergistic effect, which could cause drowsiness. They had to wait for ID verification from Bayless's dentist, a Dr. Keith Colon, who subsequently provided it. There were no copies of the X-rays, but the report said the identification was positive. The cause of death was listed as accidental, and the claim's adjustor had written all his findings in a summary, recommending full payment on both claims. Bayless had a million-dollar life insurance policy on himself, which went up to two mil because of the accidental double-indemnity clause. Ditto for the second policy his employer, the Manus Corporation, had on him. Theirs was for five million—double made it ten. Added to the personal two mil, it totaled up to a whopping twelve. I wondered what it would be like to be worth so much more being dead, instead of alive.

But then again, maybe Bayless was both.

Alex St. James

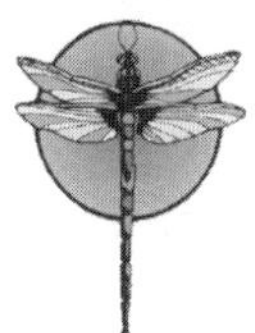

I knew I had to make an appearance at William's going-away breakfast, so I pasted on a cheerful face and headed in. William had been on staff for less than a year, so his departure didn't warrant a big restaurant hoopla event. Instead, management popped for a catered-in affair held in our lunchroom. Why they'd gone with a breakfast instead of lunch was beyond me. Maybe Bass was in charge of arranging it, and scrambled eggs were cheaper than sandwiches.

My assistant, Jordan, was already there, nursing a plastic cup of red punch. I made my way over to her, avoiding William and the bevy of women around him, saying how sorry they were that he was transferring to our sister station in San Francisco. I needed to prepare myself for when my turn came to say farewell.

Jordan alone knew how I felt about this particular personnel change. She shot me one of those "girlfriend" looks as she sauntered up. "Is that a tear in your eye, honey? I can see how broken up you are."

I stifled a snort. There were about fifteen people present. "How soon can I leave this party without looking rude?"

"Ooh," she said with a glance over my shoulder, "not soon enough."

I turned to see William heading toward us.

Jordan upended her cup to finish the last few drops, then waggled her eyebrows. "I've been here about twenty minutes. I think I've done my civic duty." She placed her hand on my forearm and whispered in my ear. "Here's your big chance to give him the send-off he deserves."

When William came up, Jordan flashed him a dazzling smile, her teeth bright against her coffee-colored skin. She was a beautiful girl, just a few years younger than I was, and I appreciated her support. I would have much preferred her to stay, but she had a warped sense of humor, and I knew she thought this was fun.

"Best of luck in your new position, William," she said with an air-kiss near his cheek. "I can only imagine how hard it's going to be for you . . . starting over in a new city where you don't know anybody."

Score one for Jordan.

William turned red. But I was enjoying the show.

"Thanks," he said. As she left, he called to her back, "Let's keep in touch."

With Jordan gone, and the rest of the gatherers seated and eating, I had no choice but to talk with William.

"I'm glad you came," he said.

I answered, with just the right amount of insouciance, "Of course I came."

"I wasn't sure if you would."

I pretended to miss his underlying meaning. "Yeah," I said, feigning weariness, "Bass has got me running around for that homeless story."

"Now that you're a big-time television celebrity, you get all the big stories."

I laughed. "Some celebrity. My face is plastered on billboards throughout the city, and I still have to show my driver's license at the bank."

He laughed. Took a drink of punch. Looked around. "I wish there was something stronger here."

"The sugar will have to hold you for now."

"Want to go out for a drink after work?"

I was about to reply that I wouldn't have time, when he said, "I'll miss working with you."

Deflecting, I said, "At least you're getting out before you have to do any homeless research. I'm really not looking forward to this one."

"Bass is a shit for dumping this one on you."

I shrugged. "I'm stuck with it."

"I made some notes," he said. "I'll get them to you later today."

"Don't worry about it. I've already got plans." That was a lie, but I didn't want to prolong our collaboration beyond this party.

William swallowed twice. "This is harder than I thought it would be—" he stopped himself. "I mean . . ."

"When do you leave?"

The puzzled tilt of his head made me realize that I'd probably asked him that before. "Friday morning."

"What airline?"

"I'm driving. I told you that."

"Did you?" I reached to ladle myself some punch. "Oh, wait . . ." I suddenly remembered. "That's right. You and umm—Tricia—are sharing the driving, aren't you?"

"Not anymore."

"No?"

William's blue eyes, the eyes that formerly had the power to weaken my knees, stared into mine as though he were trying to send some silent message to me via his gaze. "She's been transferred. To Las Vegas."

"And you're still going to San Francisco?"

He nodded.

"That's terrible. What will you do?"

He shook his head, moved a little closer and spoke quietly.

"This was a mistake."

I could have told him that back when he and Tricia "reconnected" during his business trip out to San Fran. A trip I should've taken, but couldn't. As it was, he came back filled with excitement about the city and about his new-old flame.

"Yeah," I said, "you worked so hard to get transferred. Now you have to do it all over again. But I've heard that Vegas is one of the fastest-growing cities. You shouldn't have any trouble finding a position there."

He shook his head. "You misunderstand. She—Tricia—requested the transfer."

"She did? Why?"

He gazed out at the people gathered to see him off. They were happy to have gotten a free meal, sorry to see a friend go, but tomorrow they'd all wake up and head back to work and within a week or so no one would care that William had once worked here. "She said I was moving too fast."

I held my tongue. Too fast? That hadn't been my impression when William and I came close to having a romantic relationship. Close. Yeah, but no cigar.

I smiled at that thought—sometimes a cigar *isn't* just a cigar—but as far as I was concerned, William could keep his stogie to himself.

"That's too bad," I said. I couldn't resist adding, "But things change when we least expect them to, don't they?" I glanced at the far table, where an unwrapped box sat, tissue paper spewing out around something bulky. "Did you like your gift?"

"Very much."

"That's good."

He gave me a look. If I had to characterize it, I'd say it held regret, sorrow, and just a little bit of anger. "You don't even know what they got me, do you?"

It was time for me to get out of there. "As long as you're

happy, nothing else matters," I said with a shrug. "Right?"

He opened his mouth to answer, but I stopped him by grabbing hold of his upper arm, leaning forward and dropping an air-kiss that was even more chaste than Jordan's had been. "Good luck. Wherever you wind up."

"Call me sometime," he said as I left.

"Sure," I said over my shoulder.

Yeah. Right.

When I got to my office doorway I stopped. The fat plastic bag of thrift store–junk hunkering next to my desk reminded me of the homeless plight—the feature story, yes, but my own plight as well, now that I was stuck with the assignment.

I dropped into my leather chair and stared out the window. The conversation with William left me feeling testy. I hated being a bitch, although I could be very good at it. The truth was, I did wish him well. He'd been a good friend. But nothing more.

Right about now, I was thanking goodness for that.

Sun sparkled on the river below. Almost summer. Chicagoans and tourists alike bustled across the Wabash Avenue and Michigan Avenue bridges. Right now I'd rather be shopping for shoes at Nordstrom than donning second-hand clothing and interviewing indigents.

I made a face at the bag.

My assignment could've been worse, I supposed, if this were February instead of June. Of course, then Bass would have had to provide me with a big cardboard box to sleep in.

There had to be some way to get the good story without risking life, limb, and personal hygiene. We'd tried this feature before—although never undercover—and every homeless person we'd encountered refused to be interviewed. They wouldn't even let us get close. I'd had garbage and expletives flung at me, and once I'd even been threatened with a swinging two-by-four.

Since then I'd been careful to keep my distance, only coming close to those less-fortunate folks when I shoved dollars into their paper cups.

I stood. Symbolic, maybe, but I wasn't about to sit and let the world trample over me like this. Between Bass and William—and let's not leave out Larry Farnsworth—it seemed that the males in my world were conspiring to keep me off balance.

Time to take matters into my own hands.

Staring out over the river, over the happily shopping tourists, I smiled. I knew exactly what to do.

Bass wanted a killer story on the homeless, but it was up to me to find the right angle. And when Larry Farnsworth had left me and Nicky to chitchat over dessert, the guy rambled on and on about himself. I'd let him. It was easier than investing myself fully in the conversation.

Nicky had talked a great deal about his many successes. Tucked in there was a tidbit I could use now—Nicky's *pro bono* funeral work kept him in close contact with a priest who ran a homeless shelter up on the North Side.

A homeless shelter.

I wanted information from Larry Farnsworth about my adoption. Larry Farnsworth wanted me to express some interest in his son. I'd show interest all right. Just not the romantic kind.

With a silent nod to whomever had coined the phrase "One hand washes the other," I picked up the phone.

Chapter 3

Ron Shade

Both Herbert Winthrope and Dick MacKenzie showed their irritation with me as I sauntered into the plush MWO facility about two minutes after nine. Dick pursed his lips and pointed to his watch.

"Christ, Ron. Poor Herb's been waiting here for over an hour," he said. "I thought we'd agreed on eight o'clock?" His breath smelled particularly foul this morning.

I was sure the son-of-a-bitch had said nine, but to get in an argument with a client on your second day is not good business. Still, I hate it when somebody's wrong and they're an asshole about it, and I don't get to tell them. "I could have sworn you said nine, but I'm sorry about the misunderstanding."

I glanced at my watch and the sudden expression I saw flicker in Dick's eyes told me he realized his mistake. Getting him to admit it would be a different matter, however, and I needed this interview to get off on the right foot. Plus, it was good to know that I could score as a counterpuncher once in a while. I extended my hand toward Herb, who had kind of a pudgy, soft look to him. I put him in his mid- to late-forties, carrying about fifty more pounds than he needed around his belly. His hair was clipped short in the type of crewcut that used to be big in the early sixties.

"You must be Mr. Winthrope," I said as we shook. His handshake wasn't much firmer than his gut, and when he felt mine his sour look transformed into a salesman's smile.

"Man, you got one hell of a grip, buddy," he said. Then added, "Call me Herb."

"Come on," Dick said, turning toward a row of elevators. "I've reserved the conference room on the third floor."

I resisted my urge to suggest we take the stairs, and let Herb and Dick lead me to a nicely furnished room lined with leather-bound volumes of books. As we walked in, I found myself imagining they were reference books of some kind, used to look up the proper insurance codes when underwriting a policy. But their artful arrangement had me revising that assessment seconds later when I realized they weren't actual books at all, but rather a one-piece display. They were decorative. Just for show. Like the rest of the MWO. All glitz and no substance. Everybody's friend until they had to pay out some dough, then there was only one book they pulled out: *How to Screw Your Policyholder.*

I was hoping that my host would offer to get me some coffee or maybe some ice-cold bottled water, but no such luck. Dick plopped himself down in a chair and leaned forward with his forearms resting on the table. I was reminded of a dog who's fixated on the dinner table, waiting for scraps. His breath wasn't getting any better, either.

The interview got off to a slow start, with Herb Winthrope sitting on the right side of the table, and Big Dick leaning in from the left. I took out my yellow legal pad so I could take notes. The lesson of the room hadn't been lost on me. Look like a professional, and they'll treat you like one.

"Let's talk about Robert Bayless," I said. "How well did you know him?"

Herb shrugged. "I was his insurance man."

I resisted the temptation to make a wisecrack. "About how many times did you meet with him?"

Herb leaned back in his leather chair and stroked his chin. Both of them. "Maybe half a dozen, over the course of four or five years. Most of our business dealings were done over the phone."

He must have read the skepticism in my expression, because he quickly added, "But it was him in Vegas. I'm positive of that."

I nodded, scribbling down some notes. "I'm just trying to get a view of the big picture here. Trying to put together all the information."

He pursed his lips. "You don't believe me?"

I tried a reassuring smile. "Look, it doesn't matter if I believe you, or not. I need to get a basic idea of how much proof we have. So don't get disturbed if it seems like I'm playing the devil's advocate once in a while, okay?"

He frowned and nodded.

"About how many times did you speak to him on the phone?" I asked. "Was it a regular thing?"

"Not really," he said, his voice trailing off. "But that's just the point, don't you see? It was his *voice* I heard. His *laugh.* It was a very distinctive kind of laugh." He lolled his head back and gave an imitation of a big, horsy-sounding guffaw. "I always used to hate laughing along at his stupid jokes, but what the hell. It was business."

Yeah, I thought. An insurance salesman's life was fraught with little difficulties.

"And I'd just finished his upgrade," Herb continued.

"Who'da thought that we'd end up paying out the ass on that one not six months later?" He shook his head and looked at Dick. Dick shook his, too. I almost felt obligated to join in. "I mean, if we wouldn't have been able to save some money on all those jerks who didn't have flood coverage . . ."

Dick nodded again, toeing the company line. It was easier than thinking.

"Yeah," I chimed in, mustering as much false sincerity as I could manage, "who plans for a flood if you live in a city?" Mentally I reminded myself why insurance adjustors ranked just below defense attorneys and crooked politicians on my scale of worthless humanity.

Dick gave me a rather squinty look. Maybe he was more perceptive than I gave him credit for.

"Let's get back to Bayless," I said. "Tell me about the last time you talked to him."

Herb leaned back in his chair again. "He called me twice. The first time it sounded like he was drunk. Wanted to know if he could switch the beneficiary on his life insurance policy to his son and somebody else."

"Somebody else?"

"Yeah, said he was getting divorced. He gave me a woman's name. I asked for the particulars, you know, full name, how to spell it, date of birth, address, and all of a sudden he balked. Said he'd get back to me."

"Did he?"

"Yeah, he did. About three weeks later. Told me to leave things the way they were. I laughed it off. Like I said, he'd sounded blitzed."

"You remember the woman's name he gave you?"

Herb frowned. I could see he was trying hard. It was a matter of pride for him. He shook his head. "Shit, it was something cutesy-poopsy, like Sandy or Candy, or some kind of weird nickname like that."

"Last name?"

"Christ, I don't know. It was some kind of Lithuanian name. That I do remember."

"How did Bayless explain things when you saw him next?"

"Well, like I told you, he called me back a few days later, said to disregard what he'd said before. In fact, he wanted to upgrade his policy to one million. Asked how much more the premium would be. Said his company wanted extra coverage on him, too. Five million—plus that indemnity clause."

"How much were the premiums?"

"Plenty," Herb said. He cast a nervous glance at Big Dick. "Our standard percentage of the principal averaged by our standard rates. I got it drawn up right away, but told him he'd have to submit to a physical for that much of an upgrade."

"Did he?"

Herb nodded again. "It's company policy. The doctor passed him with no trouble. Said he looked good for a man his age."

"The exam include any X-rays?"

He shrugged. "A chest X-ray probably."

"The doctor still have it?"

"He should." Herb's mouth puckered with the rectitude of the righteous. "Company policy requires that they hold on to all exam reports for a minimum of three and a half years, even in cases where the insured is deceased."

I turned to Dick. "See if you can verify that he kept them, will you?"

Dick looked annoyed at having to leave. Like he would be missing the conclusion of his favorite TV show. "Is it important?"

Like I would have asked if it wasn't. "It could be, for comparative purposes."

He got up slowly, the chair giving off what sounded like an ease of relief. "I'm on it." He strode to the door, opened it, and stepped out. I was glad to see him leave. I could sense Herb's slight relaxation, too. He leaned back and began talking in a more matter-of-fact tone.

"Little did I realize that the company would be paying out so much money so soon." He shook his head again. Without Dick there to mirror his condolences, the gesture seemed more pathetic. "We took our customary ninety-day grace period, of course."

"Okay." I raised my eyebrows. "Tell me about the sighting in Vegas."

Herb nodded. "We were out there for the insurance underwriters' convention. You know how those things are. Half the time everybody's either drunk or gambling or both."

I gave a commiserating nod. "What time of the day was this?"

He shrugged. "I don't know. After dinner sometime. Maybe eight, nine at night. You know how that fucking place is. No clocks on the walls."

"Did you have anything to drink at dinner? Alcohol-wise?"

"You trying to insinuate that I was drunk?"

"I'm asking if you'd been drinking." What a great witness this guy would be. He couldn't even handle my little interview.

Herb's lips pinched together. "Look, I know what I seen, and I wasn't drunk, if that's what you're implying."

"I'm playing the devil's advocate, remember?"

He frowned and said, "I might've had a couple of martinis, but that's all. I was sober."

"Okay, where did you see him?"

"We were in the Mirage. I was walking through the casino and I heard it. That stupid sounding laugh." He paused and gave me his imitation again. "I mean, I froze. It was like a ghost whispering in my ear. I started looking around, and then I heard it again, and saw him at the blackjack tables. He'd changed a little, grown a mustache, but it still looked like him. I couldn't believe it and wasn't real sure at first. I mean, we'd just closed out the file on him three months ago. Had some stacked blond chick hanging all over him, too." He frowned and cupped his palms in front of his chest indicating big boobs.

"So I found an empty spot at the slots and moved around so I could keep watching him." He leaned forward, acting like he was peering through a narrow opening. "The more I did, the surer I got. It was Bob Bayless, all right. That I do know. I kept watching, waiting, wondering what to do. How to handle it. Finally, I decided on a little test and crouched down where I could see his reaction and yelled, 'Hey, Bob' real loud."

He paused, smiling in a self-satisfied way.

"And?"

"And the son-of-a-bitch didn't even blink. But I could tell he heard me, though."

"How so?"

"The prick won the next hand and laughed that dumb laugh again. He tipped the dealer, then he told the blond chick to scoop 'em up. They started to go toward the cashier's booth, so I went on a parallel course." He frowned again. "There were so many goddamn people in the way, that by the time I got over there, Bayless and the bitch were gone." He leaned forward with an almost fervid gleam in his eyes. "But don't you see, that proves it. If he hadn't heard me yell his name, why wouldn't he have cashed in his chips? They beat feet outta there instead."

"You try to locate him?"

"Of course, but what could I do?" He shrugged, as if we shared the opinion that it would have been a Herculean task. "Christ, I even went back to the blackjack table and tried to ask the dealer if he knew him."

"What did he say?"

Herb shook his head and pursed his lips disgustedly. "I think the bastard was paid off. I saw Bayless tip him good. Anyway, he just shakes his head and says deals with too many people to know anybody."

"You believe him?"

"Hell, no. I demanded to see security." His face reddened. "When they came, I asked them about their surveillance tapes. Told him who I was, but they said, no dice."

"You take any other action?"

"I asked them to call the cops." His face started to look more flaccid. "When they got there, I talked to them. They took all my information and said they'd get back to me." He finished the sentence with a smirk. "They never did. We left the next day, so I reported the sighting to Dick, first thing, when I got back. But it was him. I'm sure of it." He made the big, horsy laugh imitation again. "You don't forget a stupid laugh like that."

"Do you know if the police checked the surveillance tapes?"

He shook his head. "If they did, they never told us. They probably ran a check on the info I gave them, found out it wasn't an open investigation, and filed my complaint under C, for crap."

I agreed with his assessment but didn't say so. "I'll look into that, as well."

Alex St. James

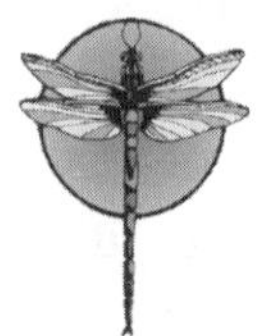

"But Alex," Larry said, "why did you call me? I'm sure Nicky would prefer to hear from you directly."

"That's the thing, Uncle Larry. When Nick and I were at

lunch he seemed rather reluctant to talk about all his charity work."

Larry let loose a sigh. "Isn't that just like my son? Doesn't want to blow his own horn."

"I thought you might run interference for me. This homeless story I'm working on needs heart. If Nick would be willing to introduce me to the priest who runs the shelter, and maybe put in a good word—"

"Absolutely. I know he'll be delighted to help you."

"I hope so. And . . ." I licked my lips before I dropped the rest of my request. "I hope you'll be able to help me, too. With my adoption information."

Long silence.

In the background I heard a news anchor's unmistakable cadence as he recited the morning's headlines. Larry was watching television. A quick glance at the clock told me it wasn't our station he had on right now. We didn't broadcast our midday news for another twenty minutes. Great. Not only was he distracted while he had me on the phone—he was distracted by a competitor.

"You know," he said finally, "Nicky's work with the homeless could make a great addition to your feature."

"I'm sure it would, but for this story—"

"I mean . . ." he drifted out of the conversation for a long moment. I waited. When he spoke again, I sensed resolve in his tone. "I'll level with you, Alex. Nicky's finally got his act together. We had some rough times there after his mother died. It took Nicky—Nick—a long time to come to terms with that. He got in with some rough crowds—did some things a father is not proud to talk about."

A little alarm chimed in my head. I remembered my parents discussing a troubled kid and their shock at his criminal activities. I'd eavesdropped as much as possible, but they were careful never to say the kid's name out loud. Despite my best efforts, I'd never discovered who they'd been talking about. Right about now I'd have to bet it'd been Nicky.

Larry was still talking. "If you were able to pull some strings and include Nicky in your story, it'd do a lot for his self-esteem."

My job was to develop and broadcast gripping features for *Midwest Focus NewsMagazine,* not wet-nurse a timid undertaker through an acute case of arrested development. I'd expected Larry to encourage me to go to lunch or for drinks with Nicky, not feature him in one of my stories.

I made a noncommittal noise. Bass wanted a story on *live* homeless people. Nick's work only came into play once they were dead.

"You'd be doing me a favor, Alex."

"And if I do you this favor, you'll be more inclined to look into my adoption information. Is that it?"

I thought I heard him chuckle. "You always were direct."

"Listen, Larry," I began, purposely leaving off the affectionate "uncle" title, "you have to understand that my first responsibility is to my station. I can't let personal interests interfere with that. Right now I'm simply looking to feature a homeless shelter with a reputation for helping get people off the streets."

"Nicky does that."

I resisted the urge to say, "Yeah, off the streets and six feet under."

"Tell you what, Alex," Larry said, desperation talking now. "Just give him a chance, okay? Just take a look. If it doesn't work, it doesn't work. But just promise me you'll think about interviewing Nicky for your show. I can't tell you what that would do for him."

"I can't promise—"

"Okay, bad choice of words. Just consider it. That's all I'm asking."

I tried to interrupt, but Larry wouldn't stop wheedling. "No pressure, Alex. Just give him a shot. Talk to him and I promise I'll take a look at your file and give you what I can. That fair enough?"

Chapter 4

Ron Shade

After the meeting was over, I made a beeline for the first Panera Bread I could find and sat at a corner table with a small coffee. I'd come to the conclusion long ago that it made no sense to buy a large size when you could go back for as many refills as you wanted. I guessed they were confident in the American public's short attention spans. A couple of giggly teenage girls sat in the opposite corner laughing and occasionally talking to each other when they weren't on their cell phones. The only other long-term customer was a guy in a Polo shirt, busy at the keyboard of his laptop. I had a small laptop myself, but I usually saved it for trips. Most of my work was done mentally or scribbling notes on paper.

My own cell phone rang and I answered it.

"Ron, Dick MacKenzie here."

I realized I'd left before tagging up with him after I asked him to trace down the X-ray thing. "What's up?"

"What's up?" His voice was petulant. "I thought you'd at least wait for me to get back before you took off. Godammit."

The swear word had come in as an afterthought. Like a guy who has to constantly remind other people that he's tough. That's usually a sure sign that the person isn't. Still, I was working for him, so I restrained my impulse to make a snappy comeback. "Sorry about that. What did you find out?"

"Nothing yet. I'm waiting on the damn doctor to call me back." He sighed. "You know how hard it is to get ahold of those bastards."

Almost as hard as a flood victim to get his house fixed after a hurricane. I longed to use the line, but for the moment, I had to stay on his good side.

"Well, I'd appreciate it if you'd keep working on it for me," I said.

"Hey, isn't that what the company's paying you for?"

The Company again. "My time is your time, Dick. You want me to run it down, I will. Just trying to keep those expenses down for you."

He snorted. "That'll be the day. Anyway, I was a bit perturbed at the way you've been going about this."

"Meaning?"

He sighed again. I'm sure it was for effect. He was trying to push his tough-guy act a bit further.

"Look, Ron, I requested your services on this because I thought you could really move this thing. Our security department handles fraud stuff and collections, but they're way out of their element trying to run down a missing person."

"Especially when he's been declared dead." It was my turn to add something for effect.

"Exactly." The bluster in his voice dipped a bit. "Like I told you, we got a lot riding on this one. How long before you get some results?"

"Dick," I put particular emphasis on the word, trying to sound as commiserating as I could under the circumstances.

"I've got to be systematic when I investigate this thing, otherwise I'll just end up chasing my tail. Plus, in order to find something solid, something we can use in court, I have to make sure I've thoroughly checked the foundation. Make sure it's sound. Understand?" He started to mumble something, but I jumped in again. "Whatever happened has its roots here, and I want to be damn sure I've checked out all the angles before I start making first-class reservations to go to Las Vegas with the company's money."

I figured the last part would get him. It did.

"First class!"

"Just kidding," I said with a laugh. "I wouldn't know what to do if I was flying anything but coach. Plus, I'd never jack up the expenses on you."

"Well," he said, his voice almost a stutter, "I appreciate that."

"Okay, buddy." I grinned to myself as I stole his line. "Show me how much you appreciate it by running down that X-ray thing." We shuffled over a few more minor details and I hung up. The coffee in my Styrofoam cup had gotten cold so I took advantage of the free refill.

I tried not to let Big Dick's whining get to me as I sipped the new coffee and evaluated just how credible Herb Winthrope had seemed. His rendition of the horsy-sounding laugh danced in my memory. If Bayless's laugh was half as distinctive as Herb's imitation, it might just stand out in a busy Vegas casino. As far as solid proof, we were still a whole lot more than six bits short of a dollar. Plus, he'd admitted he'd been drinking, which had to be factored into the identification. But Herb's description of Bayless's behavior toward the end of their association was another crack in the wall. It sounded like a man on the brink of something, but what? A midlife crisis? Maybe he was always a flip-flopper. Maybe he'd had too much booze one night and called his insurance man with an alcohol-laced solution to his unhappy life. Maybe he'd been banging Sandy or Candy or whatever the hell her name was, and maybe they'd broken it off. The increase in the policies was interesting. If you were going to die, it was good planning to up the amount of your life insurance. Herb Winthrope's Vegas sighting was a starting point. I'd have to work my way through a few more aspects of Bob Bayless's life before I could form a solid opinion, one way or another, if it was really him Herb Winthrope had seen in Sin City, or if it was just another booze-fueled desert apparition. After all, he'd said they'd been in the Mirage.

Since I was up in the northwest suburbs anyway, the next logical stop seemed to be the merry widow. I glanced at my watch. It was closing in on eleven. The girls giggled more vigorously on their cell phones. It seemed to disturb the guy with the laptop. He shot them an angry look, then continued his fixated stare at the screen. I got up. The giggling was starting to get to me, too. It was definitely time to leave.

After consulting my atlas, I managed to find my way to the Bayless residence on Eucalyptus Lane in nearby Oakton Hillside. It sounded like an appropriate address for a man presumed dead.

Before I rode by, I wanted to make sure there was someone home. I found the private detective's best friend, a row of pay phones, on the rear side of a Mobil gas station. Pulling up next to one, I dug the listing of Bayless's home phone out of the insurance file. Even though it cost me a couple of quarters just to get a dial tone, I didn't want my cell phone number showing up on any Caller ID screen the widow Bayless might have. It rang three times before a female voice said a tentative hello.

"*Si,* ah, Yes." I said, using my best fake Hispanic accent. "I call about *el caro,* ah de car."

"What car?"

"Ah, de for sale. In de paper."

"Sir, I'm afraid you have the wrong number."

"Es dis . . ." I recited the phone number, intentionally transposing the last two digits in Spanish.

"No, I'm sorry. You have the wrong number."

"Lo siento," I said, and hung up.

The quick conversation had told me two things. Someone, presumably Ms. Bayless, was home, and she was the type who was polite enough to be easily manipulated. Or maybe she just had a soft spot for Hispanics. I'd have to see how I did without the accent.

The house itself was an impressive-looking structure with a base of gray bricks and topped with a second story, covered in aluminum siding. I parked the Beater in front of it and got out slowly. No sense alarming the neighborhood. But they had to know that no self-respecting Jehovah's Witness would be seen driving around in a ride like that. With my sport coat covering my Beretta, and my necktie properly knotted and hanging at belt level, I hoped I looked like your typical Midwestern Olympia Insurance agent.

On my way up the walk I reminded myself of one of Chappie's maxims: go slow when you're feeling out a new opponent. Not that I had any intention of going a few rounds with the merry widow, but in a metaphorical sense, I couldn't afford to come on like gangbusters, either. I had to be delicate, judicious. I might need to persuade her later to okay an exhumation order.

I could hear the doorbell echoing in the house. Presently the solid inner door opened and I saw an attractive, forty-something woman looking through the glass of the screen door at me. She had light brown hair framing her face and wore a tan sweatshirt and blue jeans. She brushed an errant strand away from her face and asked if she could help me.

"Mrs. Linda Bayless?" I asked, remembering her name from the file.

"Yes."

"My name is Ron Shade," I said, holding up my private investigator's ID. "I'm working for Midwestern Olympia Insurance on a follow-up investigation. Mr. MacKenzie can verify my employment status if you want to check." I held out one of Big Dick's cards.

She opened the door a fraction and took the card. As she looked at it, a slight crease appeared between her eyebrows.

"Midwestern Olympia? They were the ones who paid the claim on my husband's death."

I smiled. "That's right, ma'am. I need to ask you a few more questions."

"I don't understand." Her tone was worried, confused. "I thought everything was settled. You people said you had that stupid ninety-day clause, and now I thought it was all settled."

"We have to do a follow-up on a few matters, and make sure everything is all right," I said. I flashed the smile again, hoping I looked as benign as possible. "I'll just need a few minutes of your time."

She exhaled hard and held the screen door open for me. I stepped inside, and she led me to a modestly furnished living room. It had blue carpeting, a long sofa, coffee table, and a pair of matching chairs. An artificial fireplace flanked the sofa. On the mantel above she had two pictures, one of a young boy and another of the same boy, a few years older in a football uniform. There didn't seem to be any photos of the dearly departed Robert anywhere. By design or necessity, I wondered.

"Please," she said, indicating the sofa, "sit down, Mr. Shade."

I pointed to the mantel. "Nice-looking kid. Your son?"

"Yes," she said.

"So how have you been?" I asked. "Any problems or anything we could assist you with?" It was one of those general, I'm-here-to-help questions. She wasn't offering me much and would probably toss me out in a second once she found out why I was here. Or would she?

"Everything is as good as can be expected." Her tone was tentative. The lady was cautious.

I popped a few more innocuous questions her way, then gradually worked my way to the meat of the matter.

"How about the funeral home expenses?" I asked. "Any problems there?"

She shook her head. "Actually, the company paid for everything. They even made the arrangements for us."

"The company? Midwestern Olympia?"

She stared at me momentarily, the area between her eyebrows creasing slightly. "No, the Manus Corporation. Where Bob worked."

"Oh, of course," I said, trying to cover. I'd been so bombarded by Dick and Herb's use of the company moniker, I'd assumed she was subscribing, too. Dumb. Perhaps it was time for a bolder move.

"I assume it was a closed casket funeral," I said. "Did you view the remains?"

She shook her head, the crease growing a bit deeper. "Mr. Shade, that seems like an odd question. Just exactly what is your assignment again?"

I smiled as gently as I could. "I'll get right to the point, Ms. Bayless. I've been engaged to look over the circumstances of your husband's death."

"Why?" The alarm was sounding. I had to try to allay her fears. For the moment.

"Actually, a lot of it's routine." I kept my voice calm. Matter-of-fact. "The company normally does a follow-up investigation in cases where a very large principal was paid out. In this case we had two double-indemnity claims." I regretted falling to Dick's level and resorting to dragging out "The Company."

"I don't understand. Wasn't all this done before?"

"Checks and balances," I said, trying for nonchalance again. "Your husband was driving downstate near Peyton when he was killed, right?" I figured reciting the facts, as she thought she knew them, would be a good groundbreaker.

She nodded.

"He was driving his own car?"

"No," she said. "A rental."

"You had more than one car?"

"Of course." Her words were a little bit clipped on that one. I was still tiptoeing through the minefield.

"Why would he rent a car then?"

She shrugged. "His Lexus was in the body shop."

"Accident?"

"A hit and run."

"Do you know why he was down in that area?"

She frowned and licked her lips. Her hands fidgeted. She had the look of a reformed smoker who really wanted to light one up bad.

"I believe he said it was a business trip," she said. There was something more in her tone, but I wasn't sure what. "He kept pretty much to himself about his work."

"He was in sales?"

She frowned again. "No, he'd been promoted to CEO. He still had accounts that he had to keep happy. But, for the most part, he kept overall control on finances."

"That was for the Manus Corporation?"

"Yes."

"How long had he worked for them?"

She seemed about to answer, then the corners of her eyes tightened. "Mr. Shade, I'm certain you must have all this information. Is it really necessary to go over it like this?"

I smiled again. "Just trying to get an overall picture of things.

How was it between you two before he died?"

"What makes you think that's any of your business?"

"He'd contacted one of our agents and said he was getting divorced. I wondered if it was troubled between you and him at the end?"

"Why are you asking me this?" The fire was growing in her tone. "What can you possibly gain by it?"

Her mouth puckered and I was certain she was getting ready to ask me to leave. Actually, I wouldn't have minded. Beating up on widows wasn't my idea of a fun afternoon. But I figured I'd try a different tactic. Angles, use angles, Chappie would always yell at me.

"Was he depressed?" I asked. "Do you think he could have intentionally run his car off the road?"

That brought a quick but bitter-sounding laugh. "Robert? Do something as noble as take his own life? Hardly."

"How would that be noble?"

The frown came back. "Mr. Shade, I'm afraid I'm going to have to ask you to leave. My son will be home soon, and I don't want you upsetting him."

I saw the opening and took it, even though I didn't feel good about it.

"That's one of the reasons I figured I'd approach you first," I said. I let it hang there while the realization washed over her. Her response was as sharp as a blade.

"You stay away from him with all this shit." The corners of her mouth twisted downward.

"I'll do my best," I said, pressing slightly. "But I do need a few more answers."

"What then. Hurry up."

"Your marriage. How was it at the time of his death?"

"Pathetic," she said. "He was seeing someone. His secretary, of all people." Her mouth twisted again, this time going from anger to disgust.

"He admitted this to you?"

"He didn't have to." She gave another harsh little laugh. "I walked in on them at the company picnic. Caught her giving him—the bitch."

I tried for a commiserating look. "I take it that caused a scene?"

The laugh again, caustic and bitter. "Did it ever. She left, and I started screaming at him. He practically dragged me to the car, tossed me in, and drove home. It continued once we got here. It got pretty ugly."

"Did he harm you?"

She shook her head. "Only by his callousness. He kept refusing to talk to me, and I was calling him every name in the book. Luckily, Chad wasn't home. Bob tried to leave and I wouldn't let him. I tried to stop him, scratched his face. He called the police."

"Sounds like it was pretty hard for you." I wanted her to feel like I saw her as the victim, and after all, in a way, she was.

She nodded, really into telling the story now. All thoughts of reticence blown away by the winds of emotion. "They came, saw his face, and asked what happened. He said he just wanted to leave. The police asked if he'd touched me. When I said no, they let him drive off."

"How long was this before his accident?"

"A few months." She sighed. "He stayed away for three days, then crawled back, all apologetic. Told me he'd stayed in a motel and showed me the receipts. Said it had been a one-time lapse in judgment at the picnic. Said they'd fired her at Manus. Told me to call to check if I didn't believe him."

"Did you?"

"No. He convinced me that we should put it all behind us. For Chad's sake." Her hands fidgeted again. "You wouldn't happen to have a cigarette, would you?"

I shook my head.

"I quit three months ago," she said, "but every now and then I just crave the feeling."

"It's good you quit," I said. "So did things get better between you?"

She shook her head, wringing her hands again. "Yes and no. He seemed like he became more focused on work. Spent time here, but always brought the company papers and reports with him." A solitary tear wound its way down her cheek. We heard the sound of a car pulling into the driveway and Ms. Bayless looked up. "You've got to go. It's Chad. I won't have him upset by this."

Since I figured asking her to agree to an exhumation order at this point was pushing it, I got up and handed her one of my cards.

"In case you want to get in touch with me," I said.

She crinkled the card, crushing it in her palm as she stood up. "Just leave. Now."

We walked to the front door and were met by the tall kid in the picture. He looked to be about seventeen or eighteen with the rangy build of a jock. A trace of reddish acne formed an uneven line along the side of his chin. His expression was perplexed as he looked from me to his mother.

"Mom? What's going on? Who's this?"

"The gentleman's just leaving," she said. It must have been the strain of holding it in, because her voice cracked as she said it. She brought her hand to her face and tried in vain to hold back the flow of tears.

I started to move by him and out the door.

"Hey." His fingers grabbed at my arm. "What'd you do to my mom?"

"Nothing," I said, brushing his hand away. "We were just talking."

"Talking? Bullshit. I'm not through with you yet, asshole." He tried to grab my arm again, with both hands this time.

"Chad, no!" his mother shouted.

"Who is this asshole?" he yelled.

I took this opportunity to pivot slightly, pushing on his elbow and pulling my arm out of his grasp. "Excuse me." I stepped onto the cement sidewalk, but the kid came after me, balling up his fist.

I'd had enough of beating up on Robert Bayless's family today, and didn't want to hurt him. On the other hand, the thought of catching one and having my still-tender eyebrow ripped open didn't enter into the realm of options, either. I reached out and caught his arm, pushing him back toward the door.

"Look, kid, I was just leaving. Now back off."

He rebounded off the door and came at me again, trying to grab me with his left and cocking his right arm back like he wanted to throw a roundhouse. I didn't wait to find out. Reaching out, I seized his extended left, encircling the wrist and bringing it down sharply. His mother screamed. I shifted my superior weight and used my right forearm as a brace, securing him in what they used to call the clamp in the army. Keeping my eye out for Ms. Bayless, I walked him to the brick wall and held him there, my face inches from his ear.

"Look, kid, I don't want to hurt you." I exerted a little pressure on his trapped arm, letting him feel that I could break it if I wanted. The pain made him stop. "Now I'm going to let you go in a second, when you've calmed down. But if you keep coming at me, I'll have no other choice but to drop you. Get it?"

"Suck my dick, motherfucker," he said.

The kid had been watching too many rap videos. I ratcheted up the pressure slightly. "One more time."

Ms. Bayless was pounding at me now, imploring me to let him go. I said I would, as long as he agreed not to come at me again. "Like I said, ma'am. I don't want to hurt him."

"Chad, leave it alone," Ms. Bayless said. "Please. Come in the house."

"We agreed, Chad?" I asked.

"Don't say my fucking name, asshole." His tone was still defiant, but I sensed a weakening that told me he realized he was way overmatched.

"We agreed?"

He started to mumble some more profane threats, so I exerted just a little bit more pressure. He rose onto his toes.

"I can't hear you," I said, using an old line from my basic training days.

"Yeah." It came out with a grunting breath. "Just get in your fucking, piece of shit car and get outta here, asshole. You ever come back bothering my mom again, I'll kill you. Understand?"

I let the irony slip by that he was threatening to kill me from a totally helpless position. But, hell, I probably would have done the same thing if the positions had been reversed.

I kept the armlock on him, backed up, instructing Ms. Bayless to open her screen door. When she did, I walked Chad inside, gave him a healthy, but subdued shove forward, and then backed away. He came to the edge of the door, his face still a picture of rage, but stopped. "If I ever see you again, I'll kill you," he said, raising his finger and pointing at me.

I figured if things had reached the woofin' stage, it was safe enough for me to walk to the Beater and leave.

"Have a nice day," I said over my shoulder as I walked across their thick lawn.

Chapter 5

Alex St. James

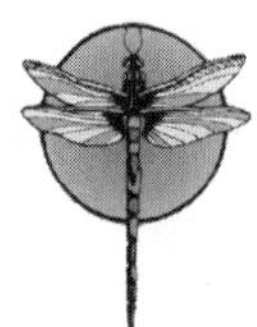

When Bass handed me the Taser instructor's card, he'd told me to "Call this guy to set up a lesson or two." I'd left several voice mails on an automated machine with a synthesized greeting, so I was surprised by the female voice when I finally got through. "Terry Hewitt?" I asked, just to be sure.

"That's me."

We talked a bit about the lessons I'd need. She asked, "Do you have an FOID card?"

I did. My last investigative skirmish left me knowing that I was sorely lacking in firearms knowledge and I'd vowed to correct that. I'd applied for and received my Firearms Owners Identification Card—required to shoot or own a gun in Illinois—despite the fact I didn't own any guns myself.

Terry and I set up private lessons at her range. One for later today and another tomorrow. She told me that this would be enough to carry me through my Taser-carrying needs while undercover, but cautioned that I should continue lessons until I felt comfortable with firearm handling.

As I hung up the phone, Bass strode in. "What are you still doing here? Shouldn't you be out on the streets?"

I couldn't tell if he was joking or not. He seemed to enjoy needling me and drew particular pleasure when his attacks provoked a rise. Today I just didn't feel like playing along. "You want a good story?" I asked. "Then let me take care of this in my own good time."

"I got a question for you. About the car I bought."

"Shoot."

"What did the guy tell you about it? I mean," Bass swagged his head from side to side. "I've been thinking about how much I paid for it. Something's wrong. Maybe it's one of those flood cars from New Orleans."

"The guy lives around here."

"Yeah, but how do you know he isn't trafficking flood cars?"

"Is it giving you any trouble?"

"No, but what happens a month from now, if it does?"

I rolled my eyes. This was *so* not my problem. "If it makes you feel better, you should call the guy and ask him."

He gave me a pointed look. "He probably wouldn't tell *me* the truth."

"I'm not getting involved here."

"Come on. He'd tell you the truth."

"Give it a rest, Bass. Enjoy the car. Quit looking for trouble."

"I'll give you his number."

"I have his number. I gave it to you, remember?" I pointed to my Rolodex. "But I don't intend to use it."

"Five-minute conversation. That's it. Ask him what's wrong with the car. Smile and look cute. He won't be able to resist."

Sexist comments aside, I couldn't let this one go. "And how is he supposed to appreciate my smile and batting eyes—" I demonstrated "—if I'm talking with him over the phone?"

"Take him out for lunch. He seemed like one of those macho

guys who'd hate it if a girl paid her own way. I'll pop for lunch and you quiz him about the car. That'll make him feel indebted to you, and he'll tell you everything. How's that sound?"

"Do it yourself." I boosted myself to my feet. "I'm out to hit the streets."

He frowned, but started for the door.

"Hey, Bass," I called. "What're you doing later?"

He turned. "I don't know. Why?"

I fixed him with a bright smile. "I'm heading out for my first Taser lesson. When I get back I might need someone to practice on."

Ron Shade

As I drove out of the subdivision, I mulled over exactly where things had started to go awry and how I could have handled them better. It had turned out badly, that was for sure, and I kind of sensed things were going from bad to worse when I saw the police car swing around and fall in behind me. I watched the rearview mirror and saw the cop talking on his radio. Seconds later, the overhead red-and-blue lights came on, and I pulled over to the right shoulder, rolled the window down, and waited.

We were in a long stretch of pleasant-looking roadway, with a grassy park on one side and a strip mall on the other. The door of the squad car opened and the cop got out. He was a young guy, short and squat, with the build of a weightlifter. At first glance his hair looked blond, but then I saw that it was dark at the roots.

Oh, great, I thought. A frosted cop.

His hand dropped down and rested on the butt of the semiauto jutting out from his holster as he walked up to my driver's-side window. I made sure to keep both of my hands on the top of the steering wheel.

"Good afternoon, officer," I said, trying to sound as pleasant as I could.

"All right, buddy, out of the car."

I nodded and flashed a grin. "You mind telling me what I'm being stopped for?"

"I said, get out of the fucking car. Now."

The profanity convinced me that he was something of a hothead. I'd been there myself and knew that my question shouldn't have ratcheted things up to the next level so quickly. I figured I'd better play it cautious.

"Look," I said, "before I do, I should probably let you know I'm wearing a gun."

That was all he needed. His fingers tightened around the handle of the big semiauto, a Glock 21 from the looks of it, and he brought the gun up level with my face.

"Get out of the car now!"

His finger was inside the trigger guard.

I slowly reached out through the window and used my left hand to open the Beater's door. Keeping both palms outward and elevated, I eased my legs out and started to get out with very slow deliberation. I thought about mentioning that I was a licensed private investigator, but decided too many words might confuse him, and I didn't want him to tighten that trigger finger. But I didn't want to get shot, either.

"Look, I'm a PI," I said, straightening up. The sound of another squad car approaching, the siren bleating intermittently, drifted in the still air. I only hoped the backup wasn't another rookie.

"Shut the fuck up and keep your hands where I can see 'em," the young cop said.

I complied, still watching that finger inside the trigger guard.

The second squad pulled behind the first one, and the officer got out. He looked older, slightly more shopworn, and hopefully more experienced. He did a quick-step to the rear of the Beater and sized things up.

"What you got, Eddie?" the second cop asked.

"Fucker's got a gun."

The older cop's eyebrows raised and he drew his own weapon, but kept it down by his leg. "That right, buddy?"

"Yeah, it is," I said. "It's on my belt, rear right side. My PI license and tan card are in my inside coat pocket."

I saw the older cop's eyes drift toward his partner's Glock. His head ticked back slightly, then he brought his own gun up. His was a Glock as well. Popular gun in this area. But he kept his index finger out of the trigger guard.

"Eddie," the older cop said, "holster your piece and pat him down when I tell you."

"But—"

"I got him," the older cop said. "Do like I tell ya."

Eddie did as he was told, and I breathed a slight sigh of relief. It could have been worse. He could have shot himself in the leg as he holstered it. Or worse yet, shot me in the leg.

I turned and placed my palms on the roof of the Beater, feeling Eddie's hands gliding over me.

"A little bit more to the right," I said, trying to inject a little levity into the situation. That turned out to be a mistake. He shoved me forward, bouncing my chest into the door post.

"When I want some shit out of you, asshole, I'll squeeze your head."

I grinned. "You think that one up all by yourself?"

He punched me in the right side. I was used to taking punches, so I kind of let my body roll slightly to minimize the impact. It was just an arm punch, anyway, and hardly affected me at all. But I didn't want him to know that. I grunted like it really hurt. Better to feign injury than risk embarrassing him.

"For Christ's sake, Eddie," the older cop said. "Knock it off."

I felt my sport coat being lifted, my Beretta grabbed from the pancake holster.

"A nine mil," Eddie said.

"Give it here and cuff him," the older cop said.

Out of the corner of my eye, I saw the Beretta being handed over. Then I felt Eddie roughly twisting my arms behind my back. He ratcheted the first cuff on my left wrist and tried to bring my right arm around but found it difficult.

"Cooperate, asshole," he yelled. "Or I'll knock the fuck out of you some more."

This guy was a piece of work. "I am cooperating."

"Take it easy," the older cop said. I turned my head and saw he'd lowered his gun again. "Use two sets of cuffs. He's too big."

"Shit," Eddie muttered. I heard him lift the flap of his second handcuff holder and felt a second cuff slip over my right wrist. Seconds later, I felt the tension and knew that he'd secured the remaining two cuffs together. He'd left my palms facing each other, instead of using the proper technique of keeping the palms facing outward. The kid had a lot to learn. The older guy holstered his Glock but still had my Beretta in his left hand. He brought it up and ran the serial number with his radio. While we waited for the dispatcher's response, I cocked my head toward him.

"How about checking my inside breast pocket? My ID and PI license are inside it."

Eddie shoved me harder against the car. The older guy told him to back off and check for the ID.

"And the license," I said, trying to sound as placid as possible. To my knowledge, I hadn't done anything wrong, but I didn't know what kind of story the Baylesses had told the cops. Probably that I'd beat up poor little Chad. I should have seen this one coming.

"So why am I being rousted, anyway?" I asked, as matter-of-factly as I could.

"Shut up," Eddie said. I felt his palm hit me squarely in the back. His other hand reached inside my coat and withdrew the black leather wallet with my PI license.

"That it?" the older guy asked.

"Yeah."

He held out his hand and Eddie gave it to him. After opening it and glancing at my name, his brow furrowed.

"You Ron Shade the fighter?"

"That's me. You been to any of my fights?"

He shook his head, glancing from the picture to my face, and back again. "Saw a few on TV."

"Good old ESPN." Suddenly I heard the approaching wail of another squad car. I was obviously the remedy for a particularly boring day shift. I said as much.

The new squad car pulled up and a big guy got out wearing a white shirt with blue chevrons, outlined in gold, on the short sleeves. He paused to place his hat on his head before he walked over to us. As he approached I silently hoped he knew what he was doing. His name tag said GILLESPE.

"This the suspect?" the supervisor asked.

"Sure is, sarge," Eddie said, twisting me around to face them. "And look what he had on him." He pointed to the Beretta the other guy was holding.

"Licensed PI," the older cop said, handing my ID to the sergeant.

"Mr. Shade," Sergeant Gillespe said, "you want to tell me your version of what happened over at the Bayless household?"

"Be glad to. But if I don't say what you want to hear, is your boy Eddie gonna punch me while I have the cuffs on again?"

The sergeant's mouth twisted downward. He looked to both of the patrolmen, then back to me. His eyes were a very pale brown.

"What were you doing around here?" It was directed toward me.

"Working a case," I said.

"What kind of case?"

It was technically none of his business, but most likely he already knew it anyway. He'd mentioned the Baylesses. I figured I might get out of the cuffs faster if I played ball.

"I'm working on an insurance investigation. Robert Bayless was killed about six months ago."

"Tell me something I don't know," he said. "What happened over at their house?"

I tried to shrug. Not an easy move when your hands are cuffed behind your back. "It's a difficult subject to broach. The widow got upset, I got up to leave, and the kid came home. He thought I'd upset his mother, and he jumped me."

Sergeant Gillespe's face tightened. "I heard you roughed him up."

I shook my head. "Not really. I got him in an armlock to keep from having to hurt him."

"You know he's a minor, right?"

I nodded. "He's big for his age."

"Sarge," the older cop said, "if this guy wanted to hurt the kid, he could have. He's a professional fighter. I seen him fight on TV."

The sergeant's eyes narrowed as he scrutinized me. "Is that a fact?"

I nodded again, figuring now was not the time to bring up the fact that I was heavyweight kickboxing champion of the world. That and a buck sixty would get me a small coffee at most Dunkin' Donuts. I'd been rousted before and had a hunch from the feel of things this one was winding down. I didn't really want to bring up George's name but figured it might end this sooner rather than later.

"If you call Detective George Grieves, CPD Violent Crimes," I said, "he can vouch for me." I rattled off the number for them.

The mention of another cop affected them. Especially a homicide dick from the big city. Gillespe handed my ID back to the older guy and told him to check on it.

"If he's not there," I called after him, "ask for his partner, Doug Percy."

The sergeant turned toward me. "What was that you said about Officer Scott punching you?"

I shot a quick glance at Eddie, whose face had turned bright red.

"Aww, sarge, he was resisting arrest," he said.

Gillespe ignored him and continued to look at me. "Well?"

"Hell, it wasn't much of a punch anyway," I said.

This must have tripped some little button inside Eddie's head because he reached out and grabbed the lapels of my sport coat. The sergeant yelled at him and he let me go, but not before shoving me back into the Beater. It looked worse than it felt.

"That's it," Gillespe said, leveling a finger at Eddie. "Go back to the station and wait for me in my office."

"But . . . He started it."

"Get outta here. Go'wan." The sarge pointed at his cruiser. The older cop was running up to us now, a worried look on his face. Eddie turned in a huff and waddled back to his car, his broad shoulders and overdeveloped traps giving him the appearance of a bowling ball with arms and legs. The sergeant watched him go, then turned to the older copper. "Anything?"

"That Grieves guy wasn't there, but his partner did vouch for Shade."

Gillespe heaved a sigh and slipped a handcuff key off a clip on his belt. "Mr. Shade, we're going to have to make a report of this incident. It'll reflect both sides of the story of what happened."

I felt the pressure on my wrists ease as he took the first cuff off.

"Just out of curiosity," I said, "what did the Baylesses say?"

I heard him give an extended exhale through his nostrils as he was unlocking the second cuff. My other arm was free and I brought my hands up and started massaging my wrists.

"Mrs. Bayless called nine-one-one. Said you'd beat up her son. The dispatch came out giving your description and license plate number."

I grinned. "And a car like this is not hard to spot, right?"

He smirked.

"We need to go back over there to get this straightened out?" I asked.

Gillespe considered this for a moment, then shook his head. "I don't think so. Since her husband's death, Mrs. Bayless has been a bit . . . emotional."

"I kinda sensed that." I rubbed my wrist some more. "Sorry if I upset her, but there were some things the company needed verification on." There I was using "the company," just like Herb and Dick. Surprisingly, I found a modicum of comfort in it. Like having a standard fall guy to blame things on when it all turned to shit.

"It would probably be best, if you need to get more information, to come back another time," Gillespe said. "Or maybe send another one of your operatives."

"This is a contract case for me," I said. "I am the other operatives. But I'm through for the moment."

His lips tightened. "Now, about this stop with my officers . . ."

I raised my eyebrows slightly and waited for him to finish. Counterpuncher.

"It seems Officer Scott may have overreacted a bit," he said.

I gave my other wrist a slight rub. "You could say that."

The sarge and the older cop exchanged glances. A hint of worry floated in the air between them.

"Mr. Shade, do you wish to make a citizen's complaint against Officer Scott?" Gillespe asked.

I considered my options, trying to figure if there was some mileage that could be gained here.

"Nah. But it'd probably be a good idea to send him to some anger management classes. And have your range officer talk to him about keeping his finger out of the trigger guard until he's ready to shoot. Sympathetic grasp reflex. Either that, or get a good civil attorney on retainer." I grinned. "I can recommend one or two, if you want."

Gillespe nodded and extended his hand. "I appreciate it. And I will speak to Officer Scott about this."

"Sounds like a good solution," I said. "Now, if I could get my gun and IDs back?"

The older cop handed me my license and turned to go back to his car. "I'll get his piece," he said, walking away.

I took one of my cards out of my badge case and handed it to the sergeant. "How about a favor?"

He looked at me quizzically.

"I need any records and reports you might have on the Baylesses," I said. "Domestics, accidents, all that stuff."

He stared at me for a moment and said, "You'll have to file a

Freedom of Information Act request."

"Sarge, come on. That could take weeks. I operate on a strict timetable." I pushed the card closer, trying to estimate if I should play the indebtedness card yet. I figured it was as good a time as any. "I mean, I'm overlooking Officer Scott's . . . overzealousness, ain't I?"

After a few seconds, he took the card and smiled. "You like to push things, don't you?"

Actually, I thought, sometimes I prefer counterpunching.

Alex St. James

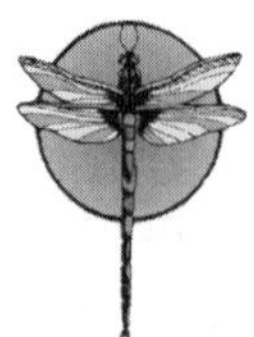

The place wasn't very big, and every inch of its musty closeness was covered with some sort of gun or accessory. There were a couple of racks of camouflage clothing and camping stuff in one corner, but the rest of the place was all rifles, revolvers and semiautomatics.

Terry grimaced when she saw the weapon Bass gave me. "Older version," she said. "The new ones are lighter, easier to conceal, and have a lot better pulse."

"My boss is a cheapskate."

She grinned. A few years older than I, she was blond, petite and full of smiling energy. Not at all what I would have pictured for a championship target shooter. I guess I expected her to have weathered skin and cowboy boots. Terry here could mingle among Chicago's glitterati without earning a second glance.

No, I amended. With a shape and face like hers, she'd garner plenty of second glances.

"This isn't a bad weapon," she said. "It's sturdy. It'll get the job done. And it's a good one to use for training. You master this clunker, you'll be a champ with one of the newer models."

"I hope I'm never in the market for a newer version."

Terry gestured me around one of the glass cases. "Ned," she said to a grungy-looking man near the cash register, "we'll be in back."

Busy cleaning a weapon, he didn't look up, but just nodded.

She led me through a small corridor to a garage-like structure attached to the back of the building. Much deeper than a garage, this had to be the range. It was a lot less impressive than I'd expected. I guess I'd imagined a shiny ultra-modern structure, like where TV cops go to practice. This place was old, its far recesses very dark. It smelled of sweat, metal and something else—gunpowder, probably.

"What about a handgun?" Terry asked. "You ever consider owning one?"

"I'm not the weapon-carrying type," I said.

"First lesson: we don't say 'weapon,' we say firearm or gun."

"Why?"

"Think about it. You pick up a hammer, a stapler, a box cutter . . ." she gave me a meaningful look, ". . . any one of them can be a weapon. We try to avoid the negative connotation by being more precise."

Uh-oh, I thought. Here comes the NRA lecture. I waited for her to launch into a speech about "types" who carry guns.

She surprised me by changing the subject. "So, why's your boss buying you a Taser? Are you his bodyguard or something?"

I laughed and explained about my homeless project.

"Hang on a minute," she said. "These things are illegal in Chicago."

"I thought only handguns—"

"Nope. Tasers, too. And if you're not in law enforcement, you can't even own this model in Illinois." She tapped the weapon Bass had given me. "Makes me wonder how he got ahold of one of these."

"Probably in some back alley."

Terry scratched her head. "I'm not sure what to do here."

"It's okay," I said, disappointed. I realized how much I wanted to try out the little gizmo. It looked like my chances were fading fast.

"Listen," Terry said, sounding genuinely concerned, "you can't go out unarmed if you plan to live on the streets."

"I guess I'll depend on my pepper spray."

She thought about it for a moment. "Be right back."

While she was gone, I looked around. A "wall" of sorts was split into five separate stations, looking like horse stalls. Beyond were targets, some placed near the shooting stalls, some farther away. To my right was a large plastic garbage can, about three-quarters full of brass-colored shells. Behind it was a broom and dustpan.

Terry came back, carrying a leather pouch. "The State of Illinois allows you to transport your Taser, as long as it's kept in a manner where it can't be used." She pulled the leather pouch around her waist—it was a fanny pack—and zipped it open. "If you carry the Taser like this, but keep the cartridge in your pocket . . ." she demonstrated, "then you're within Illinois law guidelines."

"But not Chicago's?"

She winced. "No. City ordinance. You'd be breaking the law to have possession of a Taser within city limits. But . . ."

"But?"

"If you stay out of the city on your homeless project, and you keep the pieces separate, like I have them here, and you were ever stopped and searched," she made a face that made me doubt that she really believed what she was telling me, "you could make a good argument for simply transporting your Taser."

"Transporting it while impersonating a homeless person."

"Listen, I'm not about to advise you to break the law. And I'm about as far from being sexist as you're going to get. I know that just because you're female doesn't mean that you can't take care of yourself—but you're relatively small, like me." She shrugged. "I wouldn't hang out with a bunch of unpredictable people without some sort of backup."

I decided she was right. "When do we begin?"

Terry nodded. "Good girl."

She headed to the second stall, and turned a crank that brought the paper target zipping forward till she could reach up and unclip it from its perch. The whole setup was so low-tech, it amazed me. But then again, we'd been shooting projectiles at bad guys since David nailed Goliath—maybe we had come a long way after all.

"We won't use targets for this?"

"Different ones." She rummaged through a cabinet built below the shelf and came out with another printed paper target, but this time instead of a black-and-white photograph, the bad guy was silver.

"We're targeting aliens now?"

She laughed as she replaced the silver silhouette on the clips above our head and cranked it out.

"That's not very far," I said.

"Your Taser's only got a twenty-one-foot reach. If you shoot, you better make sure your target's close." She picked up the disruptor-looking instrument and walked me through some of the specifics, pointing out the battery indicator, the sights, and the safety. "When you're in trouble, you get one shot, Alex. You got that? One."

"And if I miss?"

"Two options." She held her fingers up. "Well, three, I guess. If you fire your Taser at an attacker, and you miss, you can still use this as a stun gun. But you have to drive forward to do so—you have to make contact with the attacker. At a minimum you can't be more than two inches away for the stun to have any effect. If you don't think that's your style, you could change your cartridge." Her lips pulled to one side. "Of course, that's hard to do in a hurry, especially when you're feeling threatened."

"What's the third option?"

"Run like hell."

I laughed, but it began to dawn on me that I was learning how to handle a weapon—and I did think of it as a weapon—because I intended to put myself in harm's way. I shifted my weight, and fought the sudden flip in my stomach. Time to pay attention.

"Taser technology works by causing muscular-skeletal disruption."

This thing really *was* a disruptor. Just like *Star Trek.*

Terry clicked the cartridge, a plastic boxlike piece with a yellow facing, into the front of the Taser. "This is what you'll have to replace—in a hurry—if you miss your man. But you're not going to miss, right?"

"Right," I said, feeling less confident than I sounded.

"You aim this just like you would a firearm, but you have to remember that if your subject is wearing thick clothing, this Taser won't have any effect. Newer models do a better job of getting through clothes, but if your subject is wearing three or four layers, you might as well use pepper spray."

"And if I fire, and miss . . . or if I fire and it can't penetrate the guy's clothing, he'll be pretty PO'd."

"Yeah," she said matter-of-factly. "That's why you're not going to miss. And that's why . . ." She took up a shooter's stance and took a deep breath. A small red dot appeared low on the target's shape. Terry squeezed the trigger and fired. The Taser made an odd clicking sound as the probes shot out and pierced the alien. "You aim for where the clothes are tight."

The target shimmered and shook. Taser prongs shot right into the silver silhouette, right in the thigh.

"I should shoot him in the leg?"

"You should shoot him in the torso, right here," she swept her hand from chest to groin. "The wider the spread the more effective the charge. But if he's wearing a lot of layers on his upper body, you'll have to hit him where you can get through. Like, say, his blue jeans." She tapped her thigh. "But, remember this." She held up a finger. "This is important. Just because the guy goes down doesn't mean you're in the clear. This pulse only lasts five seconds. That's it. With no lingering effects. The instant the pulse stops, he's going to jump to his feet and come after you."

I shook my head at the plastic gun. "So, this thing buys me five seconds."

"Five seconds per trigger pull. Keep pulling if you need to. In fact, I'd advise you to just hold the trigger back tight as you can. That sends a constant pulse—one that doesn't quit until you release it." She gave me a wry look. "Or till your batteries run down. Make sure you have fresh ones. They're double-A, but they're a special kind. I'll get you some up front."

"Okay, I guess I'm ready."

"Not yet." She crouched and pulled out two pair of safety goggles from the cabinet. "I like to be careful. Especially around a first-time handler."

Terry clicked a new cartridge into position for me. "Try shooting first, then I'll have you practice changing cartridges under pressure."

I'd handled guns in the past, and I knew some basics. Still, when I aimed and fired—the clicking prongs stinging the target nice and wide across the silver man's chest—I jerked in surprise. I'd expected a recoil. There was none.

I let go of the trigger, and the clicking stopped.

"Nice shot, but you should hold the trigger," Terry said. "Here. Replace the cartridge."

As I squeezed the clips to release the front piece, she continued to teach.

"Once the probes hit someone, they become a bio-hazard. That means you have to be super careful about not sticking yourself. They'll have blood and tissue all over them." I grimaced as she went on. "And if you find the need—I can't imagine why you would—to touch the subject while he's being pulsed, you have to avoid contact in the area between the two probes. If, say, your hand comes in contact with his chest between the prongs, it's called 'touching in the beam' and you will be affected by the shock."

This was sounding like more fun every minute. "What if only one probe hits?"

"It won't," she said. "Because we're going to practice so much that you will not miss. But . . . if for some reason one of the probes does miss, or dislodge, you'll have to drive forward and shove this up against the guy." She gave me a pointed look. "While keeping the trigger pulled the whole time. Do not let up until help arrives or unless you're prepared to run."

"Got it," I said. But did I?

"Okay," she said, "let's go again."

Ron Shade

My cell phone had been vibrating in the Beater while I'd been waiting in the lobby of the police station for the sarge to get those copies of the reports for me. A better man might have had some reservations about circumventing the good old FOIA, but I didn't. One hand washes the other sometimes, and the whole idea of the Act was to make it easier for citizens to cut through the red tape. When Sergeant Gillespe came out about fifteen minutes later with a manila envelope filled with sheets of paper, he shook my hand and thanked me again for my cooperation.

I thanked him in return and he reassured me that he was going to address some issues with Officer Scott. I thought about leaving one of my cards for Mighty Mouse, inviting him to come workout at Chappie's, but decided against it. It had been a roundabout route, but I'd ended up with most of what I'd come for.

As I got back into the Beater and headed toward the I-294 ramp, I glanced down at my missed calls. One number I didn't recognize, with a 312 area code, and George's cell number. No doubt Doug had probably called him to mention that he'd received that call from the suburban PD. And naturally, George wanted to check up on me.

George was more like a surrogate big brother than a friend, and sometimes he was borderline surrogate mother. Growing up, he'd been a big influence on me, having been in the military with my much older brother, Tom. There were nineteen years separating us, and since I was the product of our father's second marriage, to a much younger woman after Tom's mother had died, there had always been an unfortunate distance between my brother and me. His experience in Vietnam had shaken him, too. Left him emotionally brittle. When he'd come back I was just a little kid, and the distance increased. It had been George who'd filled the gap, becoming closer than kin, as the saying goes, watching out for me in my final teen years, giving me the youth of America lectures to try and keep me out of trouble, and providing guidance as I finished up high school. It had also been George who convinced me to go into the army after my life fell apart and my collegiate scholarship plans went down the tubes. "Be all you can be," he'd said. "And go Airborne." When I got out after participation in a couple of desert war games, he steered me toward the PD, where I excelled until I got fired.

I grimaced as the rumination started to reflect an unflattering pattern in my life. I'd let George down, big-time. Still, I thought, you can't change the past, so you gotta work on the future.

I came to a stop light and pressed the button to check my messages. The unfamiliar number turned out to be a cool, feminine voice.

"Hi, Mr. Shade," the recording said. "It's Alex St. James from *Midwest Focus.* I was wondering if you could give me a call at your earliest convenience." She rattled off the number and thanked me in advance.

Although I'd only met her once, and that was a brief introduction, I remembered that Alex St. James was a real babe. We'd almost bumped into each other, literally, at a gas station, and her boss had subsequently called me about buying the Firebird. He'd gotten a sweet deal and she probably wanted to call me and say thanks. Or maybe she had another reason . . . Maybe she just wanted an excuse to talk to me again. I pressed the buttons and let the phone do the dialing for me. Maybe this could be a good excuse to ask her out, or something.

A feminine voice, sounding like a black girl's, answered with a "Ms. St. James' office."

"Hi, this is Ron Shade, returning Ms. St. James' call."

Silence, then, "I'm sorry, sir, what was it in reference to?"

"Don't know exactly," I said. "She called and left me a message."

"Well, she's unavailable at the moment. If you want to leave a number I'll see that she gets it."

Nicely worded, I thought. Very neutral. Noncommittal. I gave her my cell and answering service numbers.

Have to wait and see what that's all about, I thought as I turned onto the ramp of the tollway and pressed some more buttons to return George's call. His cell phone rang twice.

"Ron Shade's information and reference service," he answered. From the sound of his voice, I could tell he was driving, too.

"What kind of a way is that to answer the damn phone?" I asked, making no attempt to curtail my amusement.

"Just telling it like it is. What kind of mess have you gotten yourself into now?"

"Everything's cool."

"Yeah, right." His voice evened out with concern. "Doug called me and said Oakton Hillside PD was checking up on you."

"A minor misunderstanding. All settled, right as rain, after I told them I was a friend of yours."

"Still lying for a living, huh?"

"Hey, I want any shit out of you, I'll squeeze your head."

I heard his chuckle, crackly with the buzz of interference. "That one's not bad. I'll have to use it sometime."

"Be my guest," I said. "Say, how about we get together for breakfast tomorrow?"

Silence.

"You there?" I asked.

"I'm here," he said. The flat tone of mild irritation was back in his tone. "So what is it you want me to do for you this time?"

Now it was my turn to chuckle. "Just figured I'd buy you breakfast, is all. Maybe clue you in about my upcoming fight."

"You got one coming up? Already?"

Actually, Chappie had been dragging his feet committing to a new one, wanting to field the best offer and also let my eyebrow completely heal. But since George had won big on my last one, I figured it was only appropriate that I keep him on the string a bit. For his own good, of course.

"Could be," I said.

"Hell, I figured you wanted me to run somebody for you, or something."

"Hence, Ron Shade's information service, right?"

His laugh was lost in a sea of crackling interference once more.

"Look, I'm on the Ryan," he said. "I can barely hear you. Call me later on or come over to the house. I'll have Ellen set an extra place at dinner if you can make it."

He terminated the connection, and I was driving along listening to dead-air nothingness. Too many dead spots on that expressway. But at least I'd laid the groundwork for what I needed to do. Eventually, I probably would need his help on this one.

After coasting through my second tollbooth, dutifully holding up the transponder so I didn't have to stop and pay, I set it back on the dash and grabbed the Bayless file. Luckily, the Beater had once been a luxury muscle car, and the steering wheel had three different adjustable heights. I brought it up to the uppermost position and set the file on the base of the wheel. As I drove, I turned pages, alternating quick glances at the string of cars ahead of me, and found what I was looking for.

Being a successful PI in Chicago meant being able to work out of the box sometimes. I wasn't handcuffed by the Bill of Rights, like George was, and people hired me with the understanding that I'd find things out, one way or another. George often joked with me about it. "The difference between you and me," he'd often say, "is that in the private sector, they expect results."

And I needed some quick results if I was going to move on this thing. After all, *the company* was depending on me. I smirked as I used my thumb to press the button going through my phone contacts on my cell phone. How did we ever get through the day without them? Although more than once, I'd made people wish they had.

Francis Griggas answered with his customary tentative hello. He hated doing business over the phone, which, considering the business he was in, was understandable.

"Francis, it's Ron Shade. I need you to run down some phone records for me."

"Okay, Ron." I could hear his fingers typing on a keyboard. "Give me your code word, please."

Ultra-paranoid, Francis always assigned people an identifier, which you had to say back to him before he'd take your order. It had always struck me as a bit much, but I played along because he was good at delivering the impossible without a lot of red tape.

"Rosebud," I said, gasping and giving my best imitation of Orson Welles.

"Okay," he said. "What you need?"

I read off Bayless's cell phone, home, and office numbers from the MWO file. "I need records for those going back the last year and a half."

Unperturbed as always, Francis repeated the numbers back to me.

"You got 'em," I said. "Can you put a rush on it?"

"Do my best," he said. "Call you when I got something."

He hung up. Traffic had slowed to a turtle crawl in front of me, but as far as the investigation was going, I figured things were moving along well enough that Big Dick and the company would be satisfied. I'd still bill him for the mileage, the phone calls, and special services, of course. Hopefully, once I had enough information, things would start coming together. Right now, I had zip, but all things considered, it hadn't been too bad of a first day. Plus, I had the added pleasurable speculation of wondering what Ms. Alex St. James wanted with me.

Chapter 6

Alex St. James

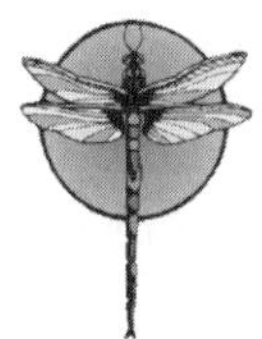

As I settled my bill and arranged for handgun lessons, I realized I had a missed call on my cell phone. Nicky Farnsworth had left me a voice mail inviting me to visit the homeless shelter where he volunteered his time.

I called him back immediately. Good fortune smiled on me when I found out that he had no pressing commitments for the rest of the afternoon and that he'd be happy to escort me to the shelter and introduce me to Father Morales. That meant I'd get going on my story, and I could avoid heading back to the office where William was probably winding up amid a slew of tearful good-byes. I'd said more than was necessary to my former colleague. Now it was time to move on.

An hour later I pulled up to Sunset Manor. The place was nice—as funeral parlors go—and I'd visited enough of them to consider myself a fair judge. This was one of the two-story models—where the mortician lives above the parlors. Expansive was the operative word. The building occupied the full city block on a busy street, with a grocery store to its immediate north and a video rental shop to the south. I parked up front, and made my way under the covered entrance to the double doors. I debated ringing the bell, but decided to just walk in.

The place was quiet as a tomb. When I'd gone Taser-ing, I'd changed from heels to athletic shoes, and now I was conscious of the *squeak-squeak* of my rubber soles against the polished tile floor. My voice echoed when I called out, "Nick?"

No sound, no movement. The lobby had a large crystal chandelier, but the four corridors stretching out from the building's center were unlit. Their dim recesses made me want to keep close to the exit. "Nick?" I called again, louder this time.

A door slammed from deep in the building, to my left.

Hard shoes clipped against distant tile. "Alex? Is that you?" A moment later he turned the corner and broke into a smile as he closed the space between us, hesitated, then hugged me. "You made good time."

I stepped back, surprised by the gesture. The hug had given me a noseful of his cologne. Somebody ought to tell him that it was to be splashed on, not showered with.

He broke away, blinked a couple of times, thrust his hands into his pockets and stared at nothing in particular. I waited for him to say something, but all I could think was that it was too quiet. I couldn't even hear the rush of traffic outside.

"A lot of new construction in the neighborhood, isn't there?" I asked, just to start conversation. "Is the shelter nearby?"

"The shelter? Oh. Yeah." His hands came out of his pockets. He clasped them together, affecting a very funeral-director-like pose, and then dropped them to his sides.

This guy needed a jumpstart. If he was this awkward in casual conversation with a female he knew since childhood, I couldn't imagine how he'd be with women in the throes of grief. "Should I follow you in my car?"

"No." It came out too loud. The chandelier's prisms tinkled.

"Okay . . . then what?" If Larry thought that his son would make a good on-air interview, he was sadly mistaken. It took effort to keep this scintillating banter going, and my patience was wearing thin.

Nick's lips tightened as though he was trying hard to remember something.

I tried again. "How about you give me directions and I'll just go there myself, then?"

"No," he said. "I mean . . . I thought you'd like to look around here a little." He licked his lips. "First. Before we go."

I understood now. As though Larry stood between us, whispering in Nick's ear, I could hear Daddy's suggestion—"Take your time, Nicky-boy. Let her get to know you."

With a pointed look at my watch I asked, "I don't want to miss Father Morales. How late does he stay?"

"He'll be there. He's always there."

There didn't seem to be much point in arguing. And, to be honest, I didn't want to pass up a chance to tour the funeral home's back rooms.

I shrugged. "Okay then, show me around."

On first glance, I decided that funeral home embalming rooms are both similar and completely different than autopsy laboratories. Autopsy rooms have a lot more people running around, and a lot more people *not* running around. This embalming room was designed for one client at a time. It was a bit more stark than the autopsy labs I'd been in—it had less personality. The Medical Examiners' staffs tended to treat autopsy labs like their offices with little reaffirmations of life—postcards, travel magnets, even utensils stored in snack cans—despite the undeniable evidence of mortality. But both settings were the same in one respect. They both carried death's pall. I could feel it pressing down on me, even as the room's chill forced my hands up to rub warmth into my arms.

"We have three more embalming rooms," he said. "There's another through that door," he swung his pointed finger to his left, "and two in the building's north wing."

"You need that many?"

"Not only do we do a brisk business here on our own, but the indigent population keeps us hopping."

"Us?"

"My staff. I have a twenty-four-hour answering service, of course, but I also have a receptionist, and several assistants. When we handle funerals, we need ushers, men to direct traffic, others to oversee the ceremonies, and I need to keep enough people on call in the event that we have more than two funerals going at once." He gave a sad smile. "In the case of the homeless, too, we need strong men to transport the remains. People from the street don't usually have their own pallbearers."

I nodded and asked a question I'd always been curious about. "Are they heavy? The caskets?"

"Very. In fact, we recently had a burial where the six adult grandchildren wanted to be the pallbearers. Three of them female." He shook his head. "We tried to dissuade the women, but they insisted. It made things more difficult for everyone. Two of my men had to pitch in at the head and foot just to get it off the transport into the hearse." Making a noise of disdain, he added, "Some people just won't listen to reason."

I moved toward the door leading to the other embalming room, thinking that if I wanted to be a pallbearer for someone close to me, I wouldn't "listen to reason," either. If it took two extra sets of hands to get the job done, then so be it. Silently, I sent kudos to the three women who'd held their ground.

"I'm surprised. I haven't seen any refrigeration units," I said. "I guess I expected—"

"Yes, well . . ." Nicky's hands came up and he picked at his cuticles. "We generally don't take visitors to our refrigeration area."

"Can I see it?"

"That's the thing," he said, continuing to pick at his fingers, "the refrigeration room is just on the other side of the embalming room next door."

"Can't we just . . ." At once I realized why Nicky was reluctant. "You have someone in the next room, don't you?"

He nodded. "I'm afraid the remains aren't suitable for viewing right now. Privacy laws and all that."

I got the picture. There was a nude dead body in the next room. "Oh," I said, injecting disappointment into my voice, "I was really hoping to get a look at all the back rooms."

"You were?"

My curiosity was at an all-time high. Here was my chance for a tour few people get to experience, at least while they're alive to appreciate it. The chances of this happening again were pretty slim and the chances of me pressing Nicky for more favors after today were even slimmer. I figured I should take advantage now.

"I think it's fascinating," I said. I knew I sounded coy, but it was no lie.

"Well, then," Nicky seemed suddenly ill at ease. "Hmm. I suppose I could . . . all right. Just a moment."

He disappeared through the metal door so quickly that I wasn't even able to get a peek. Delighted to be on my own, I started to wander about the room, examining it. There had to be something wrong with me, I decided, that I was this engrossed by the rituals of death.

There were three blue coolers on the floor next to the porcelain table. They were the kind you'd take on a picnic, just big enough to hold a six-pack of beer and a few sandwiches each. It seemed odd to have them here, open, airing out, as though waiting to be grabbed for a concert up at Ravinia.

Ravinia? Not beer, then. Wine, maybe.

A machine that looked something like an oversized blender drew me over. I'd just decided it must be a pump, when Nicky returned.

"That was quick," I said. "What's this?"

I was right. It was a pump. Nicky seemed pleased to be able to explain the process. "We use an arterial embalming process. We make two incisions in the neck of the remains," he pointed to his own neck. "The carotid artery and the jugular vein. We send the embalming fluid through the artery, and drain the blood out from the vein."

"How long does it take?"

"It depends. Most of the time, we send about three gallons of fluid and water through the remains. But, sometimes things don't go exactly right. Every body is different. We massage the remains to be sure we're getting through everywhere. And there are size and weight considerations. Clots can throw things off a bit, too."

"I'll bet." I studied the pump. "This gets everything?"

"Well, no." Nicky reached over and grabbed a long metal pole. Or at least that's what it looked like. He handed it to me. "We use this extensively."

"What is it?" The pole was over two feet long. It looked to be a stainless steel tube about a half inch in diameter. At one end was a very sharp, three-sided point with a hole at its center. The other end was open.

"It's called a trocar," he said as I examined it. "We attach a waste tube to the back end and use it to suction out the body's lower cavity."

I turned it over in my hands, tempted to spin it like some sort of morbid baton twirler might. "It's got heft."

"This is an extremely handy tool. We have to jam it, hard,

into the remains' abdominal cavity, just below the sternum."

I tried to picture it.

"Are you game?" he asked.

"For what?"

He motioned to the embalming table. "Why don't you get up there and I'll show you."

"Me? Get up there?" My voice rose and I vehemently shook my head. "No thanks." What a creepy thing to suggest. Lying faceup on a tilted table was not something I wanted to do while I still had a choice in the matter.

The look on Nicky's face made me cringe. It made me wonder what other talents he planned to demonstrate if I'd have agreed to hop onto his little table. I put the trocar back on the countertop and stepped away.

He smiled. "Just kidding."

Yeah, right.

"Let me explain," he said, picking the trocar up again. Its ultra-sharp slashed point—like that of a giant needle—made me uncomfortable.

"That's okay," I said.

"No, watch," he said, all business now. Okay, maybe I'd imagined his perverted fantasies. Maybe the place was getting to me after all. "Here." He positioned himself at one end. "This is where the head would be and this is where I'd stand to get the best leverage."

I nodded.

Wielding the trocar with both hands, he thrust it forward into the empty space where a body would lie. "See?" he said. "It's imperative that you get just the right spot, but what's even more important is that you jam it hard. Human skin is amazingly resilient. If you don't give it all you've got, you risk damaging the remains, and having to start all over again."

His explanation continued, "Once the trocar is in place, you suction out the entire area. You have to move the end around a lot," he demonstrated using a push–pull motion, "to make sure you get everything."

Made sense. "Kind of reminds me of liposuction I've seen on TV."

He made a so-so gesture with his head. "I can see that."

I would have liked to watch an actual embalming on a true dead person, but Nicky here had reacted badly when he thought I might catch a glimpse of the client in the next room, so I didn't push. "Is the embalming fluid clear?"

He pointed to a supply of containers I hadn't noticed. "I use a brand with a slight pinkish dye. It helps to preserve a more natural look." He added, "Rosey soles and pinky toes."

"Excuse me?"

With a shrug, he gestured for me to follow him. "That's a mortician's little saying. To remind us to be sure that the embalming fluid has gotten everywhere. Once the feet take on a healthy pink glow, we know we've done a good job."

Healthy pink glow. Was that a contradiction in terms, or what?

"Then you're done?"

"Hardly," he said. This time he opened the metal door wide, allowing me to follow. "We still have to work with the abdominal cavity, we have to do further disinfecting, stitching, washing, dressing, and makeup. That and the hair, takes a lot of time. So does arranging the remains in the casket. You know, it's important that they look like they're sleeping."

The adjacent room was the mirror image of the one we'd just left. The two glaring differences was the putrid smell that assailed us as we made our way in, and the fact that this embalming table was occupied. A blue paper sheet covered an adult-sized body and I made my way around it, following Nicky's brisk pace—aware of the corpse both because of its proximity and because of its smell. "Is it always like this?" I asked, wrinkling my nose.

Nicky had rushed to the next door, and stood with it open, eager to hand me through. "Unfortunately, you just experienced one of the difficulties of handling the final disposal of the indigent. We sponged down the remains with a disinfecting solution—twice—but the smell is so fully ingrained in the body that we're having a hard time getting rid of it. We have another solution to sponge on. I think it will work this time."

"I hope so," I said. "For your sake."

The refrigeration room was cold. I finally understood that term: "bone-chilling." The area was huge, a built-on section that felt like a warehouse. The ceiling soared at least fifteen feet above us, and the walls were covered with small doors looking like the old-fashioned ice boxes, with those lever-like handles that clunk shut. Where iceboxes were wood, however, these were all gleaming stainless steel. Three walls were covered with these small doors, and I started to count how many bodies could be stored here at one time when Nicky interrupted.

"I installed all this. This was how I was able to grow the business." He moved over toward the nearest wall to caress one of the silver latches, a small smile of pride on his face. For the first time, his eyes took on a hard look that I couldn't figure out until he said, "I did this myself. This was my idea. I told Ketcham for years that we needed to expand, but he wouldn't listen." Nicky's grin grew more broad as he wiped a finger along the top of the small door. "But I was right. I wish the old man was still alive today so I could show him I was right."

"Why do you need so many units? You can embalm . . . what? Four or five people at a time? But you must have forty drawers here. It's like a mini morgue."

"The work I do with the indigent," he said. When I didn't understand his train of thought, he continued, "There are a lot of homeless people who require burial. I provide a tasteful disposal of their remains at minimal cost to the county."

"How can you do afford to do that?"

He shrugged and I got the feeling he didn't like discussing money with a relative stranger. "I make . . . something . . . on each disposal. But the work buys me much, much more in goodwill."

"I bet."

"In fact, the county has been so satisfied with my services, that they're bringing all the homeless dead to me. And you know how big Cook County is."

I did. I also knew I wanted a sweatshirt. My arms came up around me again. I hugged myself, striving for warmth. "Wow," I said. "Pretty cold."

Nicky shrugged and glanced at my breasts. "You get used to it."

All of a sudden I wanted to be out of this place. But I'd made an issue out of wanting to see it, so I threw a couple of polite questions at him. "Is this an embalming room, too?" I asked, noticing the equipment on the wall's far side.

Nicky made his way over. "It can be. But we only use this room in unusual circumstances. Say we have all four other rooms in use, or maybe we have an obese body to take care of." He pointed to a set of double doors. "Those lead to a holding room and garage where we take all deliveries. All average-sized remains are brought in here, placed in a refrigeration unit, and then brought to an embalming room when necessary. Significantly sized remains are hard to handle. That's why this room is outfitted with a bigger table, and a ceiling-mounted lift." He pointed upward. "See that?"

I nodded staring at the mechanism attached to the ceiling. It really *was* an overhead lift. I had a sudden vision of a skyscraper building site with large bodies hanging from cranes, floating across the sky. "You don't need to use this very often, do you?"

"Not very," he agreed, then shot me a smile. "And we'd never use it on someone as petite as you are."

Yuck. Thanks, Nicky, I thought. That little comment would bring me cheer for the rest of the day.

Nicky must have realized his *faux pas.* "It's a good thing to have just in case," he said. "And I've found other uses for it, too. Whenever we need big pieces of equipment moved, this helps the workers lighten the load by handling the bulk of the weight. I've used it for that purpose a lot of times."

A long chain hung vertically from the apex—the point where all the weight-bearing wires met. At the chain's bottom, a gigantic hook hung, looking sinister. "What on earth do you need that for?"

Nicky reached up and draped a hand in the hook's curve. "Lots of things," he said.

I decided not to pursue the subject. And I'd seen enough. "So," I said, "how about that visit to the homeless shelter?"

RON SHADE

It was close to five by the time I got off the tollway and got to my house. I called George back and told him there was no way I could make dinner, but thanked him for the invitation.

"It's not like the Ron Shade I know to pass up a free, home-cooked meal," he said.

"Yeah, well, I wanted to go check on Ken tonight."

After a moment of silence he said, "Maybe we can make it breakfast at Karson's in the morning, instead."

I sighed, considering. "Actually, we'd better make it Thursday. I have to drive down to Furman County tomorrow."

"Furman County? That's way the hell down there, ain't it?"

"Yeah, but I'm working on a case. Guy was killed in a traffic crash down there. Or maybe not. The officer who investigated the crash is working tomorrow."

He snorted. "Well, good luck. Just remember, you piss off any cops down there, it's way too far for me to come to bail your sorry ass out."

"As usual, your confidence in me is inspiring."

We traded a few more good-natured insults as I started to feed my cats. All three of them met me at the door with a chorus of plaintive wails, and continued to follow me from room to room. I poured each of them some dry cat food goodies and detected a powerful odor in the air. They'd obviously filled up the litter boxes with a bunch of welcome home gifts in my absence, so I took care of that, too. Then I put a chicken dinner in the microwave, grabbed some cranberry juice, and sat down to go over what I had so far.

Robert Bayless's behavior seemed consistent with a guy ready to bolt. The affair with his secretary, the spats with the missus, the upgrades in the insurance polices. The description that Herb had given me suggested a man planning something. But could it have been suicide? From the description, he hadn't sounded like the type. But exactly what is the type? I looked up the policies and verified that he'd kept the beneficiaries the same. His wife, Linda, and son Chad. The other one listed a few corporate officers for the Manus Corporation. So Bob Bayless allegedly left this world knowing his family and his company would be well compensated by his demise. A comforting thought. But who was it that Herb Winthrope had heard laughing the horse laugh in Sin City? What about the other alternative? What if the guy had engineered the ultimate escape from a hum-drum life?

Of course, if Bayless had faked his own death, it would make sense to relocate far from the shores of Lake Michigan. But was Vegas a good choice? It was one of the fastest growing cities in the country, with wall-to-wall people. Nothing like getting lost in a crowd of drunken revelers. What would the odds be that someone from your past life would show up and see you? Or hear your distinctive laugh? On the flip side, everybody and their brother goes to Vegas. If you wanted to be free of prying eyes from the past, why not move to someplace like Missoula, Montana?

Las Vegas was also a big tourist spot, so just because Herbie had seen the late Bob Bayless, it wasn't a given that the laughing dead man actually lived there. He could have settled in Montana, and just have been visiting Vegas to blow some of his money. The thought of trying to track someone unknown in a city with that kind of transient population sent a shudder down my spine. Either way, this was going to be like trying to find the three double-paying bars in a slot machine.

Money . . . that was another question that had to be answered. If Bayless took the bail-out, and if he was still alive with a new identity, how the hell was he supporting himself? And the pretty young thing that was supposedly hanging on his arm at the blackjack table. Stepping away from a minimum wage, deadbeat job was one thing, but finding another career, at a middle-aged juncture like your early forties, with a new identity and a hot girlfriend, would be tricky. It wasn't likely a guy who was the CEO of Manus Corporation would be content doing the double shift flipping soybean patties at Fat Burgers or McDonald's. I'd have to get a look at Bayless's finances before his demise. Maybe he'd been socking some away. But wouldn't someone have noticed? Maybe he was skimming from the company funds. Something else I'd have to check on. I'd have to be very ingratiating to the accountant at Manus. Of course, knowing that I was looking into possibly taking back their ten million might make them less than anxious to please me. I'd have to use my charm, and if that failed, a whopper of a good lie.

Georgio, my huge, cream-colored cat, jumped up on the table and sauntered right over the open file. He paused, gave a slight mewing sound, and plopped down on his side, obscuring the papers. Little Rags, the runt, began using my shin for a scratching post, and Shasha rubbed against my other leg leaving, I was sure, a substantial amount of her white hair on my dark pants. I stretched and glanced at my clock, amazed that it was already six-thirty.

Time flies when you're having fun, I thought, and stretched again. I still had time to hit Chappie's for a light workout and then get some sleep. Tomorrow was shaping up to be a very busy day. But I had that other stop to make first. Tonight was Tuesday and that meant Ken Albrecht's therapy session would have been this afternoon. I made it a point to stop by the clinic and talk to the nurse each week to get a progress report on him.

It had been just over two months ago that the bullets had ripped apart his body and spirit. Three bullets, all meant for me, but because he'd been in my Firebird, the assassination attempt had turned even more tragic. It was one of the reasons I'd let the Firebird go at such a steal. Bad memories.

Ken's memories had deserted him. It was probably best that he couldn't recall the shooting. The third shot had pierced his skull, sending the projectile through the left side of his brain. He was relearning the basics now. Speech, movement, talking. It was rough to see such a young guy so debilitated.

It was rougher on his parents. Through their lawyer, they'd let George and me know that it would be "better" if we stopped coming around to see him. That was as they served us with the lawsuit, suing our insurance carrier for Windy City Knights

Security. Ken had been working for us when he'd been shot. His family had little choice if they wanted him to have the best therapists, but our carrier dropped us as part of the settlement, and Windy City Knights was blown away with the early summer winds. After that, we couldn't have gotten bonded with Lloyd's of London. Neither of us blamed Ken nor his family for the lawsuit. He was trapped in some netherworld, his clear blue eyes sometimes looking like there was an intelligent thought trapped behind them, waiting to get out. Traumatic brain injuries were like that. It wasn't like we hadn't seen things coming, either, and deep down we knew there was no choice. But I still felt a twinge of regret knowing that George's post-retirement plans had vanished as well.

So I had an arrangement with the nurses to get updates on Ken's progress without showing my face while he was there. At some future point, I hoped he'd recover enough that we could talk. But I was at a loss as to what to tell him. Maybe just to keep his strength and live on. Saying anything else would be the cheap way out.

I finished packing my gear in the bag and stood up. The Bayless mysteries would have to be pondered in the morning. But the main question still lingered in my mind.

If it was Bob Bayless that Herbie had seen, and he hadn't perished in the downstate traffic accident, just whose body was it that had burned to death in Bayless's crashed car? And where the hell did it come from?

Michael A. Black & Julie Hyzy

Alex St. James

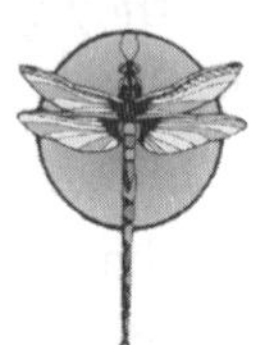

It was late by the time we got to the church, and I'd expected to be told to come back the next day, but Father Morales' face broke into a wide smile the moment he spied me and Nicky in the doorway. "Nicholas!" he called across the crowded room. There had to be at least three dozen homeless people gathered in the church basement, all taking part in some sort of lecture. It made me wonder if they all chose browns and grays to wear because it allowed them to blend in to the scenery, or if the bland clothing was all that was available to them. I'd been in enough thrift stores to know that they sold electric blue and hot pink clothing. Maybe these people's clothing had been bright and colorful at one time. Maybe it was dirt that made them all the same shade of drab.

Large, ceiling-mounted fans did an admirable job of keeping the aroma of stale humans at bay, but the rancid stench from that last embalming room was still with me. I wondered if I'd ever forget that smell.

We made our way to the priest, a large-nosed fellow with olive skin and a full head of dark hair. With his donkey-brown hooded tunic, ropes at his waist, and his indeterminate age he would've made a great Friar Tuck.

After Nicky made introductions, I said, "You're Franciscan."

Father Morales' beefy hands came out in a gesture of subjugation. "Guilty as charged. You sound surprised."

"When Nicky—er—Nick said 'Father Morales' I assumed you were diocesan."

He shook his head, called out a request to another man to take over for him, and led us to one of the few vacant tables. "I dedicated myself to the order of St. Francis when I was eighteen. But I *am* ordained."

"Do you prefer to be called Father, or Brother?"

His face was wide, and when he smiled it seemed to get bigger, though not unpleasantly so. "I'll answer to either. And whichever title will get me more donations for my shelter is the one I like best." He took Nick's hand in both of his, shaking it with genuine warmth. "It's been too long. I was so pleased to get your call." He held Nick's hand a moment longer before letting go as he turned to me. "This man has been very good to our ministry," he said. "His name, Nicholas, is precisely right for someone who gives so much. Like St. Nicholas, my good friend here has come bearing gifts more times than I can count."

That surprised me. Nicky hadn't struck me as a philanthropist. I acknowledged and congratulated him on his good deeds.

He shrugged. "I do what I can." And then Nicky gave me the floor. "Father," he began, "my good friend, Alex, needs some help with a project and I believe you'd be her best source."

I took my cue. "I work for *Midwest Focus NewsMagazine*—"

"Yes, I recognize you."

That took me aback. "You do?"

"Just because I took a vow of celibacy doesn't mean I can't appreciate loveliness. It is one of many gifts God has given you." He smiled. "And I'd venture to say you've been blessed with intelligence as well. I've seen several of your broadcasts. Quite impressive."

"Thank you," I said, but my words were nearly lost as the lecture behind me wound up and the room's murmur level grew.

"I'll take any loose change ya got." The harsh voice came from behind, as did the nudge at my shoulder. "You got some, ain't ya? Paper's welcome, too."

I turned, getting hit full face with stale body odor from an emaciated woman who looked to be at least ninety years old. Her voice, however, sounded much younger.

Father Morales' voice was a warning. "Vicki."

"I don't know how much I have—" I said, starting to dig.

"Put your money away, Alex. Vicki here doesn't need it."

If anyone needed it, this woman did. Her eyes were a watery shade of brown—nearly colorless—and her face, pockmarked and uneven, was drawn in tight, like an ugly puppet's. "I might have—" I began again.

The woman sidled closer; I instinctively pulled my purse nearer to my chest. I got the feeling that Vicki would reach in and take whatever she darn well pleased, thank you very much, and I didn't want to provide her the opportunity.

"I know you mean well, Alex, but you can't," Morales said. "Vicki, it's time for your meeting with the counselor, isn't it?"

Her eyes narrowed as Morales' arm reached around to try to turn her away from me. Before he tugged, she shot hot acrid breath into my ear. "I don't like your boyfriend," she whispered. "If you give me something, I'll like you."

Vicki winced, showing black-crusted teeth. Morales' grip had apparently gotten a little bit tighter. "These are my guests," he said. "I'll talk with you later."

The woman scuttled away, still muttering.

Morales watched her leave, apologizing for the interruption. "They're so much like little children," he said. "You have to tell them the same thing, over and over. They constantly push for more."

"I could've given her something," I said. "I feel terrible letting an old lady like that go out without helping her."

"Old lady?" Morales shook his head. "Vicki's about thirty-eight. Maybe thirty-nine. Can't remember exactly."

I stared after her. "No way."

"That's what methamphetamine will do to a body."

"My God." Horrified, I watched her make her way to the counselor who sat at one end of a long table. He pointed to an empty folding chair and Vicki sat. Before turning her attention to him however, she gave me a pointed look, rubbing her thumb and fingers together in the international sign of "give me cash."

I turned away.

"If you would have given her money," Nicky said, "she just would have gone out and gotten herself more crystal meth. She's got food and a place to sleep here. She doesn't need anything else until she's clean."

"Wow," I said. "This is a tough job."

Morales stared after the woman. "It's a calling."

The idea of spending my nights living among people like Vicki was giving me second thoughts upon second thoughts. Bass had some interesting ideas, all right. As long as he wasn't risking life and limb, they all sounded great. To him. "I guess if I'm going to get up close and personal with these folks, I should learn the rules."

"What are you talking about?" Morales asked.

Nicky spoke first. "Alex is going undercover. Living among the homeless. For a story."

Morales started shaking his head almost as soon as Nicky began. "No. No. No," he said. "This is a terrible idea. Nicholas, why are you supporting this?"

"I'm not," Nicky said.

I interrupted. "He tried to talk me out of it, but I really don't have any choice."

Morales wrinkled his bulbous nose. His big head swagged side to side. "I've taken a vow of poverty and *I* wouldn't live among them. Don't get me wrong, they need our assistance and I would never forsake them, but . . ." His eyes clenched. "They can be dangerous. Many of them suffer from mental illness. That makes them unpredictable. They are crazy—in the truest sense of the word. They harbor thoughts you and I can't even imagine. If you inadvertently make them angry, they attack. They develop animalistic tendencies. There's no reasoning with them."

The holy man's warning gave me ever more reason not to follow through with this homeless adventure. The fact remained, however, I was the new kid on the block—TV-wise—and I couldn't afford to pitch a fit so early on. Right now, I was a nobody.

In my old job, I investigated stories for Gabriela to discuss on TV. In my new job, I was still doing investigations, but they were for my own television appearances. So far, less than half a dozen. The only difference I could see was that Bass was getting a researcher and a part-time anchor for the price of one. Leave it to Bass to try to squeeze three nickels together to make twenty cents.

Truth was, I wanted to be a household name. And this story could set me apart from Gabriela. Give me my own little niche.

"I understand," I said to Morales. "I'm planning to—" I'd been on the verge of telling him about my Taser, when I remembered they were illegal in the city. "Planning to bring along a cameraman."

Nicky and Morales gave me twin looks of doubt. "What's he going to do?" Nicky asked.

"At least there will be two of us," I said, feeling a mite defensive. "He's going to film surreptitiously, and if I get into trouble, he'll have a cell phone. Plus I don't intend to carry any valuables or anything." My voice drifted off, and I realized I sounded a whole lot less convinced of the workability of this plan than I should have.

"Alex," Morales said, rubbing his temples. "There's so much

more at stake here than you getting robbed."

"When I get some of these people at the funeral home, they're diseased," Nicky said to me. "You smelled how bad it can be, remember?" I glanced around, hoping none of the local residents could hear him, but his voice rose. "Not just drug addicts like Vicki back there, but they've got AIDS and hepatitis and who knows what else. Christ, you can get bed bugs just walking in here." He gestured about the wide room, and then suddenly seemed to remember where we were. "Well," he added, quieting, "you know what I mean."

Nicky fidgeted after his little speech, making faces as though squeamish. This was a guy who pumped blood out of dead bodies for a living?

Morales was studying me. "There's no dissuading you, is there?"

I shook my head.

"When are you planning your little campout?"

"As soon as possible. I've got a cameraman on call." I shrugged. "Tomorrow, probably."

He heaved a sigh that seemed to come from the depths of his tunic. "All right then, let's take a walk." He started for the door. Nicky and I followed.

"Where are we going?"

The man from the mission had turned into a man *on* a mission. "The counseling sessions are nearing completion. Dinner's been over for some time. Shortly, the homeless folks you see here will be dispersed into the night."

"Dispersed?"

He grinned. "Sounds better than 'shoved out the door,' don't you think?" He kept a brisk pace, stopping only briefly at the basement's sign-in table at the entrance to let someone know he'd be gone for a while.

"They don't sleep here?"

We climbed metal-edged tile steps to the church's lobby—my shoes and the brother's were quiet but Nicky's clicked hollowly, echoing against the faux-marble walls.

Morales waited to answer me until we made it outside into the humid evening. Sweating profusely, he pulled a long white kerchief from his sleeve to mop his dripping face. "We can't let them sleep here," he said. "They'd never leave. We ease the rules in the winter, of course, but we don't have the facilities, or the funding to maintain a full-time transient . . . hotel." He turned to Nicky. "What do you think? Howard's corner?"

Nicky shot him a look of disbelief. "You want to walk there? At this time of day? In this weather?"

Morales' hands came up. "What choice do I have?"

Nicky gave the brother a rueful look. "I'll drive."

Howard's corner, as I came to discover was the former home of Howard Rybak. It turned out to be a wide underpass that teemed with nocturnal activity. According to Morales, Howard was the shining example of a wretched life turned around—proof that it could be done—hope for the masses.

"Here we are," Morales said shortly. "Home of the crazies."

"What did you say?" I asked.

"I know," he said, "it's not politically correct to use that term, but I've come to know these people better than most. It's an accurate assessment. One you should not forget." He turned to Nicky as we exited the black Cadillac, about two blocks from the corner. "Have you seen Howard lately?"

"He moved," Nicky answered. "About six months ago. The temporary placement office found him a full-time job."

Morales slammed the car's door and beamed. "I knew it. I'm so proud of him. And you, too, Nicky. You gave him a lot of personal attention. You made all the difference for him."

Nicky had come around, as though to help me with my car door, but I beat him to it. He shrugged away Morales' adulation. "Where do you want to start, Alex?" he asked.

"I'd like to get in touch with Howard," Morales continued. "Where's he living now?"

Nicky scratched his head. "I've got his address written down somewhere."

"Is he still local?"

"Uh . . . not sure." Nick turned to me again. "Is this really what you want to do, Alex? Look. See those folks? If you try to encroach on their space, they're going to have you for breakfast. And I mean that literally."

We made our way to the collection of people under the overpass. High above us, traffic sped by on the six-lane expressway under bright lights and reflective signs, guiding happy people on their way out for the evening, or home for the night. All of them up there had somewhere they'd been, and somewhere they were going. These people underneath weren't going anywhere.

This was a very old, very large overpass. Grisham Avenue, where we were parked, crossed perpendicularly beneath it. I'd lived in the city my entire life, and I'd never known this street existed.

There were industrial-type buildings to the west, behind us, all of which had seen better days. Farther down, past an alleyway, were a liquor store and an old gas station. This intersection was rife with dirt plots of land, broken glass. Dead trees. Debris everywhere. Streetlights at this level were nonexistent and only the remaining twilight allowed me to see the people sleeping in boxes or wandering under the viaduct. As we drew closer, I could make out at least ten people turning their attention to our approach.

"If I'm going to be undercover here, I don't think I should introduce myself," I said when Morales didn't seem to be inclined to slow down.

He threw a terse comment over his shoulder. "I'm still hoping to talk you out of this nonsense."

"This is a long way to your shelter," I said, my lungs wet with heavy air. I could only imagine what it would be like to walk the distance wearing every bit of clothing I owned.

Morales shrugged, but didn't stop. "It's only a few miles."

I didn't get it. "There's not a lot of opportunity for panhandling," I said, glancing around. "Why here? Why not closer to the hustle and bustle of the city?" We passed an old-fashioned mesh garbage can and I pointed. "There's not even any good garbage out here."

He stopped walking and turned to face me. Sweat streamed down his face, dripping from his eyebrows, slicing dark streaks down the front of his garment. "This is where they come to sleep, Alex. They're safe here at night." He panted as he spoke. "What with all the cleanup going on—the gentrification of the neighborhoods where these people have made their homes—they risk getting rousted every night." He threw his arms wide. "No one cares that they've taken over this area. Not yet anyway."

He resumed walking. Nicky and I followed.

"Where do you think I should position myself?" I asked, mentally scoping out the vicinity with an eye to where my cameraman could set up. Despite the heat, I shivered. The collection of humanity before us, swaying as they stared, reminded me of an old zombie movie, just before an attack.

"I don't think you should position yourself at all," Morales said, with more than a little spirit. "Have I not made that clear?"

"Abundantly," I murmured.

"You'll be disguised?" Morales asked.

"Yes. I have some clothes my boss picked up at the thrift store."

"Not good enough. You won't smell right. You'll be too clean."

I hadn't considered that. "Any suggestions?"

Close enough now to pick up chatter, we stopped. I realized that these folks were talking, but not to one another. Rather they were muttering to themselves. A man near to our position shouted expletives as he rooted through his belongings. A heavy-set woman at the curb chanted to the moon.

The hot breeze sent rotting garbage and fecal smells swirling around us. My hand came up to cover my nose. I'd have to watch that. Control my natural impulses.

The sun dropped and it got dark fast. I jumped when a woman shrieked, her cries coming from deep within the shadowed recesses of the viaduct. My body tensed involuntarily. "It sounds like somebody's hurting her," I said. I was ready to rush to help, but Morales gripped my arm.

"Get used to it."

There we were, a trio of clean—albeit sweaty—professionals, staring at those who society had dismissed as unworthy. The hazy moon high above made me realize how small we all were, and I felt suddenly unworthy myself. How often had I passed these people on State Street or Michigan Avenue, too caught up in my own life to think about theirs. Too smug in my assumptions that they were begging for change, only to spend it on booze, or worse.

Morales must have seen indication of my self-flagellation reflected in my expression because he said, "Remember Vicki who you met tonight. We've tried hard to help her, but the addiction is too powerful. You can't help everyone. The best we can do is hope that God will intervene at some point."

"An odd sentiment from someone who's dedicated himself to do just that."

"Each passing year causes me to become more jaded. I pray for patience, for wisdom. But I am one man, and I realize my limitations." He sighed. "I have, as you pointed out, dedicated my life to helping the forsaken. This is my life. This is not yours.

I applaud your intention—your desire to illuminate the homeless' troubles. I have, unfortunately, seen this scenario before. Your efforts will be—in the long run—superficial. Nothing but a Band-Aid solution for the homeless even while they provide a feature story for you."

That stung. I looked to Nicky, but he seemed to be preoccupied with watching the scavenging crowd. I had a sudden memory of him staring at an ant farm in our basement. His face held that same dispassionate expression now as it did then.

Morales gave me a once-over from head to toe. "I'll get you a proper disguise. Stop by the church tomorrow before you head out here." I could read displeasure on his face as clearly as though the words were written there. "You'll have to walk a roundabout course. These people may live on the fringes of society, but they're eagle-eyed when it comes to their territory. Keep a low profile and be very, very careful."

Sudden movement from beneath the viaduct shot a flock of pigeons over our heads, in a flurry of beating wings.

I ducked and realized I had no idea what I was in for.

"I will," I said.

Chapter 7

Ron Shade

I watched the sun creep up, turning the gray sky bright pink as I was finishing my morning run. The heat of the day wouldn't start for several more hours, and I hoped to be on my way downstate by then. The Bayless questions revolved in my mind as I approached "Miss Agony," the last of the three hills I covered in my five-mile runs. Even though I wasn't quite back to fighting form, I knew I couldn't let my roadwork lag. Plus, I'd been running so long that it was part of my routine. Everyone has them. Like brushing your teeth or going for a run or punching a bag. Something I went to for comfort as well as conditioning. And Bayless had to have them, too. A man might fake his own death, change his identity, dye his hair, and grow a beard, but his old routines would eventually reassert themselves. I had to figure out what had made Bayless tick, while he was still Bob Bayless. Then I'd have a key to track him.

The hill took more out of me than I would have liked. I'd lain off the running after the big fight mainly because my legs had been so sore. Getting kicked about sixty or seventy times on the thighs by a two-hundred-and-sixty-pound man will do that. But the work today was feeling better. Still not one-hundred percent, but getting into the high eighties. Another few weeks and I'd be back.

At the house I showered, dressed, and made sure the cats had enough food and water. I glanced at my clock. Almost six-thirty. If the ride down to Peyton took me the better part of four hours, I'd arrive down there at a good time to look around a bit. In addition to talking to the officer who'd handled the traffic crash, I also wanted to see the coroner. Maybe he noticed something about the body that would help. It was a fishing expedition with my chances of success about as remote as winning the Lotto, but I reminded myself that I was getting paid either way. And since it was Big Dick doing the paying, I wanted to make sure I was thorough. Very thorough.

I watched the steady stream of cars going north on I-57 as I basked in the good fortune of a reverse-commute. Everybody was heading toward the city, while I had the flat farmlands of southern Illinois ahead of me. I took it easy on the drive, conserving gas and stopping for coffee on the way down. "America runs on Dunkin'," all right. When I got off at the Peyton exit I immediately sought out Main Street only to discover that I was already on it. The town was typically rural based: a few really neat old churches, a couple homey-looking restaurants, three gas stations, a theater with one of those triangular marquees advertising the latest movie with plastic block letters. Down the block, a bright new McDonald's had a lot full of cars. It took me about ten minutes to get the lay of the land, and I pulled into the County Sheriff's Office, which was a fairly modern building. It was built out of solid red bricks and the tall framework of a metallic antenna crisscrossed its way skyward from the side of the building. A huge replica of the sheriff's police patch on framed plywood decorated the wall next to the front entrance. It consisted of yellow block letters spelling out FURMAN COUNTY SHERIFF, and displayed a tan outline of the county inside a large circular design. Some juvenile joker had taken a red Magic Marker and scrawled a capital *CK* after the first two letters of FURMAN COUNTY. It was somehow reassuring that assholes grew down here, just like they did up in my neck of the woods.

From the looks of it, Furman County was shaped like a backward L. Sort of a long slender stalk pointing north from a solidly shaped horizontal base. I wondered where, in those dimensions, the Bayless crash had occurred. On the other side of the door a red, white, and blue wooden sign structure advertised the sheriff's name on a prominent rung, along with a listing of other elected officials. Down near the bottom rung it said *Thaddeus Brunger, Furman County Coroner.* I wondered how popular you had to be to be elected to that position down here. Maybe it was a case of the electorate just continuing to dance with the one that brung 'er.

All jokes aside, I made a mental note to see him, too. I parked the Beater in one of the spots marked "Visitors" and went inside. The small foyer opened into an expansive room, with several offices on each side. Beyond that a big Plexiglas window housed a group of uniformed personnel, each sitting in front of a radio console. I went to the window and waited. Presently, one of the operators, a middle-aged woman, got up and sauntered to the counter. Her nametag said *Mildred* and the silver wire from her headset antenna stuck up in a sloping angle. Another silver wire jutted out from her earpiece positioning a tiny mic in front of her mouth. She pressed a button on an intercom, and her distorted voice asked if she could help me.

"I hope so," I said, flashing her one of my high-wattage smiles. "I'm trying to get in touch with one of your officers." I took the traffic accident report out from the file and shoved it through the slot at the bottom of the window. She took it, looked at the bottom section and walked over to a desk. She paged through a thick sheaf of papers, paused, and came back to me.

"That's Deputy MacMahan," she said, slipping the report back through the window. "He doesn't start till three o'clock." Even though Peyton was way north of Kentucky, her voice had a noticeable twang. Almost Southern sounding. The farther south you went in Illinois, the more pronounced the resonance got.

"Do you think it would be possible to get ahold of him for me?" I tried the high watts again. "I'm down here from Chicago and was hoping to talk to him about that accident. I'm doing an investigation for the insurance company." She seemed hesitant, and I quickly added, "I'd really appreciate it if you could help me out, Mildred." People usually like to hear their own name said back to them.

She compressed her lips as she debated, then told me to wait. Sitting down in front of her console section, she became less visible to me, but it appeared as though she was typing something on a keyboard. The people behind the Plexiglas all spoke in tones inaudible from my side of the window. I could see Mildred was talking into her microphone, squinting slightly when she glanced at me. I tried to figure out what she was saying by watching her lips but gave up. Finally, she got up and came back to the space on the other side of the window.

"I called Deputy MacMahan at home," she said.

I smiled. "And?"

"And he says he'll be glad to talk to you." Her mouth flashed a quick smile of her own. "As soon as he comes on duty at three o'clock."

"As soon as he comes on duty at three o'clock." The woman's smart-ass comment kept ringing in my ears. Sixty thousand comedians

out of work, and I had to get her. Maybe she was the one who kept busy with the Magic Marker in her spare time.

I glanced at my watch as I finished off another glass of iced tea at the small restaurant. Eleven-forty-five. Still a wait before I could talk to the deputy. At least, with the lengthy June sunlight, I could probably get a look at the crash site, if he was co-operative.

The restaurant was a quaint little place, with a long counter and wooden booths and tables. I'd taken one by the window so I could appreciate the scenery. The pace seemed a lot slower down here than what I was used to up in Chicago. Several men had met at one of the booths and discussed everything from farming, to the high gas prices, to the weather, to more farming. From the sound of it, they had it a lot harder than I did.

I had the file spread out in front of me, trying to figure my next move. Since I was down here until at least three, I figured I'd make a stop off at the coroner's office. I'd asked Miss Comedian Central where that was, and she told me "The Brunger Funeral Home on Main Street." I'd opted to grab an early lunch and ponder. I was actually getting good at it.

I remembered that a Dr. K. Boyd had performed the autopsy, which fit my estimation that the coroner wasn't an MD.

K. Boyd? Up in Chi-town, the use of just a first initial usually connoted a female. I wondered if that was the case here. Small-town doctor, a woman . . . Probably needed the extra cash in a place like this. With all the farmers down here they probably had more use for a veterinarian than an MD. At least I assumed she was an MD. Maybe she was both. Hopefully, she'd have a light schedule and could see me.

I decided to try Mr. Brunger first. See what I could find out from the official version. After leaving the waitress a substantial tip, using my credit card, of course, so I could bill Big Dick, I headed across the street to the Brunger Funeral Home. Except for the sign hanging from a metal rack in the front yard, the place looked like an older, large house. It was made of dark bricks and had a sloping roof that jutted out from a second story. A blacktopped driveway ran along the right side, extending into a parking lot in back. I estimated that it had been around as long as the old churches in the town, and a lot longer than the newer-looking sheriff's office. The front sidewalk was very wide, and led to a set of double doors. I rang the bell and waited. No response. I tried knocking on the door. Still no response.

"He ain't usually there this time of day," a craggy voice said from behind me.

I turned. Across the driveway a white-haired lady sat in a rocking chair on the porch next door. There was a ball of pink yarn in her lap, and her fingers nimbly worked some lengthy needles as she spoke.

I wasn't wearing a hat, so I couldn't tip it, which probably would have ingratiated me to her quicker. Instead, I smiled and stepped across the asphalt.

"Good morning, ma'am," I said, trying to sound like a city boy with manners.

She nodded and continued rocking. A pair of ornately framed, and far from fashionable glasses were perched on an aquiline nose. "Morning? I don't know where you're from, young fella, but it's afternoon 'round these parts." Her fingers kept up their rote activities.

"Yes, ma'am," I said, searching for a countrified metaphor. Something more down-home folk-sounding. "I got up before the rooster this morning myself." I saw a hint of a smirk twitch her lips. "I'm down here from Chicago."

"I figured as much. Up before the rooster, my ass."

It was my turn to smile. "I was hoping to speak with your coroner. You have any idea when he'll be available?"

Her chin jutted toward the street. "He owns that feed store down a ways. Usually don't come to the home unless he has a customer."

I looked down the block.

"The big metal building," she said. "Just past the McDonald's."

"I see it. Looks like a nice place."

Her lips pursed into a frown. She stopped the needle action and set everything down on her lap. I watched her fingers dig in the pocket of her dress. "Not for the horseshit prices he charges, it ain't. All he's concerned about is getting money from feeding your stock and burying your body." She took out a big, brown cigar and bit off the end before sticking it between her lips. "The man's a damn bloodsucker, if you ask me." She twirled the end of the cigar in the flame of her lighter, drawing and puffing. "A real shitbird."

"He must have some friends around here if he's the county coroner." I decided to try for the countrified humor one more time. "Unless, of course the county would rather just dance with the one that brung 'er."

Her stare was rueful. The tip of the cigar glowed and she blew out a prodigious cloud of smoke. "Like I said, feeding 'em and burying 'em. The son-of-a-bitch ain't nothing like his father. He helped build up this town."

What I was learning about Mr. Brunger wasn't inspiring a lot of confidence in his judgment. But still, that might prove valuable in building a case for an exhumation. I took out my pad and pen and stepped closer to the porch railing.

"Would you mind giving me your name and address?" I asked, poised.

She exhaled another gray cloud. "What the hell for?"

"Well, for my report." I tried another smile. It was bordering on desperation this time. "In case my boss wonders who I was talking to down here."

She looked down over the tops of her glasses at me and squinted, the cigar tucked into the side of her mouth. "Talking about what?"

I gave a half cough, half sigh and reached into the file. After paging through the sheaf of papers, I came across a head shot of Robert Bayless taken from his DMV file. I held it toward her. "About him. Look familiar?"

Her eyes narrowed, sending crinkly lines down her cheeks. "Not particularly. Who is he?"

"His name was Robert Bayless. He was in a traffic accident near here."

"That one got himself burned up over on the highway?"

I nodded. "You remember the accident?"

"I remember my fine neighbor having a tizzy fit about Doctor Boyd wanting to send some body parts to Springfield." She paused and smirked at the memory. "Kept him from signing the death certificate." She lowered her voice a few octaves. " 'Slowed the process down,' he said."

"Where's Dr. Boyd's office at?"

Her chin jutted in the opposite direction of the feed store. "See that big yellow house down that away? That's hers. Her father had his practice in it, too. Thank God she came home and took over when he passed."

It didn't look that much different than the other frame houses on the street. Just a humble country doctor with a limited practice and no shiny sports car. I hoped the fact that she'd sent out tissue samples was an indication of her competence. Of course, that could work against me if she'd done a real thorough job. I turned back to the old woman and thanked her, still holding my poised pen. "And now, ma'am, your name please?"

She stopped her knitting and glared at me, then said, "For your boss?"

I nodded, freezing my face in the most sincere expression I could muster.

She scrutinized me some more, looked toward the Beater, then smirked again. "If I tell you, will your boss at least give you a better car?"

This damn town was chock-full of comedians. I wondered if she had a Magic Marker under all that yarn.

Brunger's Feed Store looked fairly new and sort of out of place along the rural town's main street. But the bright red-and-yellow McDonald's next to it also seemed misplaced. Both buildings were set apart from the rest of the block, like they'd been recently added. I wondered what quaint old structures had been torn down in the name of progress. Both parking lots were full and I parked the Beater towards the back and walked to the front doors. The rear of the building had a big overhead door where a couple of men loaded bales of hay into the bed of a truck. The building itself was all corrugated metal, like an oversized shed. Probably not much need to keep it insulated in the winter. I pulled open the front door. An attached bell jingled and a jowlly looking guy with an oversized gut and jet-black hair, too dark to be natural, peered up at me. He had oversized sideburns, too, and looked sort of like an Elvis impersonator gone to seed. Late Elvis, definitely. His face quickly jerked into a smile and he asked, "What can I do you out of?" The accompanying laugh a few seconds later. Kind of a long exhalation of foul breath with his lips curled back from his teeth. The teeth didn't look all that natural, either.

"I'm looking for Mr. Thaddeus Brunger."

He licked his lips and said, "Well, you found him," and gave another of those hissing laughs, after which he extended his hand. "Don't believe I caught your name, though."

"Ron Shade." I shook his hand, noticing that he'd turned his wrist slightly, so my hand rotated on to the top of our handshake. It was a strange gesture. "You're the county coroner, right?"

"That I am." He began to look past me at someone else coming in the door. "Howdy-do, Bruce. Here to pick up a few bales?"

Behind me Bruce grunted what I guessed was a "yeah," and Brunger whisked away from me, his arm around Bruce's shoulders, guiding him toward the long wooden counter. I busied myself glancing around, studying the store. Everything was farm related, from magazines to shiny green equipment. Barrels of seed and stacked packages of nitrates lined the walls. Brunger and Bruce were leaning over the counter talking about prices. From what I gathered, Bruce wasn't too happy with the deal he got offered.

"Christ, Thad, I can't afford that," he said. "You're running me into the poor house."

Thad flashed his politician's smile again and said, "Bruce, I gotta pay my costs. Things keep going up. It ain't my fault them camel jockeys in the Middle East keep acting stingy with the spigot." He made one of the hissing laughs again, but when the other man didn't smile, Brunger lifted a hand and placed it on his shoulder. "Look, I got no problem running you a line of credit till things improve."

This seemed to satisfy Bruce slightly, and he leaned his elbows down on the counter again. After a few more minutes, he signed something and Brunger straightened up and offered his hand. He curled it under, just like he'd done mine, and I realized it was his way of seeming less threatening. Ingratiating. Everybody's friend. I was always leery of guys like that, even when they didn't look like an ersatz Elvis. Brunger came sauntering over to me, talking over his shoulder to Bruce about pulling his car around the back. When he stopped in front of me he grinned.

"Sorry. Busy time. These old farmers go by their own timetable. Now, what did you say I could do for you?"

I explained to him briefly why I was there, leaving out any mention that I was backtracking to check if Bayless could still be alive.

Brunger shook his head slowly. "I do remember that one. Bad accident. Tragic case."

"Get many of those down here?"

He shrugged. "Now and again. That stretch of road where he crashed has got a real bad curve to it. Carved out of the rocks so the road could go through. He wasn't the first to smack into it."

I took out the picture of Bayless, but Brunger held up his palms. "Whoa . . . He didn't look like that when I saw him. Burned to a crisp."

"How'd you make the ID?"

"How did we do that?" His eyes moved toward the ceiling as his fingers tugged at the waddle of skin beneath his chin. Then he snapped his fingers. "Dental records. Came down right away. Overnight mail. Actually," he took a half step closer to me and lowered his voice, even though there was no one else around, "the oral cavity was pretty well preserved, considering the extent of the burning. Good thing, too. His own mother wouldn't have recognized him."

"Any signs that it wasn't an accident?"

His dark eyebrows rose, and he got a sly smile on his face. "You thinking suicide, maybe? That affect the payout?"

It was my turn to shrug. "I suppose the double-indemnity clause might be called into question."

"How much you guys pay out? Just outta curiosity."

"About twelve million."

Brunger puckered his lips and gave a low whistle. "Shit, that's a whole ton of money, ain't it? I see now why you're looking into things." The door jingled behind me, and he emitted that cough-like laugh again. "Excuse me again."

I watched from the sidelines as Brunger made an almost identical pitch to this farmer, who had a good-sized lad with him that looked to be his son. They looked less appeased than Bruce had, and as they shuffled past me I heard the younger one mutter, "That fucker won't be satisfied till he owns this whole county."

Brunger had apparently heard it, too, and shook his head sadly.

"Time was, my father had the only mortician's business in this whole area," he said. "Population increased, and a few more sprung up. And lately, with modern medicine helping people live longer, they just ain't dying the way they used to."

"So you branched out into the feed business?"

He nodded, smiling wistfully. "These old farmers don't understand modern economics, neither. The price of gas is driving everything up."

"Hence your third hat as county coroner."

He nodded again, the smile fading. "Don't get too much outta that one, though. Unless it's something like that accident, where I can bill the county for my time and services."

Not a bad gig for a guy already in the death business. I resisted the temptation to say that maybe the stress of high gas prices would spark a few heart attacks. "Speaking of the Bayless case, I saw you did an autopsy on that one."

"Yep. Had to, since it wasn't no natural death."

"Dr. Boyd assisted you?"

He shook his head. "Yep. Well, actually, she done the whole thing herself. Just reported back to me." He pointed upward and whirled his finger. "I'm at the store a lot, you know."

"I understand. How long did you have Bayless's body?"

"Let me see." He grabbed the waddle of his double chin

again. "Must have been two, three days at the most."

"The body was transported back up to Chicago for the funeral?"

"Yeah, the company he worked for sent some guys down. Paid for everything, even my storage fees."

I wondered if he'd double billed the county on that one. "Who were these guys?"

"They worked for the funeral home. Someplace up north. Had a nice-looking hearse, anyway." He huffed out the hissing laugh and accompanying grin again. "Nice-looking, big black Caddie."

"They say which funeral home they worked for?"

Brunger shook his head. "I got the card someplace in my office. Guess I could go look for it when I get some time."

I wasn't expecting that would be anytime soon. "You remember anything else about the guys?"

"Bunch of foreigners. Russkies, I think. One bossman and two gofers. They did all the grunt work."

"How do you know they were Russians?"

"The boss, kind of a big guy, had them high cheekbones and real pale eyes." He brought his own fingers to his face and cupped his hands. "Kind of a scary-looking guy. Talked with an accent. Ordered the others around in some kind of foreign language. I just assumed it was Russian."

I heard the familiar jingling of the door and saw Brunger's eyes move toward the door. "Howdie-do, Clem." As he started to move away I snared his arm.

"Here's my card," I said, handing him one. "If you can find the card for that funeral home I'd appreciate it."

He accepted the card and stuck it in his shirt pocket.

"Call me when you find it," I said, "and make sure to send me an invoice for your time."

That perked him up and he stopped. "Yeah, I suppose I could

do that, all right."

"I'll just submit it with my expenses," I said, forcing a smile. Of course, knowing that Big Dick would be paying for it, I added, "And I'm sure it's probably gonna take at least the better part of a day, right?"

"Sure enough." He exhaled the prolonged laugh, and I got another whiff of his sour breath. He extended his hand. "Nice meeting you, Mr. Shade. I'll be in touch."

Alex St. James

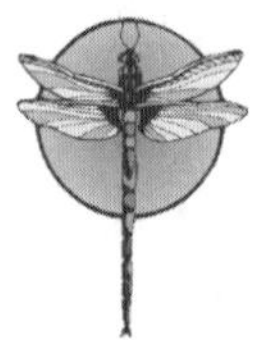

Bass stood in the doorway to my office. "So?"

I had to bite the insides of my cheeks before answering him. By the time I'd gotten home last night, it had been near midnight and the worry gremlins that prowl uneasy minds had kept me awake with all the terrible possibilities that Father Morales' tour had illuminated. I knew this homeless story was a bad idea. I knew it in my gut. And I also knew that following up on Howard Rybak's success story was the best angle for me. But Bass had shot me down when I suggested it to him first thing this morning.

"So," I said now, hoping he'd pick up on the bitterness in my tone. "I'm all set. I have a Taser and handgun lesson in about an hour, and then I'm coming back here to pick up Jesse San Miguel. He and I are going out to the viaduct this afternoon for a little reconnaissance before the big sleepover tonight."

"I wasn't asking about that," he said, frowning. Now at my desk, he pressed his fingertips on its edge and leaned forward.

In a low voice he said, "I meant about the car. Did you get ahold of that Shade character yet?"

"No."

"I told you this was important."

"I think my safety is important," I said, standing. "And you're not doing anything about that."

"San Miguel is going with you. And you've got your Taser. These homeless people are harmless. They're going to keep to themselves. All I want is for you to get down and dirty with them enough for some killer footage."

"Killer footage," I repeated. "And if I'm the one who's killed, that'll really shoot the ratings through the roof, huh?"

"God, you overexaggerate. Since when did you get to be such a scaredy-cat?"

I ignored that. "Tell you what, Bass," I said. "Let me hire this Shade investigator guy as a bodyguard. He's a big guy, and I get the feeling he'll know what he's doing—it can't cost you all that much to hire him for one night."

"It's going to cost me a whole lot more if I find out that this car I bought from him is a lemon. I swear, if he sold me one of those flood cars—"

"Do you even care?" I was exasperated, and it showed. I hated the desperation in my voice, but even Bass—with his lack of compassion and his drive to beat our rival, *UpClose Issues*—shouldn't be so glib about sending his reporter out into danger.

"I care that we get this story. And I care that I wasn't taken by a crook when I bought this car. You have your job to do. So do it."

Maybe I'd hire the guy on my own. How much could one night's protection cost?

"Fine," I said. "I'll take your buddy out to lunch after my handgun lessons and I'll find out about your damn car."

"It's about time."

"You're paying," I reminded him. "But I pick the place."

Placated by my acquiescence, he waved my stipulation away. "Whatever."

I picked up the phone as Bass turned to leave. "I'll call him right now."

But Ron Shade wasn't available today. His answering service let me know that the private investigator was out of town. Maybe this was an omen.

I left a message and decided to touch base with Jesse San Miguel to confirm our plans for the afternoon. As far as personal safety went, Jesse and I would just have to watch each other's backs. He wasn't a big guy. Though tall, he was very skinny. I could probably arm-wrestle him to the floor. But, he and I would have to make the best of it. I didn't have time to interview bodyguards, and Jesse and I needed to head out to the homeless gathering place early, while we had time to prepare.

Before I left, though, I had one more phone call I wanted to make.

"Lulinski," he answered.

"Hi, George, it's Alex."

The laconic detective surprised me by expressing pleasure at the call. He and I had worked together on a couple of our investigations that overlapped, much to his initial chagrin. Over time we'd developed a mutual respect. I trusted George with my life. More than once. And I'd do it again.

"Quick question for you," I said.

"Shoot."

"Let's say someone was going undercover . . ."

He groaned. "What are you up to now?"

"Come on," I said. "Hypothetically . . ."

"Okay, hypothetically."

"If someone was going undercover into a potentially dangerous situation . . ."

"Alex." His tone got suddenly sharp.

"Just listen. How bad would it be if she took a Taser with her?" I suddenly remembered to add, "This is within the Chicago city limits."

A long silence from the other end. It sounded like he rubbed his face. "Have you been trained in how to use a Taser?"

"Yes."

"And you know it's illegal to carry one in Chicago."

"I know."

"How likely is it that you'll be searched?"

"Unlikely."

A couple more beats before he asked, "How dangerous, Alex? And I don't want generalities. Give me specifics."

I sighed. "I'm going undercover as a homeless person."

His exclamation was about what I'd expected.

"Listen," I said, explaining. "I don't have any choice. Bass is convinced it'll bring home a Davis Award."

"That's not all it'll bring you. You ever hear of hepatitis?"

"I'm not planning to get that close to any of these people."

"Where are you going to be? And when?"

I told him.

"Shit. That's real scum. Out of my area, too. But I'll try to swing by and check on you."

"No, please don't."

He didn't reply. I quickly added, "It would tip everybody off. Besides, there'll be a sound truck out there with a couple of extra folks. And I'm taking a cameraman with me."

"And a Taser?"

I nodded, even though he couldn't see me. "And a Taser."

He smacked his lips. "Listen. You didn't hear this from me, but you be sure to keep that Taser handy. I hope you won't have to use it, but I'd rather have you facing charges of carrying an illegal Taser, than not here at all."

I swallowed. I'd expected him to say I probably wouldn't need it.

"So I've got your blessing?" I asked.

"No. But I will come check on you."

The viaduct was almost deserted. The unseasonably hot sun high above cast crisp shadows on the baking pavement. I fanned myself and hoped for the promised rain to cool things off.

As far as I could tell, there were only two people in the vicinity. One was a black man and the other was . . . hard to tell. Short and slim, the person wore so many layers of clothing that it took me five minutes of watching before I decided he was male, too. He walked bent in half, so that his upper body was nearly parallel to the ground. I finally spied a beard, which convinced me of his gender, and I could only imagine how hot he must be with all those clothes and a striped knit cap pulled tightly over his long silver hair.

I had to wonder about the rituals these people observed. According to Father Morales, they spent their days wandering, but came back here at night to sleep. Did they follow routines, have set habits, like most people did? Living with them might give me another angle for the story. At least I hoped it would.

Other than cardboard boxes, a few crates, and wooden pallets that one of the two men was pushing across the cement with his foot, I saw very little in terms of personal property. You kept only what you could carry, I guessed.

"God, the smell," Jesse said, keeping his voice low.

"This is nothing," I said, "wait till the rest of the residents show up. The combination is . . ." I struggled for the word, "intense."

"Where are we setting up?"

"Got any suggestions?" I circled the area, maintaining plenty of distance from the two men. I half expected one of them to come over and ask for money, but it was either too far for them to walk, or too hot for them to leave the viaduct's shade.

Jesse was curly haired and tall, with a tennis player's wiry build. For this adventure, I would've preferred the company of a wide receiver, but our pool of camera-wielding personnel was limited. Tonight we'd be accompanied by one of our sound techs and another camera person, but they'd be safely ensconced in a truck a thousand feet away.

"This sucks," he said, wiping his brow with the back of his hand.

I wondered how many nights I'd have to spend out here before I'd have enough to fill the feature. "Tell me about it."

"What'd you do to Mr. Bassett to get him so pissed off at you?"

I laughed, but it wasn't funny. "I don't know. Breathe, I guess."

Jesse had a miniature camera with him and he trotted up the embankment that led to the expressway above. I followed both his steps and his logic. Traffic whipped by, just above our heads, blanketing us with hot exhaust fumes. The background hum of racing cars and the lumbering power of semis reminded me how close we were to our familiar lives. And my glance back down—at the wasteland the indigent called home—reminded me of how far.

"It's not a bad view from here. I can zoom in and keep you on camera the whole time—if you're able to stay on this side of the viaduct, that is. Plus, I'll be able to get shots of the whole area."

I shook my head. "You and I will be too far apart. I think we need to stick closer together."

"Getting nervous?"

"Yeah," I admitted, "but that's not it. Bass wants up close and personal. I don't intend to sit out here any longer than I absolutely have to. I want to hear them. Listen to what they have to say." I pointed. "See that spot, right next to the battered pillar?"

Jesse nodded. The cement column I indicated looked like someone had taken a bite out of its base. Four feet up from the ground, the four-foot-wide support was crumbled, rocks and rebar poked out—but only on one side. The side that faced the street. "Looks like a bad accident," he said.

"That's exactly what it was." I made my way down the embankment. "They've had a couple of drunken drivers nail that pillar. And in the process two of the inhabitants down there have been killed. Father Morales said that the people here avoid that spot now. It seems like the logical choice for me."

"Oh, yeah. That sounds real safe."

"If we hang in here for one night, I think we'll have enough film for background and to show what life is really like on the streets." I shuddered thinking about the zombie-like atmosphere that permeated the area last night. I knew one night's worth of undercover filming wasn't going to cut it, but I couldn't consider the possibility of being out here longer than that. We'd have to take it one night at a time.

"What's your angle for this feature?"

I blew my bangs off my forehead. "I don't know yet."

Jesse set his fist at his hip and faced me. "You don't know?" His tone held more than incredulity.

"What I'm thinking," I said, my hands coming up to placate him, "is that we ask these folks about the one who made it out. His name is Howard Rybak. He used to live here and now he's holding a full-time job. He's turned his life around. If we can elicit some opinions from these people . . ."

We both turned as the black man below bellowed, "I will build an ark, Lord!" He held his arms out, began to cry as he begged—loudly—to please make the rain stop. He pounded his chest screaming expletives.

Jesse and I looked up at the clear sky. I felt my shoulders slump.

"We're going to be out here at least a week," Jesse said.

Ron Shade

I hoped that I'd have better luck, and fewer interruptions, with Dr. K. Boyd. Karen. Not a common name anymore. And the old lady on the porch had said the practice had belonged to Boyd's father. Country doctoring must have run in the family. I wondered how many autopsies she'd performed since graduating med school. From the stares the Beater was getting as I drove down the street, I realized that I'd probably have to get myself a new car pretty soon. It was all about image, even down here in southern Illinois.

I parked across the street and walked up the wide sidewalk to the yellow house. The sign above the doorbell said *Dr. K. Boyd, M.D., General Practice*. It looked weathered and old. Like it had been there a while. I was very surprised when a pretty woman with long brown hair opened the door. She was thin and looked to be in her mid- to late-thirties. The hand-embroidered letters on her gray smock spelled out her name and title.

"May I help you?" she asked.

"I hope so." I handed her one of my cards and gave a brief explanation of why I was there. "I already talked to the coroner. He mentioned you did the autopsy."

She studied the card for a few seconds, then stepped back,

holding the door. "Come in. I'm expecting a patient soon, but I have a few minutes."

Inside the house looked like any other country home. Her medical office was a section of rooms off to the right. They looked like they'd been added on or converted after the house was built. One appeared to be a waiting room with several chairs, the requisite array of magazines, and a small coffee table in the center. I followed her through it to the room beyond it, which was obviously her office. As offices go, it was neat and orderly. A huge bookcase with leather-bound volumes of medical books was immediately behind her, and stacks of journals were in cardboard slipcovers in a second case. A framed photo of her with her family, a smiling pair of kids, a handsome man, and a dog sat in the center of her desk.

"Nice-looking family," I said.

"Thank you." I saw her eyes studying my face longer than normal. "Are you a boxer, Mr. Shade?"

I grinned. "A kickboxer, actually. And not only that, I'm the world champ at the moment."

"Impressive."

"So how did you know?"

She smiled. "You have a slight build-up of scar tissue forming over your left eye. I used to live in Las Vegas, and we'd treat a lot of fighters in the ER. At least those who got hit in the face."

"Actually, I try not to get hit a lot."

She smiled again. "Maybe you should try a bit harder then."

This town was full of would-be comedians. It was like everybody was practicing their stand-up routines on me today. I waited a few more seconds to see if she was going to crack another joke or maybe launch into a lecture about the dangers of taking too many blows to the head, pugilistic dementia, and the whole bit. But she didn't. I was impressed with her perceptiveness. Maybe she'd picked up some impressions during the autopsy that could help.

"You said you were here about an autopsy I did?" she asked.

I nodded and took out the picture of Robert Bayless. I also took out the copy of the coroner's report and the neatly typed report that she'd previously done.

"Oh, yes, I remember this one." She paged through the papers, frowned slightly, and looked up. "This seemed pretty cut and dried. Why is it you're looking into it at this time?"

I decided on a cautious approach. No sense spreading suspicions too quickly.

"The company paid out a huge double-indemnity claim on this one," I said, mentally chastising myself for using "the company" excuse again. I was going to have to start limiting myself or I was going to turn into a Dick. "I'm looking into a few questionable things."

"Such as?"

She was an inquisitive lady. I ignored the question and countered with one of my own. "You listed the cause of death as multiple trauma, massive internal injuries, and cardiac arrest."

"That's correct."

Oh, great, I thought. Trying to get her to open up was going to be like getting Brunger to give away some free hay to the horse farmers. "What exactly does that mean?"

The dark eyes looked at me for a moment. "It means, quite literally, he had substantial internal bleeding. The damage was severe to his internal organs, but catching on fire caused him to expire more rapidly."

"He burned to death?"

She inhaled and smiled. "People don't really die from being burned as much as their lungs and heart stop functioning due to the inhalation of the horrifically hot air. It's not a nice way to go."

"As if any way's a nice way," I said, trying a grin. Her expression didn't change, so I added, "But I guess some ways are worse than others."

"You could say that."

"So there's no doubt he was alive when the car caught on fire?"

"None," she said. "There was soot in his nostrils and mouth. I also checked the lining of his trachea and lungs. They showed the searing that's consistent with the inhalation of intensely hot air."

"I'm surprised that the teeth survived intact. That's how you made the ID, right?"

She nodded. "Actually, the oral cavity was pretty well preserved. That's not unusual in burning deaths."

"Was any DNA testing done?"

She shook her head. "No need. The dental X-rays were a perfect match. And they just confirmed what we suspected from the vehicle's information."

"Do you think there'd be enough places left in the body at this point to do a DNA comparison?"

The space between her eyebrows creased slightly. "I'm sure there would be, unless it was cremated. They would need to withdraw marrow samples from the pelvic bone. But why would they need to? Is there some question as to identity?"

The best way to counter a question you don't want to answer is with another question. "Do you remember if there were any signs of a major disease, like cancer or something?"

She seemed a bit miffed, but answered me anyway. "None that I recall."

I smiled. "I guess what I'm asking is could the decedent have been terminally ill? Some medical condition that might have caused him to want to end it all?"

"Suicide?" Her eyebrows rose, but the dark eyes remained

focused on me. "As I said, I don't recall any evidence of that. His organs didn't show any signs of major disease, other than his lungs. He was a smoker."

"A smoker?" I opened the file and ran my finger down the columns until I found it. "I have Robert Bayless listed as a nonsmoker on his life insurance application. Are you sure?"

"Mr. Shade, it's very easy to tell the difference between a smoker's lungs and nonsmoker's, even if they have been in a fire." She canted her head slightly. "Now are you going to tell me what this is really all about, or not?"

"I already have." My voice sounded a bit forced, unnatural.

"I don't really appreciate it when people aren't up front with me," she said, getting to her feet. "Unless you want to be more forthcoming, I'm afraid this interview is over."

"More forthcoming?" I tried a quick laugh, but not as phony-sounding as one of Brunger's. "I have been."

"I doubt that. You're holding something back." She crossed her arms across her breasts and stood there looking down at me. "Believe me, I can tell."

"Well, actually." I slowly got to my feet. Starting up the rumor mill down here would be counter-productive. Doctors don't have the same instincts cops and private investigators do. "I'm just basking in my thankfulness of having followed the advice of my mother and my coaches at never having started smoking."

I tried another grin. It didn't seem to work.

I had another half hour to kill before Deputy MacMahan came on duty so I took out my cell phone to check for messages. It was on, but each time I tried to dial a number, the little screen would flash: *No Signal.* I tried moving up and down the street but nothing helped. So instead of climbing to the top of the monkey bars at the local park playground looking for that one spot where it would work, I decided to just wait till later. So much for the "Can you hear me now?" guy's commercials. Of course, my cell was a different brand than his, anyway.

I found an antiquated wooden park bench within about forty-five feet of the Sheriff's Office and sat to write up some notes. I recorded the times of each conversation and a general summary of each, along with any particular direct quotes that I could recall. This was getting to be like pushing a boulder uphill, but, I reminded myself, I was getting paid to do it. Trying to keep an open mind in this investigation was getting progressively more difficult, and I was beginning to put a bit more credence in good old Herb's identification of the horse-laugh when I saw a white squad car with the blue and red Mars lights on the top pull down the street. The tan letters along the side spelled out FURMAN COUNTY SHERIFF'S POLICE. It came to a stop in front of the Sheriff's Office Building. I glanced at my watch. Two-thirty-five. This was beginning to look promising. A big, stocky guy in a tan-and-brown uniform got out, squared a Smoky the Bear hat on his head, and ambled toward the front entrance with a bunch of papers and tickets in his big hands. I hopped to my feet and began a quick intercept course.

"Excuse me," I said. "Can you tell me what time Deputy MacMahan's working?"

The big guy stopped, regarded me with one of those sizing-up cop looks, and shifted his papers to his left hand. "That's me," he said, extending his open right hand. "And you're pronouncing it wrong, by the way. It's Mac-Ma-han."

I'd been saying it more like the old Bear's quarterback, Jim McMahon.

"Sorry," I said. "I'm—"

"The private detective come down from Chicago," he finished for me. "I figured as much. That's why I came by here a bit little early."

"I appreciate that. Can I buy you a coffee or something?"

"No thanks."

I grinned. "Hey, I'm on an expense account."

He flashed the easygoing smile again. "Nah, thanks anyway. What can I do for you?"

I took out the copy of the crash report and handed it to him. "You remember this one?"

He studied the report and nodded. "Bad one out on the highway. The guy was burned to a crisp by the time I got out there."

"How'd the call come in?"

MacMahan's eyes glanced skyward and he pursed his lips. "Best I can recollect, it was third party."

"Third party?"

He held up his paperwork and cocked his head toward the building. "Let me dump this stuff inside, and I'll show you the map and explain."

I followed him inside where he nodded at the comedian dispatcher. She reached across her console and pressed something and a loud buzzer sounded. MacMahan pushed on a solid metal door and stepped inside, motioning for me to follow. As we walked past the radio dispatch room he stuck his head inside and said, "Millie, print out a hardcopy of—" He paused and read off what I assumed was the incident report number from the accident report. "Make me ten-six, too, will ya?"

Mildred nodded and flashed me a lips-only smile, obviously still relishing her earlier witticism. I smiled back. MacMahan continued to walk down the hallway past several offices. Everybody looked pretty busy either typing, reading, or talking on the phone. He stopped and motioned to an open door that led to a report-writing room. The walls were covered with large bulletin boards with sections of huge maps tacked to them. Clusters of different-colored pins decorated the surface.

"Make yourself comfortable," he said. "I'll be back in a minute."

I stood by the table and waited, trying to figure which map was which, and what the different colored pins meant. It didn't take me long to figure out that the first map showed traffic crashes, while the second and third showed criminal activities. Just as I was trying to trace the highway route on the map to what I assumed was the site of the Bayless crash, MacMahan returned.

"I see you found it," he said.

"More or less. I could still use a little expert help."

He grinned and pointed a big index finger to one of the black pins. It was positioned at the center of the crooked line representing the highway. I suddenly knew what Brunger had meant when he'd referred to it as having "a real bad curve to it."

"Deadman's Curve, huh?" I said.

"Pretty close. Lots of fatalities there. They even had it on the TV news about two or three months before Mr. Bayless crashed there. Lots of rocks sticking up."

"You have any photos of the crash?"

He held up a manila folder. "This is our full investigation."

We sat down and he opened the folder, taking out a packet of color photos and spreading them onto the table top. "Looks like he was coming into the curve way too fast." MacMahan tapped two photos showing the extreme bend of the road that had been taken during the day. A jagged section of rock, probably thirty feet high, jutted outward like an inverted staircase. The next photo he tapped was a picture of the car and showcased the burned vehicle, the roof of which had been peeled back like a tomato can.

"After the fire was put out," he said, "we had to use the jaws of life to open it up and remove the body."

"Any photos of the body?"

His eyebrows rose, and then he nodded. He picked up another packet of photos and opened it. "Yeah. He was a goner way before we got there, though." He snapped a series of photos, each showing a blackened torso, frozen in a death spasm, its arms bending at the elbow and curled upward almost in supplication.

"What direction did it appear he was going?"

"Southeast. The highway cuts over toward Indiana. From the Interstate."

"Anybody have any idea where he was headed?"

MacMahan shrugged. "Wherever it was, he was in a hurry to get there." He took out another photo and set it carefully down on the tabletop. "We also found this inside the car."

It showed a scorched bottle.

"Booze?" I asked.

He nodded. "Vodka. His blood alcohol level wasn't that high. Point zero four, but according to his dentist, he'd prescribed some Vicodin ES for Bayless. Could have had what they refer to as a synergistic effect."

"I've heard of those. How'd the fire start?"

His eyes narrowed slightly. "Not sure. Looked like he ran over some rock sticking up here." He grabbed one of the photos from the first pack. "That must've ruptured his gas tank. After that, something ignited the fumes, most likely."

I took all this in, then leaned back. "You said something about a third-party notification before?"

"Oh, yeah." He placed the computer printout down in front of me. "This shows the time of notification. Zero two-twenty-seven. That's two a.m. See this along here?" His finger traced over a typed comment in the remarks section. *Complainant, listed above, was notified by an unidentified motorist of the crash. M/W. No other information available.*

"Exactly what does that mean?"

"The complainant, or the person reporting the incident to the dispatch center, was the clerk at the all-night truck stop." MacMahan shifted slightly and pointed toward the big map. "It's located right there on the Interstate, about two miles from the crash site. He said a white guy, about thirty to thirty-five, or so, came running up, ran in the door, and told him there'd been a terrible accident out on Highway Fourteen, and that they'd better hurry because the car was on fire."

"Some Good Samaritan lost in the night, eh?"

"Or not," MacMahan said. "Whoever it was took off without leaving any more information. The clerk said he turned around to pick up the phone and the guy had gone. He figured maybe he'd gone back to the accident scene to help, but he sure wasn't anywhere to be found when we got there." He paused and flipped up his shirt pocket, taking out a package of gum. He offered it to me. I shook my head. MacMahan unwrapped a stick, folded it twice, and popped it into his mouth. After he'd chewed a couple of times, he canted his head slightly. "I even pulled the inside and outside surveillance tapes from the truck stop trying to see if I could track the guy down, but nothing. The tapes were real grainy and the guy was wearing a baseball cap real low on his forehead. Outside, the only thing I could make out was a big, dark sedan of some sort. Maybe a Lincoln or a Caddie and an SUV. License plates on both were unreadable."

"Both cars took off at the same time?"

"Looked that way, from the tape."

I watched him for a moment. "So why'd you go to all that trouble? Wasn't it pretty cut and dried?"

His index finger tapped one of the crispy critter photos. "I just like to be thorough, Mr. Shade. It was a little thing, but it bothered me I couldn't find the original witness, or witnesses. Wanted to find out exactly what the guy saw." He shrugged.

"But we were able to piece things together anyway. Ran the plate on the crashed vehicle and it came back to a rental. The renter was Robert Bayless out of Oakton Hillside, up by Chicago. The coroner got the dental records a few days later and made the ID. One car accident. Driver somewhat impaired. Case closed."

"Any idea why Bayless was on that particular stretch of road?"

He shook his head. "We didn't really ask his family what he'd been doing down here. His work address and phone number were listed on the rental agreement, and they're the ones we talked to mostly. Said he was down here on a business trip of some sort."

"The ID came through pretty fast, huh?"

He nodded and cracked the gum as he chewed it. "The next day or two his dentist sent us down some X-rays. Matched perfectly."

I made several entries in my notebook. "Anything stand out as odd?"

MacMahan blinked quickly, like the question had stunned him. "Why do you ask that?"

It was my turn to sit back and consider what I wanted to say. "Before I went into the private sector, I was a cop. Chicago."

He raised his eyebrows.

I continued, "Now even though the State Police handle the accidents on the expressways, I handled a few in my time. Plus, we used to get dispatched to assist the state all the time. So I've seen a whole bunch of real serious crashes, and I can only remember maybe one or two that resulted in a fire."

MacMahan smiled. "You know, I've seen a whole passel of them myself, and I could probably count the number of times I've seen that on one hand." He held up a big, open palm. "And one of them was this one."

MacMahan and I talked for a bit longer, neither of us totally comfortable with the spontaneous combustion theory of the accident. When I told him the actual reason I'd been hired to look into things he emitted a low whistle. "That could mean that instead of it just being a traffic fatality, it's really something else, isn't it?"

I nodded. "Especially if that wasn't Robert Bayless in that car."

"It was definitely somebody."

"Yeah."

"Could even be a homicide."

"It could. Especially since Dr. Boyd was convinced from the autopsy that the victim was alive when the fire started. Had a scorched trachea. If it wasn't Bayless, who was it?"

"Damn," MacMahan said. "Got any theories you'd care to share?"

I shook my head. "None right now. Just a lot of pieces that don't seem to fit together real well once you start looking at them closely. You got time to take me out to the crash site?"

MacMahan grinned. "Mr. Shade, I'll make the time."

Chapter 8

Alex St. James

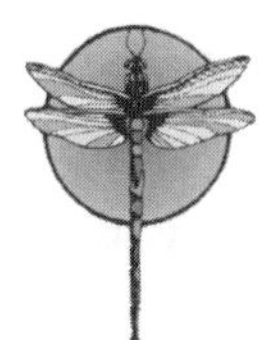

Father Morales was as good as his word. Not that I'd expected otherwise. He provided disguise—clothing for me and some for Jesse as well, which we donned in the private area of the church, so that none of the homeless guests at dinner would be aware of our transformation. The bagful of stuff Bass had given me, Morales said, was too prissy, too clean. It would've been like wearing signs with big bold letters: HOMELESS IMPOSTER.

Right about now, I would've chosen Bass's wardrobe selection over this one in a heartbeat.

My stomach gyrated as I pulled the first filthy garment over my head. I kept my mouth and eyes closed in an attempt to keep as many germs away as possible. The cotton shirt would breathe in the heat—that much was good news—but the long sleeves made me cringe. Father Morales had insisted that we conceal as much of our bodies as possible. "Homeless people are by and large unhealthy. It shows in their skin tone. You two look like prime American adults. Cover up."

I'd worn one of my own T-shirts and a pair of cotton shorts

over my underwear. The less direct contact vulnerable body parts had with these second- and third-hand items, the happier I'd be. Most everything Morales provided was brown or gray or black. But he'd let me keep the big pink hat from Bass.

"Homeless ladies like hats," he said. "You'll fit in better if you wear it."

I grimaced.

"No lice," he said as if reading my mind. "I'll spray it with disinfectant. We keep that on hand."

"I'll bet you do."

I finished dressing, resisting the screaming urge to rip the nasty clothing from my body and jump into the nearest shower. Once this evening was over, I vowed to clean out my closet and donate as much quality clothing as I could afford to part with.

Jesse, Father Morales and I met back in the church office.

"Very nice," Morales said. "You could almost fool me."

"Almost?"

He gestured toward Jesse. "Your dark complexion will help you blend in at night, but you," he turned to me. "You're too pale. Too clean. You look like a little white girl dressed like a bum for trick-or-treat. Hang on."

He left us then, giving us enough time to secret our equipment in our bags. Jesse carried his camera and accessories, and food for bribes. I had my Taser, a tape recorder and my own stash of bribe items.

When Morales returned, he carried a potted plant in his hands.

He set it on the nearby desk and dug his fingers into the soil. "Here you go," he said, and proceeded to filthy up my face.

His plump fingers worked the dirt over my cheeks, forehead and neck. "Gee, thanks," I said out of the corner of my mouth to avoid a mouthful of mud. For good measure, he plastered some over Jesse's face, too.

Fifteen minutes later, he pronounced us done. "Dinner's still being served—we've got another half hour. You hungry?"

The last thing I wanted right now was to eat. I shook my head, and coughed when I tasted dirt. "No, we better head out. We can't wait to get started," I said with a heavy dose of sarcasm. "I need to reserve my bed for the evening."

Morales shook his head, just as he'd done when I'd first informed him of the plan. "How long do you plan to stay out there?"

"All night, if we have to."

"God be with you," he said. "I know the crazies will."

Ron Shade

The ride out to Highway 14 proved unrevealing. Just a winding road that curved through a section of thirty-foot-high rocks. MacMahan's cautious brake lights ahead reminded me again that it was well known for its deadliness.

"It's on the IDOT traffic Web site as one of the most dangerous stretches of roadway in the state," he said when we got there. "Plus it's so isolated down here, somebody could crash and not be noticed for days. Luckily it was reported by that unidentified Samaritan."

I filed that piece of information for later. If you were going to set up a crash, it would be a good location to know about.

"As near as I can remember it," MacMahan said, walking along the side of the road, "his car hit this section right here." He pointed to a jagged grouping of rocks sticking up along the shoulder like an eruption of crooked teeth. "They tore the hell out of his gas tank, and maybe a spark or a cigarette ignited the fumes."

"Or a match," I said. "I remember an idiot in basic training showing me how he could put a lit cigarette out in a gerry-can full of gasoline. The flash point for the lighted square wasn't high enough to set the liquid on fire."

"It's the fumes that usually ignite," he said. "When I was in the air force in basic we had one asshole who would light his farts while everybody watched."

"Every artist wants someone to appreciate his work."

MacMahan grinned. His radio cackled and he reached up to his shoulder mic and answered it.

"Can you check on a ten-fifty on Higgins and Dundee Road?" the dispatcher asked. "Reported as PD only at this time."

"Ten-four," he said, and extended his hand. "Mr. Shade, it's been a pleasure meeting you."

"Same here," I said. We exchanged cards and I watched him roar off, his Mars lights blazing in the late afternoon haze. I turned and studied the road some more. If I were setting up a crash, how would I do it?

I walked Deadman's Curve and saw the trajectory that Bayless's car must have taken. Coming around the bend real fast and steering to the right, hitting the rocks, rupturing the gas tank, smashing into the solid rock base . . . No skid marks, according to MacMahan. Bayless hadn't even hit the brakes. But the report did mention there were a few yaw marks, indicating that the front wheels turned sideways as they skidded. I turned around and looked back at the curve from the point of impact, imagining the car speeding toward me. Then I imagined something else.

I'd been in George's office one Saturday when his partner, Doug Percy, asked if I'd seen the "good old boys" chase. Not knowing what he was talking about, he motioned me to his computer and showed me a video clip on his computer. It showed a police chase from LA that must have been filmed by a news helicopter. Several black-and-white cruisers chased a Mustang on an expressway, with Waylon Jennings singing "The Dukes of Hazzard" theme song in the background. The squad cars tapped the Mustang's back bumper several times, sending the fleeing vehicle into a circular spin out. Doug told me that it's a matter of making bumper-to-bumper contact, and twisting your steering wheel to the left. If somebody had been pushing Bayless's rental around the curb, and knew how to effect this spin out technique, it could have sent the rental into the rocks. It could also explain the yaw marks the police had found on the asphalt.

But that type of driving is very specialized. Not many people could do it. It would take someone with a lot of knowledge and a lot of skill. A pro.

Alex St. James

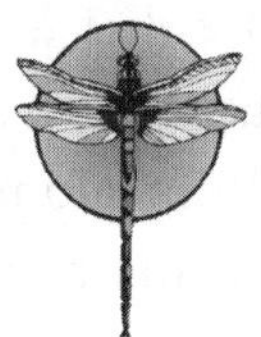

There were four of us total: Jesse, with a James Bond–like camera fashioned to look like a button on his battered hat; Rita in the sound truck, listening in on me and all the conversations under the viaduct from a thousand feet down the road; and Lew, a second cameraman, stationed in Rita's truck, equipped with a high-powered zoom lens. His job was to get both wide establishing shots and close-ups of my interactions with the homeless.

I wore a microphone attached to my collar and reminded myself that every word would be recorded, so I'd better not speak my mind about Bass tonight.

Or maybe I should.

Jesse and I made our way to the inhabited underpass, I went over the plan: blend in, keep a low profile, then use my stash of goodies—foodstuffs, mostly—to encourage people to talk. My goal was to find out more about this success story—Howard Rybak—and to find out why he was able to break free of the cycle of poverty that ensnared so many. Bass may not think this was a particularly strong angle to follow, but I did. And I knew my instincts were right. What did Howard Rybak do differently, and why didn't the rest of these people follow his lead? It was my best shot. I groped in my bag to reassure myself that I had plenty of bribe-food, and to ensure that the Taser was still there, ready for action. The last thing I wanted to do was hurt one of these folks, but . . .

No, scratch that.

The last thing I wanted was to get hurt myself.

It was twilight when we arrived. Jesse walked ahead of me by several hundred feet. We decided it best to not let on that we were "together" here tonight. Up till about two blocks ago, we'd walked together and now the aloneness of my position was beginning to take its toll on me as my loafers shuffled against the pebbly sidewalk making lonely scraping sounds.

There were more homeless gathered here tonight than there had been when Nicky and Morales and I visited. I wondered why, until a flicker of lightning flashed fast in the eastern sky. It was going to rain.

I could smell it now, feel the prickle of anticipation in the atmosphere—and I understood. The crowd had gathered here for protection from the storm.

"Great," I muttered aloud, then grimaced.

Rita would record everything I said. It was bad enough I

smelled like one of these inhabitants, I didn't want to start acting like them, too.

As I closed the distance, eyeing the bad-luck pillar where I planned to spend most of my night, I mulled over my approach to this story. Since my early days in feature researching and reporting I hadn't ever had a reaction to a story like the one I was having now. I loathed this assignment. Would give it up in a heartbeat.

But that wasn't like me.

I shook my head, causing little dirt crumbs to drop from my face. Part of the reason for my reluctance might be the fact that Bass pandered to Gabriela. But the truth was I could accept that. She was, after all, our star, and I understood the need to keep her working on stories that kept her happy and our ratings high.

Another tiny flash of lightning, high in the clouds.

Maybe it was me. My own personal reluctance. After all, the last feature I'd worked on had been . . . difficult. I'd come face-to-face with a murderer, one ready and eager to kill me.

I stared ahead at the group of zombie-like homeless folks and wondered what they'd done in their lives to bring them to this terrible place. Were they criminals, or just unfortunates with no one to take them in?

I shuddered, groped for the Taser again. At least this time I'd come prepared.

Twenty minutes after I sat with my back against crumbling concrete, my butt hurt. Jesse was to my far left, about halfway up the embankment, sitting on his sleeping bag, looking as wary as I felt. Three cars had gone by, one very slowly.

For the most part, the homeless folks kept to themselves, except for a boisterous bunch up near the top of the embankment. I had one visitor, an elderly woman who asked me if my name was Monica, and who shuffled away, wiping at her nose when I told her no.

I stood, stretching, working out the kinks in my legs that sitting on the cooling cement had so graciously provided. Next to me, a metal beam sprouted upward forty feet, to meet with the underside of the expressway above. I leaned against the metal, keeping my movements small so as not to call attention to myself. Yet.

I used the opportunity to grab a glance at the loud men tucked into the top of the embankment. There appeared to be three of them, sitting in half shadow, passing a bottle around, taking swigs. Whatever they were drinking, it kept their spirits sufficiently high that they relished sharing their every thought with the captive audience below.

One of them, surprising me with his pleasant tenor voice, sang out about winning the lottery tonight. The other two pulled the bottle out of the singer's hands and wrestled between themselves as the first guy continued to croon.

They were different than the rest of the people here. Not only were they active and rowdy, they were together. I scanned the underside of the viaduct and counted fourteen homeless folks. Every single one of them a loner. Except for the three high up above us. Maybe they would make an interesting story.

So far, I hadn't been branded as a faker, so I decided to explore. After all, the sooner I was able to produce a workable, hard-hitting, ratings-gathering story, the sooner I could return to my home, my bed, and most of all, my shower.

I looked out over the human wasteland before me. Yeah. Right.

I recognized the old black guy from earlier in the day and approached him just as he sprawled himself over a blanket of newspapers. "Hey," I said.

He'd just rested his head on his beefy upper arm and closed

his eyes. Now he opened one, and cast me a filmy glance. "I ain't got nothing you want."

"I don't want anything," I said, too fast. And too properly. I better watch that. "I . . . got something you might want, though." I dug into my bag, looking for one of the snack items I'd tucked in there.

"Don't want nothing."

"How about these?" I asked, proffering two chocolate-chip granola bars.

The guy opened both eyes and lifted his head enough to give me a stare. "You wanna give those to me?"

"Yeah?"

"Sheeit," he said, then turned his back.

A woman watched our interchange and when the grizzled old guy ignored me, I turned to her. "Would you . . ." I stopped myself mid-speech, knowing how polite I sounded. "You want some?"

Her eyes grew wide and she scooted herself away from me, mumbling something to herself about going to heaven.

Great, I thought. Two down—a dozen more to go.

Jesse had taken the opportunity to meander over, no doubt hoping to catch as much interaction as possible on tape.

This wasn't going anywhere, so I decided to take a different tactic with the bent-over man I'd seen earlier. I strode up the embankment to his "home," a portion of cyclone fence that someone either never finished erecting, or never got around to fully tearing down.

He lay on the ground, a filthy plaid blanket beneath his head. Even in repose, the poor man couldn't straighten out. He looked like a Muppet trying to form the letter "L."

"Hi," I said, for want of anything more pithy.

His body didn't move, but his eyes sought mine. "What ya want?" he asked in a nasally voice.

"Are you hungry?" I asked.

It took a minute to realize that the high-pitched squeals were laughter.

"What's so funny?"

"Am I hungry?" he said, practically hugging himself with mirth, nearly rolling on the ground. "When ain't I?"

"Here," I said, holding out the granola bars. "Take these."

It took every ounce of his effort to sit up, but sit up he did. With his legs straight out in front of him, his torso bent forward, he seemed stuck always looking down. "Whaddya want for them?"

I shoved the two granola bars at him so fast, he sat back in alarm. Which meant that his feet came up off the ground. Right about now I was feeling so white-bread, so pampered, so guilty for ever wasting a morsel of food that I wanted to empty my bag onto this guy's lap if he'd take it. "I don't want anything," I said, "I mean . . . nothing. I don't want nothing."

He snatched them from my grasp with a move so swift I almost missed it. Twenty seconds later the first granola bar was gone, disappeared into the mange of silver hair that passed for a beard and mustache. I caught a flash of green teeth, desperately chewing. He pulled open the wrapper of the second bar and warned me that once it was gone I wouldn't have any more leverage, so whatever I wanted, I better tell him now.

Not that I would've tried to stop him. The second bar was gone in almost as little time, and the guy crunched, his mouth quivering as he chewed.

"What's your name?" I asked.

He licked his lips. "Gus."

"Gus," I said, in a voice just loud enough for the others to hear, "did you know Howard Rybak?"

Gus croaked, then laughed more. "Ah! I knew it. You want something. Knew it. Knew it."

"You want something else to eat?" I countered.

"Whaddya have?"

A voice from high up. One of the three wise guys again. "Hey, Pinky. What you doing with Old Squat?" he shouted. "Don't you want some of this?"

I looked up. The guy who'd been singing before was now thrusting his pelvis my direction, emitting animated moans. One of his companions shouted, "What do you say, Pinky?"

Pinky?

I suddenly remembered the ridiculous hat I wore.

Whipping it from my head, I tossed it away.

I would've expected the tattered crowd to giggle, even laugh, but they were silent. Eerily silent.

Gus was grabbing at my bag, and instinctively I pulled away. "Hang on," I said. "There's plenty. I just want to know if you remember Howard Rybak."

"Sure, I do," he said, his fingers working the corner of my bag, reaching in. "But they're gonna get you and I want my food first."

"Nobody's going to get me," I said.

But the guy from above was making his way down the embankment, his eyes on me, his two companions following close behind.

Gus's hands had gotten to the gold and were now full of granola bars, fruit cups and other assorted items I thought the people out here might like. He acted like a selfish brat at Christmas, stuffing everything he could into his plastic bag.

"I want summa Pinky, too," a voice said.

I thought it might be the grizzled old guy come to share, but it was one of the singer's companions. He stared at me like I was the prize.

Jesse. Where the hell was Jesse?

More importantly, where was my Taser?

Just as I grabbed for it, Gus's eager fingers wrapped around its barrel. "What you got there?"

"Give me that," I said, wrenching it out of his grasp.

I heard Jesse call out from behind the three men, who sauntered closer, effectively forming a wall separating me and Gus from the rest of the gathered homeless. These three looked different, felt different, than the rest of the people here. Full of booze, to be sure, but all three were large, well-fed, muscular men. The kind who worked out with hundred-pound barbells, not the kind who socialized with hundred-pound beggars.

Gus kept grabbing at me, for protection or for more food, I couldn't tell. I stood up, both to keep out of his reach and to be able to run if I needed to. I tucked the Taser inside my shirt and stood my ground.

Next to them, I was a midget. The biggest guy had to be over six-and-a-half feet tall. He had jet-black hair, buzz-short on the sides, long in back. His two companions were nearly as tall as he was, one with a blond ponytail and tattooed biceps, the other dark complected with his right hand in a cast.

I needed to arm my Taser.

"This is my spot," I said, working up as much intimidation as I thought a homeless person might muster. "Now leave me alone."

The middle guy laughed. "You're full of shit."

Jesse yelled, "Get away from her."

Their attention diverted, they turned to face him. "Who the hell are you?"

I took that moment to grab the Taser from my shirt. My fingers scrambled to click the front arming mechanism into place. I'd done it so many times under Terry's careful tutelage that the parts came together precisely as they should with a reassuring snap.

The homeless folks had perked up, their interest engaged.

One by one, they came to their feet and crowded around. It was entertainment time.

The tallest of the three men had a deep voice, almost a growl. "Get out of here, bum." Then turning, he pushed Jesse in the shoulder. Jesse stumbled back. "We want her."

"Get out of here now, if you know what's good for you," Jesse said. Brave words, wobbly delivery.

The tall guy laughed. "Or what, punk?"

"Or . . ."

Jesse didn't finish. The three had turned toward me, but the guy with the bad hand zapped his arm back in a swift move, cracking his plaster cast against Jesse's nose. I heard the crunch, and watched him fall to the ground.

I rushed forward to help, but the blond ponytailed guy grabbed the back of my clothing, and the force of my momentum sent me sprawling to the ground.

I hit with a bump, but held tight to the Taser.

Jesse rolled on the cement, cradling his nose, crying out. Blood poured fast, like water. Puddling.

"Get up, bitch," the tall guy said.

I wasn't about to star on this grimy stage for anyone's pleasure, least of all these three bullies. Up close, I could tell they couldn't be regular street people. They were too clean.

"What the hell are you doing around here?" I shouted from the ground. "Go back to whatever hole you crawled out of."

If our cover was blown, I didn't care. Right now, these menacing men were too much of a threat and I wanted to get clear of them—no matter what. I heard a car pass and glanced around, hoping to see George Lulinski's unmarked sedan cruising by. That would scare these jokers off.

I crab-walked backward, then yanked up the microphone's head from beneath my grungy shirt. "Rita, Lew," I started to say, but the shortest of the three guys shot a meaty hand at me.

He grabbed my shirt and pulled the microphone out from its perch, jerking it high till it snapped away from the transmitter. "Let go," I said, kicking him.

"Look at what she has here," he said to his companions.

The homeless around us oohed and ahhed. Inched closer.

Jesse moaned.

I scrambled to my feet, aimed my Taser. And fired.

The probes hit, center mass. "Yes!" I shouted.

The big guy went down fast. Screaming.

I gripped the trigger, keeping the juice flowing, my voice five octaves higher than normal. "You want some of this?" I yelled. "Do you? Come on, I'll give you something to jolt your jones."

My sudden courage had nothing to do with bravery, but everything to do with giddy power. My finger gripped the trigger that put the guy in pain. I gritted my teeth and held tight. The Taser made tick-tick-tick sounds as it delivered fifty thousand volts straight into the lug's massive torso.

"Big man can't get up, can you?" I shouted, then "Rita! Lew!"—calling for help. The sound truck was far off, the microphone broken. But Lew had his telephoto lens. Couldn't they see we had trouble here?

The two other guys, horrified at the sight of their fallen comrade writhing on the ground and squealing—began to back up. They didn't get far.

Behind me, brakes screeched. A vehicle stopped. I turned, expecting to see the sound truck, or Detective Lulinski, but it was neither. As I turned, the big guy on the ground rolled to one side. One of the probes dislodged.

Two seconds and he was up on his feet, ready to charge.

But Terry's training kept me alert. I rushed him, jabbing the Taser into his abdomen, squeezing the trigger, making sure to keep contact with his body.

He went down again. I went down with him, dodging his

flailing extremities, fighting to keep the Taser tight against him, making sure not to touch him between the probes. Then I'd be down for the count, too. I felt a zing up my arm. Taser effect or fear? I wasn't sure.

I heard my name. Someone shouting for me to stop. But it wasn't Jesse calling me. Not Rita. Not Lew.

I refused to stop. Refused to let up. I held that trigger as far back as I could, feeling the rush as the tick-tick-tick sent the man beneath me into spasms. I couldn't let go. If I did, he'd get me. The part of my brain that wasn't panicking realized I couldn't stay here forever. I needed to get away.

As that thought dawned, strong arms pulled me off the thrashing bully. I fought, kicking, screaming, but I heard my name again. Closer this time. "Alex, it's me."

I turned. Nicky.

"But . . ." I said as my Taser no longer made contact. "He's going to—" I wanted to warn them that he'd recover quickly, but my words died as a giant of a man grabbed the bully on the ground and lifted him to his feet as though he weighed less than little Gus.

"Who is he?" I asked, feeling stupid. "What's going on?"

"Come on, Alex, let's get you out of here."

"But I can't . . ." I pointed. "Jesse . . ."

Nicky called, "Viktor," and the giant turned. "Bring that guy into the car."

Just as Nicky pushed me into the backseat of his Cadillac, the sound truck arrived on the scene. Too little, too late, I thought. If Nicky hadn't been here . . .

But *why* was Nicky here?

Viktor, the giant, made short work of the bad-guy bully. I couldn't see what he did to the guy, but I heard his protests, and then sudden silence. Holding my breath I waited as Viktor trotted toward the car, sweaty and triumphant, reaching down to pick up Jesse along the way.

My breath was coming in fast pants, and I worked to slow it down. "What happened?"

Viktor shrugged, answering me in a thick Russian accent. "I teach him not to pick on women," he said, then gave a wry glance at Jesse who was whimpering as he made his way into the car next to me. "Or little men."

"But, what are you doing here?" I asked. Even as the words tumbled out, I knew what had happened. Father Morales. Nicky had been vocal and adamant against my coming out here, and he'd threatened to show up to "keep an eye on things." Which is why I'd kept tonight's plans somewhat secret.

Key word there: Somewhat.

Father Morales must've told him about our plans.

"Alex." It was Rita, rushing over. "What happened? We had a problem with the feed and we were trying to fix it. Next thing we knew Jesse was on the ground and you were shooting somebody."

"It was a Taser," I said, suddenly weak. "Tell me you got it all on tape. Please."

She smiled and nodded, holding up her index finger and thumb to form an "OK."

Nicky took charge, ordered Rita and Lew back to their truck and suggested they return to the station. He promised he'd be in touch.

Viktor shoved a box of tissues at us, then took the driver's seat. Nicky climbed in next to him, leaving me to minister to Jesse. The poor guy kept his head between his legs, which I thought was a terrible idea.

Viktor drove off, though I had no idea where we were headed.

"Jesse," I said softly, rubbing his back. "Are you going to pass out?"

He shook his head.

"Then sit up," I told him. "You're losing too much blood. Let me see."

When he removed his hands from being cupped around his nose, I winced. He saw it. "Oh, God it's broken, isn't it?"

"Where are we going?" I asked.

Nicky turned, took a look at the two of us in the backseat and appeared to be making up his mind.

He shared a glance with Viktor, who shrugged.

"The hospital. Of course."

The big guy eased into the left-turn lane and hit his directional signal.

We arrived at the Edgewater Hospital emergency room just as the rain began.

Chapter 9

Ron Shade

The drive back to Chicago from Furman County had been uneventful, but lengthy. As I got close to Champaign, I remembered to try my cell phone again and found I had four messages. Three from Dick MacKenzie (screw him), and one from Ms. Alex St. James.

You know, I thought, maybe this chick was digging me more than I figured. She was a looker. Petite, with brown hair and a spray of freckles and a figure that had looked interesting in spite of the heavy jacket she'd been wearing the one time I'd seen her. Of course, it'd been right after my title fight, and I looked like everybody's favorite raccoon. As far as the message itself, though, it was pretty generic. Just a request for me to call her and her number. When I tried it, her voice gave a cool recorded answer that she was unavailable, but to please leave a message. Playing hard-to-get, I left my usual, "This is Ron Shade returning your call . . ." along with my cell number again. Maybe one of these days we'd hook up.

The next morning I ruminated about the info I'd accumulated in the prior twenty-four hours as I ran through the early-morning streets dodging the puddles from last night's rain. At least it cooled things off. It'd been way too late to hit the gym last night, and I knew Chappie would be missing me, so I planned to catch a morning workout if I could. Out of a lingering sense of frustration, more than guilt of a missed workout, I'd pounded the heavy bag and speed bag in my basement after the long ride. And this morning I'd opted for an early run again because I had to meet George. I approached the last hill and quickened my pace. I wasn't sure if I was ever going to get to defend my title, as slow as things were going, but I was determined to be ready. Being ready had helped me win when I took the last fight on a couple weeks' notice. Being ready was what had kept me alive in more than one tight spot, too. Sometimes, you just never know when things will pop up.

When I got in the door I made my way between the whining cats as I removed my hooded sweatshirt. Even though it was almost summertime, Chappie always admonished me to wear one, lest I catch cold. The sodden shirt was so soaked that I had to wring it out over the bathtub before tossing it into the hamper and grabbing a cold sports drink out of the refrigerator. My answering machine was blinking.

Francis Griggas had left me an appropriately cryptic message about "my order being ready." Good old paranoid Francis. The call back could wait until after my meet with George. I glanced at my watch and saw I'd have to hustle if I wanted to get there by eight.

Karson's, our regular breakfast spot, was at 111th and Western. With all the work being done on the Ryan, George was taking Western north, so our meetings had been working out well for both of us. I had yet to spring any requests for assistance on him regarding this case, but I did want to bounce a few ideas off his seasoned-cop's brain. He'd been in Area Two,

Violent Crimes so long I imagined he'd forgotten more about homicide investigations than most detectives ever learn. I saw his black Ford Crown Vic in the lot and knew he'd beaten me there again this morning. So much for buying him coffee. I parked next to him and went inside, nodding to the hostess who smiled and pointed to George's table. He sat hunched over the *Sun-Times* with a half-eaten sweet roll and a cup of java steaming in front of him, looking like Robert Mitchum in some forties movie. Well, actually, George was looking more like middle-aged Mitchum these days. Sort of like when he played Marlowe in *Farewell, My Lovely,* except a bit more fit and a whole lot tougher. I sat across from him and grinned. He looked up and took another sip of his coffee.

"What are you fucking grinning about?" he asked.

"Just glad to see my buddy, that's all."

He smirked. "Okay, what kind of info do you need me to get you this time?"

"That's pretty cynical," I said, smiling as the waitress came and filled my cup. "And I was even thinking of picking up the check this time, too."

"Hell freeze over?"

We exchanged a few more good-natured insults, our usual get-up-and-go routine in the mornings, and ordered our usual breakfast. Eggs, scrambled for me, over easy for him. Whole wheat toast on my side, plain old Wonder Bread for him. The only exception was I asked for water and a large glass of cranberry-apple juice.

"When did you start drinking that shit?" he asked.

"I had some on the plane out to Vegas the last time. Developed a taste for it."

"You got any new fights scheduled?"

"Not yet. Chappie wants to give the eyebrow a little more time."

He nodded and his eyes narrowed as he looked at my face. "Makes sense." He drank some more coffee and asked, "So, how's Ken doing?"

I sighed. "As good as can be expected. The nurse said he's made a little progress."

He grunted something that sounded like "Good." When he asked how my trip downstate had gone I filled him in.

He broke off another piece of the sweet roll. "I figured it must have been all right since I didn't get any calls to vouch for you from the local coppers down there."

"You know," I pointed to the sweet roll, "that's a lot of sugar."

"Yeah, yeah, you sound like my wife." In defiance he shoved the remaining piece into his mouth and chewed vigorously.

"So how difficult would it be to fake a car crash?"

He got a real pained expression on his face as he continued chewing. Finally, he managed to shift the remnants of the roll to the sides of his mouth, so his cheeks bulged like a chipmunk's. "What kind of car crash?"

I described Deadman's Curve to him and mentioned the rocks and the fire.

"Any signs of an accelerant inside the car?"

I shrugged. "Hard to say. It was totally engulfed by the time the coppers and the fire department got there. They conjectured that the gas tank got ruptured on the stones."

"Could happen," he said. "More than likely not, though."

"That's what Deputy MacMahan and I figured."

"Who?"

"The deputy who investigated the crash. Real solid, stand-up dude."

"He going to look into the possibilities of a faked crash?"

I shook my head. "Not unless I can come up with the guy who supposedly died in it."

"Okay, you lost me. I thought you said that the driver burned to death and a positive ID was made."

"That's the official version. MWO Insurance has hired me to get the Ron Shade version."

"Sounds like you need an accident reconstructionist to look over things. Maybe they can do a mock-up on a computer. The original car still available?"

"Don't know. I doubt it. It had to have been totaled."

"Well, it sounds like you're SOL, then." He smiled as the waitress set down a hot plate in front of him, then one in front of me. "But knowing you, I'm sure you'll get to the bottom of things."

I filled him in on a few more choice details as we ate. When we'd finished I made a grab for the check but he plopped his big hand down on top of it.

"This one's on me," he said. "I don't want to owe you so I'll feel like I got to do you any favors."

It was said in a joking manner, I knew, but it still stung a little. The fact was that I had intended on asking him to run some checks, and I hated to feel like our friendship was based on that. I simply nodded and tossed down a few bucks for the tip.

George and I shook hands in the parking lot, and I watched him turn left and head north. I'd relieved him of his newspaper and sat in my car, taking out my cell phone. The first person I called was Francis. I told him it was me, and that everything was cool, but he still insisted on me repeating my password.

"I've got your order ready," he said, after I'd whispered a husky "Rosebud" into the phone. "You can come by anytime and pick it up."

"Can't you just e-mail it to me?"

Silence, then, "I'd have to make it password protected."

"Forget it," I said. "I'll come by later this afternoon then." He lived way on the North Side, so it was another long trip that

I was going to bill Big Dick for. As well as the fee. "Say, Francis, make me up an invoice, too, will you?"

"An invoice?" His voice sounded strained. "You've never asked for one before."

"Yeah, but this time I need it. Got to bill my client for any expenses."

More silence. "I really would rather not. Paperwork of that sort is so traceable."

"Look, Francis, put generic computer searches on it if you want, all right? I just need it by this afternoon when I come by."

He finally agreed and I hung up. Dealing with paranoid computer geeks is not on my list of favorite things to do. I composed myself, scanned down to the number I wanted, and hit the transmit button. Moments later her velvety voice came on the line.

"Alex St. James."

I couldn't believe I'd gotten hold of her so easily. I told her so and added, "We seem to have been playing phone tag lately. What can I do for you?"

Instead of a laugh, I heard a slight sigh. Her tone sounded hesitant, on the edge of emotional. Or was she just nervous to be talking with me?

"I . . . was wondering if you'd be free for dinner, Mr. Shade. I have a couple matters I'd like to discuss with you."

Dinner? A girl asking me out? This chick was definitely interested. Old Ron Shade, world champion and professional lady killer. I took a moment to bask in the possibilities.

"Mr. Shade? Are you there?"

She definitely had a case of the jitters. I figured it was best to be brief. "Sure. Just tell me where and when?"

"Do you know where Benson's restaurant is? On Rush Street?"

Benson's . . . Now it was my turn to be hesitant. "Yeah, sure,"

I said, answering slowly. I immediately regretted letting her choose the place. Benson's would probably drain my wallet just for the valet service. Maybe I could somehow bill the thing to Dick. "What time?"

"Why don't we shoot for six?"

I thought about a way out. "Maybe I'd better check to see if we can get reservations this quickly. Any other places you'd like?" I added quickly, thinking maybe she'd agree to the Rock-and-Roll McDonald's.

"I'll take care of that," she said. "And I'm paying, too."

I started to offer a weak protest but she cut me off.

"No, it's okay. My boss is picking it up." A hint of merriment found its way into her voice.

A girl after my own heart, I thought.

"Say," she said, sounding rushed again. "I'm in the middle of something. So I'll see you there at six?"

"Sure," I said. "Call me if anything comes up."

When I terminated that call, I glanced at my watch. It was almost nine. More than enough time to hit Chappie's for a nice relaxing workout, and then a ride to the North Side to see Francis after the traffic jams had faded. I was just backing out when my phone rang and I answered it expecting Alex St. James again. But instead it was Dick MacKenzie.

"Ron, how come you haven't returned my calls?"

"I was downstate yesterday. My cell phone wouldn't work."

"Downstate? Furman County?"

"The one and only. Talked to the coroner, the doctor that did the autopsy, and the police officer who investigated the accident."

"And what did they say?"

"Pretty much what was in their reports."

"Oh, Christ, don't tell me you haven't gotten anywhere."

I resisted the temptation to say, Okay, I won't tell you.

Instead, I mumbled off some generic BS about several new possibilities that I'd uncovered. I had to keep him happy until he paid the bill.

"New possibilities? What are they?"

"Look, Dick, I can't really go over them now. You'll just have to trust me that I'm working on things. In fact, I'm on the way somewhere right now."

"Ron, you are making this one a priority, aren't you?"

"Of course. I'm all about priorities."

I could hear his heavy breathing over the phone. He was probably debating giving me the "how important this case is to the company" line. Instead, he just muttered an "Okay," and told me to get back to him as soon as I had something. His voice perked up to the old insurance salesman he was when he added, "Remember, we're all counting on you here."

I hung up and continued driving to the gym. Like I'd said, I was all about priorities.

Besides a couple of journeymen boxers who worked night jobs and trained in the mornings when they got off, I was practically alone in the boxing room. Chappie was out doing something, so we were left to our own dedication. The gym was composed of three long, parallel rooms, dividing the place into three sections. Several women swayed to some hard rock in the aerobics class next door, and in the room adjacent to them, die-hard lifters pumped iron with our resident body builder, Phil Brice. My winning the championship seemed to have inspired everyone there to work harder. Brice announced he was going into training for the Mr. Midwest title, and a couple of the boxers began begging Chappie to set them up in some smokers at the Aragon. My buddy Raul, who'd won, then lost, the light-heavyweight kickboxing title, had been coming in more often as well. Unfortunately, Chappie's young protégé, Marcus Smith, had been killed in a drive-by shooting. Initially, I'd wondered if he'd gone to workout at another gym, but then heard word on the street that he'd fallen in with some bad dudes. His death, which had involved the ubiquitous gangs and drugs, had come about a week later. Chappie took it pretty hard. It was like a light somewhere had been extinguished, leaving his world in a little more darkness. Marcus's mama had signed the paper to donate his organs, so she felt that at least a little good had come out of the tragedy. But I'd been slightly irritated by the doctors who'd been hovering around us in the waiting room, giving the poor old woman the soft-soap about how important it was, and how organs were in such short supply.

"It could help save another young man's life," the doctor had said. Chappie had been on the verge of going after the guy when Marcus's mama agreed. I wondered if it wasn't just another form of flim-flam. The law of supply and demand, taken to the ultimate degree.

I worked the speed bag, concentrating on the various rhythms, as I worked the case in my mind. A trip to Bayless's former place of employment was definitely in the cards. So was a trip to the dentist. The one who'd confirmed the ID. If something was fishy, a whole lot of people were either real stupid or involved somehow. That meant some pretty big payoffs. Of course, with a double indemnity of ten mil, there was plenty to go around. Still, I couldn't afford to show my hand too quickly. Better to give the appearance of plodding ahead, then dazzle them with some speed and footwork right before the round ended.

With that brilliant thought, the round bell rang, and I stopped for my minute's rest. The other boxers, who'd been working the heavy bags, stopped, too. We all stood in silence as the music, the Bee Gee's "Staying Alive," wafted in from the other room. An iron pumper's primal scream sounded as well. He'd either completed a tough set, or gotten a hernia. Chappie would be more than a little peeved at me for missing last night's workout. He'd been training our Russian kid, Alley, for another bout, and Chappie liked for me to help out. Alley's name made me think of Alex St. James, and I suddenly felt an urge to check my cell phone just in case she'd called back wanting to change our plans. Maybe she'd want me to pick her up instead of meeting at Benson's . . . Maybe I should have suggested it . . .

I decided that the gentlemanly thing to do would be to call her and extend that offer. Of course, it meant driving the Beater. I pondered that and decided she wasn't the type of girl who'd be overly impressed by a flashy car. Still, when this case was over, I'd have to go car shopping. After all, I had an image to uphold. Slipping off my bag gloves, I headed for the locker room, eyeing the bouncing female forms as I walked past them. Chappie's daughter, Darlene, usually led the classes, but she'd gone back to law school and was seldom there anymore. He'd hired a couple of other young lassies to fill the gap. The one today was named Norma Rae. I hadn't figured out if that was her first and last names, or only the first two. She looked like she'd had enough plastic surgeries to send a couple of the doctor's kids through college, although she was buffed as hell, in an extreme sort of way. I'd talked to her a few times, but her main focus was on Brice, who also looked cartoonishly chiseled. Together, they made the perfect couple to put on the cover of *Muscle & Fitness Magazine*.

I sat on the bench inside the locker room and turned my cell phone on, getting ready to call Alex when the text along the screen told me I had a voice message.

Did I want to check it?

Of course I did, and pressed *Yes*.

"Mr. Shade." The voice was flat-sounding and twangy. "This is Thad Brunger, from Furman County. I have that information you requested. If you can call me back at . . ." He left me two numbers and added that if he couldn't be reached at the first one, the second was his store.

I ended up dialing them both, since the first one went almost immediately to a voice message. Brunger answered on the third ring of my second call.

"Ah, Mr. Shade. I was hoping you'd get back to me relatively soon. I found the name of that funeral home that picked up Mr. Bayless."

"Great." I stood and searched the shirt hanging inside my locker for a pen and paper. "What is it?"

I heard one of those sudden exhalation sounds and remembered the man's disconcerting laugh. I guessed it was supposed to be ingratiating, or something.

"Before we get to that," he said, "I'd like to discuss my fee. I believe you mentioned you'd be willing to pay for my time looking the information up?"

"Absolutely." I found my pen, and scanned the room for some paper. I walked over to the waste can and pulled out a plastic soft drink bottle, peeling off the label as I spoke. "What would you feel is a reasonable amount?"

"Well, ordinarily, I charge ten dollars for any copies of reports," he said. "And since I had to get up extra early to search through the files here, meaning that I had to open the feed store a bit later than usual, I feel that twenty-five dollars would be appropriate."

I had to hand it to the shithead, he wasn't shy. I folded the peeled label in half, giving me a slip of white on which to write.

"How about fifty?" I asked. "Would that cover it?"

"Why, ah, certainly." His voice had a glow of satisfaction. "Shall I send you an invoice?"

"I'll need that," I said, thinking of Dick hitting the roof and screaming about being bilked by a public official. But grease made things go faster, and Dick was too big a boy not to know that. "If you can give me the name now, and send me an official invoice, I'll get started on your reimbursement."

Long silence. I could tell his huckster nature was in a tizzy. If he gave me what I wanted, there'd be no guarantee he'd ever see his money.

"Mr. Brunger, remember that I'm building a case here. I have to have receipts to go in the file. I may need to have you deposed at a later date as well, which, of course, would be more money."

That seemed to whet his appetite. "Of course." I could almost hear him licking his chops. He quickly added, "I'd be happy to help out in any way I can."

"Good, good," I said in my most reassuring tone. "Ah, the name?"

"It's Sunset Manor." He read off the address. It was in Edgewater.

"The card say anything else?"

"Ah, yeah. It says: 'Where we treat the dead with the dignity they deserve.' "

And how about the presumed dead?

ALEX ST. JAMES

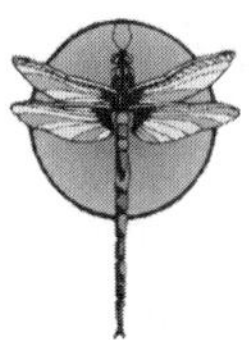

Bass came into my office just as I was ending my call. I motioned for him to sit. He scowled, but complied.

"Thanks," I said into the receiver, "keep me posted."

He waved a note in the air. "What's this?" he asked, then

used the note to fan his nose. "You look like shit. And you smell worse."

I'd been up most of the night with Jesse. Nicky and Viktor took their leave shortly after dropping us at the hospital's door, but before they drove off, Nicky told me—three times—to let him know when I needed to be picked up. I told him—three times—not to worry, that I'd find my own way home.

In fact, I hadn't gotten home at all.

We were stuck in the emergency room for hours, until the triage nurse decided Jesse's injuries were the next most critical and assigned us to a doctor. We waited there again, where I dozed, only to be wakened by Jesse's whimpers of pain.

He refused to let me call his family until we knew what was up. He claimed that he didn't want to unduly upset them, but I suspected that he was angry with me, and he saw my presence at his side as recompense for getting him into this mess.

No matter. I wouldn't have left him anyway. Not till I knew his prognosis.

At five in the morning, Jesse went into surgery. Broken nose, just as we suspected. The good news was that it was a clean break and after he healed, he would have no physical indication of the injury. His family showed up at six. Amid a lot of wailing and crying from his mother and sisters, and after explaining the situation to a demanding father, I'd snuck out.

And now Bass, furious, in front of me, was more than I cared to handle.

"Do you have any idea who I was on the phone with?" I asked.

"No. Am I going to have to get the cleaning service to fumigate this office?"

"Edgewater Hospital."

"Okay, so?"

"So Jesse's been injured," I said. "He's just gotten out of surgery."

Bass opened his mouth, but I interrupted him.

"I'm sure your heart bleeds for the guy, but let me put this in terms you'll understand: Jesse got hurt investigating the homeless story. The story you assigned us to. Know what that means?" I didn't wait for his answer. "It means that the station could be liable for his injuries. Oooh," I said with a fake shudder. "Liability."

That got his attention. He stopped waving the little paper. "What the hell happened?"

I gave him a rundown. "That's why I left you that note this morning." I pointed to it. "I thought I'd be out of here before you came in. I wanted you to call me, even at home."

"You're going home?"

"Look at me," I said. "I am not spending the rest of the day here looking and smelling like this. And, to answer your question, yes. You should have this office fumigated. Today. While I'm home sleeping." He opened his mouth again, then wisely shut it as I continued, "I'm going home to get some rest before I go meet with your buddy, Ron Shade, tonight. Or did you forget about *that* little assignment?"

I knew I was sniping, but it felt good.

Bass kept his voice neutral. Smart man. "You mean to ask him about the car?"

"Yep."

Nodding, Bass stood. "Okay. Sounds good."

"One other thing," I said as he made it to my door. "I want to hire him as a bodyguard when I go back undercover."

"What? How much is that going to cost?"

I held up a finger. "Don't quibble on this one, Bass."

To his credit, and my immense surprise, he didn't.

Ron Shade

I hit the showers after hanging up and left the serious working out to those of a more dedicated variety. I just didn't have it this morning. No zip. Maybe the run had taken too much out of me. I reminded Brice to make sure he told Chappie I'd been by. He nodded as he did curls with an Olympic sized barbell with forty-five-pound plates on each side. His biceps bulged with veins the size of garden hoses. Outside I strolled around to the back of the building adjacent to the alley and down to where I usually parked my car. The Beater had been blessed with a plethora of FOP and IPA stickers, since it had originally belonged to George's partner, Doug Percy. Although the body had more Bondo holding it together than a Baghdad taxi, no self-respecting copper in the entire city of Chicago would dare slap a parking ticket on it with all those police stickers. Thank God for good old Chicago alleys, as well. Too many places in the city, even on the good old blue-collar South Side, were getting the gentrification treatment. Alleys were literally being eliminated as homes became required to have front drive access to their garages. Sometimes change is for the better, sometimes not. I knew I'd miss them when they were gone. As I got in I thought about my date tonight with Alex St. James, and how I really would have to go car shopping soon.

The drive north went relatively well, despite the lane closures that the Illinois Department of Transportation had so thoughtfully provided. George liked to say we had two seasons in Chicago: winter and construction. Luckily, I fit in between the rush hour of people getting to work and would hopefully beat the rush of those same people coming home. I used the rationale as another reason to have cut my workout short. Plus, I didn't want to be totally worn out in case things went well on this date tonight. But maybe I was reading more into it than I should. Still, I had a date with an angel, and if I kept my expectations low, I wouldn't have to worry about being disappointed. I resolved that all I would hope for would be a pleasant dinner, with equally pleasant company. Still, I did make a silent vow to work out even harder tomorrow night.

I circled the block around Francis's North Side neighborhood for fifteen minutes before a space finally opened up, and that was by an alley. I gambled that the stickers might buy me enough time to make the quick pickup and be gone. Most of the garbage bins looked empty, so I didn't have to worry about it being pick-up day. Francis lived on the top floor of a brick three-flat and it took me another five to dash down there. Inside the foyer I rang the bell and waited, looking up at the small, black plastic half moon that I knew was a camera he'd installed. When his voice came over the speaker and asked who it was, I yelled, "Take a look at your goddamn camera."

The buzzer sounded a few seconds later and I pushed through the door, taking the stairs two at a time until I got to the top. I was pleased that I wasn't even winded when I got to the third floor. But I was feeling a bit hot under the collar having to rap on Francis's door again.

"May I have your password, please?" the voice on the other side said.

I swore under my breath and was about to pound my fist on the door again, when it opened and Francis stood there with a simper on his face. He was wearing blue jeans and a T-shirt and looked like a refugee from one of those old *Revenge of the Nerds* movies, except that he wore wire-rimmed glasses without any duct tape holding them together and his hair hung down around his shoulders.

"Sorry," he said. "I couldn't resist." He stepped aside and ushered me in, glancing in the hallway before shutting the door. "You know, of course, that neither I, nor any of my staff will ever ask you to repeat your password in public."

"Staff? What the hell are you talking about?"

"Never mind. It's a computer thing." He walked briskly through a narrow hallway that was stacked with books, reams of paper, old magazines, and tons of comic books. A large-screen plasma TV sat on top of its cardboard box, a DVD player hooked up and on the floor next to it. Stacks of plastic slipcases were piled on a coffee table next to a comfortably distorted easy chair.

"Excuse the mess," he muttered.

"Man, I thought I was a pack rat."

He turned to frown as he stopped by his desk. It looked like a smaller version of the living room, except his monitor and computer weren't stacked on cardboard.

"I'm a bit concerned about this invoice you wanted," he said. "I don't like to do anything traceable."

I took a deep breath. "Look, I just need it to turn in for expenses. You can put anything you want on it. You got my numbers?"

He frowned again and bumped up his glasses on his nose. "Of course." He dug through a stack of papers next to his printer. "I worked really hard on these, Ron."

"I'm sure you did." I reached out and he gave me the pile. I shuffled through the sections of papers on top and scanned them until I found the one I knew was for Bayless's cell phone. It had numerous calls to what I recognized as his office, an occasional one to his house, some scattered other repeated numbers, but the one that stood out the most had an 847 area code. "You run down these phone numbers like I told you?"

The question seemed to wound him. "I told you I worked hard, didn't I?"

Now it was my turn to frown. "Then work a little harder and show me where they're at, will ya?"

He peeled back the tops of a few pages and inserted a slim index finger into the sheaf. "Right here."

I looked up the 847 number and saw it came back to one Candice Prokovis. Francis had been thoughtful enough to list her address as well.

"Can you get me the records of this number, too?"

"I can," he said, "but I wish you would have asked me that before."

"How could I ask you before when I just got the number now?"

He licked his lips and bumped up his sagging glasses again. "That cell phone number you gave me was no longer in service. Neither is this one."

"You already checked it?"

He shook his head, causing his shaggy bangs to fall on top of the glasses. "I just wanted to see if it was still active. It wasn't."

I glanced at my watch. No telling how long I had before someone pitched a bitch about the Beater partially blocking the alley. "Can you put a rush job on it and do it now?"

"I suppose." He scratched his chin. "You're going to pay me extra, right?"

"I'll pay you double if you can get it for me before my car gets towed out of that no parking zone."

"Oh, okay." He scurried around behind the desk and sat down. His fingers flew over the keyboard and he looked up. "What did this chick do, anyway?"

"Don't know yet."

More finger flying. "There must be some reason why you're

so hot to trot in finding out about her."

I couldn't believe the little bastard was trying to pump me for information. The fewer people who knew my business, the better I liked it.

"Well," I said, "there is."

"Oh yeah? What is it?"

"You check out the last name?"

"Prokovis? What about it?"

"It's a Lithuanian name."

"Yeah, so what? Mine is, too."

Griggas Lithuanian? I bought a few seconds with a nonchalant shrug before I figured out a reply. "Well, you know what they say about those Lithuanian girls . . ."

Alex St. James

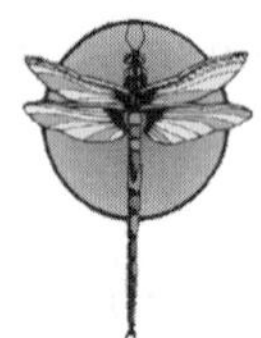

Deciding on what to wear for my meeting with Ron Shade was easy. After having spent too many hours in disgusting duds, I was ready to sparkle. This wasn't a date—far from it—but I needed to feel feminine again. Not to mention clean. As I walked my fingers over the tops of my "nice clothes" I decided that tonight, I'd be dressing for me.

So it didn't take long to choose the black sleeveless number I'd only worn twice before, to a Christmas party and a New Year's Eve bash. Same year, different gentleman callers. Although I could hardly use the term "gentleman" to describe either. I held out the princess-cut garment and smiled. A bad-luck-date outfit if there ever was one. Which made it ideal for the business dinner tonight.

Sleeveless meant I'd have to carry a shawl or sweater in case the restaurant's air-conditioning was set to frigid, but the sleek lines of this dress always made the most of my rather buxom shape.

The four-hour nap I'd gotten was plenty to make me feel refreshed, but not enough to jolt me into insomnia later. I felt good. I showered, and, not wanting to bother with hair frustration tonight, twisted my wet locks into a quick French braid.

I called Edgewater Hospital and learned that Jesse had been released. When I called his house, his mother reamed me out in fast Spanish, and hung up on me when I tried to apologize. It wasn't my fault, but try telling a distraught mother that.

Shaking off the sourness from the phone call to the San Miguel residence, I got dressed, added some of my favorite jewelry to the mix, splashed on a bit of *Heavenly* cologne and with a few minutes to spare, I gave George a quick ring.

"Violent crimes," he answered.

"I hope not," I said. "What happened to your ever-cheerful 'Lulinski'?"

He chuffed. Half annoyance, half laugh. "Where were you last night? I drove by about ten-thirty and couldn't find you. I thought you said you'd be out there late."

"Yeah," I said, drawing the word out, "that was the plan."

I told him all about the three big guys—their taunts, their attack, my Taser response, and Nicky's welcome appearance just in the nick of time—and I could tell he was scribbling notes. "What time?" he asked.

"Geez," I said, thinking. "Had to be around nine, I guess. I'm not sure. I wasn't wearing a watch." Right now I was wearing one. I needed to be out the door in the next three minutes.

"I'll see what the report says."

"I don't think there was a report." I grabbed my shoes, slipping on the black sling-backs as I cradled the cell phone and hopped.

"You didn't call the police?"

"No," I said, feeling defensive. "What was the point?"

His exasperation shot out in a noisy exhale. "The point, Alex, is that maybe the guys who bothered you have a sheet. Or a warrant." The next noise I heard sounded like angry scratches—a furious pen obliterating notes. He sighed, more gently this time. A squeak—as though he leaned back in his chair. "Tell me again about your 'rescue'?"

When I explained about Nicky and Viktor showing up just as I nailed the guy with the Taser, he asked, "How did they know you were out there?"

"I think Father Morales tipped them off."

Now he said, "Hmph," and then, "The timing's a little too perfect, don't you think?"

"What do you mean?" I asked, but by the time the words left my mouth, I understood. "You think Nicky and Viktor were watching, just waiting for me to get into trouble?"

"You said the three big guys didn't look like your average homeless people, right?"

"Yeah."

"And that they seemed to single you out."

I'd just reached for my purse. Now my stomach dropped as Lulinski's inference became clear. "You think Nicky arranged for them to bother me?"

"I think it's worth considering."

"But . . . why would he do something like that?"

"Good question. You said he made it clear he didn't want you going out there."

"I can't see Nicky putting me in danger."

"If he arranged this—then you never were in danger."

I thought about that. "No," I said, gathering my purse up

again. "That doesn't seem to be in his character. He's been trying to get a date with me, not scare me off."

Lulinski laughed. "And you, Alex, are much too trusting. You were the damsel in distress and he was the knight in shining armor."

"Shining Cadillac, you mean."

"You like him?"

"Like? You mean—to date the guy?"

"Yeah."

"Eeyoo."

He laughed again. "Well, there is one good thing about you not filing a police report."

"What's that?"

"At least you weren't arrested for carrying the damn Taser."

Chapter 10

Ron Shade

When I got back to the Beater I was delighted to find that it had totally escaped the vigilance of the city's meter maid force. I patted the dashboard and made a mental note to buy Doug a beer or something the next time we all got together. It had been less frequent now that Windy City Knights Security had gone belly-up. I kind of missed the old days of working the hotel security job whenever it suited me. I'm sure Doug did, too.

After finding the nearest coffee shop I double-parked and bought myself a medium to-go cup. Using the steering wheel as a desk, I sorted through the calls Bayless had made in the last month before his untimely demise. Most were to Candy, whom I had pegged as the secretary, and his work number. Which meant he either spent a lot of time out of the office, or he'd called for some other reason. I looked at the last day and saw the same pattern of numbers called. The girlfriend, the office, the girlfriend again, and a couple to another number I didn't recognize. It had a 773 area code, which meant it was in the city proper. I jotted it down on a piece of paper and checked out Candice's cell phone records. They pretty much mirrored Bayless's, except in reverse order. But there was one on the day of Bayless's accident that looked familiar. It was the same one Bayless had called with the 773 preface. Deciding against coincidence, I punched in the numbers on my own cell phone. I missed the days when all you had to do was dial the old 696-9600 and the free service would give you the name and address of the listing. But that service had gone the way of so many other good things, brought down by the ubiquity of the Internet. I hit the SEND button and listened to the rings. After two, one of those computerized menu things answered and reassured me, in a very calming voice, that my needs in this time of crisis would be well attended to because I had reached the Sunset Manor Funeral Home, "Where we treat the dead with the dignity they deserve."

It took me about fifteen minutes to get to Edgewater and find the place. Sunset Manor was one of those big, sprawling buildings that had probably been built in the 1920s using decorative flagstones and an artful, but solemn, two-story design. There had obviously been an expansion recently, judging from the newer-looking brick section along the back of the place adjacent to the parking lot. As it was, the place took up damn near the whole block, dwarfing the grocery store across the street and the video rental shop farther down. The sign in front was big, metallic, and in need of a retouch job, if you looked close. The windows hadn't been washed recently, either. At least the two long black Caddies that sat in the lot looked shiny and clean, though. A nice-looking red Corvette, equally immaculate, sat alongside them. I parked in the lot, which was almost empty, and wondered what kind of procession would be led by a Stingray. A fast one, no doubt.

The front of the place had an awning spread out over a set of double doors, which were locked. Undeterred after ringing the bell several times, I tried a few substantial pounds with the meat of my hand. Just as I was about to give up, one of the front doors whipped open and I saw a paunchy-looking guy with an angry expression on his face. He had slicked-back brown hair and a long nose. His lips twitched like a frustrated rabbit's and I caught a whiff of overapplied aftershave.

"What the hell you want?" he growled.

It was times like this that I wished I wore a pork-pie hat. I could have set it back on my head in an ingratiating, friendly gesture.

But since I was hatless, I mumbled a greeting and took one of my cards out of my pocket and handed it to the man. He made no move to accept it.

"What the hell were you pounding on the door like that for?" His voice hadn't lost any of its irritation.

"My apologies," I said. "My name's Shade. I'm working an insurance investigation and I was looking for the proprietor."

My explanation seemed to confuse him. The lips twitched again and his eyes narrowed. "Insurance?" He drew the pronunciation out into the three syllables. "What kind of insurance?"

"We had a client who died back in November. He was killed in an accident and the wake was held here."

His head bobbled slightly and canted to the side. "Six months ago? What are you doing coming back after all this time?"

"Just routine stuff," I said, trying my best to look ingratiating without the hat. "Are you the owner, sir?"

The "sir" must have got him. His head straightened up and his lips curled back into an almost cocky sort of look.

"Yeah."

"And may I ask your name?"

The eyes narrowed again. "Nick. Why?"

"Nick?" I asked, leaving the rest of the implied sentence hanging there. He made no move to answer so I had to ask it. "What's your last name?"

He rolled his tongue over his teeth and squinted. "Jones," he said. "Let me see that card again."

I handed him my card and he read it, lips moving over each word, and stuck it in his pocket. "Who you asking about again?"

"Our client was named Robert Bayless." This time his eyes stayed focused, but I saw a small twitch at the corner of his mouth.

He shook his head. "Doesn't sound familiar."

"You had to go downstate to pick up his body. He was in a car crash. His employer picked up the transport tab. The Manus Corporation."

The tip of his tongue protruded ever so slightly out of the corner of his mouth and he licked his lips, making a fair pass at looking thoughtful. Like he was actually trying to recall the transport, then shook his head. "We do a lot of services here. Sorry. It doesn't ring any bells."

"I can understand that. Lots of dead people, eh?"

He shrugged again. "Everybody dies."

I tried a smile again, not thinking it would do much good. "I just need to verify some details. I promise it won't take much of your time at all."

He took a half step back and pulled the door toward his retreating figure. "Yeah, well, look . . . I'm kinda busy right now. In fact, I was just on my way out. Business."

I nodded, still trying to be as ingratiating as hell. I stretched and looked toward the parking lot. "No problem. I can come back another time. Say, that your Corvette?"

His eyes flicked toward the parking lot. "Yeah."

"Nice car. Always wished I could afford one."

I saw his gaze drift out toward the Beater. He smirked. "Looks like you need one. That piece of shit yours?"

"My other car used to be a Firebird," I said.

His smirk got bigger and he stepped back again, starting to close the door. "Call me for an appointment."

"Business must be pretty good if you can afford a 'Vette and two Caddies."

"Yeah, well, like I said, everybody dies." The door slammed shut. The sickeningly sweet smell of his pungent aftershave still hung in the air. I guess a guy who spent most of his time around dead bodies wanted to make sure the stink didn't linger on him. But this guy stunk anyway, for a different reason.

I sat behind the wheel of the Beater, pretending I was studying a map, while I waited for Nick to leave on his important business. He did, but it was close to forty minutes later. It was a small lie, and certainly an understandable one, considering he was trying to get rid of some guy at his front door. But when he did leave, he got in one of the Caddies and left the 'Vette. I saw him staring at me as I continued to pore over the map. Looking up as he slowly passed, I waved and made a small hold-on-a-minute wave. His head swiveled to the front and he gunned the big engine, disappearing down the street. Instead of following him, I backed up, drove into the funeral home lot, and copied down the license plates on both cars. Maybe I could persuade George to run a criminal history check on him. There was something about the guy I didn't like, and it wasn't that he had a red Corvette. I made a mental note to tell him my Corvette joke at the conclusion of our next interview. It was guaranteed to piss him off.

I glanced at my watch and assessed the time factor. I was up on the North Side, and the Manus Corporation was maybe thirty miles west, through heavy traffic. Even if I started now, I wouldn't get there inside of thirty minutes, and that was with a little bit of luck and no traffic jams. But that would put me in rush mode, considering that I'd have to conduct as thorough an interview as I could, and figure they might not welcome me back the next time. After all, they might realize that I was trying to look into taking their whopping double-indemnity millions away, if I could. Of course, they might realize that right off the bat and refuse to give me diddly. And, at the moment, time was tight. It would be better to go there in the morning and make it clear that I had the whole day to languish in their waiting room making their receptionist miserable. Ruin a receptionist's day, and her indignation will usually seep up to the corporate boss's office like rising flood water. I thought about the poor people that MWO had cheated out of an insurance settlement by exercising the no flood damage loophole and decided that I'd call it a day.

Besides, I still had to drive home and get my ass downtown for my dinner with Alex St. James. I smiled at the thought. A date with an angel.

Yeah, Mid Western Olympia's dirty work could wait.

Trying to find a parking space near Benson's was more problematic than third-year calculus. And I never got past advanced algebra. I circled the block several times looking for a space, any space, that I could squeeze the Beater into. I figured I could brave a no-parking zone somewhere and hope the FOP stickers did the trick, but the prospect of maybe giving the lady a ride home didn't gel with worrying some overeager meter maid would call for Lincoln Towing. In the end, I found a parking garage about two blocks away and swung in. They had a valet parking service, which meant a tip on top of the hefty charge, but what the hell. The guy looked at the Beater and frowned, probably figuring a dude driving this clunker wouldn't tip for shit. I grinned at him and said, "Take good care of my baby," and pointed to the FOP stickers. He glanced at it and nodded.

It was one of those cool late-spring, early-summer evenings where the temps float in the low 70s and it reminds you of the joys of the seasonal changes. The sky was clear, and even though I couldn't see any of the stars because of the extra hours of daylight and the ubiquitous city lights lining the skyline, I knew they were up there twinkling down on me anyway. I clapped my hands together in anticipation and picked up my pace. Tonight, I thought, anything might be possible.

After all, she had asked me out. Forward thinking on her part, obviously, but most likely the sign of a real modern woman. The kind who sees a good thing, something she wants, and isn't afraid to go after it. Or him, in this case. I wondered if she'd be just as forward-thinking about first dates?

Shade, old boy, I heard an imaginary British voice saying inside my head, you just may have done it again.

Benson's was one classy joint and the maître d' eyed me almost suspiciously as I walked in. Like he wanted to tug on my necktie to see if it was real. I'd even worn my famous gold chain tie clip, which was known to make most women weak in the knees as soon as they saw it.

"May I help you, sir?" The guy had a prissy face, with a tiny mustache. His mouth twisted into what might have passed for a smile, but I could sense the condescension behind it. Sure, I was wearing a sport jacket instead of a suit, and my shirt wasn't white, but I felt like asking him if he'd ever tried to shop for a shirt with an eighteen-inch neck.

"I'm supposed to meet a friend here," I said, flashing a confident grin. Yeah, I belong here, Roscoe, and don't you forget it. "A Ms. Alex St. James."

The maître d's manner softened a bit and he turned, holding up a delicate hand and wiggling his fingers in a "come hither" gesture. I followed along, feeling like the bear being led into the circus tent. This place was already making me itch.

To my right when I'd first walked in was a separate room with an undulating bar of polished wood, equally polished tables and chairs, and the feel of old money interacting with new. It wasn't very crowded, and even the bartender looked bored. The bottles lining the back of the bar looked untouched. I followed the maître d' into the dining room, where booths lined the perimeter and well-dressed people sipped wine from long-stemmed glasses. The place had a 1940s ambience that almost made me check for Bogey and Bacall sitting in a back table somewhere. Off to my left a waiter dressed in white stepped back quickly as he lifted the metal lid of a serving tray, touched a long rod to something, and some flames shot upward. He replaced it and a line of smoke filtered through the air.

"What's your fire coverage on this place?" I asked. "I got a buddy who sells insurance."

If the maître d' heard me, he didn't let on. He just kept walking me through the maze of tables. He stopped at a booth and looked down.

"Madam, is this the man whom you were expecting?"

Alex St. James looked up at me and smiled. "Yes, Herman. Thank you."

She looked gorgeous, with her hair pulled back and done up in a French braid. Her dress was black and sleeveless and she wore a silver necklace that held a cylindrical blue stone captured inside four tiny pillars. I checked to see if her freckles descended from her face to her shoulders, but from what I could see, they didn't.

"Hiya," I said, slipping into the booth across from her. She'd sat with her back to the wall, which is the seat I take out of habit, but who was I to argue? At least I had a babe watching over me.

"Would you care for another Riesling?" Herman asked her.

A half-empty wineglass sat on the table in front of her. "No, one's plenty. Thanks."

Herman turned to me. "And for you, sir?"

Since I didn't drink, I ordered an iced tea.

Alex picked up her glass and brought it to her lips. "So the man of steel doesn't imbibe? I told you my boss is picking up the tab, right?"

I smiled. "I'm in training." That usually satisfied people, or else they asked what I was training for.

"What kind of training?"

"I'm a professional kickboxer. Besides being a world-class Private Investigator, I'm also a world champion."

Her eyebrows rose. "Is that why your face was so bruised looking when we met at that gas station back in March?"

"Yeah," I said, then added, using my best Marlon Brando imitation, "but you shoulda seen the udder guy."

That made her smile. Things were looking up.

Before I could come up with another witticism, Herman was back and placed my iced tea on the table without comment. "Would you like menus now?" He spoke only to Alex, which was fine with me. When she said we would, he whipped a pair of leather-bound menus from under his arm and placed them in front of us with the aplomb of a high-class poker dealer. He straightened, nodded, and turned. I picked up the menu as I watched him walk away.

"I think he likes you," I said.

"No, I've just been coming here a long time." She took another sip of her drink. "Anyway, I'm glad you could make it."

"Me, too."

"You're probably wondering why I asked you here to-night . . ."

She left the end open, full of promise. Did I dare hope that she would be this forward?

"The question did enter my mind," I said, thinking, but I bet I can guess the answer.

"Well, I have a business proposition I'd like to run by you."

Business? In a romantic place like this? My libido suddenly felt like it got punched in the gut. Or maybe a little bit lower. I was at a loss for words.

"But first . . ." She let the sentence hang a split second, "there's something else I'd like to ask you."

Ah, I thought. Here it comes . . . The windup, and the pitch. My killer charm has done it again.

"What's that?" I punctuated the question with another high-wattage smile.

"It's about your car. The one you sold to Bass, my boss. The Firebird."

I semi-shuddered thinking of how to explain that I was only driving the Beater temporarily. Just until I had time to get something better. I cleared my throat. "How does he like it?"

"Oh, he's wild about it," she said. "But . . ."

The great eraser. "But?"

She looked down at the rim of her glass. "He's curious as to why you let it go for such a low price."

This was getting ticklish. Did I tell her about Ken? I definitely didn't want to scare her off if she was interested. But the truth won out.

"Lots of bad memories," I said. I gave her a thumbnail of how I got the car as payment for catching Paula's killers, and then how Ken had taken a bullet meant for me on a stakeout. The space between her eyebrows creased slightly as I told her about my surreptitious checks on Ken's rehab progress.

"That poor guy. It must have been terrible for him," she said, reaching forward to pat my hand. "And for you, as well." It felt electric and sent a charge through me. A good charge.

ALEX ST. JAMES

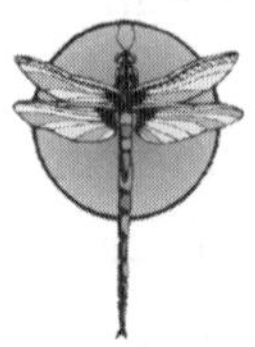

To say I was relieved that this Ron Shade fellow walked in at Benson's looking a lot less beat up than he had when we'd first met, was an understatement. Despite the fact that he seemed uneasy while the maître d' hovered, I could tell Shade was a man comfortable in his own skin. That was nice. Too often, these gym rat–types were all muscle and no personality.

But, as I listened to his tale of the Firebird's history, I realized he wasn't the gym rat–type at all. Broad shouldered and muscular—yes. Needing me to fawn all over him—no. Thank goodness. He had strong features and a kind face. I liked him. And from his animated, vivid descriptions of how he and his cop friends handled situations, I trusted him, too. Which made the prospect of a successful business arrangement even better than I'd hoped.

He seemed so shaken by the telling of the story of how his friend had been shot and permanently disabled—by a bullet meant for Shade's brain—that I patted his hand. He looked like he needed it.

With a smile that told me he was grateful for the gesture, he shifted in his seat. It dawned on me that dredging up all this negativity had to be tough for him. I figured he'd appreciate a change in subject from one so personal to something more neutral, so I thanked him for his candor and decided to get to the real reason for tonight's meeting. "Do you have any evenings free in the near future?"

Our waiter stepped up to the table before Shade could

answer. He introduced himself as Jorge, then asked, "Have we decided?" in cozy waiter-speak.

"I know what I want," I said, looking at my dinner companion. Shade seemed suddenly discomposed and, worried that I was rushing him, I quickly added, "But I think we still need a few minutes. Is that okay?"

"As you wish," he said, blending away.

Shade took a long sip of his iced tea. "Evenings?" he asked.

"Yeah." Elbows on the table, I leaned forward, keeping my voice low so as not to be overheard. He leaned in to hear me. "First of all, I have to apologize," I said.

He started to shake his head, dismissing any apology, but he didn't know what I was going to say, so I continued.

"When I arranged this on the phone with you, I was . . . distracted. I'm sorry. I'm sure I sounded a bit . . . scattered."

"No, not at all."

He was being kind. I smiled, but didn't want to come across as too eager to hire him. Sometimes men got the wrong idea when I warmed up to a subject. They often mistakenly thought I was warming up to them.

"Why don't I give you a chance to look at the menu before I take this any further," I said. "Would you like an appetizer?"

"What did you have in mind?"

I reached a finger to point over the top of his leather-bound menu. "This first one. It's a combination. Chicken skewers, beef kabobs and a sampling of ribs."

"I don't eat pork."

"Okay," I said, wondering what that was about. "Then, whatever you like."

He shook his head, closing the menu. "I think just dinner will be fine."

"They have the best steaks here," I said.

Jorge sidled back to the table, hands clasped behind his back.

This was one of those places where the waitstaff never wrote anything down. I think they saw it as classy. I found it unnerving. But they hadn't messed up a single order of mine yet. "Are we ready?" he asked.

Shade canted his head in my direction. "Ladies first."

"I'll have the filet mignon," I said, "the king cut. Medium rare, with a side of creamed spinach. Salad with ranch dressing on the side, please."

Shade started speaking, so softly I couldn't understand. Jorge bent closer. "Sir?"

Again, Shade ordered. And I realized he was speaking Spanish. Or trying to. Jorge listened patiently and repeated the order in English. Porterhouse, well-done, with asparagus. No salad. "Very good, sir," he said. *"Gracias."* He drew the menus out of our hands and drifted into the background.

"I'm impressed," I said. "Where did you learn Spanish?"

He blushed. "I used to know a Cuban girl. But she said I mumbled too much when I spoke."

I'd thought the same thing, but didn't say so.

"You've got a good appetite," he said.

My turn to blush. "Why not? My boss is handling this tab. He really wanted me to find out about the Firebird. I just have to decide how to break it to him."

His eyebrows twitched. "Is that why you asked me to this dinner? Or, is there some other reason?"

I took a sip of the remaining wine. "There is another reason." I sighed, thinking about poor Jesse's nose. Thinking about what Detective Lulinski had suggested about Nicky arranging for the attack. "And I know this is terribly short notice, but could you be available for the next several evenings?"

This time, his lips twitched, breaking into a slow smile. "Well, that depends."

I held up a finger, amending. "Not tomorrow night. Tomorrow I have too much other stuff to do, plus I need to connect with the filming staff at the station. But, let's say the day after. Would you be available for, say, three or four nights? For bodyguard work?"

"Whose body am I guarding?"

"Mine."

Now he looked confused.

Jorge swung my salad onto the linen tablecloth before me. I speared a tomato, but waited to pop it into my mouth until I'd told Shade about the homeless feature, the terrible conditions under that viaduct, and last night's altercation. "I had to Taser one guy. The others ran off when my friend's son happened to show up."

As I alternately talked and worked at my salad, Shade asked questions, good ones. He was a pretty sharp guy.

I finished by recounting my theory—well, Lulinski's—that the altercation might have been an elaborate setup.

"So, who arranged for the punks to harass you?" he asked.

I shook my head. I had no real proof that Nicky had done anything of the sort. And I didn't want anything to get out until I was sure. The last thing I needed was to get on Larry's bad side before he looked into my adoption information. "It was just a theory we tossed around."

Our steaks and sides arrived exactly as ordered. We settled into small talk as we ate, but I'd filled up on salad, so I didn't finish mine. I waited till Shade cleared his plate before I asked for mine to be wrapped up. "I'll be eating dinner on my boss for two days," I said. "And enjoying every morsel of it."

Jorge returned with a tidy little bag, and a tray laden with dazzling confections, "Do we care for dessert?"

"Not for me, thank you. Mr. Shade?" I asked. "Is there something you'd like?"

He demurred, his expression unreadable.

"Nothing at all?" I pressed when Jorge left. "Coffee?"

"No, thanks." He seemed disappointed, and I couldn't figure out why.

When Jorge dropped the bill off at the table, I picked it up. Shade offered to leave the tip, but I refused. "Nope. The whole thing goes on the company tab. And I'm an excellent tipper." I placed a credit card in the folder and winked. "Former waitresses always are."

"You were a waitress?" he asked as our bill was swept away.

I nodded. "In college."

"I'd like to hear more about that."

I smiled, knowing he was just being polite. Probably feeling uncomfortable because I paid for dinner. But I wasn't about to bore him with tales of my adventurous youth. "Some other time," I said with a smile.

Jorge placed the folder back on the table. I figured the tip, signed, and pocketed my credit card. As I did, my watch slid over my wrist, turning so I got a look at its face. It was later than I thought, and I'd promised my sister Lucy I'd call her tonight. "Maybe it's a good thing we didn't have dessert," I said, with a pointed glance at my wrist. "I gotta get going."

He slid out of the booth and stood. "You need a ride home?"

"Valet parking," I said. "Thanks anyway."

Again, he seemed disappointed.

Then it dawned on me. "Oh," I said with sudden realization. "A contract. I almost forgot. I'm sure you'll require a contract and a retainer, won't you?"

"I'll draw up one of my standard contracts and send it to you," he said as we made our way to the front of the restaurant.

"Wonderful," I said, digging in my purse. "Let me give you my card."

"I still have the one you gave me before."

When I looked up and smiled, I caught another unreadable

expression on him. "Great," I said, thrusting my hand out.

He stared at the hand for a moment before we shook, as though the gesture surprised him. That surprised me. He gave a slight smirk.

"It's been a pleasure, Mr. Shade."

"Ron."

"Ron," I repeated. "I look forward to working with you."

Ron Shade

And so it goes, I thought as I walked along State Street under the streetlights. A handshake instead of a kiss. Still, the evening hadn't turned out to be a total washout. I'd obviously misread Ms. St. James's "interest" in me as something more than professional. A good lesson, and after all, it wasn't such a bad thing if your ego got an ass-whipping every once in a while. I reminded myself of my original expectation of hoping to have a nice conversation with a pretty girl over dinner. Nothing more, nothing less. I'd certainly gotten that, and a new gig as well. Bodyguarding her on this homeless story—it sounded like something I could do in my sleep, and it would give me some extra cash to go shopping for that new car.

I was wondering how her boss—Bass, she'd called him—would react when he found out about the Firebird's history. But it wasn't like I'd sold him a lemon, or anything. Hell, I hadn't even gotten rid of the extra baggage myself. Memories of Paula and now Ken floated in my thoughts as often as the moon in the sky.

Tomorrow I'd hit Manus Corporation bright and early, and then corral good old dentist whatshisname about the "positive ID." The more I thought about it, the more this case was like being under a pier and noticing that half the underpinning was rotted away. A few well-placed taps and the whole structure could come tumbling down. I just had to figure out where to tap.

Chapter 11

Ron Shade

There was no need to skimp on the roadwork the next morning because I'd been in bed right after Letterman's Top Ten List. I ran at a brisk pace, as if to outrun the hint of disappointment that still lingered from my date. I had failed to impress her, that's for sure, and I realized that I'd misread what I thought were clues in her asking me to dinner. For her it had been a business thing. Nothing romantic. I'd let my oversized ego bounce around the ring talking trash, while reality crept up and delivered a knockout punch.

Well, I thought as I ran up Miss Agony. Perhaps it had been a unanimous decision rather than a knockout. Maybe a majority one . . . Her eyes had lit up a few times at a couple of my witticisms. But in the end, the result was still the same. She didn't seem that interested.

But new tasks awaited, and I was champing at the bit to go after the Manus Corporation. After all, I was the guy who could cost them more than the guy on that old Lee Majors TV show.

Michael A. Black & Julie Hyzy

Alex St. James

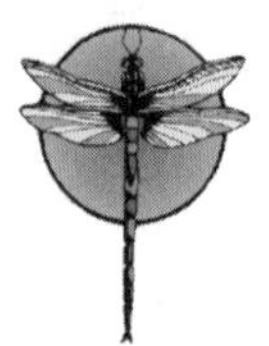

"So how do I tell Bass that his new baby, the Firebird, was involved in one homicide and another attempted homicide?" I asked.

Jordan sat across from me in my office, a bemused expression on her café-au-lait face. "What are you, crazy? You don't tell him *none* of that. Make something up. Tell him that this Shade guy is independently wealthy and . . . this is . . . chump change to him."

"You know that won't work."

She took a moment to stare out the window over the Chicago River, giving the view a wry shake of her head.

"What?" I asked with more than a little annoyance in my voice.

Turning to me, she kept up the head shakes. "You are just too honest, girl. You need to develop some lying genes or something. All that do-good, tell-the-truth shit is going to get you in trouble."

"It already has."

She didn't ask what I meant. She knew. We'd discussed Detective Lulinski's supposition that Nicky Farnsworth had arranged for the little altercation under the bridge, and we both agreed the theory had merit.

"So . . ." she said, leaning forward, eyes sparkling, "how did the rest of it go?"

"The rest of what?"

"Your big dinner last night. With the private investigator."

"Actually," I said, "it went great. I hired him."

Her dark eyes went flat. "That's *not* what I meant."

I knew what she meant. "Jordan . . ."

She didn't heed the warning—she pressed up against my desk to give me the lecture. "Just because you had some bad luck with men recently . . ."

"Is that what you call it?"

"That's all it is. Just a string of bad luck," she said. "If you go thinking it's more than that—if you go thinking it's *you* that's the problem—then you will never have a chance."

I held a hand up. "Okay, you're right."

She sat back, pleased with herself.

"But," I amended, "that doesn't mean I have to be interested in every eligible man I meet." I furrowed my brow, thinking.

"What?" she asked.

It hadn't even occurred to me to find out if Ron Shade was available. "I just wasn't thinking of him that way."

She held up her left hand and wiggled her fingers. "What about a wedding ring?"

I shrugged. "Didn't notice."

"Girl, you are so out of practice. Did he ask you anything personal? Like 'Are you seeing someone?' "

"Of course not."

She twisted her mouth, surprised. "Okay, then, no big loss. He's probably taken. Or gay. But that doesn't mean I'm letting you off the hook."

I laughed. "No?"

"Uh-uh. I'm making you my project. I'm going to find you a man by—"

Bass broke into the conversation, bursting into my closed-door office without knocking.

Jordan took one look at his face, stood, and inched her way out with a wide-eyed "Glad it's you and not me" expression.

She said, "Looks like you don't have to worry about ruining his good mood with your news, sweetie."

"What's she talking about?" Bass asked.

"Don't worry about it."

"Guess what I found?" he said, waving several sheets of paper in the air over his head.

"Shush," I said. "You're shouting."

"Of course I'm shouting. Look at what that Ron Shade character sold me." He thrust the pages at me.

A quick glance told me that Bass had been busy researching news articles on the Internet. These were printouts of stories run several months before in the local papers. Four articles in all, each told the same story of Ron Shade's Firebird being involved in a shooting on the city's southwest side. Ken Albrecht had taken a bullet to the brain, just like Shade had told me last night. I flipped through the stories twice. No mention of Shade's girlfriend, Paula, and *her* troubles with the car.

"Has the car been giving you trouble?"

"No, but—"

I handed the sheets back to him. "I don't see the problem then."

Bass snapped his fingers against the pages. "He didn't tell you any of this, did he? I knew it."

"As a matter of fact," I said, "he did."

I wished I had a camera to catch Bass's expression. Total shock. "He did?" he asked in a small voice.

"Yeah," I said. I pointed to the chair Jordan vacated. "And now that I've done your dirty work, why don't you have a seat? There are a couple of things we need to discuss."

RON SHADE

After making the trek to the northern suburbs once again, I circled the building that housed the Manus Corporation three times, writing down plate numbers and checking the place out. There were only half a dozen cars in the lot, which struck me as odd for a company that was listed as one of the up-and-comers in *Crain's Chicago Business.* Of course, the most recent millions had been forked over by MWO, rather than earned. Maybe Bob Bayless had been worth a lot more to them dead than alive, in which case they might not be too happy to see me. I parked the Beater on the far side of the lot, so if anybody looked out of the big sparkling glass windows, my car would be obscured by theirs.

The building had kind of an artsy design to it. It was only one story, but it sort of reminded me of the Frank Lloyd Wright house in Beverly. A triangular roof, with one side sloping down sharply, contrasted by an elongated slope on its other side, squatted over a dark brown building. Lots of nice, big windows. The sidewalk curved in a semicircle through some lushly maintained grass, and a row of well-trimmed hedges stood guard along the front, next to the front entrance. I pulled on the door and it opened with oiled precision, accompanied by a single, semi-strident beeping sound.

Inside, a pretty woman glanced up from a thin computer monitor that faced away from the door, and smiled at me. She had brown hair to her shoulders and very nice teeth.

"May I help you?" she asked.

I was impressed enough by the surroundings, and her professionalism brought it up to a new level. Her dynamite looks didn't hurt any, either. "Hi, I'm Ron Shade." I handed her one of my cards. "I need to speak to someone about Robert Bayless."

She looked at the card and I thought I saw a glimmer of something. Recognition? I'd never seen her before. Maybe she was impressed with the card. Or me. After all, I had run about four miles that morning.

"I can see if Mr. Prince will talk to you," she said. "Since you don't have an appointment."

Scratch her being impressed. Maybe I need to get a few more workouts in with Brice, I thought.

She purred into the phone in a tone so low that I could barely discern what she was saying. But I was virtually certain she'd said something like, "It's the private detective, Ron Shade . . . About Mr. Bayless's death."

She hung up quickly and smiled up at me again. "He'll be with you shortly, sir. You can have a seat in our waiting room. Would you care for a cup of coffee while you wait?"

I shook my head and retreated to the area she'd pointed at. It was a good-sized room on the right. A television playing CNN at a low volume from a wooden cabinet, and several comfortable-looking chairs formed a small semicircle in front of it.

I stood behind one of the chairs and pretended to watch TV as I slowly checked the room out. It was set up to look like a library of some sort, with a bunch of leather-bound volumes lining some built-in bookshelves. The book spines all had the token look of a set of The Great Books. Made for decoration and not for reading just like at MWO. The floor had several Persian-design rugs over finely polished wood. Directly in back of me a doorway framed a small corridor and farther back, I could see more rooms. If anyone was working in them, they must have been in stealth mode. I listened for the traces of floating conversation, the ringing of phones, the tapping of fingers on keyboards, but nothing. The place was as quiet as a morgue.

"Mr. Shade," a voice from my left said. I turned and saw a thin, blond-haired man in his mid-thirties moving toward me with an extended palm. "I'm James Prince. CEO here at Manus. What can I do for you?"

I shook his hand and was surprised at his grip. He either had a bit more strength than his sparse body appeared to have, or he was trying to impress me. Or maybe he was nervous. I squeezed back with slightly more returning pressure than I normally use to let him know that I was not easily impressed. I caught a minute wincing on his face.

"I'm doing some follow-ups for Midwestern Olympia Insurance. About the death of one of your employees." I waited a few beats to gauge his reaction to the name. "Robert Bayless."

His eyebrows rose simultaneously and his eyes shot down and to the left. "Good old Bob. Shame what happened to him. Real shame." He looked back at me and smiled. "Perhaps we'd be more comfortable in my office. Would you care for some coffee?"

"No thanks," I said. "Your secretary already asked me."

I thought I heard her murmur "Administrative assistant" under her breath as I walked by.

Jim Prince's office was down a second hallway, and I estimated that the long corridor that we turned onto was the extension of the one I'd seen from the waiting room. The place was far from labyrinthine. He sat behind a neatly arranged desk, with a telephone, a date book calendar, and a paper-thin computer monitor. Numerous plaques hung on the wall behind him, and two padded chairs were off to the side. He motioned me toward them and I sat. On the opposite wall were several pictures of Prince with a group of men and women on what appeared to be a south-of-the-border fishing trip. In one they held the body of a swordfish. In another they held some longneck beer bottles. I recognized one of the men in the pictures as Robert Bayless. I asked him about it.

"Yeah, that was good old Bob, all right." He clasped his hands together and leaned back slightly. "Our company trip to Cancun. Lots of good memories on that one."

I studied the photos for a telltale blonde in the vicinity of Bayless, but saw none.

"How long after that one was taken did he die?"

Prince's eyebrows rose again. "You know, I'd have to think on that one a while. The whole thing was such an awful event, I've tried to replace it with happier memories." He unclasped his hands and pointed toward the photo array. "Hence the photos of the Cancun trip. That's how I'd like to remember him." He heaved a sigh. "I assume you've lost people close to you, Mr. Shade?"

"A few."

"Then you know how hard it is to talk about certain things, I imagine."

I could think of about ten million reasons why he wouldn't want to talk to me. I merely nodded in agreement.

"So let me ask you this," he said, leaning forward in his big padded chair. "What's MWO's renewed interest in this? I thought the whole matter was settled. We deposited the check a while ago."

I'd planned on this question, so I shot back my cryptic answer. "Just routine. Making sure all the *i*'s are crossed and all the *t*'s dotted."

It took him a moment, then he made a snorting half-laugh sound. I grinned back. Two mid-level corporate buddies, sharing a good joke, each one knowing the other was about to toss some bullshit.

I glanced from one wall over to the next. "What exactly did Bob do around here, anyway? I'm assuming you took his place?" I figured multiple questions, like a good punching combination, would keep him off balance.

"Why, yes, I did replace him," he said. He raised his eyebrows. "You see, I'd been his assistant, so it was only natural that I take his place."

"As CEO?"

"Right."

"So, what exactly does a CEO do here at Manus?"

He exhaled loudly through an accompanying smile. "Way too much," he said, and punctuated it with a forced laugh. "We're basically in medical supply. We have numerous accounts and work with all kinds of doctors, hospitals, and medical research facilities."

"Medical supply?"

"Correct."

"That's a tall order." I glanced around again. "The place doesn't look that big. Where do you keep your inventory?"

He did the exhaling smile again. "We're not that kind of a company." His head canted slightly to the right. "If I had to make an analogy, I'd say we're more like a middleman. When a doctor needs some sample drugs, test results, or basic office examination equipment, he or she calls us. We're familiar with the market, know which vendors to approach, order the stuff and ship it to him."

"Or her," I said.

"Right." He made an agreeable nodding gesture. Sort of like a trained seal.

"Wouldn't it be simpler and cheaper for the doctor to go to the vendor himself?"

His mouth twisted with a mild case of the "I'm getting irritated" look and he shook his head. "Not if you understand the way the system works. Believe me, we know how to get the best products, the best deals. Our clients love us."

I figured I'd softened him up enough with the jabs. Now it was time to follow up with a straight right. "What was Bob Bayless doing so far downstate when he was killed?"

The question hit him like a body blow. After a few beats he responded. "I wish I knew. I think he was going to check on some colleges in that area. His son was about that age."

"Nice kid. Athletic."

"He is." He was back to nodding agreeably.

"Bayless was a good family man?"

"The best."

"Funny . . ." I went for effect as I raised my eyebrows in a look of confused skepticism. "I heard he was banging his secretary." I cocked my head toward the front of the building. "She still work here?"

He shook his head.

"Was she let go, or did she quit?"

"Mr. Shade," he said slowly, "we're a small company, although we'd like to cooperate with MWO, our employees do have certain expectations of privacy." He glanced at his watch. "It wouldn't be ethical for me to talk about her."

"Then don't. Just steer me toward her and I'll do the talking."

He shook his head. "I'm afraid I can't do that."

"Because?"

He started to say something, then stopped, sighed again, and smiled. "All right, I can tell you this much. Candice is no longer with the company."

"Where'd she go?"

"I have no idea."

"Come on, nobody called for references? How about giving

me her last known address?"

He looked away, his mouth drawing into a tight line—his obvious defense mechanism.

"I'm afraid I couldn't do that, even if I wanted to," he said. His accompanying smile had all the sincerity of a used-car salesman. "Our company policy forbids us to divulge any information about our employees, even former employees, without a subpoena. Otherwise, it could open us up to civil liabilities."

I nodded, letting him think he'd won one. "You guys paid for Bayless's body to be transported up here from downstate, right?"

His eyebrows rose again. "Yeah." The tip of his tongue shot over his lips. "Like I said, we're sort of a big, extended family here at Manus. We look out for each other."

"That's commendable." I looked around.

He swallowed hard. "Look, Mr. Shade, I'd like to help you but I do have a company to run." He stood up. "So unless you can think of anything else that I can help you with . . ."

I stood, too. Lawyers weren't the only professionals who asked questions they already knew the answers to. "What funeral home did you use for the transport?"

His head jerked back slightly, like I'd brushed him with a jab.

"I . . . can't recall right now," he said a little too quickly. "I'd have to look that up."

"Okay." I handed him one of my cards. "When you find out, I'd appreciate it if you'd call me."

"You can count on it," he said, the smile back now that I was moving toward the door.

I'll bet I can, I thought.

I turned as I got back into my car to see if I could detect anyone peeping out one of the windows trying to catch a glimpse of my ride. If they were, I sure didn't catch sight of them. But I accomplished what I'd hoped to. There was something going on here, and I knew who was involved. Mostly.

It was like having a bunch of pieces to the jigsaw puzzle, but missing an exact replica of what I was putting together. And another big question loomed: why? If Herb Winthrope's ear had been correct, and it was Bob Bayless's horse laugh he'd heard in that Vegas casino, what was the motivating purpose behind all this pretense and subterfuge? They'd obviously involved a lot of people, and someone along the way had substituted a body that had been mistakenly identified as Bayless. A body that had been warm before it ended up in that smashed-up car on Deadman's Curve. What was holding all these pieces together? And who stood to gain the most?

Mrs. Bayless got rid of a boob of a husband and was rewarded with a two-million-dollar parachute for a new start. But she didn't seem to be part of the equation. Manus, and James Prince, got a larger settlement. About ten mil. While it would be like winning the Lotto to a guy like me, to an up-and-comer business featured in *Crain's,* it was probably small potatoes. So how had Bayless convinced everyone to go along with this elaborate scheme? What kind of ace was he holding? And how had the ID been faked? And whose body had ultimately ended up a well-done hunk of meat cooling in a downstate morgue? I glanced at my watch. A little after ten. A good time to visit the dentist.

Dr. Keith Colon's office looked less than impressive. It was located in Rogers Park and occupied a section of a strip mall down from a cleaners, a used bookstore, a restaurant called Poppa's, and a 7-Eleven. Plenty of parking, but not too many cars. Most of them were in front of the convenience store. I parked right in front of Colon's place. Maybe the Beater being there would make passersby think his rates were as low as his name.

I pulled open the door and stepped inside. The waiting room

was small and unoccupied. Behind a small glass window, a sharp-looking blonde in a light blue medical type smock smiled at me.

"May I help you, sir?" Her voice was anxious, like I was the first catch of the day.

"Is the doctor in?"

"Yes." Her reply was punctuated with a wide smile. Her teeth looked pretty good, but I figured it would be a bad business move to employ someone whose teeth weren't.

"I'd like to see him for a moment, please." I handed her one of my cards.

"Do you have an appointment, sir?"

I shook my head. "It's business. An insurance problem." She nodded, and I figured the vague answer would get her moving. Dentists made most of their bread and butter from the insurance payouts. Rising from the chair, she walked back toward an open hallway, leaving the desk and phones unoccupied. It would have been much simpler to use their interoffice phone system. Maybe they didn't have one . . . Or maybe she'd been forewarned by the good doctor to notify him as soon as a guy named Shade came in. The second possibility, while reeking of a conspiracy theory, seemed the most likely. She came back with a swarthy-looking guy close behind her. He was dressed in the same light blue medical-type outfit. His hair was dark brown and feathered back like a rock star's, with a greasy sheen to it. Or maybe it was just too much mousse. I estimated him to be in his early- to mid-thirties. His face had a narrow look to it, and I noticed he was either trying to grow a mustache or he'd missed large spots with his razor. A pair of dark eyes, like a hawk's, sized me up quickly as he extended his hand.

"Mr. Shade," he said as we shook. "I'm Dr. Colon. What can I do for you?"

"Perhaps it would be better if we spoke in your office?"

He nodded and glanced at his watch. He was either pressed for time or nervous at me showing up. Either way, he wasn't exactly the kind of person I would want leaning over me, looking into my mouth.

He turned to the girl. "Janet, let me know when Mrs. Ferguson arrives, okay?"

She nodded and watched me out of the corner of her eye as I walked by.

Colon's office was even messier than mine, and that was saying a lot. Normally, I view the clutter on a person's desk as a direct indication of his intelligence, but in this case it told me something else. Especially the stack of riverboat casino advertising letters that he quickly set a bunch of papers on top of. I knew in a heartbeat why the doctor's office was so messy. The man obviously had other, more pressing interests.

He motioned to a chair in front of the desk and smiled. "Excuse the mess. I've been in the process of getting some paperwork done."

I grinned. "Reminds me of mine."

We sat in an awkward silence for a few more seconds during which time I took out my small notebook and stared at him. It seemed to unnerve him further.

"Ah, look," he finally said, "I'm very busy. Patients. You mentioned an insurance problem?"

"Was Robert Bayless your patient?"

"Bayless . . . Bayless . . ." He glanced toward the ceiling in a gesture meant to look like pure concentration. "Yes. Bob Bayless. He was killed a few months ago, right?"

"He was. I'm looking into a few things for Midwestern Olympia Insurance."

Two deep wrinkles formed in the space between his eyebrows. "I was under the assumption that he was killed in a traffic accident."

"The actual cause of death was from multiple trauma and asphyxiation. He burned to death."

Colon sighed and looked down at the stacks of papers covering his desk. If this guy could find anything in a hurry in that shit pile, I was the tooth fairy.

"Yes, I do remember now," he said. "I had to assist with the identification."

"Did that prove hard to do?"

He shook his head. "Not really. They contacted me because he'd been coming here for some work. I had recent X-rays and sent them down there. They matched up exactly. Or, so I was told. Case closed."

"Almost," I said.

His head quivered fractionally and he squinted at me. "How so?"

"How long had Bob Bayless been your patient?"

He ignored that I'd answered his question with an unrelated question. He tilted back in his chair and looked up at the ceiling again. I got the impression that he was a really bad actor trying to make me think he was consulting his memory banks. When he leaned forward again, he spoke so decisively that I knew he'd had the answer all along. He was just stalling for time.

"Two months," he said.

"What was he having done?"

He took a deep breath and canted his head to the right. "Mr. Shade," the eyebrows rose in unison, "I'm dealing with a sensitive issue here. I'm not sure I should be discussing a patient's history with you."

"Why not?"

"Well," the word came out like a mild bark, "there's a matter of confidentiality. HIPAA laws and all that."

"Doctor, the patient is deceased," I said. "There's no

confidentiality anymore."

"Still, I feel like it's violating a sacred trust we had."

"Doctor, come on."

"All right." He pursed his lips before he continued. "He was having some mandibular malocclusion. I put some veneers on his anterior molars, and also on his laterals. The latter was more cosmetic than medicinal, but with the insurance paying . . ." He tried a quick smile, saw it had no effect, and continued, "I also did some amalgam fillings in his second and third molars and I made two extractions."

"How did they match up the X-rays? Through the fillings?"

He heaved a theatric sigh, pursed his lips again, and said, "It's a detailed process involving several aspects, but not all that difficult. I'm sure, given a set of the two X-rays, even a layman like you would be able to do it."

The guy knew how to shovel the horse shit. I gave him that. But this was telling me other things that were significant, so I tried another angle. "Who contacted you about doing the ID?"

His head jerked back ever-so-slightly and I could tell this was one question he hadn't anticipated. "Uhmm . . . I believe it was his . . . his . . . Mrs. Bayless."

"Not the Furman County Coroner's Office?" I asked, letting just a little sound of surprise creep into my tone.

"Yes, maybe it was them." He nodded, licked his lips. "I do believe . . ."

I made a show of flipping through my notebook. "Oh, wait a minute, I was wrong. It wasn't the coroner. It was his place of employment. The Manus Corporation."

He snapped his fingers and flashed a weak smile. "That's right. They looked in his insurance file and found my office listed."

I made it look like I'd scribbled something down. "You see the body?"

"No, why?"

"Just wondered, him being your patient and all. Dying in such a tragic way."

"The identification was done downstate. They used the X-rays. It was my understanding that he'd been burned pretty badly."

I nodded. "I have photos if you want to see them."

He shook his head and glanced at his watch. "Excuse me a moment." Picking up the phone, he pressed four numbers and waited. "Jan, has she called or anything?" Listening, he nodded and licked his lips again. I was going to have to bring him some ChapStick when I came back. "Okay. Thanks." He set the phone back in its cradle. "I'm sorry, Mr. Shade, but my next patient's almost here. I have to get the examination room ready."

It was good to know that the good doctor's intercom system was in working order. I took out one of my cards and handed it to him. "Thanks for your time. You have a card with your number on it?"

"You can get one from my assistant." He was all business again, standing and smoothing back his greasy-looking hair with his palm. I sure hoped he washed up before Mrs. Ferguson arrived.

The girl, Jan, gave me one of his cards and I tried to strike up a conversation with her about directions. She replied in typical airhead fashion, but I had the gut feeling that she was smarter than she was pretending to be. After all, she was bright enough not to use the intercom before. The conversation meandered slightly. Suddenly Colon opened the door separating his back offices from the front and did a double take when he saw I was still there. "Janet, I need you to pull that file."

She looked like the teacher had just caught her passing a note to a girlfriend in class. I apologized for keeping her from her work and left. But I didn't go far.

I sat in the Beater and watched the front entrance of Colon's office for fifteen minutes. When no one went in, I knew what I'd known all along. There was no Mrs. Ferguson coming in to get her teeth scraped by Dr. Greasy. But I had made him nervous enough that he'd concocted a story to get rid of me. People make excuses to get rid of me all the time, but in this case it was getting to be a habit with everybody I interviewed.

I shifted into gear, backed out of the parking space, and drove through the strip mall. At the last building, the 7-Eleven, I hung a right and went around the back. A lane for deliveries ran parallel to the front aisle and had spaces where employees could park without taking up spaces reserved for customers. A particular concern when you have adjacent stores that have different types of clientele. In the double spaces behind Dr. Colon's office I saw two vehicles and wrote down the plates on both. One was a Toyota Celica and the other was a shiny silver BMW. Somehow, I didn't figure the good doctor for a Toyota-type of guy.

Alex St. James

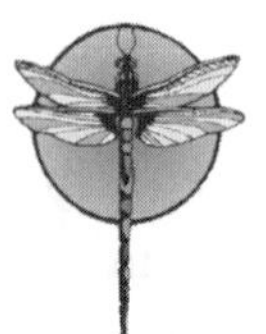

"Thanks, Rita," I said into the phone, then hung up. I turned my attention to Bass who still sat across from me. "We're ready to roll."

He held up the index fingers of both hands, waving them like windshield wipers gone mad. "Wait just a second, here. You haven't held up your end of the bargain."

"You are *not* getting out of watching this footage."

"Then give me the rest of the dirt on the Firebird."

"Footage first," I said. I heard the tiny *chip* that signaled a new E-mail. A glance at the monitor confirmed it. "It's here now."

"This better be worth it."

I started to swivel the monitor to face him, but he stood and came around to my side. "Better this way," he said, watching from over my left shoulder.

With a shrug, I double-clicked on the icon and last night's adventure came to life on my screen.

"What the hell?" Bass said.

"Give it a minute."

Jesse's movements as he traipsed up and down the embankment in low-light conditions made it difficult for the camera to focus. Which in turn made it difficult to watch. A significant headache began to brew as I tried to keep track of the people in the scene.

"This guy is one of our top cameramen?"

I shook my head. "He's new, actually. Fresh out of school. But he was the only one who volunteered for this extracurricular activity."

After about thirty seconds of camera-panning, where Jesse took close-up shots of the area and the people there, Bass said, "Get to the good stuff. This atmosphere garbage is boring as hell."

"Ya think?" I asked. "You wanted a homeless story. This is it." I tapped the screen.

"Don't do that."

"Do what?"

"The screen. You touch it, you ruin it. These screens are only a couple years old. I don't want to have to go buy you a new one because you don't know how to take care of it."

I shot him a look, but he ignored it.

We watched, as still more nothing happened.

"Can't you fast-forward?"

I sat back in my chair, striking a pose and gasping—for effect. "But you insisted that we talk with these people. You insisted that this would be our next Davis Award story."

He ignored that, too. "Get to the good stuff."

"The 'good stuff' as you call it, is brutal."

His eyes remained riveted to the screen. "Brutal brings in viewers. Fast forward."

I did.

Together we watched the entire scene play out like an angry tableau. As the three men approached, my body reacted as though I was back there. I tensed. My heart rate kicked up, my breathing grew shallow, and sweat tickled my lower back.

Bass made noises. A couple sounded like *tsk,* and the others were variations on his customary grunts of displeasure.

"What?" I asked him when the playback finished. My own displeasure reared its ugly head and I could feel myself spoiling for a fight. "What are you weirding out about?"

"Christ, we can't use any of this without the worry of getting sued. What were you thinking with that Taser?"

"What was I thinking? They were going to attack me."

"Were they? From what I've seen on this tape, a smart attorney could make a case for you attacking them."

"Look what those guys did to poor Jesse."

"Yeah, and we'll probably be receiving a lawsuit letter from his attorney any minute now." He frowned. "He called in his notice, by the way. He quit."

"I hope he's all right. Poor guy."

"Poor guy? He's a wuss." His lips tightened up and he glared at me. "When I gave you that Taser it was for self-defense only. Not for you to go play Lady Blue." He crouched down and mimicked holding a weapon and adding a mock tremor to his hands. "You want some more of this, big boy?"

"That's not how it went."

He continued mimicking me. "I got plenty more for ya."

"Bass, that's low."

"For crying out loud, Alex, what you just showed me is shit."

"What do you think I've been trying to tell you?"

He blinked, his brow tightening.

I was getting angry. "I can't get anything out of these people. Unless you let me follow the success story—Howard Rybak—then this is the best we'll come up with. There . . . is . . . no . . . story . . . here."

Bass backed up enough to give me room for my vehemence, but he wasn't about to give up. "No," he said. "There's a story all right, you just don't seem capable of exploiting it."

I stood. "You know what? You're right."

He jerked back. "You admit it?"

"Since I'm not capable of 'exploiting' the situation properly why don't you have our TV star, Gabriela, spend a night out there and see what she brings back?" My voice rose, but I didn't care who heard me. "Or better yet, why don't *you* spend a couple of hours sitting on the curb next to upchucked whiskey? Talking with people who've forgotten the simple comforts you and I take for granted? People who can't work their way out of the hell they're in because society has given up on them? See what it does to your sensibilities." I took a furious breath. "If you have any."

"Listen, we gave you this chance to be on-screen. You don't want it, fine. We'll send you back to your desk to do research with your tail between your legs."

I laughed. Really laughed. "This *is* my desk, Bass. I haven't moved an inch. I still do my own research. You're getting a two-fer here. And *you* know it. You want to 'send me back' to my old position? Fine." I sat. "Here I am. Now find somebody else to go play campout for your award-winning story."

He sat in the chair opposite me. We stared at one other. I couldn't figure out why Bass hadn't stormed out of my office. Until he said, "So, what's the rest of the story on my car?"

The car. Of course.

"First—"

"No," he said. "I watched the clip. Now you give me the information."

I shook my head. "The reason you watched the clip was because I want to change the focus of the feature."

He wisely kept quiet.

"I told you there's no story here," I said. "But I can make this one work. If you give me a little leeway."

"Keep talking."

"I'll go back out there," I said, then amended, "Just once. I want to follow up on the homeless guy who made it. Howard Rybak. He's the one that got out of the gutter and broke into the middle class. The success story."

Bass looked skeptical. But not as skeptical as usual.

I hurried to continue. "It could work. And if he talks to me, maybe he'll get some of his cohorts to open up, too."

"Okay."

"Okay?"

"What do you want, an answer on an engraved platter?" He settled himself in the chair. "Now, your turn. And this better be worth it."

I thought he'd go crazy when he heard about the car's history: the drug money; the original owner's demise; the manner in which Shade had earned the car as payment. But all he said was, "The trunk was punched?"

When I answered in the affirmative, he stood. "Damn it."

"What's wrong? It's been fixed, or you would've noticed it by now."

"I wanted a pristine car."

"It's used, what did you expect?"

"Not one with a goddamn punched trunk."

"Yesterday you were worried that it was a flood car. It's not."

He headed for the door, muttering.

I was about to call after him, to argue that he should be happy that the news wasn't worse, but I stopped myself before inserting the foot in my mouth. I'd gotten what I wanted. The feature focus was right where I wanted. It was time to call Nicky and find out how to reach the elusive Mr. Rybak.

Chapter 12

Ron Shade

It was getting way past lunchtime, and I was feeling it. I turned into the first decent restaurant I saw and went in. The place was bright and cheery, with pseudo chandeliers and big windows that let the sunshine in. I settled in a booth and ordered an iced tea and a chicken delight, substituting cottage cheese for the fries. After the waitress brought the tea and left, I mulled over where to go next. Obviously, both Manus and Dr. Colon had been stonewalling, but was it because they had something to hide, or because they suspected I was working to take their big payoffs back? That argument might have worked for Manus, but not the good doctor. He hadn't received any hefty insurance payoff. Or had he? Substitution of dental records to ID a badly burned corpse would have to carry a heavy price tag. Plus, whose records were they? The man in the car, I told myself. If I could find out who he actually was, I might be on my way to cracking this thing wide open.

I sipped the iced tea and thought. I needed leverage to get inside their defenses. In the ring, Chappie would tell me to either bore in on a reticent fighter or make him come to me. One thing was certain. I had a lot more of the pieces for this jigsaw, but was still missing the overall picture. Once I could determine who all was involved, I'd pick them off, one by one, starting with the weakest link first. My gut told me that might just be Colon. He had the look of someone who's overextended and in up to his neck. If I could figure out who that damn body actually was, I'd have enough to persuade him to sing to the state's attorney. Then the house would start to collapse. I needed to check him out on the sly. Get the financial scoop. And nobody had better access to the kind of databases that contained all that than my buddy, Big Rich.

Rich Stafford was a reporter for the third largest newspaper in the city, *The Chicago Metro.* He and I had been fast friends for a number of years, and I had steered more than one juicy story his way. He returned the favor by using his newspaper sources to look into things from a whole different angle. Usually, he got back to me real quick, too. I took out my cell and called his office number. It rang several times and I checked my watch. It was Friday, and he should have been there getting the weekend edition ready for the printers. Instead, I got his voice message system. I left a quick one, telling him to call me and left my cell number, even though I knew he already had it.

Just as I was slapping the phone shut the waitress brought my food and I tore into it, finishing the whole thing, except for some slices of cantaloupe, which I despise. I tried Big Rich again, hoping that he'd just been on a trip to the men's room before, but got the same voice mail message. This time I didn't leave any message. I thought for a minute and debated whether or not to call George.

Whenever I needed a favor done on the side, George was there for me as well, but lately he'd been complaining more. He mentioned that they'd started checking on "unauthorized use of certain departmental equipment." As one of the premier detectives they had, I knew he would be beyond any watchdog's eyes, but he had also been studying hard for the sergeant's test. He'd taken and passed it several times, but promotions came in waves, and the political process tended to rear its ugly head from time to time. I knew he'd pass it again, and maybe this time the promotion would come through for him. I hoped so. He deserved it. Still, I didn't want to give his boss, and my nemesis, Lieutenant Bielmaster, any reason whatsoever to go after George. In the end, though, I knew I needed his help. I dialed his cell number, vowing to keep my request small and insignificant.

He answered on the second ring with a cheery, "Good afternoon."

"Good afternoon? What the hell kind of way is that to answer the phone?"

"You know," I heard him sigh, "I'm in such a great fucking mood today, that even a smart-ass comment from my favorite boy wonder ain't gonna shake me. Now what can I do for you?"

It was uncharacteristic of him to be so forthright. And sound so happy. "Everything okay?"

"Sure. Couldn't be better, buddy."

Buddy? Now I had the feeling that something was really amiss. "You sure you're okay?"

"Ron, buddy, friend, world champ, what do you need?" A bit of heavy dramatic inflection set off the last part. "Just tell me. Because whatever it is, I'm here for you."

Not one to look a gift horse in the mouth, I answered. "I was working a case and wondered if you had time to run a couple plates."

"Sure. What are they?"

Something was definitely off kilter. He never ran plates for me without a lecture on how much I owed him, how much I was going to owe him, and how he could get in real trouble if Bielmaster ever caught him doing unauthorized favors for me. I read off the two plates from in back of Colon's place. I still had the ones from Manus, but planned to save those for next time.

"Got 'em," he said. "Any more you want me to check on for you, my liege? How about CQHs on them?"

This stunned me. It was as if he was doing a parody of Jeeves the butler, or something. I'd had about enough. "You gonna tell me what the fuck's going on with you, or what?"

His deep laugh came over the phone like the ticking of a bass clock. "Well, I guess since you are responsible for my good fortune," he said, "it is only right that I share the news with you." He paused, and I heard him yell to somebody else. "Hey, Pers, it's Ron-boy on the phone."

"Tell him thanks from me," I heard a distant Doug Percy yell back.

"You hear that?" he asked. "Pers says thanks, too."

"I heard it, now tell me what he's thanking me for."

More deep laughter. "Everybody in the squad's on cloud nine. In fact, we're all thinking of knocking off a little early and going out drinking in your honor."

"Well, if somebody's wife had a kid, just remember, I ain't responsible."

"Nah, nothing like that. We just got word today that old Bielmaster's pulling the pin. He's been off for the last two months recovering from that bypass, and that mini heart attack you put him through, and we were expecting him to return next week." He laughed again. "Then they made the announcement at roll call today and passed the envelope. He's putting in for retirement."

"Wow. I sort of never expected him to leave. Figured they'd carry him out on a stretcher someday."

"Yeah. Me, too." The glee in his voice was unmistakable.

"Everybody in the division's happier than a pig in shit, and we owe it all to you."

"Me? Why?"

"Well, you blew the lid off the crock of shit he'd been sitting on regarding his innocent little daughter. I think he was so embarrassed the way that one turned out, that he ain't got the guts to face anybody around here no more."

I'd found Bielmaster's supposedly abducted daughter and brought her back, safe and sound. He'd fired me, but not before it was revealed that she'd been a willing participant in the scheme. It also called into question some criminal sexual assault charges that Bielmaster had trumped up against her boyfriend years before. I'd handled it as best I could, trying to make sure that no one got hurt. Bielmaster had seen it differently, and refused to pay my fee.

"And then when your collection agency put a garner on his paycheck and word got out about that," George continued, "it's been like laugh central around here. He's lost face. Totally."

It was also something that I'd never intended. "How's his heart condition?"

"Who cares? Word is that he's up for having another stent put in, or something. All that matters is, he's outta our hair. Right, Pers?"

"Thanks again, Ron!" I heard Pers shout.

"Look, I'll run these and see what I can find out. Do the criminal histories, too. Is tomorrow soon enough to get back to you?"

"Yeah." I was still stunned. "Fine."

"I mean, for you, I'll try to have them tonight, if you want to stop by the bar."

Bars were places I took particular pains to stay away from. "Can't. Got a date at the gym tonight."

"This is going to be a night of major celebration. I can tell.

And if I'm able to still drive, I just might come banging on your door at three in the morning with the info."

"Don't wake the neighbors," I said. "Just leave it in the mailbox instead."

We chatted for a few more minutes as I left a tip, got up, and paid my bill. I still had that dumbfounded feeling. An institution was toppling. Not that I'd be sorry to see Bielmaster go, but he'd been such a regular fixture when I went to see George, that it felt somehow unnerving.

I guess I should be rejoicing, I thought. Like the building falling on the wicked witch, or something.

Since I was still on the North Side, and had the beginnings of the afternoon rush about forty minutes away, I decided to take a detour downtown and stop by to see Big Rich in person. If I could get him working on Dr. Colon and Manus, and maybe ask George to run a couple more plates from there, while we were still in the honeymoon period, I could hit the ground running after the weekend. It would also give me time to work that bodyguard thing for Alex St. James. I started saying "Mo' money, mo' money, mo' money" like they did on the old *In Living Color* TV show when the homeboys ripped off the ATM machine. Plus, Bielmaster would have to pay off the lien the collection agency put on him before he could start getting his retirement checks. Maybe there was some justice, after all.

After finding a parking lot close to the *Metro*'s building, which was no easy trick downtown just north of the river, I walked at a nice clip up to the front doors. They'd instituted a restricted entry system, and I gave my card to the security guard at the front desk.

"Ron Shade to see Rich Stafford, please," I said, smiling.

The guard nodded and picked up his phone. He dialed a number and I could tell he'd gotten the same voice mail message that I'd gotten earlier.

"Looks like he ain't in," he said.

"He's gotta be. I just talked to him last week. He was working on a story and he never leaves the building. He's like Nero Wolfe."

"Who?"

"Never mind. Is there anybody else up there I could talk to, to leave a handwritten note for him. It's real important."

He glanced down at my card again, pursed his lips, and made another call. After speaking into the receiver to at least three different people, he finally had a semi-long conversation with someone. Holding the phone out toward me, he said, "This is Mr. Foley, his editor."

I took the phone and greeted Mr. Foley as warmly as I could, ending with, "Big Rich around up there?"

"Actually," I heard the voice say, "uh, what did you say your name was again?"

I told him. "The big guy and I go way back."

"Yeah, he did mention you. You're the boxer, right? Just won a championship?"

"That's me." I didn't want to break rhythm and tell him I was a kickboxer.

"Okay, well, I guess it's all right to tell you then. Rich is in the hospital. Had open-heart surgery Tuesday."

The news hit me like a body shot. "What? Is he okay?"

"He actually died on the operating table three times," Foley said. "They managed to bring him back, but his blood was so thin from all the damn aspirins he's been taking, that they had a helluva time getting the bleeding stopped."

This was sounding bad. Very bad. "How's he doing now?"

"He's in cardiac recovery at St. Francis. Should be there another week or so. I have a number if you'd like to call him."

"Please," I said.

As soon as I walked outside I went to the Michigan Avenue

Bridge. Cell phone reception was generally sporadic in the Loop, but you could usually get a signal by the river. The call went through and I asked for his room. It rang about five or six times before he answered, sounding weaker than I'd ever heard him.

"Hey, you son-of-a-gun, how are you?" he said. It seemed to take all his breath just to get the sentence out.

"I'm fine," I said. "How about you?"

"Could be better."

"I'll bet." We chatted for a minute or so, and I could tell the conversation was weakening him more. "You up for visitors yet?"

"Sure," he said. "But maybe tomorrow, okay?"

"Sure thing, buddy." I told him I'd be by at eleven.

Alex St. James

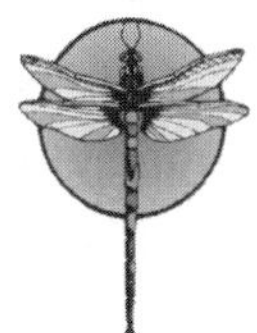

"Nicky," I said, working a smile into my voice as he answered, "It's Alex. I just wanted to call and thank you again for your help the other night."

"Oh," he said with an aw-shucks so deep that even the telephone line couldn't disguise his pride, "I'm just glad that we happened to be there when we were."

I'll bet.

I said, "But I have to admit, I'm disappointed that I didn't get more accomplished. One of the main reasons I went out was to talk with the homeless and get their take on Howard Rybak."

"Rybak? Why?"

"He's the success story," I said as if that explained everything. "He'd make a great feature for the program, and if I'm able to interview him—get his insights into how life on the street affected him—I might be able to give up my homeless disguise."

"You aren't going back out there?"

"I wish I could say I wasn't." I said to gauge his reaction.

"Alex, come on, you had a close call yesterday. Too close. If I hadn't been there . . ."

"You and your friend, Viktor," I added.

"Yeah. If we hadn't shown up when we did, you could've been in real trouble."

"I was pretty lucky."

"You were," he said. "Very lucky. I wouldn't attempt it again if I were you. It's too dangerous for a woman to be out there alone." His voice rose. "You understand?"

"You've got a point," I said as I doodled the words "set up" on my blotter. "The problem is, Father Morales lost contact with Rybak. And you did, too, right?" I didn't wait for him to answer. "So I have to rely on his former colleagues to get my story."

"No," he said sharply. "Listen, you can't keep going out there."

"Believe me, I don't want to."

I waited for him to offer to double-check Rybak's contact information, to say he'd try to hunt him down, to promise me he'd look into it, but what he said was, "You know I can't be out there every night to watch over you."

I pulled the receiver away from my ear and frowned at it. Jordan appeared at my door just then and shot me a quizzical look. I motioned her to sit while I returned to the conversation.

"And I couldn't ask you to put yourself out that way," I said, in my best grateful-damsel voice. "In fact, you're right about how lucky I was . . . I have to tell you, it scares me to think what could have happened if you were just a few minutes later."

Jordan mouthed, "Nicky Farnsworth?"

I nodded, held up a finger. "How did you know when to be there? I mean, wow . . ." I was laying it on thick here, "you and your friend jumped right in. Did you know it was me you were rescuing, or were you just being Good Samaritans?"

"Alex, you know how much I think of you. And you know I'm furious with your station for putting you into this situation, so I took it upon myself to ensure your safety out there."

I cooed into the phone—it made Jordan giggle.

"I asked Father Morales to let me know when you'd be out there," he said, "and he told me about that bright pink hat you were wearing, so I'd be able to spot you. Good thing we got there when we did. Two minutes later and," he gave an audible shudder, "I don't even want to imagine it."

Something clicked in my brain—I needed clarification. I said, "I'm surprised you didn't intervene sooner."

"I would have," he said with rallying pride, "but we just pulled up that minute." He waited a beat—repeated: "That minute."

"Wow," I said again. But what I thought was: "Gotcha."

Jordan reacted to the face I made, leaning close, mouthing questions. I held her off as Nicky continued, "So you understand, Alex, this isn't a game. One minute could mean the difference between life and death. Promise me you won't go out there again."

"Will you try to find Howard Rybak for me?"

He hesitated. "Sure."

"Thanks, Nicky. You're a gem."

"So we're agreed. You won't go out undercover with the homeless again?"

I bit my lip and didn't exactly lie. "If you're willing to help me locate Howard Rybak, I have no need to go undercover again. And believe me, I don't want to."

We made a little small talk, I thanked him again for his timely assistance and I mentioned wanting to speak with his father soon about my adoption. Unaware of my growing displeasure with him, Nicky chatted with glee, suddenly switching gears. "Say, Alex," he said, and I could hear what was coming next, "if you're not busy Friday—"

I waited, working on appropriate rejection lines.

"I was thinking maybe you'd enjoy a night out. Dinner? Movie? Dancing?"

"No wakes that night?" I asked lightly.

"Not this week. I usually have a couple days' notice. So if Friday's not good, maybe Saturday?"

"Uh . . ." I made noises as though consulting my calendar. "It looks like I'm tied up both days. Sorry."

He mumbled something I didn't catch.

I bit my lips shut, but to no avail. "Thanks for asking," I added, hating myself for being polite. I knew he'd read it wrong, and he did.

"Maybe next week," he said, obviously cheered.

"Maybe." Sometimes I just couldn't fight ingrained habits.

When he hung up, Jordan held out her hands. "What was that all about?"

I summarized most of it, then got to the meat of the matter.

"You know the guys who broke Jesse's nose?" I asked.

"Yeah?"

"They called me Pinky. Because of my pink hat. I didn't like the way they singled me out, so I took it off. But Nicky here says that that's how he recognized me and how he knew to come to my rescue." I pointed skyward. "But I didn't have it on when he got there. I didn't have it on for a long while before he got there."

Jordan raised her eyebrows. "So he's lying about how he

knew it was you?"

"Worse. The pink hat was the key. That's how the bullies knew who to target." I chewed my bottom lip—thinking. "That's how Nicky set me up."

"Wow," Jordan said. "But why go to so much trouble?"

"That's what I need to find out," I said. "He worked pretty hard to arrange all that. And I don't buy the 'damsel in distress' reason so much anymore. If it were that alone, he'd be trying harder to get me to go out with him. I think it's something else."

"Like what?"

I had no idea. And I said so.

"You really busy those nights he asked you out?"

"Nope. I lied through my teeth."

She grinned. "There's hope for you yet."

Chapter 13

Ron Shade

A dead man who came back to life, a misidentified, unidentified corpse, employee privacy, lawsuits, HIPAA laws, Bielmaster retiring, and Big Rich down for the count . . . All of a sudden I felt I was treading water in the eye of a hurricane. And the guys coming for me in the rescue boat would probably use one of those long, hooked staffs to push me back under. I needed a workout, bad. By the time I got to the gym that night, I was determined to work out more than just a few frustrations of the past two days on the bags. I packed my stuff in my locker and suited up in my usual gray sweatpants with my protective cup on the outside. It fits better that way if you're not wearing trunks, except it looks a bit ungainly. Instead of the regular sweatshirt with the sleeves chopped off that usually tops off this outfit, I put on my vinyl top. It's guaranteed to make you drop at least ten pounds of perspiration during the course of a good workout.

As I walked through the other rooms, I could tell people were watching me. I felt like the king of my domain, taking a stroll through the village streets clad in my underwear, but tonight I was going for results, not fashion. When Chappie saw me his face spread into a wide grin.

"Well, well, well, looks like you come to do some serious working tonight."

"I was hoping you'd let me spar a few rounds." I nodded toward Alley who was holding the heavy bag for Raul.

He leaned forward, his fingers checking my eyebrow again. I saw the area around his eyes crease slightly. "Don't think that be a good idea just yet. Give it another week. Or two."

As if sensing my frustration, he added, "But we are gonna do some pad work up there." He cocked his thumb toward the ring to our right. I stared up at it thinking it looked like an old friend just across the shore. He grabbed the focus mitts and started to slip his hands inside them as we walked to the steps leading up to the apron.

"You warmed up?" he asked.

"Absolutely."

He stepped on the bottom rope and I ducked through it. Chappie called to Alley to set the ring timer and we began our movements, Chappie holding the heavy mitts out in front of him, directing me to jab, jab, jab, right cross, hook, uppercut . . . We continued this until the bell rang signaling the end of the three minutes.

"Not too bad," he said. "But we gotta go a few more now."

I nodded, concentrating on getting my breathing back to normal in the sixty seconds. I usually judge how good of shape I'm in by the length of time it takes me to recover between rounds. Of course, after only one round, I would have been really disappointed if I hadn't recovered quickly. It wasn't anywhere near as hard as being in a real fight, either. Having another guy trying to hurt you with every punch, intent on knocking your lights out, adds a bit more to the equation.

The timer signaling the end of the minute's rest period sounded and Chappie slapped the mitts together and motioned me toward the center of the ring. We'd gone about two minutes when, out of the corner of my eye, I noticed Brice come in.

"Hey, Chappie," he called. "Telephone."

"Tell 'em I'll call 'em back. Can't you see I'm busy?" His tone was angry, but his dark face never lost its concentration or sight of me.

"Okay," Brice said with a shrug. "But it's Saul."

Saul Bloom was our promoter and he usually didn't call unless it involved a big-money deal he was setting up.

"Shit," Chappie said. "I been waiting on him to call me. Might have a good match for Raul in the works."

"Take it then," I said.

He shook his head. "He can wait till we finish this round."

We continued our dance around the square jungle, framed by the trio of elastic ropes and ring posts. Chappie concentrated on boxing moves and then stepped back slightly, telling me to throw some kicks. It felt good to have my instep slap against the mitt as he held it at head level.

"Gimme a hook kick," Chappie said, after I'd thrown a roundhouse, and I pivoted slightly and brought my heel against the padding as he brought up the other mitt. The bell sounded and he grinned. "You lookin' good, champ. Like a million bucks."

Yeah, green and wrinkled, I thought.

He turned and yelled down for Alley to come take his place. I leaned my forearms on the top rope and scanned the room. Raul was nowhere to be seen, and Alley stood talking with some big guy with short-cropped hair and a craggy face. The man's body had the look of lean muscularity, like a big linebacker. If he could move and hit, he'd be formidable. He was looking directly at me with an amused expression. His mouth twisted downward as he said something, and I saw Alley say something back accompanied by a head shake. The big guy smirked, nodded, and turned away, walking out of the boxing room with a slow deliberation.

Alley grabbed the focus mitts from the spot on the apron where Chappie had left them and hopped through the ropes. "Hi, Ron," he said.

I nodded. "So who was that dude you were talking to? New member?"

Alley shook his head. "I no tink so."

"You know him?"

He shook his head again. "No. You?"

I always got a kick out of the kid's struggle with English. Of course, it was a helluva lot better than my Russian.

"Why would I know him?"

"Vell, he ask me 'bout you." He finished working his hands into the mitts. "Ask me if you Ron Shade, da shampion."

I grinned. "He must've heard of me, huh? He say why he wanted to know?"

Alley shook his head. "He say, you no look that tough. He was . . ." His face scrunched up slightly. "How you say . . . Stuck up?"

"Arrogant?"

"Da," Alley said, nodding and grinning. "Arrhagant. In Russian we say *pridurok.* I tell him he wrong. You tough. Very tough. I no like him."

My mind replayed the scene I'd witnessed. Their communication and ease of conversing. "Was that guy Russian?"

He nodded. "He Russian-speak good."

"He was a big dude." I grinned, appreciative that Alley had "defended" my tough-guy rep, but ready to get back to the task at hand. "You think he's bad?"

"Bad? Bad guy?"

I shot my gloved fists out in a quick combination. "You know. Bad."

His face got serious and he stepped back, lowering his hands and patting the place on his forearm with the tattoo of his unit in the Russian Army. "I see his arm. He *Spetsnaz.*"

That was one bit of Russkie that I didn't need translation for. I knew it from my own army days. It was the word for the Russian Special Forces.

About an hour and a half later I was walking out of the gym, mulling over how much I'd let that damn Russkie's comment get to me. "Not that tough." I was used to people trying to play mind games with me, especially in the fight game, where a lot of your preparation is purely mental. People talk trash and try to get your goat, try and bait you, and try and bolster themselves. Normally, those kinds of comments didn't get to me. I used them for fuel during my training, when motivation ebbed and you needed that little extra push to get you over the hump. I would take the snide remarks, and make a vow to shove them down my opponent's throat during the actual fight. Most of the time, it worked like a charm. But this one had been sort of anonymously delivered. A reflection by an asshole, told to me by a friend. Maybe what bothered me was that I wouldn't get a chance to show that big jerk how wrong he was. That was the payoff for me the other times. This time, it was like getting slapped and not being able to slap back. I didn't even know who the big bastard was. But if he came back to the gym sometime, I'd make sure I mentioned that he looked a lot like the guy I took the championship from. "He was a Russkie, too," I imagined myself saying.

But if this guy was *Spetsnaz,* he did have certain bragging rights. I'd been a U.S. Army Ranger, but I couldn't lay claim to being the elite of the elite. That belonged to the Green Berets.

Still, talk was cheap, and I didn't need to prove anything to anybody.

I smiled as I turned in back of the building and started down the alleyway to where I'd parked the Beater. Maybe the second-hand insult coming so quickly after my "failed" dinner with Ms. Alex St. James had rubbed my bruised ego the wrong way. I'd just about decided to forget about it when a shadow moved off to my right. A man stepped out from between the Dumpsters against the back edge of the building. He was tall and rangy looking.

"Hey," the man said in a low voice. "Give me wallet."

He'd pronounced it "Vallet," with a foreign-sounding twist to it.

I never brought my wallet or my gun to the gym for fear of somebody stealing them from my locker. Now I was being stuck-up for something I didn't even have. And tonight, I stood to lose a whole lot more. In the pale ambient lighting of the alley I saw the glint of a gun barrel in his right hand. A four-inch, stainless steel revolver.

"Sure, sure," I said, adjusting my feet into a boxer's stance to make a narrower target. "You can have it." His head tilted back slightly and the light reflected off the planes of his face. High cheekbones, like an Eastern European thug's. But there was something more in that face. Something that told me, deep down, that this dude meant to pull that trigger whether I gave him the wallet I didn't have or not. That's when I pivoted, swinging my big gym bag up and into his right hand. The flash of the muzzle shot out a foot, with a piercing blast. I continued my momentum, releasing my grip on the bag and concentrating on getting both my hands around his gun hand. Just as I got control of his wrist with my right, the gun went off again, the hot spray from the cylinder burning my left palm. Securing my grip over the cylinder and barrel, I twisted my hand down sharply, snapping it from his grip.

His left elbow collided with my temple and I saw a mosaic of black dots swarm in front of my eyes momentarily. Luckily, I was used to getting hit, so the blow didn't affect me that much. I had no desire to take another one, so I gave him an elbow of my own, right in the gut. It was harder than I'd anticipated. This guy was like a rock. He tried to snake an arm around my throat for a choke hold, but I brought my chin down. I felt two hard punches hit me in my back. Kidney shots. I slipped out of his encircling arm, but his leg whipped out and almost caught me squarely in the groin. I was used to blocking cheap shots like those, too, but the gun dropped from my hand and skittered a few feet away on the asphalt.

I crouched and sprang upward, using my body to propel him away from the area where the gun had fallen. He took two awkward steps back, regained his balance, and jumped toward me again. That was a move I was totally ready for, and I shot out a jab, catching him on one of his prominent cheekbones, then sent in a whistling right cross that flipped his head the opposite way. He stumbled back, colliding with a huge Dumpster and I moved forward like I'd caught him against the ropes. His right hand moved down to the front of his pants and came up quickly holding the tapered silhouette of a knife blade. I stopped advancing as he lunged forward. I felt a sharpness slice through the sleeve of my jacket and scrape over my arm.

Two steps back and I bumped into a couple of plastic garbage cans which I rolled around and pushed over, placing a barrier between him and me. The city had long ago gone to these big, plastic monstrosities which could be hooked onto a special lift truck and emptied. Gone were the old cans with the removable lids which I could have used in this case. My adversary stepped nimbly around the scattered garbage, and came at me, holding the blade poised by his body like an experienced knife-fighter.

A bunch of long, fluorescent lightbulbs extended from the lip of an adjacent can. I grabbed one of them and swung it at his face, like a tennis backhand. He brought his left arm up to block, but the bulb shattered, sending a hailstorm of tiny shards at his face. This stopped him long enough for me to deliver a front kick to the inside of his foremost leg. I hit him with the sole of my shoe in more of a stomping motion. It sent him down and I moved to the right, circling back to where the gun was. His knife hand shot out, trying for my legs as I went by, but he missed. I took my eyes off of him long enough to scan the ground for the gun.

I saw it, three feet away.

So did he, apparently, and we both scrambled toward it. Since I was on my feet already, I got there milliseconds ahead of him, reached down, snatched the gun, and brought it up as I fired. The flash was equally impressive this time, and through the ringing in my ears, I heard him grunt as he grabbed his gut. He took two stagger steps toward me, the knife curling out from between his fingers and clattering to the ground. His mouth was wide open, sucking in air as bright light engulfed us both.

I heard the roar of an engine and swiveled my head in time to see a big, dark SUV barreling toward us from the mouth of the alley across 99th Street. It looked like it was heading right for me, and it wasn't slowing down. A red flash glowed on top of the dash. Seconds later something tore through the windshield and I realized what it was. Another gun blast.

I sprinted across the alleyway, vaulting a four-foot fence and hitting the ground running in the yard on the other side. A bullet smacked into the garage close to my head and I held the revolver under my arm as I ran, firing twice. I rounded the corner and realized I didn't know how many rounds I had left. How many had I fired? Was it a six-shot, or only five? As I waited by the garage, out of the line of fire, I prayed that it was one of those new eight-shooters.

I heard someone yell something I didn't understand, and after a few seconds more, the SUV took off south down the alley. I made my way around the other end of the garage with the intention of emptying whatever bullets I had left into the car, but a solid seven-foot stockade fence loomed in front of me. Good thing it hadn't been on the other side or I would never have gotten over it in time.

Something warm ran down over the back of my left hand and I saw it was blood. I checked my forearm and, to my chagrin, saw that his knife had indeed caused a deep gash on my forearm. But that wasn't what I was disappointed about. I'd worn my special, Imperial Palace jacket that Chappie had given me on our last trip to Vegas. The time I'd won the championship. The delicate black cloth had a jagged rip across the sleeve, and the whole lower portion was sodden with blood. But at least it was just my own blood.

I moved back into the alley, picked up my gym bag, and headed back to Chappie's to call 9-1-1.

Alex St. James

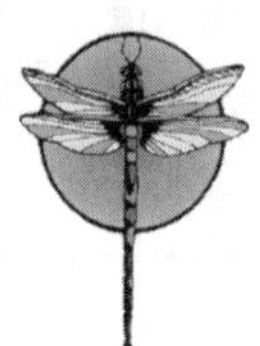

That evening, as I dialed Larry Farnsworth's home phone number, I remembered Jordan's admonishment to be less forthcoming with the truth. Larry hadn't returned any of my prior calls. I'd left four polite, hopeful messages—twice with his assistant, twice on his voice mail. The most recent had been two days ago. Although I wasn't exactly a client, I thought I deserved the courtesy of a return call.

Larry answered mid–fifth ring. "Hello?" His voice was groggier than an eight o' clock phone call warranted. It almost sounded like he'd been drinking.

"This is Alex, Uncle Larry," I said unnecessarily. I was pretty sure just about everyone had Caller ID these days. "Are you okay?"

"Fine," he said too quickly. "Why, what's the matter?"

I could tell I'd woken him up. Surprised him. Set him off kilter. Damn. His demeanor was all wrong for a friendly call asking a favor.

This had been a mistake. "Nothing, I just wanted to call and say hello. I'll try again some other time when it's more convenient."

"It's convenient now," he said brusquely. "You're calling because I haven't gotten back to you about your adoption, aren't you? I've got other things on my plate, you know. I have paying clients who depend on me to look after their interests."

Shoot. I'd not only bothered him, I'd put him in a bad mood.

I scrambled to come up with another reason to have called, one that wouldn't hurt my chances of getting adoption information later. "I was worried that you were okay," I said. "Because I knew you'd return my calls if you could."

Jordan would be so proud of me.

"Hmph," he said, but his tone softened. "Makes sense. Never thought of it that way. Been such a long time since . . ."

He didn't finish the thought.

"I'm glad you're all right," I said, prepared to end the call there and then. The good will this little conversation provided might pay dividends later if I didn't press my luck now.

"Nice of you to call."

"Well, you take care, Uncle Larry."

"Say," he said, "have you talked to Nicky lately? Was he able to help you out with that story you were working on?"

Evidently, the man wasn't as groggy as he sounded. And, just as evidently, Nicky hadn't told Daddy about his just-in-time damsel-in-distress rescue.

"He's been helping me a lot," I said with manufactured warmth. If my embellishing made Larry a little bit happier with his son, I was glad to do it. "In fact, you should ask him about the excitement on Grisham Avenue the other day."

He coughed. "Not too exciting, I hope," he said with a phlegmy laugh. "What happened?"

"I'll let Nicky tell you all about it," I said. "I'll tell him you want to hear the whole story."

"You'll be talking with him soon?"

"I plan to call him again tomorrow."

"Oh," he said and even over the connection I could hear the smile in his voice. "I didn't know the two of you kept in touch so regularly."

I pressed my lips shut to keep from answering the begged question—from correcting what I knew Larry assumed. I hated being disingenuous, even by omission, but I was tired of being ignored.

Keeping my tone light, I answered without answering, "And you and I should probably keep in touch regularly, too. I know you're busy, but . . ."

"I haven't forgotten, Alex. I just haven't had time to devote to investigation." For the first time since we started talking, Larry sounded sincere. "There are a couple of big cases at work that I've been called in on. I haven't had a moment's rest all week. But soon, I promise you, I'll take a look at your file and let you know where we stand. Fair enough?"

"More than fair," I said. If he had as heavy a caseload as he claimed, I could empathize. Momentum could be destroyed when starting a new project. After all, I'd only recently broached the subject to him. "I'll call you in a week or so, just to check in."

"Better yet, why don't you and Nicky set a date and the three of us will all go out. I should have my portion of this case taken care of by next Thursday. Let's all go out for an early dinner on the weekend." He sniffed and made a noise like he was thinking aloud. "Early enough to give you and Nicky time to do something else afterward. My treat."

The thought of me and Nicky "doing something else" repulsed me with such vehemence that I shuddered. "Sounds wonderful," I said. "In fact, Nicky's been helping me with another matter."

"Oh?" he said with a little too much enthusiasm.

"Nicky is trying to help me locate one of the homeless folks who he helped. This guy made a new life for himself. Maybe you know him. Howard Rybak?"

Larry gave a grunt. "Doesn't sound familiar. But then again Nicky's always helping someone. This time, I'm glad he's helping you."

Ron Shade

On my run the next morning I reflected on the whole incident. I was going much slower than usual, not so much because of my injury, but because the shoulder rig I was wearing with my Beretta 95F was rubbing my side with acute irritation. I don't normally run with a gun, but after last night's encounter, paranoia had gotten the better of me.

Chappie had insisted on accompanying me to the ER, where a very nice, young, female doctor cleaned up my wound, gave me a tetanus shot, and a latticework of stitches. Chappie kept shaking his head.

"Can't believe this happened. We never have no problems of that kind by the gym. You know who this cat was?"

I shook my head. "I'm pretty sure I winged him, so he might be showing up at a hospital for a gunshot wound."

"I see the motherfucker, I'll kill his ass," Chappie said. "If you didn't beat me to it."

Two uniformed coppers from twenty-two came by and took the report, telling me they'd put out a city-wide on the car. I wished I could have gotten the plate for them, but I mentioned that it might have a couple of bullet holes in it.

After getting the release, and a prescription for antibiotics and pain, if I needed it, we left. I had Chappie drive me to my house so I could pick up the Beretta before I went back for the Beater at the gym. I needn't have bothered because a host of police and evidence techs were processing the scene, complete with big, portable spotlights. I walked them through the fight, and showed them the signs.

"The blood there is probably mine," I said, pointing to a trail across the alley. I'd also left a bloody handprint on the fence and side of the garage. They found some more splatterings in the vicinity of where my assailant had been, which increased my belief that I'd hit him with at least one of the rounds. As it turned out, I'd had one shot left. The gun was a six-shot, Smith & Wesson, three-fifty-seven Magnum. Second only to the new fifty calibers and old Dirty Harry's gun for leaving big old holes in people.

Now, I crested a hill and felt a throbbing in my arm where the stitches were. Maybe this run hadn't been the brightest idea I'd had, but I was committed to finishing. I just took a shortcut and headed back around. Best to vary my usual routine until I figured out if the attack had been a random act of violence, or something more specific.

In my business I'd made plenty of enemies, but something was bugging me about this one. In that instant before I moved, I'd sensed something. Maybe it was the expression in the man's eyes, but something in my gut told me that he was going to fire. But if the dude had been intent on killing me, wouldn't it have been simpler to just shoot me and then take my wallet? It was almost as if they wanted to make it look like a stick-up gone bad. Plus, if there were two of them, why did one hold back, watching from across the street with the get-away ride? That seemed to add a bit of sophistication to a simple stick-up. Maybe they didn't think I was that tough . . . The guy's accent. He'd said, "*Vallet.* Give me your *vallet.*" And an hour or so before that, some *Spetsnaz* asshole was in the gym scoping me out. Co-incidence? I didn't think so.

Spetsnaz . . . Russkies . . . Hadn't Thad the Cad mentioned a bunch of Russkies had picked up Bayless's body from Furman County? Things were suddenly taking on a new urgency with this one. I had to get to the bottom of it fast, or keep looking over my shoulder. I was going to have to lean on the sweet-smelling jerk at the funeral home. As I rounded the last turn before heading down the block toward my house, I checked the cars on both sides of the street. The same ones as when I'd left earlier. The two Russkies had known I worked out at the gym, but so did a lot of people. It was advertised in the window and most likely would come up in a Google search from some of the articles that had been written about me. I always mentioned Chappie. But not where I lived. I'd have to work to keep it that way.

As I showered I heard my phone ringing, and when I checked

the message it was George. His voice sounded agitated on the tape.

"What the hell is this, you get cut up and shot at and you don't call me? I got two dicks from Violent Crimes that need to interview you ASAP. Call me as soon as you get this, dammit."

Good old George.

I dialed his number and he answered on the first ring.

"You all right?" he asked. There was a lot of angry frustration in his tone, but an undercurrent of concern, too.

"I'm fine. Now who are these two dicks who want to talk to me?"

"Norris and Cate. Good guys. They knew that I know you, so they reached out this morning. Said you got stabbed."

"Slashed is more like it. But I think I winged the asshole."

"You did. They found the car. Abandoned in an alley a few blocks away. Blood all over the interior."

"Any leads?"

"Nah, stolen earlier that night. Taken from a garage. The owner didn't even know it was missing. My guess is they had another car parked nearby the dump site for a clean getaway."

I considered this. That showed more sophisticated planning and foresight. Steal a car to do the dirty deed, one that won't be missed for a while, and then leave it when you're done and drive calmly away in your own ride.

George's voice interrupted my reverie. "I'll bring the guys over now for the interview, okay?"

"Give me a bit. I just got back from a run. I need to shower."

"You ran?" I heard him laugh. "You tough bastard, you."

"Keeps me outta the bars," I said. "Take them over to Karson's and I'll meet you guys there in about forty."

It took me closer to an hour, but that was only because I wanted to make sure no one was following me. No one was. By the time I got to the restaurant, I was chiding myself for being so extra-cautious. But, I reflected as I got out and scanned the parking lot, that's what kept me alive this long.

Paul Norris and Lincoln Cate turned out to be a salt-and-pepper team as well as a couple of good guys, like George had said. After the introduction and hand shaking, they got right down to brass tacks.

"You think this was a random thing, Ron, or could it be related to something you're working on?" Cate asked. He was a black guy who looked to be in his early thirties.

"I was just asking myself that question on my run this morning," I said. The stall was automatic. I never liked to share details of what I was working on, who my clients were, with cops, except for George. It was bad for business to reveal that kind of stuff offhand. But in this case, I couldn't afford not to. If those two guys had been gunning for me, I needed to call out the troops to start beating the bushes. I gave them a quick rundown of the Bayless case, and also mentioned the Russians, the funeral home, and the *Spetsnaz* joker who'd stopped by the gym.

"Spetz-what?" Norris asked. He was the white guy, and a bit shorter than his partner, but just as young.

"Spetsnaz," I said. "The Russian Special Forces. Supposed to be some real bad dudes."

Cate grinned. "Not so bad if you disarmed one of them and shot him to boot."

"He's good with kicking the shit out of big Russians," George said. He proceeded to tell them how he'd won a bundle on my fight with Sergei.

"This guy wasn't as tough as Sergei," I said, "but he had pretty good moves. Good street fighter."

"We got the word out to all the local hospitals," Cate said. "If the motherfucker's gut-shot, he's gonna need to see the docs."

"Plus we had our ETs go over the car with a fine-tooth comb," Norris added. "You know it was a steamer, right?"

"Yeah."

"The gun you took from him turned out to be hot, too," he said. "Taken in a burglary a few months ago. We got some partials off the ammunition. We'll need you to give us some elimination prints."

"Mine are on file," I said. "Plus, I didn't touch any of the shells."

He nodded.

After another chorus of promises to keep me in the loop, Norris and Cate left in their unmarked. George stared at me from across the table.

"So how come you didn't call me last night?" he asked, his head tilting to the side slightly.

I watched him take a long sip of his cold coffee.

"There wasn't any reason to," I said. I motioned for the waitress. "It wasn't that big of a deal."

"Some prick tries to ice you in an alley and it's no big deal?"

"I handled it."

"Yeah, and got your arm all sliced up in the meantime."

I realized he was just feeling like my surrogate big brother, a little PO'd for me not running to him after a fight. In a lot of ways, George had been more of a big brother to me than my real older brother, Tom. But calling him last night hadn't been in the cards. The main reason was I had Chappie with me, and he and George were like oil and water. "I must have been out of it more than I realized. I apologize."

He smirked. The waitress arrived to freshen up our cups, and asked if we wanted to order something else. George looked at me expectantly. "It's my day off, so I could go for some eggs."

We got our usual and he leaned his elbows on the table. "I got those damn printouts you wanted at work. Didn't think you'd need them till Monday."

"No problem. I've got a couple things going this weekend anyway."

"Such as?"

"What, are you checking up on me?"

"When you maybe got some guys gunning for you, yeah."

"This is a bodyguard thing tonight for a reporter. Ever watch *Midwest Focus*?"

"That news program? That the one with the babe reporter?"

"Alex St. James."

He frowned. "I thought her name was Gabriela, or something."

I shook my head. "I have the enviable task of guarding her delectable body while she goes undercover as a homeless person."

He grinned. "Sounds like a nice gig. Right up your alley." Then his expression got totally serious. "Just do one thing for me, okay?"

I raised my eyebrows. "What's that?"

"Keep your peter in your pants. I don't want you distracted and thinking about romance until we bring down these guys that are after you."

"Well, that won't be much of a problem. I had dinner with her the other night and she's a first-class ice princess."

"Oh yeah?"

I nodded. "Tried all the Shade charm, and it had absolutely no effect."

"No kidding?" He feigned amazement. "She a lesbian?"

I chuckled. "I don't think so."

"Well, maybe she's smarter than I gave her credit for," he said. "I'll have to start watching that show."

Before I could think of a good comeback, the waitress came with our food.

★ ★ ★ ★ ★

Visiting hours at St. Francis started at two and I was informed by a strict-looking nurse that because Big Rich was in the intensive care unit, the visit couldn't last more than five minutes. As we walked down the hallway I brushed her arm.

"How's he doing?" I asked.

"Not bad," she said. "He needs to quit smoking if he wants to live, though."

"I've been telling him that for years."

She frowned. "He tried to fool us the other day. We walked him to the bathroom and helped sit him down, then we left him and the next thing we heard a crash. When we opened the door, he was on the floor." The frown deepened. "He'd snuck a cigarette into the washroom with him. Lord knows where he got it and the lighter, but it put him right down."

"That sounds like Rich," I said. "He can be resourceful when he wants to be."

We stopped by the entrance. "Well, don't give him anything like that, sir. I only shared that with you to convey the delicate nature of his condition. All right?"

"Yes, ma'am."

When I walked in I saw him propped up reading the *Metro,* his long hair pulled back into a ponytail and the thick glasses perched on his wide nose. He looked up and smiled, but it was perhaps the weakest smile I'd ever seen.

"How you doing, buddy?" I asked.

His head lolled to the side. "I'd be doing a lot better if I could grab a smoke from you." Just saying those few words seemed to wind him.

"I'll bet. But you and I both know that ain't gonna happen." I looked around the room. It was small and sterile, with a ceiling-to-floor-length curtain drawn around the bed. Numerous wires and IVs were hooked up to his chest and connected to a bunch of monitors. I watched an erratic line trace his heartbeat across one of the screens.

"Didn't think so."

I didn't know if I was supposed to shake hands with him, but he held his out and I took it. His grip was incredibly feeble, even though his hand was massive.

He shook his head. "They tell me if I want to live . . ." He paused and took a breath. "I gotta quit smoking and lose some weight."

I nodded. "Sounds about right."

"But I told 'em," pause. "That ain't living. Much." He tried to laugh and it was a mistake. He motioned for me to hand him a pillow stacked next to the bed. I did and he grabbed it to his chest and held it there. His mouth opened and for a second he looked like a fish out of water, gasping in the open air. He lowered the pillow.

"You okay? Want me to get the nurse?"

He shook his head. "Had to cough."

I remembered my visits to Bielmaster when he'd been in for his heart operation. He and Rich were about the same size, but Rich was younger. He seemed to have fared worse, though.

"They split me open from here to here," he said, bringing his hand from just under his throat to mid-belly. "Almost bought the farm on the table."

"What brought this on? Were you having pains?"

He shook his head. "My belly swelled up to like three times its normal size. My nuts, too. Had to go in, and they rushed me into surgery."

The nurse came to the edge of the door frame and stood looking at me.

"I take it my five minutes are up?"

She nodded.

I turned back to Big Rich and held out my hand again. "If

you need anything, except cigarettes, you call me, okay?"

He nodded, and as I left, trying my best to look cheery, I saw his eyes misting over. He'd fallen from the mountain and was working his way back up. I hoped he had enough drive and sense to do what they told him and drop about a hundred pounds. The cigarettes would be rough, too, for a guy who acted like a human chimney. But seeing him there, holding a pillow to his chest so he didn't blow out his staples, might be enough motivation for that. I hoped to God it would be.

I thanked the nurse and went down to wait for the elevator. You couldn't take the stairways in hospitals because you could never find them. The down arrow light clicked off with an accompanying chime and I got in, pressed "L" for lobby, and watched the doors slide shut.

I silently wished Big Rich luck and reflected on how we'd been friends for years, but really barely knew each other. Strange. One other thing was glaringly obvious as well. He'd be in no kind of shape to help me with the Bayless case. My cell rang, snapping me out of the reverie. I answered it with a gruff hello.

"Mr. Shade?"

"Yes." The voice was feminine and familiar.

"It's Alex St. James. I just wanted to touch base with you about tonight. Do you know where the Grisham Avenue viaduct is?"

"Not really."

She gave me a more exact location. "They congregate under the viaduct there. We figure to set up about seven-thirty."

"I'll be there." I pulled out my notebook and pen. "Give me a description of those knuckleheads who attacked you before. I'll run some checks to see if they match any previous crime patterns." As she gave me the description I could tell she was a little impressed. My checks would consist of a phone call back to George, using another favor, but what the hell. It sounded good. Or at least I thought it did. She surprised me with her next comment.

"Actually, I had a detective friend look into that already," she said. "It looks to be an isolated incident, but then again, how many homeless people are going to be reporting things to the cops?"

"Probably not too many." This was one smart chick.

"Which is why I have you, right?"

I agreed, and she rattled off what she'd be wearing. "You may not recognize me. I'll be undercover as one of the homeless. Just look for the blue baseball cap."

I thought about saying if that was the case, she'd be the best-looking bag lady on the block, but George's warning to me stuck. Keep it professional. Especially now. So, I simply replied, "I'll make sure I find you."

My aimless driving took me toward the gym, and pretty soon I found myself edging down the south end of the alley where the incident had occurred the night before. I pulled in back of Chappie's and stared out the window, re-creating last night's every move in my mind. Getting out, I retraced my steps. The Beater had been there. I looked across the street. *Vallet* Man had been in the shadows next to a small cement wall. He'd known I was coming, and must have known I was headed for the Beater. He also had the element of surprise. The other guy had been in the SUV somewhere as lookout, or maybe backup. They figured I'd go down easy . . . Not so tough . . . Tiny shards of the broken glass still littered the dark asphalt where I'd smashed the florescent bulb across the guy's face. I looked harder, trying to see where the bullet that had been fired had hit the ground, but it all looked the same. Just a lot of uneven, worn blacktopping, ground away by the friction of thousands of tires.

As I walked toward the front doors I looked around, cognizant of every car, every pair of eyes within shooting distance. The Beretta on my hip felt comforting as well. If anybody came at me again, I'd be ready.

Inside, I heard the familiar sounds of the gym: weights clanging, music playing, and a distant *thump, thump, thump* of a speed bag. When I got to the boxing room I saw it was the man, himself, beating out the rhythm. His dark eyes caught a glimpse of me and he stopped abruptly, the bag smacking the board and then slowing appreciably. Sweat glistened on his shaved head.

"Hey, Champ," Chappie said. "What you doing in here?"

I shrugged. "I was in the neighborhood."

"Hey, now, don't you be thinking about working out today." He shook his head and made an "Uuuu-aah" sound. "You need to be resting and letting that arm heal. Last thing you want is to pop some of them stitches."

"Yeah, I know." I looked around. "Alley here?"

Chappie shook his head. "He came in this morning, did his work, then went home to sleep. Working the night shift tonight."

Alley had a job as a janitor and trained at odd times. For him, a real treat was to have a night off so he could come to the gym and spar with Raul or me or some of the regular evening guys for a few rounds. "The kid's got heart, I'll give him that."

"What you looking for him for?"

"I wanted to ask him about some guy that came in last night," I said. "Before I was attacked. Alley said the guy was Russian."

Chappie's eyebrows rose. "Well, he oughta know." He looked at me. "You thinking he the dude that tried to stick you up?"

I shook my head. "It wasn't him, but he might've been with him. My guy had some kind of foreign accent."

He shrugged. "Lots of those 'round here now."

"Too many to believe in coincidences," I said.

Chapter 14

Alex St. James

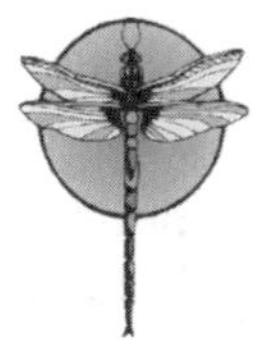

I caught an aproned Father Morales peeling potatoes next to a giant stove. Large window box fans placed strategically around the humid kitchen made lots of noise but did nothing to cool the area. Morales plopped a bald spud in the nearest stainless steel pot and reached for another when I called out a hello.

"Alex," he said with surprise as he wiped his brow. "What are you doing here?"

"Bad time?"

"Not at all, I just didn't expect you." Morales stopped what he was doing, banged his potato and knife on the countertop, and stared at me with intensity. "I heard what happened the other night. You could have been killed."

Not if I was right about Nicky's involvement, I thought. "I got lucky," I said, then turned the conversation away from my safety. I wasn't in the mood for another lecture. "Who were those three guys?"

He grimaced at the remaining pile of potatoes, turned off the heat beneath the stainless steel pot and wiped his hands on his apron. "Don't know," he said. "I've been trying to place them. From what Nick told me—"

"That's another thing," I said. "Why did you tell Nicky when I'd be out there?"

"Why not?" he asked. "Isn't it good that he showed up?"

"Of course," I said. I wasn't about to share my suspicions that Nicky had engineered the episode, but I didn't want to risk a repeat performance, either. "I just was surprised to see him."

Morales smiled. "So you're finished with your project? No more living among the homeless?"

"What I'm actually interested in," I said, deflecting, "is contacting Howard Rybak. I understand he used to stop in here all the time. If you've got his address . . ."

"Will that keep you from doing this 'undercover work' you're so set on?"

"It might."

"You're a bad liar," Morales said. "But let me think." He pursed big lips. "The last time I tried to reach him, I discovered his telephone had been disconnected. I'm afraid the address I have is out of date."

"I'd still appreciate it, if you wouldn't mind."

He wiped his hands again. "I think I have it in the office here. Give me a minute. Have a seat, if you want."

"Thanks."

My Catholic guilt sent me to the pile of potatoes, and I began peeling the one Morales had started. He was doing me a favor, I reasoned. No need for him to fall behind on his work to help me out.

By the time I'd gotten to my tenth potato, I'd begun to perspire. Hair strands stuck to the side of my face, and I pushed them away with the back of my hand.

I turned to glance at the door where he'd gone. What was taking so long?

There were only two potatoes left to be peeled by the time Morales finally got back. He noticed my handiwork immediately. "Alex, how can I ever thank you?"

I dropped the knife and wiped at my sweaty face. Peeling potatoes was not hard work, but this kitchen was a steam bath. It amazed me that Morales wasn't thinner. "You can thank me by putting me in touch with Howard Rybak," I said with a smile, pointing to the paper in his hand. "I take it you found it."

He made a so-so look with his head. "This is the most recent address I had on file. But, like I said, last time I tried to reach him there I had no luck."

I took the paper. North Side, a bit farther east. I wasn't familiar with the area, but I knew I could find it. "Thanks."

"Nick doesn't have anything more up-to-date, either."

"You never know," I said.

"No," he said, heading back to the potatoes. "I just got off the phone with him. He rattled off the same address when I asked."

"You called him? You told him I was here?"

"Not at first," Morales said, looking flustered. "I just asked him for the address, but then after he gave it to me, he asked me why I needed it. That's when I mentioned you. Was that the wrong thing to do?"

I took a breath. "It's fine," I said. I'd asked Nicky for the address, too—though he hadn't been able to rattle it off for me. "I just know how busy he is. I don't want to cause him more work."

"Nick is always very busy," Morales said. "Which is why his help with the indigent is so admirable. He makes time for them in a way that most successful businessmen would not."

I stared at the note in my hands thinking of Morales' phrasing. "How is it that Nicky was able to just rattle the address off?" I asked.

"Nicky found the apartment for Howard."

"He did?"

"I'm telling you, Nicholas Farnsworth is truly our Saint Nick."

"I had no idea he was so involved."

"I hope this information helps you," he said, then added, "and as long as it keeps you from camping out among the homeless, I feel as though I've done some good."

I pocketed the note Morales gave me and thanked him. "You've helped a lot. I'll make sure to mention your work on behalf of the homeless in my story."

"God's blessings on you."

He returned to his potatoes, and I returned to my musings.

As I walked to my car, I heard the toot of a horn. I turned. Nicky pulled up in a red Corvette.

"Hey, good-looking," he said.

Damn it. Morales' phone call had brought him around like a bird dog. Or maybe a hound dog. I really didn't want to stop, so I waved and kept walking around the car's far side.

The Corvette's passenger window whirred down this time. "The good father told me you're going back for more under the viaduct," Nicky said.

So much for priest's keeping secrets. Maybe I should have told Morales my plans within the boundaries of confession. But since Nicky was here, I figured I'd poke around a little. "I'm more interested in interviewing Howard Rybak. I guess you had his address all along, huh?"

He glanced forward, and into his rearview mirror. "I . . . uh . . ." he licked his lips, "you see, I didn't want to give it to you because I knew the address was no good. I told Father Morales that Rybak moved, but actually, he left for parts unknown." He continued to ease the 'Vette forward to match my pace. It sounded like a racehorse champing at the bit. "Look, Alex, you need to rethink going out there again. Didn't you learn your lesson the last time?"

I smiled coyly. "Actually, I learned plenty."

"What's that supposed to mean?"

"It means that this time I'm bringing my own security." I looked at my watch. "In fact, I need to go meet him now."

"Security? Who is this guy?"

"How do you know it's a guy?"

That flustered him. "Is it?"

This was fun. "Yes."

"When are you going back 'undercover'?"

"Next week," I lied. "At the earliest."

Nicky snorted as he did a quick glance at the mirror again. "Well, I hope this security guy is better than the last wimp that was supposed to be protecting you."

I was angry that he'd refer to poor Jesse that way. "This guy's no wimp. He's a professional kickboxer and a private detective." Not that it was any of his business.

"He's a what?"

"A professional kickboxer."

His lips separated like he needed more air. "What's his name?"

"Ron Shade."

He blinked twice. "Shade?"

Something was strange in the way he said it.

"You know him?" I asked.

His cheeks puffed out slightly and he shook his head. "I guess you don't need me then." The big tires of his Corvette spun until they caught on the asphalt, leaving a dark spoor of tread.

His abrupt departure was unnerving, although welcome. I shook my head at the smell of the burned rubber. He was a grade-A jerk even if he was the son of a family friend. Still, his behavior was odd. Like his reaction didn't fit with the situation. Was he jealous because I hadn't swooned over his invitations to dinner? Or maybe that I didn't fall all over him after his dubious rescue the other night. And I was beginning to suspect that there was more to his elaborate theatrical production than just impressing me. Maybe there was a story lurking here after all.

Ron Shade

I hummed "Over the Rainbow," substituting "under the viaduct" as I walked toward the towering section of elevated roadway at the Grisham Avenue viaduct. It was supported by some huge cement pillars adjacent to a sloping hill of wild grass. The human detritus that littered the expansive underbelly looked like a rag-tag bunch of discarded clothing. As I got closer, I saw a nondescript van with one too many antennas on top. It had to be the *Midwest Focus* camera vehicle. Alex had said they'd be lingering close. Figuring she might be inside, I paused next to it and rapped on the back doors. I heard a couple of voices inside abruptly stop talking. The windows were all smoked glass, totally opaque from the outside. When no one responded, I knocked a bit harder. Finally, a bearded, male face popped out and asked me what I wanted.

"I'm Ron Shade. Alex St. James hired me to—"

The guy cut me off. "Yeah, yeah, I know. She's over there already. With the blue hat on."

In the fading evening light I saw her svelte form. I thanked the van geek and strode toward the lady in the blue hat. I was only about fifty yards away. She'd arrived early, because it wasn't even seven-fifteen yet. Maybe she was going to pay me by the hour and had to round everything off. In any case, I decided to have some fun. Instead of acknowledging her, I kept walking right past, letting my eyes linger on her. In a few seconds she was right beside me.

"Hey," she whispered.

I did an exaggerated jump. "Beat it, panhandler."

She frowned. "Come on, don't tell me you don't recognize me."

I made another exaggerated show of studying her, during which her lips scrunched together and she looked like she was about ready to smack me. I reached in my pocket, took out my wallet, and removed a dollar bill. "Here, go buy yourself some deodorant."

Her eyes widened in anger and she literally snatched the buck out of my hand and shoved it into her pants pocket. "Very funny."

"Ms. St. James?" I asked, doing my best to imbue surprise into my tone. "I'm sorry. I thought you were a good-looking bag lady."

Her expression softened slightly and she rolled her eyes. "Give me another dollar."

"What?"

"I don't want to make it too obvious that we know each other. I'm supposed to be undercover here."

I got my wallet out again and looked through it. I had only fives, tens, and twenties. I took out a five and handed it to her. "Here, you can buy the coffee when this thing is through. What time is that going to be, by the way?"

"I'm hoping to creep away by midnight. We should have all the shots we need by then." She glanced around, then tugged the sleeve of my field jacket, pulling me toward an alley. "I'm not real concerned about those three guys anymore, but anyway, that's why you're earning a paycheck tonight, right?"

"Roger wilco," I said, and watched her move away, back toward the viaduct. The pants she had on were tight enough to show the outline of her ass, which made me regret my promise to George. But then again, I was dealing with a classic ice princess anyway.

I decided to get the lay of the land, which was something I always do when working a particular place. I combed through the alley area, then went around to the embankment a bit farther down. The expressway roared above us, buttressed by angular concrete blocks that extended the roadway over Grisham. Where the elevation ended and the bridge part began, an unintentional shelter from the elements had resulted. It was sad to think of people living under there. But then again, the homeless had always roamed the city, except in the old days they'd been called bums.

I walked back toward the congregation, checking out the businesses and houses on the block. Mostly empty lots, but farther down were a neighborhood liquor store and a dilapidated gas station that had more reinforcements in the windows than Fort Knox.

I looked at the motley collection shuffling through the Dumpster in back of the liquor store. One guy came out with a rolled up bag of potato chips. His teeth had almost as many gaps in them as the street had potholes. He stuffed his treasure into his pocket and continued digging. One guy staggered along the sidewalk and came up to me.

"Hey, mister, spare any change?" His bleary eyes stared at me like a lost puppy's. Maybe he'd seen me giving money to Alex. I felt sorry for him, but I knew if I got made as an easy mark, they'd be on me like a horde of seagulls. And I was here to do a job, which meant I couldn't afford any distractions.

"Beat it," I said, using my cop voice. "Before I call for a squad car."

The guy's eyes widened. "You the po-lice?"

"Yeah, now scram."

He scurried off and I pondered the wisdom of my ruse. It might make the locals less responsive to Alex St. James's camera needs, but it would make my job a helluva lot easier. An ounce of prevention, my mother always used to say.

Not that I wasn't totally prepared for tonight. On the contrary, in addition to having my Beretta and enough extra mags to fight a small war, I had my trusty pepper spray, a kuboton, my folding, double-bladed knife, and a set of nunchucks tucked inside my belt on the left side. In the hands of someone who knows how to use them, they could reduce a threatening crowd to mishmash in about thirty-five seconds. I strolled down toward the grassy knoll, looking for Alex. Now that I had my bearings, and spread some intimidation around, I figured I'd better keep an eye on her. After all, that was what I was getting paid to do.

Alex St. James

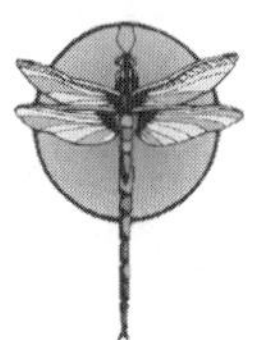

It was with an unpleasant sense of déjà vu that I settled myself under the viaduct a second time, disguised as a homeless woman. What a way for a girl to spend a Saturday night.

Rita and Lew were, again, stationed in the sound truck, though this time they parked a little closer to the action.

With Jesse still recuperating, I needed another camera person. The only one willing to take on the challenge was Hal, a longtime employee, about thirty years older than Jesse, and about sixty pounds heavier. Hal was a gem, but I worried for his inability to be discreet. The guy was a nonstop talker. Homeless people needed a gentler touch.

I'd made some significant adjustments to this outing. I decided against the smelly clothing from Father Morales. In fact, I'd thrown that stuff away. I couldn't help but wonder if he'd really given me those malodorous items as part of his plan to dissuade me from going. Tonight, I wore the used garments Bass had originally provided—they were clean, at least—and I chose not to let Father Morales or Nicky know my plans for a repeat engagement.

Again, Jordan would be proud. Nicky had asked me when I planned to revisit the viaduct, and I'd lied and told him that I wasn't even considering going back till next week at least.

This time, I had control. I made sure that everything was perfectly arranged. And, the best part, the part that made me feel the most secure, was Ron Shade's presence on the scene. For the first time since I'd been assigned this story, I felt safe, with someone who knew what he was doing watching my back.

Hal, sporting his miniature camera, walked the location three times before sitting on a grassy patch to the far side of the cement incline. "Gotta sit on the grass," I heard him say to little Gus, "my back aches, and I got a touch of sciatica." He looked around. "Where do I go if I gotta go?"

Gus inched away. I didn't blame him.

Shade had disappeared. I sat with my back to the metal post, my butt perched on the edge of the cement pillar, and tried to see where he went. I didn't want to be too obvious—the last thing I needed was to have the local population pay too much attention to my actions—but it was disconcerting to have him out of sight.

I pretended to be fascinated with the streetlight over my left shoulder, and used the time to scan the viaduct's underside. I couldn't see him anywhere. Not that my subterfuge mattered. The folks beneath the expressway were all involved in their own matters, whether it be babbling to themselves, sorting their belongings, or sleeping.

"Looking for someone?" a male voice said.

I spun. It was Shade.

"There you are," I said. "Where did you go?"

"I wanted to get a feel for the place. Check things out."

I frowned slightly, thinking about what might have happened if those three boors would have shown up, but then realized that the chances of that were minimal since I'd thrown Nicky off the scent.

"In the army we called it recon," he said. "Short for reconnoitering."

"The importance of familiarizing oneself with the surroundings for those just-in-case moments?"

He nodded. He was wearing an old military field jacket that looked older than he was.

"Is that from your army days?" I asked.

He shook his head and pointed to USMC stamped in black letters above the left pocket. "It belonged to my buddy George. He was in the marines back in 'Nam. Now he works for CPD as a detective."

"George? What's his last name?"

"Grieves. Why?"

I smiled. "I've got a friend on Chicago, too, who's a detective and his name is George. But his last name is Lulinski."

"Good Irish name," he said with a grin.

"Speaking of names, do you know a Nicky Farnsworth?"

Shade considered the name, looked pensive, then shook his head. "Doesn't ring any bells. He a cop, too?"

"Hardly."

Loud grunting caused us both to look up. A man, high up on

the embankment stood bent in half, pants around his ankles, holding his stomach, moaning.

"Oh geez," I said.

"Real classy joint you picked." Shade grinned. "But I guess you're dressed for it."

I looked at him. "You know, you don't look much like a homeless person."

"Don't you think I look scruffy enough?"

The last thing I wanted to do was offend my security detail. "Well, I guess every homeless person started out clean at some time."

At that he'd smiled. I thought about Jordan's suggestion to think of this guy as more than the hired help, but recent events, and the desire to get this story done without distraction worked more powerfully on me than the prospect of dating again. It was easier to think of Shade as a big brother–type.

He was brawny and powerful-looking. He looked more like the three guys who'd accosted me than the people who actually lived here. "You're here to get a story," he said with a shrug. "I'm here to make sure you stay safe." Thrusting his chin toward the rest of the inhabitants he said, "These people aren't paying me a bit of attention. And that's good. You go about what you need to do, and I'll make sure it stays quiet."

And so I did.

The first person I talked with didn't know Howard Rybak, or maybe she just didn't care to admit that she did. I could've sworn the name registered when I'd asked her. The second person, a man who looked to be in his seventies, stared at me with close-set vacant eyes. I sat next to him—not too close—this guy reeked so badly of body excretions my eyes watered. "Dunno," he said, when I mentioned Rybak's name. I was about to turn, relieved to get away, when he asked, "He the one got new teeth?"

I didn't know what that meant, or if he was even talking to me. His gaze seemed fixed somewhere over my right shoulder.

"I'm not sure," I said. "Howard. You know him?"

The elderly guy must've had something stuck in his own tooth because he worked his stubbled, doughy face back and forth, side to side, like a masticating giraffe.

My nose seemed to take on a life of its own, fighting to leap off my face.

"What's your name?" I asked, holding the back of my hand near my face.

He stopped chewing. "Brewster."

"Brewster. That's a nice name."

More chewing.

"I'll be right back," I said, jumping to my feet. I scurried over to the curb. Even with hot stinky air blowing up from its sewers, the street was a way better place to breathe. I leaned forward, hands on knees, working air in through my nose and out my mouth.

"What's wrong?"

I lifted my eyes to see Shade there, looking concerned. "Holy geez," I said. "That guy stinks."

He chuckled. "I told you. These homeless people aren't like you see in movies or on TV. These people live out here. They eat, sleep, they . . ." he shrugged and glanced up toward the scene of the pants-dropping. "They do everything out here."

"Yeah."

"You okay? You going to throw up?"

"No," I said with asperity. "I'm not a wimp." I softened my tone as I straightened. "I just needed a few breaths. Something to clear this . . . ick . . . out of my nose."

"It can stay with you," he said, commiserating. "I've been there."

"I think there's smell memory," I said, turning to face Brewster again, gearing myself up for another round of aromatic questions. "Do you wear aftershave?"

"Not usually."

"Men's cologne?"

"Why, you planning on buying me a present?"

I laughed.

"No," I said, "it's just that there's this guy I know who wears too much cologne. Every time I see him, I smell him for the rest of the day."

"Maybe you should ask your boyfriend for some of his strong smelling stuff to give to that dude."

"He's not my boyfriend," I said, shooting him a disparaging glance. "Believe me."

"Well maybe that guy's available." He grinned and pointed toward Brewster.

"I'm worried that his fragrance is going to stay with me even longer." With that discouraging thought in mind, I returned to talk with Brewster, staying far enough away to keep the nasties at bay.

"Howard Rybak," I began, trying to jar Brewster into awareness with mention of the name. "You know him, huh?"

He stared at some middle distance. Chewing again. But his eyes reacted.

"Hard times out here?" I asked.

Nothing.

"How long have you been on the street?"

Brewster stopped chewing. Blinked. "What year is this?"

I told him.

"Twenty-two."

I couldn't stop my exclamation. "You've been out here for twenty-two years?"

He didn't seem to be bothered by my shock. "Not just here. I been places. Been lotsa places." His mouth worked the phantom food. "Seems longer than twenty-two years. Seems my whole life."

All of a sudden discussing the success story that was Howard Rybak seemed cruel. I was about to stand—to find another interviewee—when Brewster looked me straight on. "Wish I could get the good deal he got."

"Who?"

"That guy."

"Rybak?"

He nodded, his gaze zooming off again. "Wish I could get what he got. Even if I might get dead." Brewster spread his lips, pointed to rotted out teeth. "New ones. Good ones. He looked real good."

"Rybak did?"

Brewster sighed. "Nice teeth. New ones. He come back to show us. Brought us food. And then he was gone. If I got new teeth, I'd be gone, too."

At that the old man started to cry. I was completely at a loss of what to do, how to react. I couldn't very well put my arm around him. Nor would I want to. He'd probably see it as an attempt to steal something.

I got up, brushed my backside and thanked Brewster.

He didn't even know I left.

Hal intercepted me on my way to talking with a woman curled up in a fetal position.

"You getting anything worthwhile?" he asked.

Disgusted, I shook my head. "Don't know."

"Who's this guy you keep asking about?"

I explained.

"So you think that if you can track this guy down, you might be able to avoid living among the undead?"

Casting a glance around all the people I'd thought of as zombies, I agreed. "That's the plan."

"Tell you what. I'll see what I can come up with—I'll talk with some of the folks near me."

"Thank, Hal," I said. It couldn't hurt.

He climbed up the embankment and I headed to the pillar.

When I got close to the fetal-positioned woman, I thought it might have been Vicky, the woman who'd coerced me for a handout at Father Morales', but it wasn't. This woman was about the same size and build, but older. A lot older.

"How are you doing?" I asked her.

"Why?"

I lowered myself to sit next to her. She had an unpleasant scent around her, but it was nowhere near the world-class stink that surrounded Brewster. "Just want to talk," I said.

"You talk different."

I'd given up the imperfect grammar. It was difficult to maintain, and until right now, apparently unnecessary. No one under this bridge cared how I talked. They went about their business as though they expected oddities, and when some surfaced—me, for example—they took the new development in stride.

Either that, or they were all so out of it that no one really noticed.

Except this woman here. Maybe she noticed other things as well.

"What's your name?"

She sat up, stared at me for a long, uncomfortable moment. "Ugly bitch."

Taken aback, I didn't know what to say.

She laughed, showing teeth almost as bad as Brewster's. "No, I ain't being rude. That's what everybody calls me around here. But you ain't from here, are you?"

"I'm from nearby."

"Sure," she said, rolling her eyes. She worked her mouth, a

lot like Brewster had. I wondered if it was a symptom of bad dental hygiene, or a ghost movement, prompted by wishful memory of eating real food. Whatever it was, it gave her a moment to think as she scrutinized me. "Name's Iris."

"I'm Alex," I said, encouraged by the interaction. "So, Iris, how long have you been on the street?"

"You don't wanna know."

"I do."

She licked her lips. "You ain't here to be my friend, so why don't you cut the shit? What is it you want? You looking for action? Cuz me, I like men, myself. But if the price is right—"

Revulsion must have showed on my face because she stopped herself. Got angry.

"Then what the hell do you want, Miss Priss? You come down here. You talk to us. You gotta be here because you want something. Because if you—"

I cut her short. "I want information."

That took her aback. She twisted her face into an exaggerated frown, but I could tell I'd piqued her curiosity. "What the hell kind of information do I have that can do you any good?"

"For starters," I said, "does the name Howard Rybak mean anything to you?"

Her eyes narrowed. "Shit."

I waited.

"Who are you with?" she asked.

I knew better than to bullshit. I pointed to Hal, who was desperately working on chatting up Gus. "Him."

She gave me another hyper-frown. "Ain't what I mean."

"Then what do you mean?"

She stared at me, squinting as though trying to read a hidden message in my eyes. "Us . . . here," she gestured to encompass everyone in the immediate area, "are in the dog pound. You know?"

I didn't but I nodded.

"And sometimes they come getcha." She snatched at my arm but didn't touch. "Now is it good that they getcha, or is it bad?"

Trying desperately to follow her logic, I said, "I guess that depends on who's getting you."

Her eyes lit up. "You're a smart cookie."

"Did somebody 'get' Howard Rybak?"

She nodded.

"Who was it?"

I'd gotten used to the smell, so when she leaned in close, it didn't bother me. But her whispers shot hot, rancid breath—a new nasty scent—my direction. "Sometimes it's like . . . like a nice family, picking out a puppy to take home," she said with a knowing look. "But most times, well, most times it's money-grubbers who want to steal what we got. So they lead us away and promise us treats and tell us they're our friends." Another look. "But the whole time they're just fixing to put us to sleep. Like dogs."

When she leaned away again, I tried to put it all together. "Which way was it for Howard Rybak?" I asked slowly. "Did he get the good home, or is he . . . being promised treats?"

Treats in exchange for what? I wondered. This made no sense. Why would anyone promise homeless people "treats" just to lead them away? Taking them from their homes, such as they were, required dedication and commitment if the goal was to find them better lives. It was an enormous responsibility. And it didn't make sense.

"So *who* you with?" she asked me again.

I shook my head. "I'm just looking for Howard Rybak."

"No treats for Howie," Iris said. "No treats no more."

"Why not?"

"He's gone."

I knew that. "Gone where?" I asked.

Her face crinkled into a frightening smile. "You're the smart cookie. You figure it out."

Chapter 15

Ron Shade

Bright and early Monday morning I was heading north on the tollway once again, en route to MWO. I'd spent most of Sunday at my desk trying to sort out the who's and why's of this thing. I was convinced that the horse laugh Herb Winthrope had heard in that Vegas casino was indeed, the presumed dead Robert Bayless. He'd obviously set up his demise to start a new life in parts unknown, and somehow he'd managed to recruit a host of characters to help him. That was what was bothering me. How had he done it? Offering someone a cool million seemed like an easy enough answer, and his life insurance would have provided plenty of cash to spread around. But would it be enough? And what gave Bayless enough control or leverage over the insurance money distribution and everybody on board? How much dough had Bayless promised to spread around? And how much had he kept for himself and how would he arrange that? I kept thinking of the old maxim, crime always follows the dollars.

The obvious defect in the plan was that he'd involved way too many people. Possibly the Manus Corporation flunky that

I'd talked to and Dr. Colon for the false ID. And then there was the disposable, breathing, body that conveniently took Bayless's place in the wrecked car. Who was he, and where did he come from? Since the corpse was picked up by some Russians, and it was most likely some Russkies who'd tried to take me out, the funeral-home guy who smelled like a cologne ad was probably in on the fun, too. And a funeral home like that one probably wouldn't have too much trouble procuring a body, even if it was still breathing. That was a lot of people. Like any big conspiracy, it was only as strong as its weakest link. All I had to do was find that link and work on breaking it. Which I aimed to do.

My answering service had relayed a call from Dick MacKenzie last night. He wanted a progress report.

Well, let's see, Dick, I imagined as I drove. I've been downstate, found a few holes in the scheme, and made some people nervous enough to try to kill me. How's that for progress?

Our real conversation was much more protracted, with me explaining just about everything I'd learned thus far.

Dick scratched his forehead, which looked more wrinkled than a dried-out prune. He heaved a sigh. "So what you're saying, in effect, Ron, is that you pretty much confirm our suspicions that this claim is fishy, but you're lacking any cold, hard proof."

He hadn't phrased it as a question, so I made no effort to answer him.

His eyebrows rose in unison, exacerbating the prune effect. "Well?"

"Well, I'm confirming your suspicions that this claim is a little fishy, and I'm lacking any cold, hard proof." I grinned. "At the moment."

His lips worked together, like he was busy chewing something, or else trying to contain the mouthful of words he was thinking of spitting at me.

"I need more time," I said, figuring I'd better not go out of my way to antagonize him.

"I expected more from you," he said. "With all the business we toss your way, the big retainer fee we pay you, the least the company could expect is some exclusivity."

Exclusivity? I never liked that word. I wanted to ask him if he had other clients. Like it was okay for him to divide his time and make money, but for me it was violating some horseshit sacred trust called "exclusivity." But, I took a deep breath, held it for a few seconds, then slowly exhaled. "I could argue that this entire matter eluded your original adjustors, but I won't. I could also mention that I was called in because *the company* screwed this one up, and now wants me to bail them out." I paused. "But I won't. What I will do is tell you that I've got a personal stake in this one now."

"Personal?"

"I've made some people pretty nervous. Some guys tried to whack me the other night."

"My God." His forehead crinkled again. "You don't think they'd come after anyone here at the company, do you?"

His concern for my welfare was touching, but I knew when to capitalize on an opening. "Not if I can run them to ground first. I'm working on it."

He nodded, his lips compressing inward now, like he was contemplating a trip to parts unknown until this was settled.

"I'm pretty sure that dentist, Colon, is involved," I said. "And some knucklehead who owns the funeral home that took care of the body. There's still too many variables, though. We need to make an end-run play."

"How do we do that?"

"I need some more time to bring Bayless back, alive and well. Or at least some kind of proof that it isn't him in that cemetery plot pushing up daisies."

His eyes narrowed. "You think you can do that?"

"I'm ready for round two, with your blessings, of course." I'd already set a few things in motion, but I figured I'd give him the false pleasure of giving his imprimatur.

"Go for it," he said, using what he probably thought was his best Sylvester Stallone as Rocky imitation.

When I got to my car I sat in the parking lot and called George on my cell. Luckily, there hadn't been any murders, rapes, or robberies yet, and he was in the office.

"I was just gonna call you," he said. "Cate and Norris need to talk. Plus, I got that info you were looking for. Want to stop by and get it? I'll buy you lunch."

Obviously, I was still riding the crest of the wave for the Bielmaster thing. I decided to press that advantage before it ran out. "Hey, how about running a couple more for me?"

"All right." From his tone I gathered that the golden goose was on precarious ice.

I gave him the rest of the plates I'd collected from the Manus parking lot and asked him to see what he could find out about Candice Prokovis. I gave him the address Francis had given me.

"Who's she?"

"Used to be the dead-guy-who's-still-alive's secretary."

I heard him chuckle. "I'm sure glad you're handling this one. I'd never be able to keep all that crap straight."

"Believe me, I've got it all on a big flowchart. Think you could get me an I-Clear DL retrieval image of her? And one of my buddy Bob Bayless, too?"

"Sounds like a violation of the Drivers' License Privacy Protection Act," he said.

I hesitated. "Does that mean you ain't gonna do it?"

I heard him chuckle. "Nah, that's a federal law. Nobody minds if you stretch them a bit, right? Look at your income tax return."

"A license to steal."

"Damn straight."

It sounded like the good mood lingered, so I figured why not push the envelope? "Hey, one more thing. I'm pretty sure her license is going to come back as surrendered to a foreign state. See if you can get me her new address."

"Anything else, Prince Ron?"

"Nah, that'll do for now," I said.

"You know," he said, "on second thought, why don't you bring your royal, high-maintenance ass over here so you can buy *me* lunch?"

"What's up with Cate and Norris?"

"They spent the weekend checking all the hospitals and clinics for a guy with a gunshot wound."

"Any luck?"

"Plenty, but none of them looks like our guy. They also talked to that Farnsworth asshole. He denies ever meeting you."

"Farnsworth? Who's that?"

"The fucking guy who owns the Sunset Manor Funeral Home," he said. "Plus, he also says he don't have no Russians working for him."

"He told me his name was Jones. The son of a bitch lied about that, he's probably lying about the Russkies, too."

"No shit. But the guy's father is a lawyer and told him not to say anything else."

"Shit. A lawyer."

"Don't worry, I'm in the process of checking him out. I should have that info for you, too, by the time you get here to buy me the biggest, fattest steak sandwich we can find."

"I'm on my way," I said, but what I was thinking was I needed to get hold of Ms. Alex St. James, pronto.

Alex St. James

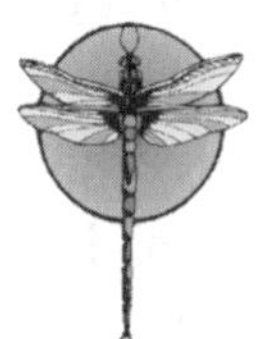

The next day, after lunch, I struck out for Howard Rybak's last known address. By the time I'd gotten home from the "reconnoitering" under the viaduct it had been after two. I'd talked with several other homeless folks, and come up mostly empty. So had Hal. Except for the occasional mention of teeth and gifts of food, nobody knew anything about their old friend Howie. And no one had a clue where he'd gone. Even after I'd pressed Iris for more information, she'd confessed that she didn't know for sure, though she was convinced that his "escape" only served to set the dogcatchers after him again.

Why hadn't Nicky provided Rybak's address when I'd asked for it? I pondered that question as I stood before a six-flat apartment building in a rundown section on Chicago's North Side. What had once been a pristine neighborhood of well-maintained three-flats and bungalows, with the occasional apartment building thrown in, was now a collection of boarded-up homes with black soot from old fires, dirt front lawns and empty lots where someone had obviously said, "Enough!" and begun razing.

This was not yet one of Chicago's rediscovered gems waiting for gentrification. This was a slum. The apartment building before me set out like a very wide red brick "U." Three stories tall, there appeared to be two apartments per floor on each of the building's three sides. That meant eighteen apartments in all.

At the center of the squared-off U was a courtyard that, at some point in the building's history, probably boasted a carpet of grass, clipped shrubbery, and a sea of proud hostas. Now four small fields of dirt bisected by two broken sidewalks, with a tree in each of the area's quadrants, made up the sum total of the landscaping.

I made my way to the center door, the base of the U, hoping something in there would direct me to the building's office. Just as I made it to the wood-framed glass door, a dark-haired man emerged. Pale, forty-ish, with salt-and-pepper hair and mustache, he looked clean-cut enough to not belong in this area. He waited in the doorway, chewing and cracking gum, until I walked up, his furry eyebrows upraised.

"Excuse me, are you the landlord?"

"How 'ju know that?"

Despite the North Side address this guy talked like an original southsider.

"Lucky guess," I said.

He gave me the once-over. "You ain't wanting to rent," he said. "You wouldn't last a week in this neighborhood." He made a show of looking up and down the street, still chewing the wad of gum. When I caught sight of his brown teeth, I started to wonder if it was tobacco in there. "You here by yourself?"

I started to answer, thought better of it. "Do you have a few minutes?"

He stopped, snagged the wad of white between his incisors. It was gum, after all. "You a cop?"

"I want to ask you about Howard Rybak," I said. "If you have a few minutes."

"Rybak? That shithead."

"He used to live here, didn't he?"

The landlord opened his mouth to answer, then stopped himself. "You got a name? What's it to you? Rybak your uncle or something?"

I introduced myself. "And you are . . . ?"

"Joe Smeraldi," he said. "My brother and I own the place. We share this, and another property and a plumbing business." He shrugged and looked at the place over his shoulder. "We keep an apartment here between us in case we got to spend the night ever. It ain't too bad. But we both live someplace else." Giving a mock shiver, he smiled.

So this is what an absent landlord looked like. For some reason I always pictured business-suited rich men in corner offices, ordering evictions between sips of caffeinated beverages.

As though he read my mind, Joe added, "I ain't no slumlord. We keep this place nice for the people we rent to. And we're careful about who we let stay here, too. My brother Tony and I figure a couple more years and the yuppies are gonna move this direction. Then we're gonna sell. Make a bundle."

"About Howard Rybak," I began.

"Hang on, you want a cup of coffee or something?" Joe stepped back into the miniature foyer that housed a broken tile floor and eighteen mailbox slots. He used a key to open the door immediately behind him. "I ain't no masher, and I was just going out for another six-pack, 'cause I'm running low. 'Course, it's not like I need it." He patted his pregnant-size stomach. "I can't tell you much, but you still ain't told me why you're looking for the guy."

Joe Smeraldi's easy demeanor and pear-like physique reminded me that sometimes in this business it's better to go with your gut. I said, "Sure," and followed him in.

The ground-floor apartment smelled of damp carpeting, cigarettes, and Lysol. There was no clutter. There was almost nothing. A fake-woodgrain, two-chair table sat atop green linoleum in the kitchen, a folded newspaper, crushed beer can and full ashtray dead center. "You want something?" He opened the fridge. "How about an Old Style? Got one left."

"No," I said, too quickly.

"I got a Diet Coke in here, too."

"No thanks."

He popped open the beer and took a swig, grabbing a chair and gesturing for me to take the other. The table wobbled when he planted his elbows on its edge. "So you never said why you're asking about Rybak."

I started in, describing my plans for the feature story. I was interrupted twice when he found out I worked with Gabriela—is she really that pretty in real life? Is she single?—to which I answered yes, and yes.

That apparently made his day. Grinning, he said, "Tell me what you want to know about Howard. You think I'll be on TV? Maybe get to meet Gabriela?"

I fingered my brown hair. Blondes *did* have more fun. "When was the last time you saw Howard Rybak?"

Smeraldi rubbed his chin. "Dunno."

"A year ago? Six months?"

He chewed the inside of his cheek. "Definitely before he left. He was past due on his rent by about a week or so, and I stopped by here. Couldn't find him. My brother, Tony, tried three times that week. We figured he was trying to ditch us, but . . ." he spread out his hands.

"But . . . what?"

"He was gone. Like gone for good, gone. There was food left on his table, like he was planning to come back, and when Tony and I finally decided we better come in and have a look-see, it was all maggoty. Looked like the inside of my garbage cans after a week in the sun."

Well, thanks for that visual, Joe.

He continued, "I was thinking that maybe we were going to find old Howard dead in the bedroom or something, but Tony says that we would of smelled him by then." Joe gave a little shrug. "Tony's older'n me."

I wanted to ask him why Tony's age had anything to do with it, but he went on. "I don't know what happened to the guy. This had to be like around December. Yeah. It was around Christmas. I was thinking that maybe he was late on this payment because of the holidays and all, but then I was thinking that he didn't have nobody to buy nothing for, so what was up with that? That's when me and Tony went in."

"And found the old food?"

"Yeah. All his stuff was still just where I woulda' left it if I was living there, and so we waited a month, figuring he'd come back, but he never did."

"Why did you wait?"

"Security deposit," Smeraldi said. "We take a first and last month's rent up front just in case of something like this. Usually when people skip out, they take their stuff with them, though."

"I thought he had a job in the area."

"Yeah, I thought so, too. He put it on the reference sheet, you know. Tony made me go over there to talk to them."

"Who did he work for?"

"Some funeral home."

"Sunset Manor?"

He snapped his fingers. "Yeah, that was it. How 'ju know?"

Another lucky guess. This one felt a little bit too lucky. How come Nicky hadn't mentioned this tidbit? "The guy who owns the funeral home, Nick. He supposedly arranged for Rybak to rent this apartment."

Smeraldi gave a snort. "That guy."

"What's wrong with him?"

Squint. "You ain't here because he told you to come, are you?"

"No," I said. "In fact, I had to get this address from somebody else. Nick wouldn't give it to me."

"Figures," he said. "There's something weird about that guy. And not just that he pumps blood out of dead bodies. When I went to go talk to him—to see if he knew anything about Rybak—he got all jumpy and said that the guy had taken off on him and left no forwarding." Smeraldi shrugged. "I didn't expect he was going to be any help. But then I asked him what I should do with all the stuff left in the apartment."

I sat up. "Do you still have it?"

"That's the thing," Smeraldi said. "This funeral guy tells me to dump it all. Give it to Goodwill or toss it. But what if the guy comes back? I asked him. I figure if I hold onto his stuff, I got some leverage here. The place stayed vacant for three full months before I was able to re-rent. If Rybak wants his stuff, he's going to have to fork over the back rent."

I could feel my excitement mounting. Something was wrong. Definitely wrong here. But there might be a chance of finding a clue in Rybak's personal stuff. "So you kept it?"

"You gonna go running to the funeral guy?"

"No."

"I told him I dumped it all. He came here twice to make sure I did. I said yeah, and he went away. Haven't seen him around since. But, I kept everything. I figure I'll sell what I can. Make a few bucks. Not that there's anything real good in there."

"Can I take a look?"

Smeraldi's eyes narrowed. "What are you looking for?"

I lifted my shoulders. "Not sure. I'll know it if I find it. And . . ." I thought fast. "If I find anything I want to take, I'll pay you for it."

He didn't seem convinced.

"It'll be easier than you having to take the whole bunch to the flea market."

"And you said something about me getting on TV about all this, huh?"

I hadn't said that, exactly. But it wasn't impossible. "Could be."

"With that Gabriela?"

I couldn't lie this time. "No. This one's my story. If you're on at all, it'll be with me. Sorry."

With a grudging nod, he stood. "Eh, you're a babe, too. Just in a different way. Come on. I have his stuff in boxes in the basement."

Scant light filtered in from the dank basement's tiny above-ground windows, the sunshine marred by dirt and criss-crossing spider webs. There were four coin-operated washing machines and dryers at the room's far end and a series of padlocked wooden stalls at the other, each numbered to correspond to an apartment. The area was surprisingly free of clutter, except for some dilapidated furniture that took up most of one corner. Piled there so as to take up minimal floor space, the stuff was pressboard-cheap and covered with gray dust.

"I keep Rybak's stuff in my locker," Smeraldi said as he moved to one of the big doors and pulled out his keys. "Had to empty the one for Rybak's apartment so the new people could load their stuff."

The door swung open, scraping against the concrete floor. Smeraldi walked in and tugged at a pull-chain lightbulb. Not nearly enough illumination to see into the stall's far corners. But it'd have to do.

"Is all of this his?"

He started to pull boxes from the right side. "Nope. My brother and I keep stuff down here we don't want the wives to see." I expected some self-conscious gesture, but he offered none. "Nothing terrible. Just some girlie magazines. I got a bunch of *Playboy*s down here that're collectors' items. Worth big bucks."

"Isn't it a little damp down here for paper?"

"Yeah, I know. But I got them protected. I check 'em every so often. Here . . ." He tugged at a capped brown box with built-in handles. "Here's one of Rybak's boxes. He's got maybe two . . . three more. His furniture's the stuff we passed in the other part of the basement. Too big to fit in here and too junky to worry about anybody stealing it. But if you see something you like . . ."

I doubted I would.

Taking the box from Smeraldi, I lifted the lid and rearranged myself so I wasn't blocking the solitary lightbulb's glow. While I scavenged, he pulled out another box and several plastic garbage bags.

"You want a chair to sit while you go through this stuff?"

Chalk one up for the gallant Joe Smeraldi.

"Thanks," I said.

He pulled up two and sat next to me. Whether to help me search, or to ensure I didn't steal anything, I didn't know and didn't care.

A half hour later, I wiped sweaty dust off my forehead. As I'd expected of a formerly homeless guy, Howard Rybak hadn't accumulated much clothing. Blue jeans and work shirts mostly. But then I found an open three-pack of men's briefs. Polo by Ralph Lauren. One pair missing. I held the package up. "He wore designer underwear?"

Smeraldi held up both hands. "Don't ask me."

Further digging unearthed an opened pack of matching designer undershirts. One missing. "You'd think he'd spend his money on the basics before he'd start buying designer stuff," I said, half to myself.

Smeraldi took the packages. "These'd be too small on me." He patted his beer belly again and it dawned on me that he was proud of it. "I wear forty-eights. You want 'em? Maybe your boyfriend fits in a thirty-six."

Thinking about my feature story, I said, "Yeah, I'll take them." Who would've expected a homeless fellow to shop for high-end stuff? Designer underwear that, presumably, few would ever see. It was odd and quirky, but it was just the sort of detail that viewers might like. "How much do you want for them?"

He made a so-so shake of his head and suggested we keep looking and hammer out a final agreement once I picked through the whole stash.

An hour later I decided I'd gotten all I could from this venture. There wasn't a lot of personality here, and no indication of where Howard Rybak may have run to. Why would a man who had been homeless for years, who'd been given a chance at a more normal lifestyle, give it all up? It didn't make sense. Nor did the fact that when he took off, he left his belongings. Then again, maybe he took as much as he could carry.

But I didn't think so. He'd left his toiletries: his shaver, toothbrush, comb, nail clippers. The argument could be made that if he was returning to the street, he wouldn't need all that, but he'd left a five-dollar bill in one jeans' pocket, a couple of singles in another pocket, and the pocket of a spring jacket had a ten. Would he really leave the money here?

Joe Smeraldi's eyes lit up when we uncovered the cash. I had no doubt that the moment I left, he'd be back down here, scrounging it and calling it fair play.

There was one item in one of the jeans' pockets that I decided was worth keeping. It was a dental appointment card, reminding Rybak that he had a six-month cleaning scheduled for this month. Dr. Keith Colon. This meant that Dr. Colon had seen Rybak in December. Just about the time he disappeared. Maybe he could offer a clue.

I knew my feature story was supposed to be about the homeless. I knew that I'd strong-armed Bass into letting me focus on

Rybak's "success." Right about now, however, this investigation had morphed from a second-string feature into a much bigger story. What I had here was a solid missing-persons case.

Chapter 16

Alex St. James

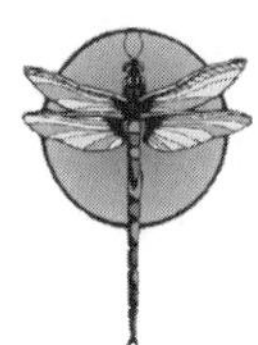

Monday morning, I pulled into the small asphalt parking lot that served a strip mall in Rogers Park. Dr. Keith Colon's business took up one of the smaller storefronts of the shopping area, its generic "Dental Practice" sign in unlit red neon above the door. Just after nine in the morning, the place should've been open.

I tugged at the glass door, but it didn't budge. Cupping my hands over my eyes, I peered in and caught sight of a young woman walking around in the back of the office, behind a reception window. I knocked.

She glanced up, startled, then took a look at her watch and frowned. Coming to the door, she turned the deadbolt with a loud metallic click and held the door open for me. "Sorry," she said. "I forgot to open up. Do you have an appointment?"

"Actually, I'm just here to talk with Dr. Colon. Is he in?"

Looking perplexed, she shook her head. "His first appointment's at nine-thirty, but he usually comes in a little early. What's this about?" The way she sized me up, I bet she thought

I was here to apply for her job.

"You know," I said, affecting my new lie-all-the-time persona, "a friend of mine has his dental work done here. But before I switch over, I thought I'd stop by and talk with the doctor . . ."

I let the thought hang there, hoping she'd pick up. She didn't. But at least the suspicious glares were gone.

"You say he'll be in soon?" I asked.

"Who's the friend who recommended us?" she asked.

This girl was sharper than I gave her credit for.

We were still standing in the doorway, and I gave a sideways look into the waiting room. "Can I come in?"

"Sure," she said, stepping out of my path.

Once inside, I meandered toward the near corner. Taking a seat here would put me in position to see into the back office. When Dr. Colon arrived, I'd know it. "Nice magazine selection," I said. I picked up a copy of *Entertainment Weekly,* sat and opened it as though ready to read.

The girl bit her lip, but smiled. "I have some filing to catch up on, so I'll leave you here."

"Thanks."

She started away, then stopped. Definitely something on her mind. "While I'm filing, maybe I should pull your friend's chart for Dr. Colon to refer to before you talk with him." Her forced smile left me no option.

"Sure," I said, wondering why this was such a big deal. "His name is Howard Rybak."

"Oh." She smiled.

"Do you know him?"

"No. Well, I'm sure I met him when he's been in. I just don't remember him."

"What's your name?"

"Mine?" Suddenly happy as a clam to talk with me, she produced a genuine smile. "Janet."

Acting on a hunch, I decided to push my luck just a bit. I affected a conspiratorial tone. "You expected me to say something else, didn't you?"

She laughed like we were girlfriends now. "No, it's just weird, is all. The other day some guy came in here asking about somebody, too. I thought maybe you were here for the same guy."

"Guess not," I said.

"I hope Dr. Colon doesn't get all shook up about it like he did with the other guy."

"Shook up?"

"Yeah," she said. "I guess it's hard though, you know, to know what to say and what not to say when there's all these privacy laws."

"Yeah," I said. When Janet moved toward the files I hit her with another question. "Does Dr. Colon do a lot of work for the homeless?"

"Oh!" she said, her eyes wide. "Okay, I remember Howard Rybak now. *He's* a friend of yours?"

"Sort of," I lied. "I work for a television program and we're doing a story on his success getting off the street and into mainstream America."

"Wow," she said. "Cool."

"I understand he's been here for his dental work. I assume that means Dr. Colon takes care of other indigent people."

She shrugged. "Some. He doesn't really like to, but it's good for business. Goodwill and all that." Wrinkling her nose, she said, "But some of the homeless really stink. Usually they try to clean them up a bit before they bring them here."

"They?" I asked. "Who's they?"

She canted her head. "I don't know exactly who they are. Helpers, I guess. Maybe workers from a soup kitchen."

I thought about Nicky's friend Viktor. He didn't strike me as the type to volunteer helping with the homeless out of the goodness of his heart. "Was one of them a big guy?" I asked, describing Viktor as I remembered him, "With a Russian accent?"

"I think so. Could be."

"Does Nick Farnsworth come here, too?"

"Oh sure, all the time. He's one of our patients." She clapped a hand over her mouth. "Shoot," she said between her fingers. "That's probably against the law to tell you."

I waved away her worry. "I won't tell anyone."

"Thanks."

The waiting room wasn't exactly bustling with people, so I decided to find out how many indigent people Dr. Colon treated in a given month, when a back door slammed.

"Janet?"

His voice boomed, and before Janet could answer him, the dentist himself appeared from around a back corner. He was about my age, but looked like someone caught in the disco age, with an allover tan and shiny blow-dried hair. His quick assessing glance convinced me that if we'd been standing under a revolving mirrored ball and flashing colored lights, this guy would've asked me to do the hustle.

"Oh, hello," he said, masquerading his surprise. Shooting a furious glance at Janet, he smiled in my direction and tried for smooth. "I didn't realize I had a new patient. I'm sorry to have kept you waiting."

"No problem. I'm not here for an appointment," I said. "I just stopped by to ask you about one of your clients."

His face went from placid to stricken.

"Not Bob Bayless," Janet said quietly. "She's here about someone else."

Bob Bayless. So that was the name that had "shaken up" Dr. Colon. I wondered if this Mr. Bayless filed a malpractice suit.

"You want to talk with me about a patient?" Dr. Colon asked.

"Why? Who are you?"

Janet ran her hand down Dr. Colon's upper arm. "It's okay. She's from a TV show. Her name is . . ."

At that moment, I realized I hadn't introduced myself. "Alex St. James," I said, moving forward, hand extended.

Dr. Colon seemed unwilling to touch me, but he relented. "Who are you here to ask me about?"

"I'm doing a story on the homeless," I started to say.

Dr. Colon's tanned face blanched.

"Is something wrong?" I asked.

"No, why? What do you mean you're doing a story on the homeless? Why are you talking with me then? I'm not homeless. Do I look homeless?"

Janet seemed as taken aback as I was.

I switched to my soothing voice and worked up a smile. "No, of course not. I just know that you help so many homeless people by offering them free dental care."

"Who told you that?"

This man was as jumpy as a patient anticipating a root canal.

"You do help the indigent, don't you?" I asked. "For the good of the community?"

He nodded.

Janet piped in to help. "She's doing a story on one of the people we treated here." Turning to me, she continued, "Didn't you say he made a new life for himself? That he got a job and everything?" Addressing Dr. Colon again, she said, "I think that if Ms. St. James does a story on how you help others, it could be really good for business."

"What's wrong with business? We have plenty of patients."

"Keith," Janet said very quietly.

He snapped out of whatever paranoid fever he was in and said, "I'm sorry, Ms. St. James, but I just don't have time to spend discussing my patients. They have rights, you know.

Privacy rights. Even my indigent patients."

I knew I wasn't getting anywhere with this guy so I shot him my best conciliatory smile, and shrugged dramatically. "Sorry to bother you."

He nodded and followed me to the door.

Just as I grabbed the handle, in a Columbo-type move, I turned around. "Here," I said, digging out a business card from my purse, "just in case."

He took it. "Just in case of what?"

"Well, maybe you can tell your Russian friend that I'd like to talk with him," I said, then remembered the appointment card I'd found among Rybak's possessions. My elusive quarry was scheduled for a cleaning in a couple of weeks. "And I have a feeling you'll be seeing Howard Rybak before I will," I said.

Dr. Keith Colon backed up. His voice was just above a whisper. "Get out of here."

Ron Shade

I turned into the restaurant parking lot on 79th Street and looked for the little white Ford Escort that Alex St. James had been driving when I'd first bumped into her in that gas station a few months back. When I had finally gotten ahold of her on her cell phone, she'd seemed as anxious to meet with me as I was with her. Maybe that old Shade charm was taking hold . . . Sort of a delayed reaction on her part. It wouldn't be the first time some pretty girl had done a flip-flop. But my hopes of this dissolved as I caught sight of her tiny little wave to me as she paced behind her car, talking on her cell. She looked about as excited as the morgue attendant when he sees the funeral hearse coming.

I pulled the Beater up next to her and caught a glimpse of her stare. I'd forgotten that she hadn't seen my working ride before. Of course, since I'd gotten rid of the Firebird by selling it to her boss, it was also my only ride until my next big paycheck arrived.

"Hi," I said, getting out of the car.

Still on the phone, she nodded fractionally and continued to talk to someone. I gathered it was her boss.

"Yeah, yeah, I know, Bass," she said. "I'm meeting with Mr. Shade now. He just pulled up, in fact."

Back to "Mr. Shade" again, I thought. Nothing personal, just business. But that was okay. I needed her to use her reporter databases to do some behind-the-scenes corporate digging, since Big Rich was down for the count. Maybe if she needed something as well, one hand could sort of wash the other.

Now wasn't that a pleasant thought . . .

She hung up and placed the phone in the back pocket of her pants. She was wearing jeans, and although she filled them out quite nicely, I was a little surprised she'd dressed so casually. She must have read my face and said, "Doing some field work today."

I grunted an approval. "Hungry?"

She shrugged. "I could go for a salad, maybe. Coffee for sure."

She almost smiled, and I silently admired the contour of her cheeks. I even dug the spray of freckles.

A hostess took one look at us as we walked in and gave us a booth near a row of windows. When the waitress came by we both ordered coffee. I offered to spring for the salad she mentioned, but she shook her head.

"Let's wait on that," she said. She took hers with just a small shot of cream. I kept mine black. "You said you had something on your mind, Mr. Shade?"

"You can call me Ron."

She smiled and sipped her coffee. Judging from her expression, if I was waiting for her to mention my name, my coffee was gonna get mighty cold.

"Well," I said, "I did have something to ask you. Why did you ask me if I knew a guy named Nick Farnsworth the other night?"

The question seemed to catch her interest, and she considered it for a moment. "I was having a conversation with him. When I mentioned your name he had this . . ." She paused to consider her response, then shrugged. "Reaction. Like he knew you, or something. Why?"

I ignored her inquiry for the moment. "And your relationship to him is . . . ?"

She smiled. "None of your business."

I smiled back. This was a girl after my own heart. Never tell anybody anything, if you don't have to. "Look, I'll level with you, okay? I just need to know if you're going out with him, or something."

She rolled her eyes. "No, no, no, not ever. His father's an old family friend, and he tried to fix us up."

"His father the lawyer?"

This time she looked surprised. "How did you know he's a lawyer?"

"Because my buddy George said a couple of CPD dicks questioned him and his father, the lawyer, told him to exercise his right to remain silent." I shook my head and grinned. "Lawyers, you got to love 'em. I rank them just below snail slime." I almost said whale shit, but thought better of it. This was one high-class chick and I didn't want to risk offending her. Especially since I was about to ask her assistance. "Even if he is an old friend of your family."

She made a dismissive gesture. "He's not that good of a friend." Her eyes suddenly had a lingering sadness in them, then she smiled. "So what's your connection to Nicky?"

"Nicky? You sure he isn't a sweetheart?"

"He may be to somebody, but not to me. Why were the police questioning him?"

I debated about how much to tell her. Stalling, I plucked a napkin out of the holder and began to roll it up, like a parchment. What the hell, I thought. If she's going to help me, I might as well be honest. "The other night, when I was coming out of the gym, two guys tried to kill me."

"Oh, my God." Her eyes widened as she said it. "And they think Nicky was involved?"

"Maybe. The two of them sounded like foreigners. Russians, I think. Farnsworth supposedly sent some Russkies downstate to pick up a body for a funeral."

Her eyes narrowed and for a second I thought she was going to rip the napkin out of my hands.

"Mr. Shade," she began.

"Ron, remember?"

Frowning slightly, she continued, "Mr. Shade, perhaps you'd better tell me exactly what it is you're working on. I think we may have more in common that you realize, as far as this case."

So I told her about the late Bob Bayless and watched her reactions. Her brown eyes stared at me, as if sizing me up from across a ring. "Bob Bayless?"

"You know him?"

She shook her head, looking confused. "No. But I heard his name. Today."

Now it was my turn for confusion. "You did? Where?"

She told me about her own investigation into finding Howard Rybak. "I found an appointment card in his belongings, so I visited his dentist, to see if he knew anything about Rybak's whereabouts."

"Don't tell me. Dr. Keith Colon?"

Alex nodded. "This is getting weird. While I was there the receptionist mentioned that the dentist was upset because someone was asking about Bob Bayless." She shook her head. "I know that's the name I heard. And you think this guy Bayless is still alive?"

"Alive and well, and gambling periodically in Las Vegas."

She took a long sip of her coffee and the waitress magically appeared to warm up the cups for us. "So if he's alive, whose body was it in the crashed car?"

"That's the twelve-million-dollar question." I grinned. "But one thing's for sure. If your buddy Nicky works at a funeral home, he's got access to a lot of bodies."

The space between her eyebrows creased slightly. Her forehead was pretty much line free. The sign of an untroubled adolescence, they say.

"But you also said the deceased had signs of smoke inhalation," she said. "That means . . ." Her voice trailed off.

"That somebody had access to a body that wasn't quite cold yet," I said.

"I hate to think Nicky would be involved in something like that. I mean, we grew up together."

"People change."

She glanced out the window, obviously considering something. When her eyes darted back to me, she looked serious. "You said the two guys sounded like Russians?"

"Yeah."

The tip of her tongue swept over her lips. "Remember I told you about the first night under the viaduct when we got attacked by those guys? It was Nicky who showed to rescue us. He's the one who set the whole thing up. And at first I thought he just did it to impress me. Now, I don't know."

Maybe this Farnsworth guy had more nuances than I'd figured. I couldn't argue with his aspirations, even though his methods needed work.

"His friend's Russian," she said. "And he was carrying a gun, too. Nicky said he was some kind of security guard, or something."

Things were definitely starting to pull together. "You know this friend's name?"

She shook her head. "Viktor, I think. I can try to find out."

"That would help. I also need your help on something else."

Her eyebrows rose.

"There's a corporation dealing in medical supplies called Manus," I said. "I'd like them thoroughly checked out."

"The reason?"

"Bayless worked there, and they got a huge insurance payoff. I went to see them and something didn't smell right."

She canted her head. "I thought *you* did that kind of work, Mr. Shade?"

"I do, but mostly that consists of me finding somebody who specializes in finding out certain particulars. Somebody who has access to all sorts of private databases, who can do in one hour what would take me a month of Sundays."

"Somebody like a reporter?"

"Yeah. My buddy, Big Rich Stafford of the *Chicago Metro*, usually helps me out in that regard." I tried to gauge her reaction. "I've given him many an exclusive story from my findings, too. He's out with a heart problem at the moment."

She smiled. "So I wasn't your first choice, then?"

She certainly would be, if she were available. But I couldn't come right out and say that. She might take it the wrong way. "Like I said, there could be a hell of a story here."

The brown eyes rolled upward, sweeping over the ceiling for

a moment. "Actually, I had something I wanted to ask your assistance with. Are you any good at locating people?"

I grinned. "They used to call me Daniel Boone when I was in the army."

"The man I'm looking for is named Howard Rybak." Her lips compressed slightly. "At one time, he was one of the homeless over on Grisham. But then he straightened himself out, got cleaned up, found a job . . ."

"Sounds like an old Frank Capra movie. Now he's gone back to the streets?"

"I'm not sure. I wanted to use him in my documentary segment, but his landlord says he left unexpectedly."

One hand does wash the other, I thought. "Sounds like it's right up my alley. Give me his full name and last known address and I'll check it out." I only hoped I could tap George for one more favor before my luck ran out.

Alex St. James

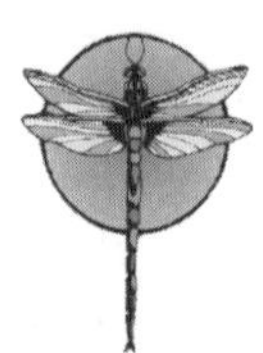

Back at the office, I did my best to avoid Bass. He was getting antsy for his homeless story, and I was getting antsy to get him off my case. My lunchtime discussion with the private eye, Ron Shade, led me to believe that there was a lot more story here than I'd originally assumed. He'd said as much, of course, but people always do. They'll say whatever they think necessary to get themselves on television, or in this Shade fellow's case, to get the information he needed.

Private eyes apparently weren't all sneak-in-the-office-after-hours-types that movies would lead audiences to believe. His job, to identify people who could provide information, in order to solve his cases, sounded an awful lot like mine. I'd always fancied myself a detective of sorts. But the fact that a couple of Russians tried to take him out was also a part of his job description. That part, he could keep.

Bass thundered in. Well, as much as a man of his stature can thunder. "Another date?" he asked.

"I was researching my story," I said.

"Uh-huh." Bass dropped into one of my chairs. "Research." He snorted. "Sounds more like a date to me. Lunch with that private dick who sold me the lemon car, and who you've hired to protect you. On the company's dime, no less."

I stared at him for a long moment. I knew that unsettled him so I held out a little longer than necessary. When he squirmed, I broke the silence.

"What do we know about Manus Corporation?"

"Never heard of them."

I nodded in dismissal, then turned to my computer screen, knowing Bass well enough to know that he couldn't suppress his curiosity. "Why?" he asked.

"Well," I said slowly, as I began an Internet search, "they might've benefited from the death of one of their key executives."

"So what?"

I shrugged. "So, the guy isn't really dead. And the body who took his place might very well have come from a local homeless shelter." I'd been thinking about Iris, the crazy woman under the viaduct and her comments about the dog pound. I'd passed them off as the ravings of a lunatic, but there was a deep fear in her eyes that I couldn't dismiss. "I think this Manus may be tied in with our story."

"What do they do?"

"Checking now," I said. Shade had given me some company basics, so I included enough keywords to keep my browser's hits focused. "They're a medical supply company," I said, then, "eeyoo."

"What?"

"Body parts. They market body parts."

"Is that legal?"

I didn't answer right away.

Bass squirmed again, but this time with a look of distaste on his face. "You can order parts from the Internet?" He looked out the window as though to clear his mind of some unpleasant image. "I thought there were waiting lists for those. I thought that hospitals decided who got what."

"No ordering," I said, as I clicked through the company Web site. "They're a clearinghouse for body parts."

"Clearinghouse? Like that million-dollar-prize place?" Bass stared. "Like someone might show up at my house someday with a van and tell me I've won a liver?"

"It'd be a winning day for all of us if they brought you a heart."

He didn't comment, so I kept clicking. "No. They 'obtain' parts—it doesn't say how—and manage the inventory for hospitals." Manage inventory. Saying it aloud, even with the buffer of sterile corporate-speak, still made me feel icky. "Whenever a patient needs a transplant, the hospital contacts Manus. It's . . ." I faltered, ". . . more efficient than the hospital trying to match patients up on their own. I guess."

"Inventory?"

"Yeah," I said, still uncertain about what I was reading. "I hate to ask this, but how does one go about determining the shelf life of a body part?"

Bass stared out the window again, frowning. "I don't like it."

"Nobody likes anything to do with death, Bass." I read a

small paragraph about the thorough testing and quality-control procedures each donated body part must pass before being released to medical professionals for transplantation. The Web site boasted all the expected articles on heart, lung, liver, cornea, and kidney transplants, but there were also parts I never expected to see. Bones. Femurs were available, as were a variety of tibia, fibula, and patella. The list went on. "Wow," I said, reading some of it aloud. "They use these for research and medical schools, but they also use them for actual transplants. Can you imagine all the lives that are saved by these donations?"

"You sure they're all donations?"

"What else would they be?" I asked. I kept clicking around and then mused aloud, "I'm surprised there isn't a link to the registry of organ donors here. I've signed up with that organization. The Secretary of State runs it."

"You have? Are you nuts?"

I stopped what I was doing. "Of course I'm a donor. I signed the back of my driver's license, I had it witnessed and I'm on the organ donor registry. If the donation of my organs can help someone else—once I no longer need the organs, that is—then I'm all for it." This topic was one I felt strongly about. I placed both hands on my desk, and I held eye contact with him. "I plan to use everything I've got till I'm old and gray and I plan to die peacefully in my sleep when I'm in my nineties. Or later. But things don't always work out the way we plan, Bass. I could get hit by a truck tomorrow. And if I do, I don't want to take parts with me that could possibly help someone else."

"If you get hit by a truck tomorrow, you better hope the paramedics don't read the back of your license."

"Why not?"

"You think they'll work as hard on someone who's an organ donor?" He shook his head. "I think you're asking for trouble."

"And I think you're wrong." I returned to the screen.

Bass made a noise and gestured toward my computer screen. "Sounds like a company of vultures waiting to swoop in the minute someone's dead."

"They're streamlining the process. In fact," I added, returning to the list of browser hits, "they're not the only company doing this. It's a whole industry."

He made another noise of disgust. "How do we know they're not swooping in early?"

I flicked a glance his way as he turned to me. "They wouldn't—" I started to say, but then stopped myself when I remembered Shade telling me about the dead guy with burned lungs. He'd been alive when placed in that car to burn. And homeless Iris with her dog-pound analogy. Bringing lonely, orphaned dogs to the pound to die.

I shivered even though the room was warm.

"It's getting to you, too, isn't it?" He smirked. "Admit it."

I didn't answer him right away. "Can you check on this company for me? You have contacts informed on local businesses, don't you?"

Bass squinted at me. "Give me the name, location, whatever you've got. I'll see what I can do."

When he left I reviewed my conversation with Ron Shade. He'd asked about my connection to Nicky Farnsworth. I hadn't told him about my adoption quest, but I wasn't quite sure why I hadn't. After all, he was a private investigator. Maybe he could find my birth parents for me without Larry Farnsworth's help. That'd be nice. The sooner I put distance between me and Nicky, the happier I'd be. I'd tried to give Nicky the benefit of the doubt since we were adults now, but Shade's intimations dredged up an old memory.

It'd been years since I thought about the incident that had separated the Szatjemskis and the Farnsworths. We were at our house for one of those family get-together nights that sent the kids to the basement while the parents played Pinochle or Rook.

This time, Nicky brought along the ant farm he'd gotten for Christmas. Generally sullen and unpleasant, Nicky was not our favorite guest, but this time he was animated—eager to get to the basement to show us his gift.

Downstairs, he held the double-glassed display case high, out of our reach. "This is mine," he said. "I get to do whatever I want with it."

Face upturned to study the busy ants, Lucy waited patiently.

When Nicky finally deigned to bring it to our level, he placed it on the table in front of himself and pointed. "See how they carry stuff?"

Lucy nodded. I squirmed next to her wanting to get a better look. "They never stop moving," I said.

"Yeah, they do," Nicky said. He pulled a book of matches from his pocket. These were the fancy boxed kind, with wooden sticks instead of the paper kind my dad picked up at restaurants for free.

"What are you doing?" Lucy asked. "We aren't allowed to have those."

He rolled his eyes. "That's because you don't know how to handle them. I do. Just watch."

I wanted to run upstairs to tell my parents that Nicky had matches, but before I could get even one step from the table, he'd poured out some of the dirt and ants onto the table.

"What are you—?"

The question died on my lips as he struck the first match.

I started to yell, "Mom!" but he stood, blew out the match and shoved a hand around my mouth.

"Shut up," he said. "I told you I'm not setting your damn house on fire."

He used a bad word. That shut me up with shock.

"Watch." He touched the burnt end of the match against one of the ants. It crackled, hissed and the ant stopped moving.

"What are you doing?" Lucy yelled. "Don't hurt the ants!"

Nicky pulled away from her grasp. "It should have made a bigger noise. You slowed me down. The match wasn't hot enough." He struck another one.

"Mom!" This time I hollered as loud as I could.

The parents came running and within minutes the mess was sorted out. Nicky got a scolding—not much of one to my mind—and his dad took possession of the matches and the ant farm. They went back upstairs to their cards.

"You are such sissies," he said when we were alone again.

Maybe if Nicky hadn't been so angry. Maybe if I hadn't called for the parents.

Maybe if our dog, Buttons, hadn't gotten up from her pillow just then, looking for someone to scratch her belly . . .

I shuddered. It had happened over twenty years ago and the incident still made me cringe. With a look of fury on his face—something I'd never seen on anyone before—Nicky turned on the dog. He grabbed her collar and dragged her across the floor—she fought and twisted the whole way.

"Stop that!" I shouted.

Lucy cried and begged him to stop.

"You want me to stop?"

We both shouted, "Yes!"

"Okay, fine." With that he released Buttons, grabbing her front paw, the white one. He yanked hard, pulling her to the ground. She squealed and fought with her remaining paws. "Let's see what your dog looks like with only three legs." He used his free hand to hit her in the face.

"Stop it!" I grabbed him with both arms, kicking and screaming, trying to knock him over and trying to make him let go. He held fast, and Buttons cried out again, in a high-pitched whimper that translated to great pain.

I bit down hard on Nicky's shoulder. My mouth came up full of flannel, but in my little girl rage protecting my dog, I hoped I'd drawn blood.

He let go of Buttons, who backed up and bared her teeth.

Nicky held his shoulder and cursed me out. I'd never heard such words.

Lucy ran for my parents.

The Farnsworths trundled down the stairs again and this time Nicky worked up tears, telling how I went wild and hurt him, giving his parents the wide-eyed innocent look and explanation that shouldn't have fooled them, but did.

My dad came over and I told him what really happened.

Larry Farnsworth glared at me with a look intended to induce shame for ratting on his son. Mrs. Farnsworth started to move toward us, but her husband said, "It's time we went home."

They left. And our families never got together again. I think my mom and Mrs. Farnsworth might've kept in touch. But when she died, our families lost touch completely.

Until I called Larry Farnsworth about my adoption.

And it seemed that Nicky hadn't changed, after all.

Chapter 17

Ron Shade

I'd used my last bit of the goodwill from the Bielmaster situation by calling George on my cell as soon as I was out the door from my lunch date with Alex. Luckily, the streak still had a little more play in it.

"A fucking homeless guy?" he said. I could hear the irritation beginning to creep into his voice more and more. Pretty soon we'd be back to normal.

"I know it's a big favor, buddy," I said.

"That's putting it mildly."

"But I'm on the way over to Bridgeport Sam's to get that thick steak sandwich on the griddle for you."

"Oh yeah?"

"As we speak," I lied. "In fact, I'm risking a ticket from one of Chicago's finest because I didn't even take the time to put my earpiece in my cell phone before I called."

I heard him sigh, then punctuate it with a laugh. "Make sure you order fries for me, too. I'll see you over there." He hung up.

In reality, I knew the computer check on Rybak wouldn't

take more than a few minutes, but I was hoping it would turn up something. The prospect of searching through a bunch of shelters and other Grisham Avenue viaducts had me holding my nose already. I cut back east on 79th Street until I got to Halsted, then headed north to Bridgeport. It had been Mayor Daley's neighborhood, and that of his father, the first Mayor Daley. Richard J. and Richard M. Both had done a lot for the city, and both were pure Chicago. My father, who had been a dental technician, had worked on the original Mayor's bridgework and knew him personally. I'd never met either one.

When I got to Sam's place, one of the original greasy spoons for the working-class area, I saw George's unmarked squad-car already sitting in the parking lot. I parked the Beater next to it and went in. Sam's hostess, a tough-looking gal named Wendi, nodded to me. "He's over in a booth."

I went down the narrow aisle toward the back. George was already working on a long steak sandwich and a heap of fried potatoes. I sat across from him and nodded.

"Took you long enough," he said.

"I was meeting somebody over by Ford City."

He shrugged and shoved some fries into his mouth. "I figured you weren't that interested."

I grinned. "You would be so wrong."

"Norris and Cate called me. No word yet on your armed robbery case. They're still checking all the hospitals."

"Maybe he's treating it himself."

He shook his head as he chewed. "Not with the amount of blood he left in the car. That puppy's gonna need a doctor, for sure. Or else he's dead, in which case, we'll eventually find the dumped body."

"Unless he's cooling his heels in good old Sunset Manor Funeral Home," I said. "They looking into that?"

"That Farnsworth asshole's booked up. Funeral home's

closed and he ain't been home." He shrugged. "We'll find him. We put the word out in the district."

"Be nice to check that place out."

"No PC for a warrant."

"Well, I got something on those Russkies that work for Farnsworth," I said. "One of them is a big guy named Viktor."

"Last name?"

"Something Russian-sounding."

"Well, shit." He smirked. "That narrows it down."

"You get that other stuff I asked you for?"

He grinned and took an enormous bite of the sandwich. His mouth full, he set the sandwich on his plate, held up a finger, wiped his hand on a paper napkin, and picked up a nine-by-twelve envelope.

"It's all in here," he managed to say after shifting a load of food to one cheek.

The waitress came by with a menu for me, but I told her, "Just coffee."

"He's gotta pay for all this," George added, holding his hand above his plate. "And I ain't even thought about what I want for dessert yet."

"If there is a dessert," I said, grinning. "I'll base that decision on the quality of the information herein."

"Then tell the chef to start preparing cherries jubilee," he said.

The girl smiled, but the look in her eyes told me she thought we were nuts. When she left to get my coffee, I undid the prongs of the metal clasp and opened the flap. Inside were several sheets of paper. The first two were full-page color reproductions of Robert Bayless's and Candice Prokovis's Illinois driver's license photos. The third one was a printout of Candice's driver's license listing from the Secretary of State. The address matched the one I'd had in my notebook, but it was the last line that was the most important. It read, *Surrendered to foreign state—NV,* and listed an address in Henderson.

"This is fantastic," I said. The waitress set a mug down in front of me and filled it with hot coffee. I waved off cream and sugar but told her, "Tell the chef that's got to be nonalcoholic brandy on that dessert."

She gave me a questioning look, then glanced at George, who laughed.

As she walked away, he said, "What the fuck are you talking about now? Nonalcoholic brandy?"

"You're on duty, right?"

He nodded. "Technically, yeah."

"Well, cherries jubilee is a flaming dessert. They light the brandy after they pour it over the ice cream."

"It is? That's news to me. Maybe I'll just have a milk shake instead."

"Had your cholesterol checked lately?"

"Nah," he said, stuffing his mouth with fries before picking up the sandwich again. "Been too busy doing favors for a friend."

I smiled as I watched him eat. When he had done a little more chewing, I ran my fingers over the papers still inside the envelope and asked, "She live there alone?"

"With her significant other, I assume." George smirked. "Unless it's her brother and they changed their name." He pointed to the envelope and I withdrew another sheet and started to read it. "His name is Robert Barstow. Looks to be about fifteen years older than her. No Illinois record for him."

I was getting a lot for that steak sandwich. This would probably be all I needed to run down the elusive quarry. Bob Bayless, won't you please come home, I hummed silently to myself.

George must have sensed my feeling of triumphant satisfaction because he said, "Ain't you gonna look at what else is in there?"

I raised an eyebrow. "Rybak?"

He licked his lips and nodded.

I sorted through the next few sheets and skimmed them.

"He's dead?" I asked.

He nodded. "Found him yesterday in a dumpster behind a 7-Eleven on Grisham. At least what was left of him."

"No IDs?"

"Plenty of IDs," he said. "In a jacket just laying there next to the dumpster. The body inside had been burned beyond recognition."

"Set on fire?"

"Yep. They conjectured that he was trying to ignite some debris, maybe to cook something, or maybe just to stay warm. Got some lighter fluid on his pants. Went up like a Roman candle."

"They confirmed the ID?"

He nodded. "Dental records."

This was beginning to sound like déjà vu all over again. "Who was the dentist?"

He reached over and plucked the paper from my hands. Now I was going to have to worry about being able to read it around the grease stains. His big finger moved down the report. "A Doctor Colon." He read off the familiar address.

"They do an autopsy?"

"Sure, this morning. Had to. No way it was a natural death."

"And lemme guess. I'll bet they found he was alive when he started on fire, right?"

He raised his eyebrows. "Very good. You must be what they call, physic."

"That's psychic," I said, "and am I right?"

He looked at me for a moment, then grinned. "Sure are. How'd you know?"

"I'm physic, remember?" I said. "Anybody claimed the body yet?"

"Probably not." He looked on the report and shook his head. "Nah, says here they turned it over to someplace that buries a lot of the homeless. County contract, or something."

"What do you want to bet it was Sunset Manor?"

That got his attention. "Sunset Manor?"

"Can you check?"

His nostrils flared and I knew he was following me. He took out his cell phone, punched in a number with rote quickness, and waited. When someone answered, he read off the ME number and asked what funeral home had picked up the body. From his expression, I knew it was good old Sunset Manor.

I was right. It was just like déjà vu, all over again.

Alex St. James

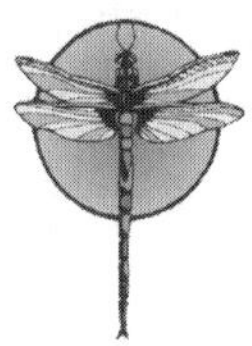

Bass had come up with a couple of interesting pieces of information on Manus, information that I couldn't wait to share with Shade. I called him and arranged to meet him at Home Run Inn Pizza on Archer, after work. I doubted he'd have found Howard Rybak this soon, but I thought I had enough on Manus to warrant a meeting of the minds.

Because I was early, I kept an eye on the front of the restaurant, but he showed up only about five minutes after I'd settled into one of the tall wooden booths. He was wearing the same outfit from this morning, jeans, a black T-shirt and a beige camouflage flak jacket that I knew covered his gun. "Hi," I said, waving.

His chin lifted in acknowledgment, and he made his way toward me.

He stopped and glanced at the booth's open seat. "Do you mind if we switch sides?"

"How come?" I asked, but I already knew the answer.

"I don't like sitting with my back to the door."

"Figured as much," I said, gathering my purse. I didn't like sitting with my back to the door, either, but this seemed more important to him than it was to me. At least at this juncture. "Sure."

"Thanks."

"What do you like on your pizza? Or would you prefer to do the buffet?"

His face lit up. "They've got a buffet?"

"I guess that's settled."

The waitress came up just then. We both ordered iced tea and she invited us to help ourselves at the buffet whenever we felt like it. Shade got up immediately. I followed.

When we were both settled again, I pulled out my notes on Manus. "You aren't going to believe this," I said, then stopped. This wasn't good dinner conversation.

He'd taken a big mouthful of mostaccioli. "What?"

"Maybe this ought to wait till we're finished eating."

He gave me a quizzical look, wiped his mouth, then pulled an envelope out of his flak jacket. His movements were heavy with reluctance. "Here," he said.

I tried to take the envelope, but he held fast. He had blue eyes, I noticed, and they were boring into mine.

"Howard Rybak," he said.

"You found him?" When I heard the excitement in my voice, I realized that until this minute I hadn't actually expected to find Rybak anywhere. Shade still held tight to his end of the envelope. "Wow, are you quick! This is unbelievable. I didn't think that—"

I stopped when I saw his face.

"This may not be what you wanted to hear," he said.

"What is it?" I asked. He finally let go, and I dug in to grab the envelope's contents. I shook my head. "You didn't find him?"

"I'm sorry, Alex," Shade said.

By the time I pulled out the police report, I knew what it would say. "Oh," I whispered softly, running my fingers over Howard Rybak's name. "He's dead."

"You didn't know him, did you?"

"I never met the man, and despite my best efforts, I didn't get to know him, not one little bit." I shook my head. "This is all wrong. Things aren't supposed to work this way." I stared down at the report. "What happened?"

Shade told me.

"A fire?" I asked. My tone was incredulous. "But he had an apartment. He had a place to live. Why would he take refuge in a Dumpster?"

"Sometimes the homeless are unpredictable."

"He wasn't homeless!" My voice came out too loud, too strident. I had no idea why I felt so strongly. I tried to calm myself by focusing on the report's findings but something caught my eye. "He had smoke in his lungs?"

Shade nodded.

"He was . . . alive when he burned?"

"Don't get too worked up," Shade said, "because I don't think that was really him."

"But it says that the ID—"

"I know what it says, and I know what my instincts are telling me. Rybak turned up dead two days after you started asking about him."

"Yeah . . ."

"In a fire . . ."

I kept silent.

"Take a guess which illustrious dentist did the identification."

"No!"

"Yes."

"We need to go talk with him," I said. I looked down at my plate and realized I'd stopped eating. I was starving and the pizza here was the best in the city. I grabbed one of the squares of sausage and mushroom that I'd heaped on my plate and took a big bite.

"I agree," Shade said. "But before you get your hopes up about your story and Rybak's well-being, I have to tell you I think it was his body they placed in the car to take Bob Bayless's place."

I shook my head as I finished chewing. When I swallowed, I said, "That's a stretch."

"Think about it. Rybak's missing, right? For just about the same amount of time that Bayless has been 'dead.' Bayless, who worked for Manus, needed a body to take his place if his disappearing act was going to work." Shade had become more animated, but his voice had gone lower. I had to lean forward to hear him.

"Don't you think that's too much of a coincidence?"

"Not when you factor in the common denominators." He held up his index finger. "Sunset Manor, your buddy's funeral home, recovered Bayless's body from downstate." Holding up another finger, he continued, "Both Bayless and Rybak have been identified by the same dentist, Dr. Colon, a guy who gets very shaky when you ask questions about his patients."

"I've noticed that." I felt confused. "But, come on. What are the chances that the guy I'm looking to find is the same guy who winds up dead in your investigation?"

"Pretty good, when you consider that Sunset Manor is the common denominator. You told me you heard about Rybak from Nick Farnsworth, right?" Shade ticked off another finger. "Sunset Manor is picking up the 'current' Howard Rybak's body when he's cleared by the Medical Examiner for burial."

I sat back in the booth. "Wow. So you're saying Nicky Farnsworth is in on all this. That he helped engineer Robert Bayless's fake death."

"Yeah. And he and his Russian friends have been killing people in the process, to cover their tracks. They probably took poor homeless Rybak in, gave him a few bucks—"

I jumped in. "Set him up in an apartment. Gave him a job—at Sunset Manor."

Shade looked surprised, but pleased that I was following along. "Yeah. And they took him to the dentist to set the wheels in motion for the big switcheroo."

"But why? What's in it for Nicky?"

Shade shrugged. "Follow the money."

"The money," I repeated. "This *is* starting to make sense."

It was Shade's turn to look confused.

"Look at what I found." I pulled out the information I'd gathered on Manus, and the information Bass had gotten me, as well. My mind started to put the pieces together, even as I spread the papers out before Shade. "Hey," I said suddenly.

"What?"

"What brand of underwear did Bayless wear?"

Shade made a face. "How the hell should I know?" He immediately softened his tone. "Why?"

"When I was going through Howard Rybak's things, I found designer underwear. I mean, what homeless guy is going to go out and buy Ralph Lauren underpants and shirts with his first paycheck? I thought it was weird at the time . . ." The poor guy.

He thought he'd hit the lottery of good luck. Instead, he'd been set up. "There was a set missing. I bet they made him wear it the day they put him in Bayless's place."

The thought depressed me. I looked down at my favorite pizza and suddenly had no appetite.

Shade seemed to sense that. "What were you going to show me?" he asked.

I glanced over at his plate. "You finished eating?" I asked.

"More or less."

"This may seal it for you." I showed him the market Manus cornered. "Body parts," I said. "And who would have the best access to them?"

"A funeral home?"

"That's not the worst of it," I said. "Over a dozen times in the past two years, the company was cited for providing 'less than perfect' specimens. My boss, Bass, uncovered this tidbit. It's off the record. He tapped into his cache of cohorts to find out the dirt." I licked my lips, finally putting it together. "Donors are usually young, healthy people who've had a terrible accident. But some of the bones and organs provided to the research labs and to hopeful patients have been—diseased." I looked up at Shade who was sitting in rapt attention. "There's a lot of money here. A lot. How much you want to bet that they're taking donations from homeless people—without their consent?"

Ron Shade

Alex St. James didn't get into the Beater right away. Her passive expression turned to one of delight. "What a perfect car for a private detective," she said. "I meant to tell you that the other day, but I got so worked up in my conversation with Bass, that I forgot. This is a great car."

I hadn't quite thought of it that way, and I wondered if she was being sarcastic. She took a few minutes to walk around the car before climbing into the passenger's side, where I held the door open.

"This is a cool car," she said. "My parents had one like it when I was a kid. What year is it?"

I told her. As I slid behind the wheel, I gently patted the angular dash. "They don't make 'em like this baby anymore."

"No, they don't," she said, as she fastened her seatbelt. "They say the type of car a person drives is an extension of his personality, don't they?"

"Well, remember, I sold my Firebird to your boss."

"Believe me, I remember. Firebirds and Corvettes are—" Rolling her eyes, she stopped herself. "Never mind." She glanced around the car's interior. "I like this one better."

As we were driving, she was on her cell phone trying to get a cameraman to meet us at Dr. Colon's office. After several unsuccessful attempts to get hold of whom she was looking for, she finally let out a sigh of exasperation and began searching in her purse.

"Problems?" I asked.

"I can't get hold of any of our on-call camera people." Her tone was tinged with exasperation. "That's the problem with not being network. If you don't book somebody in advance, you can never get hold of them when you need them."

"I could pull into a Best Buy or Circuit City and you could buy a camcorder."

"Wouldn't work. Which one of us is going to be the cameraman? Besides, I need some professional-looking video if I'm going to use it."

"Makes sense."

She held the phone to her ear and after a moment said, "Bass?"

Although I could only hear her side of the conversation, it was obvious that her boss didn't like being disturbed at this time of the evening. Alex pleaded her case with an urgent eloquence and hung up with a satisfied smile. "Hal is going to meet us over there in half an hour."

"Half an hour?" I looked at my watch. "It's already almost six. We'll be lucky to find the good doctor in at this hour."

"Then we'll call his emergency service number," she said. "I'm sure he has one, being a dentist."

"But he's a crooked dentist."

"Which we still have to prove."

"Listen, if it's one thing I know, it's people. Like I told you, they're panicky. Getting sloppy. Running scared."

"And Colon's the weakest link," she said, lowering her voice and doing a fair imitation of me. Then, returning to her normal tone, "Do you think you'll be able to get him to cooperate?"

"Piece of cake. He's in too deep. The advantage we have is I can threaten to drag him to the cops if he doesn't. We're going to give him his only out, unless he wants to go down for murder and face the needle."

She compressed her lips. "I hope you're right."

"Trust me," I said.

Her cell phone rang, interrupting our conversation. It was Hal, the cameraman. She gave him our location, and probable ETA. When she hung up I glanced over her way.

"He's on his way," she said. "Should be there in about twenty minutes."

"We'll be there in five. But that'll give me a chance to go in and soften the good doctor up."

"Don't you mean 'us'?"

"But of course."

As we approached, the lights were all on in Colon's office, which, given the still available light on this fine late spring evening, was hardly noticeable. Instead of pulling into the strip mall, I continued on down the block. Alex looked out the window and then to me. "I think you just went past it."

"I know. But the last time I was here, I noticed the good doctor parks his shiny, silver BMW in the back. I figure if it's there, he's there."

"He drives a Beemer?"

"Obviously the fruits of his ill-gotten gain," I said, making a hard right and then another one as I came to the alley. It had the same potholes that I'd bottomed out on the first time, so I took it real slow, sparing the Beater's undercarriage as much as I could. As I drew closer, my heart sank. No BMW.

"Maybe he went out to get something," Alex offered. "He left the place lit up."

"Maybe," I said, hawking the back door as we rolled past. "Maybe not."

A sliver of light ran down the side of the rear door. It was ajar. I pulled down to the corner and into a spot by the currency exchange. Alex glanced at me as I shifted the Beater into park and shut it off. I leaned over and opened the glove box. A half dozen receipts, the owner's manual, a collection of candy from the various charitable organizations, some latex gloves, and a tire gauge came tumbling out.

"Oh, my God," Alex said, laughing. "It looks just like mine."

I ignored her and fished around in the remaining items inside the glove box, searching for what I wanted.

"Do you need some help?" she asked.

"Un un," I said as my probing fingers found my Mini-Maglite flashlight. I held it up for her to see.

"We going to wait here?" she asked.

"Un un," I said, opening the door and sliding out. I felt for my Beretta. "You're going to wait while I prowl the place."

"Prowl the place?" Her tone reflected a humorous skepticism. "Who writes your dialogue?"

I reiterated that she was to remain in the car. I'd purposely left the keys in the ignition. "And lock the doors. I don't like the looks of this."

"The looks of what?"

"An open back door," I said. "But if we're lucky, we might get a chance to poke around in Colon's files before we catch up with him. Now, stay here."

She kept protesting until I assured her I'd come back for her once I was certain the building was clear. "Besides, what I'm about to do is totally illegal. It's called criminal trespass. You wouldn't want to be involved in breaking the law, would you?"

"Only if it's for a good cause," she said with a smile.

I smiled back and walked nonchalantly toward the rear entrance of Colon's office. As I drew closer, the slice of lighted space became more apparent. Why would he leave the place unsecured? Maybe he'd left in a hell of a hurry. Or maybe he hadn't. I paused to put on my thin, leather driving gloves, so I wouldn't have to worry about minimizing my skin contact with any smooth surfaces. I used the flashlight to push the door open all the way and stood off to the side, peering in by just exposing the very edge of my face. If anybody appeared, I could pull back and be out of any line of fire. Staying behind cover whenever possible. An old Ranger habit.

A long hallway extended before me, solid metal doors indicating three rooms along the way. At the end of the hallway, I could see the reception area, which looked deserted.

I waited and listened and thought I heard a voice. Seconds later, it became apparent what it really was.

A radio was playing somewhere inside. Elevator-type music. The voice was a disc jockey introducing the next bit of light jazz.

No movements.

I hesitated before taking that step inside, and removed the Beretta from its holster, holding it down by my leg. Better to be safe than sorry. I snapped the safety off and headed down the hallway. I checked the knob of the first door. It turned easily and the door opened. I let it go all the way to the wall, figuring there was no way anyone could be behind it unless they were Flat Stanley's first cousin. The room was dark, except for the light spilling in from the hallway. A room without windows. I swept the flashlight beam around and saw nothing but a lot of cardboard boxes with medical company logos on their sides. I moved to the adjacent door and tried it. It turned out to be a very large storage closet.

Third one's gotta be the charm, I thought.

As I moved down the hallway, the sound of the music grew a fraction louder. For some reason I recognized the song. A jazzed up version of "The Best is Yet to Come." The third door was unlocked as well, opening into another windowless room. This one wasn't filled with boxes. Two bodies lay on the floor, their hands tied neatly behind them, dark circles of blood ringing each of their faces, the expressions frozen in that last look of horror.

Dr. Colon and his pretty, young secretary.

ALEX ST. JAMES

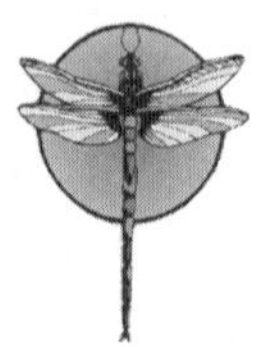

From my perch in his passenger seat, I watched Shade move like a big cat—smooth, alert, confident—as he pulled on a pair of gloves and made his way into the office through the open back door.

It drove me nuts to sit here and wait.

I hated waiting.

To keep myself occupied I reviewed our recent discussions, and I thought about my conversation with Dr. Keith Colon. He struck me as kind of a wimpy guy. Shade insisted that Colon was the weak link in this organization and that we should press him for answers because he was the most likely to give up the goods. He was right.

I had to admit, I'd been skeptical at first, but Shade's reasoning—his convincing argument that Howard Rybak had taken Bob Bayless's place in the burning car made sense. More than that, it struck that indescribable chord of truth. I knew it to be true, I knew it down deep. And now I was fully committed to seeing this story to its end.

Once Shade had made it through the doorway, and his shadow disappeared into the brightly lit office, I hadn't seen or heard anything.

I tapped my fingers on the door's edge. I tried to make myself think about other things, even as I stared. Maybe I'd have to start the car and unlock the door if he came running. Maybe he'd appear and gesture me in.

Maybe I'd be stuck sitting here and waiting. Like a girl.

Let the big, brave private detective have all the fun. Make the girl sit out in the car and wait.

I hated waiting.

But what could I do? Shade warned me that what he was doing was illegal. He'd even pulled on a pair of driving gloves to keep from leaving his prints. That much I knew. And I knew that if I followed him I'd inadvertently touch something, probably without realizing it.

And then I remembered the treasure trove of Shade's glove compartment. Among the piles of junk that had spilled out were latex gloves.

I opened the compartment. Three gloves total—I wondered about that—but not long enough to slow me down.

Grabbing the keys from the ignition, and being careful to leave the doors unlocked in the event that we'd have to get in quickly, I tugged the gloves on, and made my way to Dr. Colon's back door.

I couldn't believe how my heart pounded. I felt a rush, like a kid doing something forbidden, and for a moment I faltered. Shade probably wouldn't be happy to see me—but why should he get all the fun of interrogating Colon? I wanted to be there. I deserved to be in on it.

I felt a rush of excitement, fear, and impulsive determination.

My gym shoes were nearly silent on the floor tile. I could see all the way to the front of the office, and it looked like all the doors were open along the way. A radio played, but otherwise the place was silent as a tomb.

Where was Shade?

I took a quick look into the first room. Dark, empty. Nothing. It was too quiet. Shade should be talking to someone.

Unless he was going through the files, as he threatened he

might do. The thought of such an illegal search gave me the jitters, but I wanted to see those files, too.

I passed the second open room, a storage area, and was about to enter the third room, when from within, Shade shouted. "Don't move."

I peered around the doorway, to see who he was talking to.

Shade's gun pointed straight at my face.

"Goddamn it," he said, lowering the weapon the moment he saw me. "Do you want to get killed?"

"No," I said, my voice shaky and angry at the same time.

"Then why the hell didn't you stay in the car like I told you?"

"Because you don't get to tell me what to do."

"I do if it's for your own good."

"You don't get to decide what's for my own—" I suddenly spotted two bodies on the floor behind him. "Oh my God."

"Let's get out of here," he said, pulling his cell phone from his pocket.

I couldn't drag my eyes away from the scene. "They were shot in the head."

"Yeah," he said, grabbing my elbow.

"Oh my God," I said again, resisting him. A sudden memory bubbled up, and I could see how these two died. I'd watched someone get shot in the head before. Up close and personal. "Who did this?"

"If we get out of here, we can call the cops and maybe they'll find out," he said, his voice losing all friendliness. "You're contaminating the scene just by being here."

His tone got to me. I held up my hands. "I put gloves on, okay?"

My voice shook. Dr. Colon and his receptionist lying dead on the floor, pools of blood surrounding their broken skulls, reminded me so much . . .

"Yeah, well, what about your shoes?"

I glanced down. I hadn't thought about that. "Yours, too."

"It's a hell of a lot easier to explain one of us being in here, than two." He shook his head in apparent disgust and politely pushed me down the corridor to the back door.

This time I allowed it.

Outside, I closed my eyes for a moment, centering myself. I could imagine the gunman, easily. I could imagine his dispassionate actions. Who did he kill first? I hoped it was the receptionist. Then she wouldn't have had time to be terrified.

"You okay?" Shade asked.

I nodded.

"Never seen anything like that before, huh?"

"Actually," I felt bile rise up the back of my throat. "I have."

He didn't ask and I didn't offer. This was not the time for a Kumbaya meeting. Shade turned away. In a moment he was on the phone with the police, holding a finger against his opposite ear when a loud car on the next street boosted its bass.

I pulled out my cell phone to call George.

Still shaky, I said, "Hi," when he answered.

"What's wrong?"

I opened my mouth to speak but for a long moment nothing came out.

"Alex?"

"It's another . . ." I bit my lip, and leaned my butt against Shade's fender. I was vaguely aware that he'd completed his call and had come over to me. There was concern in his eyes. "It's another murder," I said finally. "A double shooting this time."

Shade lifted his eyebrows.

"Where are you?" George asked.

I told him.

"I'll be right there."

When I disconnected, Shade asked, "Who'd you call?"

"My police detective friend, George."

He looked at me for a moment. "*Another* murder?"

"Long story."

Shade was taken aback, but we didn't have time to discuss it. Nor did I care to. The first wave of police officers arrived, followed by evidence technicians, and detectives. A couple of them joked about waiting for the medical examiner.

We both agreed to tell the truth. We were there to question Dr. Colon, we found the back door open, and we investigated. Two detectives sidled up to Shade and didn't look like they were glad to see him.

One of them said, "You again? How come whenever there's a dead body we find you nearby?" He looked over at me. "And always with some girl."

I frowned at that. The other one looked ready to take me, too, but George Lulinski was suddenly there. "I got her, guys," he said, leading me away.

"Detectives Reed and Randecki," I heard Shade saying. "Nice to see you two again."

They both frowned and took Shade with them.

As soon as we were out of earshot, George said, "I could ask you the same question. How come whenever there's a dead body, you're involved?" He slung a glance back at the departing threesome. "And who's the guy?"

Ron Shade

It was close to two in the morning when they let Alex and me go. Not that we technically couldn't have walked out at any time, since we weren't under arrest. But I've usually found that whenever I try to flex my constitutional muscles with the cops, they end up making things more difficult in the long run. Especially when Reed and Randecki were involved. It was also one of the reasons I didn't bother to call George right away. Didn't want it to look like I ran to him, my surrogate big brother, whenever I ran afoul of the law. Besides, the last time there'd been a bit of a row, with George threatening to punch Randecki's lights out because he suspected me in a murder. A murder that had been a lot like this one.

Luckily, neither of them was the primary, so they had a vested disinterest. Plus, Alex's friend, George Lulinski, seemed more than up to the job of keeping our powder dry. He seemed like a helluva nice guy, too. I felt I could talk to him. And besides, neither Alex or I had anything to hide. We were the complainants. Discoverers of a violent crime, just doing our civic duty and reporting it to the lawful authorities.

But try convincing yourself of that one after you've spent a solid four hours sitting on a hard chair in an interview room up at Belmont and Western, waiting for someone to come take your statement. I understood the motivating procedure for keeping us separated. It was standard procedure for crime witnesses, but I really needed to talk to Alex. Luckily, Lulinski walked in and offered me a cigarette. I shook my head. He shrugged, shook one loose, and stuck it between his lips. So much for our public servants adhering to the restrictions of the clean air act.

"I know I'm sort of in your house," I said, as politely as I could, "but I really hate the smell of cigarette smoke."

"Me, too," he said, taking out his lighter.

"How about if I mention that I'm a professional athlete and I'm in training?"

He held the lighter in his hand, gesturing as he talked, but not lighting the square. "Yeah, I heard something about that.

You're that fighter buddy of Grieves over in One, right?"

"One and the same," I said.

He scratched his chin and slipped the lighter back into his shirt pocket. The unlit cigarette was still between his lips and it bounced up and down as he talked. "I heard about you. You're supposed to be a pretty straight shooter. Now, what I want to know is how you got Alex involved in a homicide. And a double, at that."

"That was her idea. I told her not to follow me in."

"It doesn't matter much, now, does it? With her sitting down the hall in a room like this."

The good-cop-guilt-trip didn't work well on me, and I told him so. I'd been around long enough to know how things worked in the world of police. He grinned and took out the lighter as he stood.

"It was worth a try, though, wasn't it?" With that he flicked his Bic, held the flame to the end of the cigarette, and started to leave the room as he inhaled. I had to put my trust in somebody and since Alex seemed to think highly of this guy, I said, "George."

He turned, his eyebrows elevated.

"What do you want to know?" I asked.

He turned and smiled, pausing to grind out the cigarette on the cinderblock wall before coming back to the table.

"Details of the case you're working would be nice." He sat in the chair across from me. "And I'd appreciate it if you hurried, unless you want me to have a nicotine fit."

I grinned. "I appreciate your restraint." As quickly as I could, I ran things down for him, starting with the Bayless investigation, my conversations with the widow, Dr. Colon, and Nick Farnsworth. "It was shortly after that conversation that a couple of his Russian friends tried to whack me in an alley. They got away, but I put a bullet in one of them."

"And who's working that case?"

I gave him Cate and Norris's cell numbers, as well as George's. "Grieves can vouch for me, if you question my veracity."

"Your what?"

"Never mind, I was just in a literary mood." I paused and licked my lips. "I know it's asking a lot, but could you give Alex a note if I write her one?"

His mouth sort of went sour, but he nodded. "What I'd really like to do is talk with this Farnsworth guy. You know how to get ahold of him?"

"Alex might know," I said. "Apparently they were childhood friends, or something. But she knows he's a shithead." I took out my notebook and pen and wrote on a piece of paper: *The next weakest link is Bayless, and they're getting sloppy tying up loose ends. We've got to move fast. Are you up for a quick trip to Vegas?*

I signed it *Ron,* and made no effort to fold it or conceal what I'd written. Lulinski took it as if he wasn't going to look at it, but I was sure he'd read it as soon as he left me alone in the room again. I only hoped it worked.

Chapter 18

Alex St. James

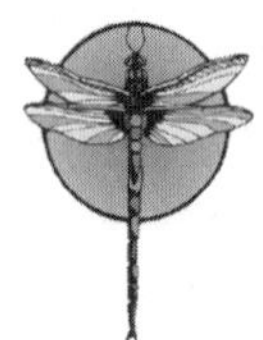

We made it to Midway Airport by seven o'clock the morning after next. Too bad our flight wasn't scheduled till three-fifteen. We'd gotten there early in the hope of catching an earlier flight, but there were none available with standby seating. There aren't any places to sit and wait at Midway, until you get past security. Since we were early, we couldn't check our bags right away, and we were stuck meandering the small check-in area with occasional traipses downstairs to the bathrooms in baggage claim.

Southwest Airlines was my favorite way to fly, despite the crazy A, B, C seating system. We'd all gotten in the A group for our three-fifteen departure, but before our plane took off, I asked Shade to hold my place in the boarding line, while I walked off to put in another call to Jordan.

She'd been surprised by my sudden travel plans when I told her yesterday. Shade had made a good case for taking off the morning after we found Dr. Colon, but I needed a day to get the travel approved and to get a cameraman to accompany us.

Hal sat in a chair with his back to the window, claiming that he didn't feel like spending an hour standing in line just to get his choice of seats. The truth was he knew we'd save him a spot and he had no problem leaving us to do the dirty work. Hal dozed frequently. His big head bobbed up—startled—whenever he lost consciousness, and his bottom lip hung slack.

I made my way past him as Jordan and I talked. I asked her to do a little more investigative work on Manus while I was gone. She agreed. "By the way," she said, "your uncle called this morning. He was trying to get ahold of you."

"My Uncle Moose?" I'd already told him and Aunt Lena that I'd be out of town for a couple days.

"No, your Uncle Larry."

"I don't have an—" I let my voice trail off. Good old "Uncle Lare." I was really beginning to regret using that appellation when I was trying to butter him up for my adoption quest. And now he'd called my work claiming to really be my uncle. That was odd. "Did he say what he wanted?"

"No. He seemed worried, and when he found out you were going to Vegas, he got upset."

"You told him?"

"Not me. Frances. She took the call when I was away from my desk. I guess your Uncle Larry didn't feel like leaving a voice mail and Frances let it slip where you were. She said he got angry and wanted us to call you right away to tell you not to go."

I'll bet, I thought. Nicky must have confided in him—which meant Uncle Larry was now on the list of bad guys. "If he or Nicky Farnsworth calls back, don't tell him anything else. As far as the world is concerned, I'm heading to Lincoln City, Oregon."

"Where's that?"

"It's on the coast." I sighed. "Anyway, thanks for the update. I'll call you if I get anything."

"You got to go?"

"No, Shade's motioning to me. He must want something."

"You go, girl." Her tone was so light it took me a minute to realize what she meant.

I started to say it wasn't that kind of a trip, when she added, "Try to stay out of trouble," and hung up.

Ron Shade

I motioned to Alex St. James, who was on her cell phone once again, and she held up her hand for me to wait. I was glad she wouldn't be yapping on the damn thing during the flight, since most likely we'd be seated next to each other. At least that was the plan. And it probably wouldn't have been an issue at all if we'd gotten her boss to pick up the tab for some first-class tickets. But instead, she'd insisted on flying on Southwest, her "favorite airline." For my money, all they did was cut bad jokes and make you wait in line according to number, then scramble for your seat. Not that I minded scrambling, but I hated to wait. And that seemed like all I was doing lately. I'd pressed to leave immediately after we'd found Colon and his hygienist stretched out in that pool of blood, but Alex had to get the trip approved and arrange for her pain-in-the-ass cameraman to accompany us. Just what I needed: some guy with a bladder control problem dragging me down. We'd lost some of the element of surprise already, but at least the bad guys didn't know we were coming. I needed to work that advantage.

And in all fairness, the extra day had turned out to be sort of a godsend for me. I'd spent the time briefing George, who was furious I hadn't called him last night. Luckily, Lulinski had already given him most of the scoop, and all I had to do was fill in the blanks. Plus, I approached him about his daughter taking in the mail and feeding the cats while I was gone. She'd done this before and spared me the expense and trauma of boarding them at the vet's. After throwing things in a suitcase, I grabbed a couple hours' sleep before getting up extra early to meet Alex at Midway at seven. We'd managed to get reservations on a flight with three cancellations that took off at three-fifteen, but we hoped to find an earlier one. As luck would have it, we didn't, and we'd already spent most of the day waiting and trying to avoid airport chow as best we could. At least we'd been able to check our bags at noon and get through the security checkpoints. But now we were back to playing the waiting game, and I had to hit the bathroom, but some grandmother with a little squirming tyke was inching up on me in the A line. If I left to go, then it would be back to the end once again. I motioned yet again, and, once again, she held up her hand to let me know she'd be there in a minute.

Like I said, I'm a man who hates to wait.

It wasn't helping things that I hadn't packed my Beretta, either. I felt practically naked without it. I hadn't taken it the last time for my big fight back in March, but this time I was working a case and might end up needing it. I wasn't licensed in the state of Nevada and didn't want to risk losing the gun if I got involved in a shooting. So I had to make other arrangements, although I had an idea about how to maybe get around that.

That extra bottle of water I'd drunk to wash down my fast-food lunch was really starting to get to me, and grandma looked like she sensed an imminent move on my part. Alex heaved a sigh and looked like she was finally starting to wind up her phone conversation.

"Excuse me, young man," grandma said. "Are you going to be here for a few more minutes?"

"It looks like it," I said.

"Good, would you mind holding my place in the line?" She grinned knowingly at me. "I have to take my granddaughter to the washroom. She has to go."

I grimaced as I nodded. I knew the feeling.

Alex finally hung up and came sauntering over, stopping to smile and exchange a few words with grandma and grandbaby. I guess the kid didn't have to go that bad after all. But I sure the hell did.

I glanced at my watch and hoped for the best. I could hardly wait to get on that damn plane.

Finally Alex sauntered over to me with a "What?"

Before I could answer, the Southwest attendant stepped over and started announcing that they'd be allowing handicapped individuals and people with small children to board in five minutes.

She raised her eyebrows questioningly. "What do you need?"

"A short line in the mens' room," I said.

Alex St. James

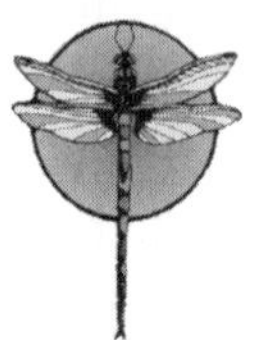

On the plane, I made myself small, trying to keep my arms away from the large male bodies that walled me into the tight cocoon of middle-seat airline travel. The overbooked flight left me no open seats to claim later, and so I'd resigned myself to three and a half hours of minuscule movements between muscular Shade and beer-belly Hal.

I glanced out Shade's window as we passed through a sunlit blanket of white clouds. He had gallantly offered me the window seat, and although I would have loved that, it made much more sense to put the smallest person in the center.

Shade read a novel, Hal slept and occasionally snored.

"Bayless," I said.

Shade turned to me. "What about him?"

"If you're right, and he's the next weakest link, don't you think whoever is running the show will be after him?" I thought about the glistening pools of blood on the dentist's office floor. "Don't you think he's in danger?"

"No," he said, shutting his novel and keeping his voice low. "I don't think anyone realizes that we've put it all together. Not yet, at least. That's why I wanted to fly out as soon as possible."

I took a deep breath. No sense in putting off the inevitable. "I've got some potentially bad news for you."

"What?"

"Nicky probably knows we're headed to Vegas."

"How the hell can he know that? Did you tell him?"

I sat up as straight as my cramped quarters would allow. "Of course not."

"Well then, how—"

"One of the station's assistants inadvertently told Nicky's father where I was going."

"Shit." He stared out the window, working his jaw. Little clicks of tension broke the silence between us. "This changes things."

"But," I said, "I can't see Nicky being a threat."

Shade turned to me, a warning in his eyes. "Just because you've known the guy since you were a kid doesn't mean that he isn't capable—"

"I don't mean that," I said, interrupting him. "I think Nicky's perfectly capable of all the terrible things we suspect him of. I just don't see him as someone to be afraid of. He's kind of a wimp."

Shade made a noise that might've been a laugh. "Wimps get desperate, too. That's when they get dangerous. He's got a lot to lose and if he's calling the shots . . ."

"That's the thing. I don't think he's in charge."

"Then who is?"

"I have no idea."

"We can't discount the possibility that Bayless is involved in the whole thing, but with him being in Vegas and all these bodies popping up in Illinois, it's probably a good bet that he's on the periphery. Your buddy Nicky's the one with the association to dead homeless guys."

"All the same," I said, "I don't know . . ."

Shade continued, "Think about it. He's got unlimited access to the body parts market, which you found out about, and he's hired the muscle to take care of any problems that come up."

We were silent for a while, listening to the muted roar of the 737's engine.

"I still don't know how you think we'll find Bayless in a city as busy as Las Vegas," I said.

"I have my ways."

"And when we find him?"

"When he finds out what happened to Dr. Colon, he'll be willing to sing like a canary. Especially once he knows Nicky and his gang are on their way."

I gave him my best skeptical look. "And if Bayless doesn't sing?"

"Then we find out what his buttons are and we push them," he said. "Hard."

With a menacing grin like that, he looked positively scary. I realized that I would never want to be on this guy's bad side. I checked on Hal. Still fast asleep. He snored loudly, then slid sideways to lean against my shoulder. "Great," I whispered.

"Why did he have to come along?" Shade asked. "He's just going to slow us down."

"Bass insisted."

"Your boss doesn't like me much."

"Bass doesn't like anybody much."

"I thought you said he'd fight you about paying for this trip."

"Yeah," I said, marveling. "Go figure. Bass is a guy who doesn't like to be 'taken.' He thinks that since you weren't up-front about your car's history, you tried to 'take' him."

Shade considered that. "I thought just giving him a good price was enough."

The cabin attendant came by with little packets of peanuts and boxes of snacks with hearts printed all over them. "I love Southwest," I said, when I found Oreos in the box. I tore open the package and popped one in my mouth saying, "Best cookie ever invented."

"I heard they took out the trans fats in those."

I stared at him and shook my head. "Don't mess with my Oreos."

He laughed. "Or what?"

"Or I'll take them on," I said. "Believe it. I may not look it, but I'm tough."

"Oh yeah?"

Since he clearly didn't know me, and I didn't feel like arguing, I took the opportunity to shove a second cookie in my mouth. "You'll see."

"When we find Bob Bayless, I'll need you to be ready," he said.

"Ready for what?"

"That's the thing. We don't know exactly. Not yet. We've got Nicky figuring into the equation now. He's a variable I didn't count on. I want to run over all possible scenarios with you, so that we're prepared."

We talked until the cabin attendant returned with our beverages. Shade and I had cranberry juice, Hal woke up long enough to ask for coffee. He dragged the back of his hand against his mouth and thanked her.

"Look," I said, pointing out the window. "Snowcapped mountains."

Shade turned to look out. "Beautiful."

Hal wasn't paying attention.

"We need you to be ready to move, too," I said.

Hal took a long drink of coffee, still not fully awake. "Where am I moving?"

I started to answer him, but he drained the cup, pushed up his tray table and stood.

"Forget that now, I gotta go."

Shade followed him with his eyes. Hal headed for the front of the plane where the attendant reminded him that there could be no line for the washroom. She directed him to the back. He shrugged good-naturedly as he passed us.

I stretched and stood.

"You gotta go, too?" Shade asked.

"No, just appreciating the space."

When I sat again, he said, "Your friend Hal's going to slow us down. Mark my words."

I sighed. "You're probably right. But without footage, I don't have a story."

"Here's the thing, Alex," he said. "All I have to do is prove Bayless is still alive. If we capture him on tape, we'll have proof. But if he rabbits, I'm going after him, with or without you." He glanced back toward the washroom. "Or Hal."

"Well then, I'll just have to make sure we keep up."

Shade lifted an eyebrow.

Ron Shade

All I remembered doing was leaning my seat back after we finished talking and I was out like a light. I didn't know if I snored on the way, but the quick combat nap was all that I needed. I felt a gentle pushing at my side, and hoped I didn't mention any girl's name, because when I snapped awake I saw Alex St. James giving me a sideways look.

"We're on the descent now," she said.

I turned and looked out the window. Mountains and a fleeting glimpse of what I figured was Lake Mead were visible down below. I moved the seat to its upright position and stretched the best I could.

"How long was I out?"

She shrugged. "Only about ten minutes."

"So, did I snore or say anything really embarrassing?"

"No more than usual," she said, with a self-satisfied smile.

I figured it was better not to inquire further.

The plane canted and we saw the Strip, the huge hotels looking like real expensive toys spread out in a cluttered sidewalk. I wondered what Vegas would be like in ten years if the building craze continued. Chappie's remark on my last trip had sort of stayed with me. "Shit, when I was fighting out here, wasn't nothing around 'cepting Fremont and a few big hotels. Now there's wall-to-wall people."

And one of them was Bayless. I checked the copy of the *Sun-Times* in my carry-on gym case. Still there.

"You really think he'll be intimidated enough to cooperate

when he sees that?" Alex asked.

"One headline's worth a thousand words, and this one's a doozy." It read, in big block letters: DENTIST AND ASSISTANT SLAIN.

We were descending now, the ground getting closer and closer. I started a slow count, estimating that we'd touch down in about fifteen seconds. We hit the tarmac in ten, harder than I thought we would. The big turbines turned it up a notch as they began to spin in reverse, and I felt the pull on the brakes. The plane slowed and everybody breathed a collective sigh of relief, whether they wanted to admit it or not. The pilot's voice came over the intercom.

"Ladies and gentlemen, welcome to Lost Wages."

As soon as we'd deplaned, we headed to the washrooms before making the hike to pick up our luggage. Naturally, Hal went in first. I glanced at Alex and told her I'd watch the carry-ons if she wanted to go to the ladies' room. "Unless you figure the men's room would be quicker."

She smirked and as she walked away, said, "Don't think I wouldn't."

I shifted my gym bag to my right forearm and took off my watch to reset it to Nevada time. It was only four-forty-five here. I refastened my watch and checked my cell. The screen showed a missed call from George.

"How's things in sin city?" he asked. The reception was iffy, but it always was on the Ryan.

"Hot and nice," I said. We went by an island of slot machines. "What's up?"

"Just wanted to let you know, our buddy Nick Farnsworth still isn't anywhere to be found." He laughed. "Of course, maybe he's out helping the homeless."

"Yeah, right," I said. "I think I might know where he is.

Someone at Alex's office tipped his lawyer daddy that we were out here."

I heard him sigh. "Not much point in asking daddy lawbucks where he's at, either."

"Keep checking under some rocks," I said. "And maybe with some of the airlines. You guys can get access to passenger lists, right?"

"If I ask sweetly."

"I guess I can forget that, then. Anything on that Russian dude?"

"Nope, but I'm looking." His laugh was bitter. "You got any fucking idea how many Russkies are named Viktor?"

"More than three?"

"Yeah, a lot more. But, we did get a line on the dude you shot."

"Great, who is he?"

"John Doe. At least we're pretty sure it's the same guy. The ET's lifted a blood print from the dashboard. Norris said they told him the guy must have been close to bleeding out from the amount of blood that was in the car. So they're still checking all the hospitals. My guess is he'll turn up in the morgue or on a dump."

"Or maybe in Sunset Manor. Why don't you get a warrant for that place?"

"With what as probable cause? The fact that you think the guys that attacked you were Russkies?"

I sighed. We were still marching down the long aisle toward the shuttle tram, and Alex St. James and old Hal were ahead of me. "No ID on the print yet?"

"Nah, nothing. We're running it through the FBI now. Maybe he'll turn up with an arrest record in another state, if we're lucky. Then I can run his known associates and maybe get a line on our buddy Viktor."

He pronounced the name with a heavy accent.

"I didn't know you spoke Russian," I said.

"I don't. I was imitating Schwarzenegger. Wanted to make you feel at home. He's the governator out there, ain't he?"

"That's California. We're in Nevada. And he's Austrian."

"Close enough. Besides, he played a Russian copper in *Red Heat* with Belushi. Anyway, if it's possible these assholes are in Vegas, you watch your ass."

"I always do, but why'd you mention it?"

"The way this thing's playing out, these guys ain't your typical street punks."

"So?"

"They had the foresight to have another ride stashed and ready for their getaway. And the way they did that dentist and his secretary . . . Lulinski told me it looked like a couple of professional hits." The rest of his sentence faded away.

I considered this. Very cold-blooded. Very *Spetsnaz*.

"Ron, you there?" His voice brought me back.

"Yeah, I lost you for second."

"Yeah, I'm getting to a bad spot. I said, don't discount the possibility that they might already be out there. Like I told you, nobody's seen hide nor hair of Farnsworth lately, and it fits with what you told me."

"I hope they are," I said. "I'd like a rematch with the dude who tried to run me down."

"Yeah," he said, "just remember that you're dealing with some sociopathic motherfuckers."

I grinned, even though I knew he couldn't see it. "Maybe I'll have this thing all wrapped up for you by the time I get back." I caught up to Alex and Hal at the shuttle doors. She looked up at me as I talked.

"Hey, I'm serious," George said. "You ain't licensed to pack in Nevada, buddy."

"Don't worry. I got that covered."

"Huh? How?"

"Never mind," I said. "Any word on the demise of the good Doctor Colon?"

"Cause of death for both was a close contact wound to the back of the head. A couple of cold-blooded dispatches. Office was ransacked, but you already know that, don't you?"

"So, most likely the killer was looking for something, then?"

"Probably, but that's an assumption. Still, we'd like to talk to Farnsworth about Colon. There's got to be some connection with all this. I mean, Colon fixed the teeth of the homeless and Farnsworth buried them."

"And sometimes not in that order," I added.

"Like I said, watch your ass."

"I will."

"And, Ron . . ."

"Yeah?"

"Don't do nothing illegal as far as carrying a gun. I don't want to get a call to wire you any bond money."

"I told you, I got that covered," I said. "I'm on my way to see a bondsman."

I hung up on him, fished out the card I needed, and began punching in another number.

"Who are you calling now?" Alex asked.

I glanced toward the big window to the right. I could see the shuttle tram making its smooth run along the cement track toward us. "A guy I know from the army. Lives out here."

"Can't we get our luggage first?"

"Relax." I finished putting in the long-digited number and pressed the SEND button. "It's not even off the plane yet." I pointed in the direction of the monorail shuttle that would take us to the baggage claim section. "Besides, we still have a long walk just to get to baggage claim."

The phone rang twice before a gruff male voice answered. "Licardo bail bond."

"Hey, Tony, it's Ron Shade."

"Ronnie." His voice immediately warmed up. "What you been up to? How's Chi-town?"

"Actually, I'm in your backyard. Just landed at McCarran."

"No shit? What, you got another fight out here, or something?"

"Or something. I wanted to touch bases with you." Alex St. James turned away from me, as if she couldn't care less about my conversation. "I'm working a case and might need some local assistance."

"Does it involve a bail jumper?"

That was the Tony I remembered. Always looking for an angle. All business. "Sort of. Only there's no bail on this one. It's a missing person case."

"Sounds intriguing."

I could almost hear his mental wheels whirling, trying to calculate how profitable this would be for him. "I thought I'd drop by your place after I get my car. You still at the same address?"

He repeated the Desert Palm Street address that was on his card.

"Yeah, come on by. It'll be good to see you again."

As I hung up I spied the shuttle through the huge Plexiglas windows, unloading the departing people on the other side of us.

"Why did you say that?" Alex asked as the doors for our side opened.

"Say what?"

" 'Touch bases.' " The three of us stepped inside and sat on the area next to the window. "I've always thought it was 'touch base.' "

I considered this for a moment and realized she was probably right. Since I'd always been too busy punching bags or running track growing up, I never took the time to learn the rudiments of the national pastime.

"Well, ordinarily it would be," I said, as the shuttle closed. It was just her, me, and Hal in the car, so I shot out a super-quick jab. "But when you're as fast as I am, you say 'bases.' "

Luckily, the shuttle lurched forward and I grabbed the long metal pole for support, sparing me any further demonstrations.

Alex St. James

A tram ride later, and just as we entered the enormous baggage claim area, Hal had to make yet another pit stop.

On the phone again, Shade gave me a look that said, "I told you he's going to slow us down."

I turned away, rolling my eyes when I knew he couldn't see me. They were *both* slowing us down.

Let Shade make his important calls. He was probably a player, and I didn't mean the kind who sat at a Baccarat table. Chances were he was "touching bases" with a girlfriend—or twelve—to tell the poor dears that he landed safely.

None of which was helping my story.

I wanted to get moving.

"I'll be with the luggage," I said, loud enough to break into his conversation. He signaled me to wait, but I shook my head. "You wait for Hal."

Striding toward the cavernous carousel area, I finally felt like

I'd accomplished something. At a minimum, I was moving. Coupling the daylong wait at Midway with my inability to move freely on the plane for the past several hours, I was tense, irritable and wanting to break away. Now.

Getting the luggage would help.

My bright purple suitcases popped over the top of the carousel, and I scurried to retrieve them. Hal and Shade would have to find their own, since I didn't pay close enough attention to their belongings to recognize them now. I snapped up my wheelies' handles and started back. Shade spotted me from across the room and changed his trajectory.

"Where are you going?" he asked.

Still walking, I pointed toward the rent-a-car counter. "Somebody has to get us organized here."

"Just wait till I get my stuff."

I didn't stop. "I'll be in line right there." I pointed. "Where's Hal?"

Shade yanked a thumb over his shoulder. "Playing the slots."

"For crying out loud. Doesn't he know we're here to work?"

"Go get him then, while I get my stuff."

"No," I said, "you go get him." Shade had followed me to the rent-a-car location, and I was already in line. A long one. My voice betrayed my impatience. "Tell him to get his butt over to the luggage with you and then both of you meet me here."

"Yes, ma'am." He saluted.

"Hop to it, soldier." I fought a smile as I turned away. At least someone was finally listening to me.

Just as I was making the final arrangements for the car, Shade came waltzing up with the luggage and Hal in tow.

"You win anything?" I asked him.

He shook his head sadly.

Good.

Shade and I battled a bit over the hotel arrangements. He

wanted to go check in as soon as we got our car, but I felt it was just one more delay. As the woman behind the rent-a-car counter processed an extra driver, Shade persisted.

"But what if they give our rooms away?" he asked. "Then what do we do?"

"Our rooms are reserved," I said. "They can't give them away."

"You better hope you're right." He shook his head. "I mean, it'd be a real shame if we had to double up." He wiggled an eyebrow at me.

"I'd manage to find a room for myself," I said, looking over my shoulder at Hal who stood about thirty feet away, surrounded by luggage. "But you two would make interesting roommates."

Just then the counter clerk handed us our paperwork.

I grinned at Shade. "Don't forget, he snores."

"Just the same, I'd feel better if we got ourselves settled."

I bit my lip. Another delay.

Shade, Hal and I took the shuttle to the remote lot where Shade insisted on upgrading from a Taurus to a big cream-colored Cadillac Escalade. Another delay. While we waited, he told me that his trainer, Chappie, said, "A champ should always ride in a Cadillac." Truth be told, I was impressed by his world-champ title, though I was loathe to admit it at the moment. I was hungry, tired, and more than a little bit annoyed by the constant drag on our time.

Shade drove, Hal took shotgun, and I sat in the back. I was starting to feel like the useless female again. But then, just before we pulled out, Shade turned around. "Okay, your call. I think we should get our rooms because we need a base of operations. There's no telling how long we'll be at the Bayless house, and the last thing we need is complexity when we're tired tonight. Plus it's good to have somewhere people can reach us to leave messages." He fixed me with an earnest stare. "But it's up to you."

"I'm just worried. It's already after five. How are we supposed to find where Bayless lives? I'm sure all the official buildings are either closed by now or will be soon."

He dug into a pocket and pulled out a note. "Here."

It was an address for a Robert Barstow. "This is Bayless?" I asked.

"Yep." Before I could say anything else, he pulled out pictures and handed them to me. "And here's the happy couple."

They were copies of Illinois drivers' licenses for Robert Bayless and Candice Prokovis. I was amazed and nearly speechless. Coupled with the address, Shade had eliminated the biggest challenge we faced. Finding these people. "How did you get these?"

He smiled as I handed the papers back to him. "I got friends in low places."

"I'll bet you do." Suddenly ebullient, I grinned. "You're good."

He wagged an eyebrow. "You have no idea."

I was about to quip back, but Hal chimed in, "So where are we going first?"

They both looked at me.

"Let's go check in."

Chapter 19

Ron Shade

I was beginning to feel like spending time with this high-maintenance gal was like going a couple of rounds in the gym, with one hand tied behind my back. All she did was complain and find fault. We were like two bull goats, butting heads over which way to go on the mountain path. I glanced in the mirror and saw her pretty face staring back at me. Well, maybe not a bull goat . . . She smiled at me. No, definitely not.

"Aren't we going the wrong way?" she asked a moment later.

I'd taken a left on Koval, instead of a right, and then another left on Las Vegas Boulevard. We were going past the Luxor with the Mandalay Bay coming up on the right. "Nope."

"But we're going south. The Venetian is back that way."

Of course, she was correct, but I'd be damned if I was going to admit my mistake in front of Ms. High Maintenance. "Yeah, I know. But this is a special route."

I drove down Las Vegas Boulevard until we went past the big sign telling us to drive carefully and come back soon, and turned around.

"There it is," I said, "Welcome to Fabulous Las Vegas, Nevada. It's one of my favorite sights." Naturally, this elicited an exasperated sigh from Alex St. James.

"Aww, looks like the old Klondike Casino is closed," I said.

Another sigh, this one more exaggerated. "That's a real tragedy . . . And this has what to do with our assignment again?"

"I always like to drive past this spot," I said, by way of explanation.

"Wonderful. Now can you do something to avoid some of this traffic?"

It was getting pretty heavy, so I edged over to turn right at Tropicana and take the back way in.

"Are you *sure* you know where you're going?" she asked, her voice lilting with sarcasm.

"Yeah, like the back of my hand. This ain't the first time I been out here." I pointed to the MGM and said to Hal, "I had a fight in that place once."

"Great," he said. "Say, how soon till we get there? I got to go to the bathroom."

So much for male solidarity. I shot a quick look back at Alex. How did I get stuck with these two? But at least she was easy on the eyes. Plus, I got a feeling that under that ice-princess exterior beat the heart of a real sweetheart. Maybe someday I'd find out. I glanced at her in the mirror again, and this time she looked away. Then again, maybe I wouldn't find out.

Now it was all beginning to come back to me . . . My early morning runs along the streets east of the Strip. I cut over on Koval and took it north. The traffic was noticeably lighter, so we reached the back entrance to the hotel in about ten minutes. I still needed to get to Tony's place before we went Bayless hunting. I parked in the special section that allowed us express check-in and left the luggage with a bellman. I slipped the guy a twenty and told him which rooms we were in. I figured after my unintended detour, time was of the essence, and the expense account would handle it.

Back in the car, I swung out the back way and went over to Sands and hung a quick left. Once we crossed under the expressway, Sands morphed into Spring Mountain, and I took a chance and turned right on a street called Polaris. I actually was lost but didn't want to admit that in front of Alex St. James.

"Where are we heading now?" she asked, as if she was reading my mind.

Just as I was about to nudge Hal to hand me the map, I saw Desert Inn Road and grinned. "To see my buddy Tony." I turned left and we were on our way.

His bail bondsman office was in a strip mall, which accounted for part of the reason I drove right by it. The other part was the scarcity of address numbers. By the time I saw one, I knew I'd overshot it. Swearing, I slowed down and executed a left, then a U-turn, then a right.

"Going to take in another of your favorite sights?" Alex asked.

She had a good metaphorical jab; I let it slip by. If I admitted she was getting to me, I'd lose, and I hated to lose at anything. Once we were close to the strip mall, I saw the sign advertising Licardo's Bail Bonds in big white letters. How I'd missed it the first time was a mystery.

The buildings were all yellow brick, anchored by a big grocery store at one end and some kind of retail place on the other. In between were a series of smaller shops, restaurants, and Tony's place. The windows had *Bail Bondsman* painted on them in a huge colorful swath. It was glass across the front and the door had a large window, through which I saw Tony sitting at a desk talking on the phone. He grinned as we walked in, and I heard him say to whomever was on the line, "I gotta go." He hung up, stood, and came around the desk to give me an exaggerated hug.

"Ronnie, you're looking good, kid."

He was several inches shorter than me, and he'd gained about fifty pounds since we'd rolled in the desert sands shooting at bad guys together. He'd let his dark hair grow a bit longer, too, and now sported a mustache. He smiled at Alex and asked, "And who might this charming young thing be?"

"Tony Licardo," I said, "meet Ms. Alex St. James."

They shook hands, after which he said, "Charmed." He then gave her an up-and-down once-over, and added, "That Ronnie, he sure knows how to pick 'em."

I thought she was going to explode from the look in her eyes. Either that, or deck him. I let out a quick laugh in the hopes it would break the tension. "Actually, we're all here on business. Oh, by the way, this is Hal."

Tony and Hal shook, and Hal asked if he could use Tony's washroom.

"It's down the hall and to the right," Tony said. He turned back to us as Hal took off. "What brings you out to Vegas?"

I gave him a thumbnail sketch of the case, making it as brief as I could.

He cocked his head back. "So, lemme get this straight. This Bayless guy is not wanted, and presumed dead?"

I nodded.

He sighed. "So, there's no bond up?"

"Right. I need to find the guy and convince him to come back to Chicago. Either that, or get some proof he's alive and well."

"You need me to help you find him?"

"Not exactly. There's some pretty bad dudes on his trail, too," I said. "And since I'm not licensed in this state, I didn't bring my piece with me."

"And?"

"And, I thought since this case does involve a certain amount of danger, you might see your way clear to sort of hire me temporarily and loan me a gun that works."

He considered this for a moment, then said, "Ron, I got a business here. I'm bonded. I let you go around carrying in my employ, without the right permits, and I'll be in deep linguini."

We heard the toilet flush and Hal came ambling back toward us. Tony gave him a disgusted look. "That's your backup?"

I'd figured he might be a bit resistant so I pulled out the heavy-duty artillery. "What about all those times I saved your life?"

He smiled. "Yeah, I ain't forgot those." His big hand gripped his chin and his brow furrowed. After a minute of concentration, he brought the hand away, jerking his finger in the air like he was tapping an imaginary button. "I think I got it." He pulled out his cell phone, looked up a number, and called it. "Ross? Tony. What you doing?" He listened, grinned at us, and said, "Great. I got a special job for you. Bring the van, too." When he hung up, he held up his thumb and index finger in a circle. "Ross can go with you. He's one of my best skip tracers. We got a fabulous surveillance van, too. You can use it all, and he'll be packing the heat. He's got a concealed carry."

I nodded a "thanks" and smiled back. I could tell from her expression that Alex St. James wasn't too impressed, but this was probably as good of a deal as we were going to get in this town. I only hoped it would be enough.

ALEX ST. JAMES

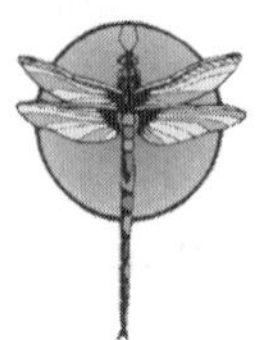

I desperately hoped we'd find this Bayless guy before Nicky and his Russian friends did and that the skip tracer's presence would prove unnecessary. He wasn't a bad-looking guy. Sort of tall and angular, wearing a free-flowing Hawaiian shirt. I placed him in his late forties. He was smoking when he came inside the office, but extinguished it as soon as he saw us standing there. His van was as impressive as Tony bragged. It had windows made for looking out, but not letting anyone on the outside look in. Inside, he had a couple of comfortable chairs, a small refrigerator, several TV screens, and a retractable curtain behind the front seats.

Ross generously offered Hal a spot in his surveillance van. That was quite a coup for us: He'd have plenty of room to spread out his equipment, and he'd benefit from the van's back windows' one-way glass. Things were starting to come together, finally. It felt good.

Shade showed him the address, and Ross said he knew exactly where it was. We followed him in the Escalade for the twenty-minute trip, the air-conditioning keeping us cool. I felt some of my tension recede.

The Barstow home looked like every other home in the area. Unremarkable architecture, pebbled front yard. Nothing like the green lawns and careful shrubbery of home.

"So, what do we do?" I asked when Shade and I parked in front of the house. Ross's van pulled up one driveway behind us.

"I like the direct approach myself." He held up the front page of yesterday's *Sun-Times*. The bold headline announcing the double murder was eye-catching, but the smiling pictures just below, of Dr. Colon and his receptionist in better days, told the story. "Think this will get his attention?"

"You're sure this is his house?" I asked.

But Shade was already out of the car, newspaper in hand. He went to look in the garage window, then—bold as brass—strolled over the pebbled lawn to the front door.

I followed him up the short path and stood beside him. Shade pressed a thumb against the doorbell, hard. He held it there and from deep within the home's recesses, I heard the chime.

We waited. No movement, no dog barking, nothing.

Shade pressed the bell again. Longer. This time it chimed twice.

We waited again.

"Do you think they're just not answering?" I asked.

"No trace of a car around." He leaned sideways, peered into the front window, then pounded on it. A moment later he answered me. "I don't think anyone's home. So," he said, dragging the newspaper from under his arm, "we should leave a calling card."

He folded the newspaper so that the headline faced out, and snugged his business card between the door and the jamb. There was no screen door, so he wedged the folded newspaper in such a way that when someone inside opened the door, the newspaper would land faceup at their feet. That was the plan, anyway.

We returned to the car. I glanced over at the quiet van but didn't signal at all. If anyone was watching—like a nosy neighbor—they'd notice our attempt, but probably not associate us with the van.

Shade put the Escalade into gear and we took off. "Where are we going now?"

"Hang on."

He made a U-turn and came back to park across the street from the Bayless home. Just before he shut off the engine, my cell phone rang. It dawned on me that we should've rigged up walkie-talkies. My phone didn't have that capability, and when Hal came on the line when I answered, I wasn't surprised.

"Oh," he said. "I thought you were leaving."

"Nope. Just don't want to crowd that side of the street."

"How long you planning on waiting here?"

I asked Shade. He shrugged and pressed buttons to lower the windows. "As long as it takes."

Hal heard him through the line because he whined at me, "That's no answer."

"Why?" I asked. "You have a date?"

I was trying to be funny, but Hal huffed into the phone before answering, "Yeah, I got a date. With my urologist back in Chicago next week." His voice was so loud I held the phone away from my ear. "Until then I have to take a piss every hour or so and this little stakeout is killing me."

I closed my eyes and pulled my lips in tight to keep from sniping. I wanted to ask why in God's name he volunteered—in fact, lobbied—to come on this trip if he wasn't physically able to carry it out. Three other people from his department put their names in for the trip, too, but Bass picked Hal. I hadn't argued. There wasn't time. And, I saw no reason to. Now, I wanted to scream.

Shade grabbed the phone from me. "Improvise," he said. He hung up, handed the phone back and stared out the window at the house across the street. I could practically read the words, "I told you so," rising in an imaginary thought bubble as little waves of steam emanated from the top of his head. He was pissed. But not as much as I was.

"Why did you do that?" I asked him.

He looked at me as though I'd spoken Greek.

"Why did you rip the phone out of my hand?" I asked again.

"You looked like you were frustrated. Overwhelmed. I took care of it for you."

"I was handling it."

"Oh, you were?"

"Yeah, I was." This guy got my back up like no other. "Hal is my co-worker and my . . . problem. In the future, I'll handle my own problems, okay?"

"Fine."

"Fine."

We sat quietly for a long time. Hal ambled out of the van at one point and took a walk down the street. I had no idea what poor tree or bush he'd target, but in about fifteen minutes he was back. Our windows were open and the heat crept in. I knew Shade didn't want to keep the motor running for fear of overheating the big engine. "I'm a closet environmentalist," he'd said. "Hate the thought of all those fumes in the atmosphere."

I couldn't argue with that sentiment, but Ross kept his van humming, and as I pulled my T-shirt away from my sticky skin, I gazed enviously, imagining its cool interior.

Dusk began to settle slowly, bringing temperatures down a little. I realized I'd snapped at Shade. He really wasn't a bad guy. I decided to patch things up. He had a small pair of binoculars suspended around his neck.

"Mind if I look at those?" I asked, pointing to them.

Without a word, he lifted them over his head and handed them to me.

"So . . . Ron." I grimaced.

"What's wrong?"

"I don't know. It's silly, but I don't think of you as a 'Ron.' You're 'Shade' to me." I made a little helpless gesture. "Do you mind if I call you 'Shade'?"

This man had a very nice smile, I was glad to see it. "Don't mind at all."

"It suits you."

"Thanks. I guess."

A few more minutes ticked by.

"I never figured you for a country-and-western type," I said, breaking the silence.

"What are you talking about?"

"Garth Brooks. You said something earlier that made me believe you're a fan."

"Actually, I'm very eclectic in my tastes."

"Oh?"

He settled back in his seat to talk. "Chappie, my trainer, turned me onto Motown. You know, Diana Ross and the Supremes, Marvin Gaye, the Temptations."

I'd pegged this guy as someone who listened to hard rock. He was more into oldies.

He continued, oblivious to my musings, "George and my older brother Tom, are big Elvis and Sinatra fans. I guess I caught the bug from them." He studied the Escalade's ceiling as though his memories were recorded there. "Rounding it all out is Linda Ronstadt, Garth and then of course, Shania Twain, who was the object of my delayed adolescent fantasies." He looked over to me and smiled. This time, when he wasn't trying to be cute, he actually was. He looked almost embarrassed by his admission.

"Nice mix."

"What about you?" he asked.

"Music? I guess Train, Green Day. The Rolling Stones. And The Mon—"

Headlights swung up into the Bayless driveway. We both watched as a dark-colored BMW pulled forward and the attached-garage's door began to rise.

"Here we go," Shade said.

The driver appeared to be female. She doused her lights and hit the button for the automatic door to lower. "What now?" I asked.

Shade smiled. "This is the fun part. We give her a couple minutes to get settled and then—we pay her a visit."

I took a deep breath. My heart raced. Shade looked cool, relaxed, almost eager to move. His eyes sparkled in the scant light, and he kept a tight eye on the home's front door.

"How long?"

Without averting his gaze, he said. "Just long enough to let her—"

The front light came on and the door opened. As the woman stepped out, the newspaper we'd placed there dropped. She picked it up and read it, at arm's length, her face well illuminated from indoors. I focused the binoculars. "It's her," I whispered.

Shade turned to face me. He draped his right arm around my shoulders and pulled me a little closer. "I don't want her to notice us watching," he said. "So let's try to look like a couple having a serious talk. You keep an eye on her. Tell me what she does."

I nodded, put the binoculars in my lap, and scooted a little closer. Shade's breath was cool and minty.

Candice's hand came up to her brow as she continued to scan the article. "She looks nervous," I said.

"She should be."

With a look up and down the street, Candice headed to the curb.

"I think she's coming to talk to us." I instinctively startled backward, but Shade kept his arm snugly in place, preventing me from making any suspicious movement. "No, wait. She's going to the mailbox," I said.

"Anyone else around?"

"No."

His fingers skimmed my upper arm. It gave me tingles, and for a moment I questioned my sanity. This was the closest I'd been to an attractive man in a long time, and his touch—in this case, totally platonic—still caused goose bumps. Geez, what was wrong with me? I forced myself to remember that I was on a stakeout and not at a teenage makeout session.

He brought his face closer to mine. "Anyone else in the house, that you can tell?"

I cleared my throat. "No."

Candice Prokovis, aka Candice Barstow gathered a handful of mail and headed back inside. She shut the door behind her.

"All clear," I said.

Shade pulled his arm back immediately. "Sorry about that," he said. "I just thought—"

I waved off his apology. "Don't worry. I get it. Made total sense. I'm just glad you were thinking."

His lips twitched and he turned back to watch the house. "I just wish I would've thought about the mail before. Should've taken a look at who's in touch."

"Isn't that illegal?"

He shrugged. "I wasn't going to take anything, just have a quick look. But then again, if one of the neighbors caught us . . ."

The minutes ticked by.

"I wonder how Hal's doing," I said. "It's been a while since he . . . uh . . ."

In profile, I saw Shade's eyebrows rise. "Yeah, it has been." He checked his watch. "Time's up."

"For Hal?"

"For Mrs. Barstow, or whatever she's calling herself these

days." He turned to me. "You ready? It's not too late to back out."

"Back out? Me?"

He nodded.

"No way."

"Okay then," he said. "Let's get Hal and Ross and head in."

I called Hal on his cell and told him we were going in to visit Mrs. Barstow and that he should take the camcorder. To his credit, he and Ross were out of the van and ready to move moments later.

The four of us trekked up the front walk, Shade in the lead. He rang the bell and again I heard the door's chime.

Candice Prokovis, looking a lot like her Illinois driver's license, opened the door.

"Mrs. Bayless?" Shade asked.

She nodded.

I would have assumed she'd insist her name was Barstow.

"You might as well come in," she said with a resigned sigh. Widening the door, she stepped aside when she saw all of us. "We've been expecting you."

Chapter 20

Ron Shade

She'd cut her hair shorter and had obviously eased up a bit on the bleach bottle, but Candice Prokovis looked pretty much like her old Illinois driver's license photo. She held open the door, and Alex and I stepped into the air-conditioned coolness of the house, followed by Hal and Ross. Hal was quietly filming the whole thing, and he hadn't even asked to go to the bathroom yet.

"May I call you Candice?" I asked.

She edged over to the sofa but didn't sit down. Her lips compressed and she nodded.

"The game's about over," I said. "We need to talk to your husband."

"Who are you?" She directed the question toward Alex.

"I'm Alex St. James. I'm a reporter for *Midwest Focus News-Magazine.*"

Candice looked from her to Hal, who had the camcorder on his shoulder recording, and then to me. She tapped the newspaper. "I assume you're the one who left this here?"

"Like I said, Candice, the game's over. You can see what the stakes are. I know you're in over your head. These people don't play around."

This seemed to perplex her for a moment, then she regained a modicum of composure and straightened up. "Just what is it you want with us, Mr. Shade?"

I let her question hang there, trying to make it look like I knew more than I did. After a sufficient pause, I said, "It's time for Bob Bayless to go back to Chicago and face the music. Co-operate with me, and I'll see what I can do."

"Cooperate?" Her voice sounded brittle.

It was my turn to nod. "Like I said, those kind of people don't play games. That paper shows it. They're cutting out the weak links, eliminating any trail back to them, and, let's face it, you and your husband are next on the hit parade."

Twin patches of color stained her cheeks, but she silently considered my words.

"Where is your husband?" Alex asked.

She'd broken my rhythm by asking, and it threw me totally off my game. Candice's attention immediately shifted to her. I guessed she'd erroneously assumed I wasn't getting anywhere.

"He's not here right now."

"Where is he?" Alex repeated.

The other woman's eyes shot down to the carpet, then up again. "Maybe I'd better call him." She took a cell phone out of her jeans' pocket and dialed a number. After a few rings, it was apparent Bayless had answered. "Hi, it's me." Pause. "Yeah, they're here now. I'm talking with them." She listened some more. "He's got two reporters with him and some other guy."

I really need to get on that phone, I thought. Maybe if I could talk to Bayless, I'd be able to get him to see the light.

"Bob," Candice said, "they brought a Chicago paper showing that Dr. Colon and his receptionist are dead. Murdered. He says we'll be next if we don't cooperate."

Whatever he said next took a long time. Her end of the conversation was filled with "Un-huhs" and "Un-uns," but it was too vague to follow. And then, "All right, I'll put him on." She held out the cell phone toward me. "It's my husband. He wants to talk to you."

I couldn't believe how well this was going. I felt like a fighter who suddenly gets his second wind in the seventh round, just as his opponent loses his. I wanted to keep my greeting salutation as neutral and unthreatening as possible, so I just said, "Hello?"

"Shade? It's Bob Bayless."

He didn't sound like a dead man. "I know. We need to talk. I'm here to help you."

"Help me?"

"Yeah." I paused, listening for any background noises. Nothing was distinct, which made me think he was in a room or a car. "You got some bad-ass people on your trail. They're obviously eliminating loose ends to their little escapade, and you and your wife are probably in their sights. Do they know where you live?"

"What?"

I took a chance. "Farnsworth and his Russian buddy. Do they know where you set up house?"

I heard his breathing. He was obviously thinking. Probably wondering how far he could trust me.

"Bayless, they're here in Las Vegas," I said. "There isn't much time. Where are you at?"

"I'm . . . by the Strip."

That nailed things down, all right. "Yeah, so are a million other people. Where exactly?"

More silence, then, "Okay, Shade, listen. I'll meet you. I want to talk this over first."

"Meet where?"

He cleared his throat. "Well, I can't come home, if you found me this easily."

"I'm good." I continued to press him, "But I can't stop the clock. You agree to come back with me now, testify about your involvement, blow the whistle on their little parts-by-number scheme and they'll probably go easy on you. You don't, they'll find you, and I don't need to tell you what'll happen then, do I?"

"No," he said, "you don't." Another pregnant pause. "Okay, listen. I'll talk to you, like I said, but nobody else. No reporters, or anything. Not at this point."

"Fair enough," I said. "Where?"

"Go to the back entrance of the Arabesque at Sahara and Paradise," he said. "You know where that is?"

"Yeah. Is that where you're at now?"

"Park in their garage, and then call me at this number." He read off the digits slowly. I scrambled to get my pen out and write them on my hand. Candice shoved a piece of notepaper at me. "I'll be watching. If I see you're not alone . . ."

"Relax," I said. "I will be."

"Let me talk to Candy again," he said. I handed her the phone. She listened intently, and then said, "Okay." She hung up.

I looked at Alex. I didn't like the idea of leaving her alone here, but she would have Ross.

"You all right with staying here?" I asked. "He wants a solo meet."

"I figured as much." She smiled. "Don't worry. We'll be fine."

The same pluckiness that had irritated me earlier now gave me a sliver of reassurance. She looked like she could take care of herself. But meeting a walking, talking dead man alone and on his home ground had me feeling a bit uneasy. After talking with Bayless I was even more convinced he'd taken an easy exit from his humdrum wife and now it was all catching up to him. I turned to Ross and canted my head in Alex's direction as I asked, "You mind staying here and watching the store till I get back?"

"No problem," he said.

"You packing?" I asked the question, even though I knew the answer.

"Yeah. You?"

I shook my head.

"Here." He raised his right foot and placed it on the arm of the sofa. Pulling up his pantleg, he withdrew a chrome snub-nosed revolver from an ankle holster. I was beginning to like this guy more and more. "Take my back-up piece, just in case."

It was a five-shot thirty-eight Smith and Wesson. I automatically flipped open the cylinder and checked the load. "You aren't going to need it?"

He shook his head and lifted the bottom of his billowy shirt, displaying a big semiauto in a pancake hostler. "If I can't hit 'em with this, I ain't gonna. Nineteen shots."

"Ah," I said. "I prefer the Beretta myself."

He shook his head. "Nah, there ain't nothing like a Glock."

I grinned and held up the revolver. "Except a Smith."

Alex, Ross, and I all double-checked that we had each other's cell phone numbers, and I walked toward the door. There was a lot about this arrangement that was making me uneasy. I guess it showed. As I pulled open the door, Alex spoke.

"Shade . . ."

I turned.

"Be careful," she said.

Chapter 21

Alex St. James

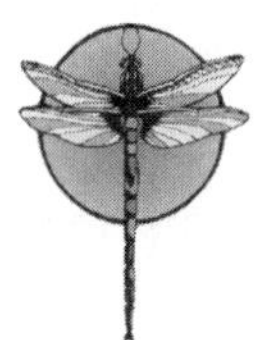

I watched the Escalade pull away with more than a little disquiet. I didn't like the way things were shaping up. Shade was gone and much too fast. We hadn't had a chance to decide our best move together. But then again, I couldn't blame him for not consulting me. In his line of work he made solo decisions all the time. I was the same way. Maybe that's why he and I constantly butted heads. We were both accustomed to a certain autonomy, and authority.

And I couldn't diminish the fact that he was here for Bayless. Plain and simple. Once he got Bayless cornered, once he proved the dead man was still alive, Shade's job was done, and his money earned. Mine continued until I got my story.

Stepping away from the front window, I worked up my best empathetic smile. "Candice," I said, as I gestured for Hal to position himself in the living room's corner to film. "May I ask you a few questions?"

"Questions? About what?"

I wanted to snap at her dull stupidity—but courtesy won out.

I kept my expression passive, my tone nonthreatening. "About your husband's involvement in black-market body parts. About his purported 'death,' and why he felt the need to flee Chicago and take on a new identity."

Candice blinked at the camera, looked away. "I don't have anything to say."

I waited a couple of beats.

She'd crack eventually, but these things often took time.

Ross winked at me, then moved past Candice, positioning himself in the doorway that led to the back of the house. "Want to stay out of the picture," he said. "I don't want to be identified on film. It'll hurt business."

"Sorry," Hal said. "Close quarters like this, I don't have much choice, unless I keep a tight close-up on the lady. You want that, Alex?"

I shook my head. "We can edit you out," I said to Ross. "Don't worry."

He didn't look happy at the prospect. "How about I sit in the kitchen and wait till you wrap this up?"

"Go ahead," I said.

I turned to Candice and gestured to the seat beside her on the sofa. "May I?"

Her look was glum. "Sure."

"You understand," I began softly, "that the Manus Corporation benefited from Robert Bayless's death. They collected ten million dollars in insurance money."

"Yeah?" she said, the way some people say, "So?"

This woman wasn't getting it.

"These aren't nice people. They won't want to give that money back," I said. "There are ten million good reasons why Manus would like to ensure that your husband stays dead."

She stared at her hands, folded in her lap. She was a thin woman, and the skin between her knuckles stretched so tight it looked ready to split.

I glanced up to be sure Hal was getting all this. Returning my attention to Candice, I said, "You're in danger. But if you work with us, we can help keep you safe."

A loud thump and clatter from the kitchen caused us all to jump. "Ross?" I called. "You okay?"

No answer.

"Ross?"

His voice was muffled. I couldn't make it out, but it sounded like he said he was okay.

The interruption cut some of the tension in the room. She seemed softer all of a sudden, more relaxed. I decided to try another tactic. "Listen, we know about the body parts operation that Manus has going. We know about Nicky Farnsworth's role in acquiring . . ."—some things were difficult to say aloud—". . . homeless people for . . . inventory." The truth was we didn't actually "know," we'd surmised. But the evidence all pointed in one direction; and I knew I had to press my advantage or lose her entirely.

She finally met my eyes. Another subtle shift.

"Come on, Candice. Work with me here. Your husband must have known what was going on. That's why he had to fake his death. Manus doesn't want him alive. Not with all he knows about their operations. Not with ten million dollars on the line. People are looking for you. Bad people."

Candice looked at the camera, then back at me. If she broke now, it'd be perfect dramatic timing for our feature. Instead of fighting an emotional outburst, however, she said, "Nobody will look for us. We're safe here."

I sat back, surprised. "Don't you understand what's going on? We've uncovered a terrible travesty. And your husband is the key to unravel the whole conspiracy. You aren't safe. No one is."

"So? What does that have to do with me?"

Struck by her insolence, I lost my words for a moment. When I regained my composure, I spoke slowly. "Don't you get it? Your husband's former colleagues are cold-hearted killers. They target innocent people. With real lives. Lives that Manus has stolen in order to harvest body parts. For profit." My voice started to rise, because the thought of what they'd been doing—for years—sickened me. "These diseased parts are being sold to hospitals who believe they came from healthy donors. I can't imagine anything more horrific than the scam Manus is perpetrating on trusting people. Vulnerable people, who are grasping for hope." I sucked in my cheeks, biting them to keep from losing control on camera. "I think Manus is despicable. If you have any compassion whatsoever, you've got to see how horrific this is. We're going to bring them down. All of them. With or without your help."

Candice blinked a couple of times. "Then, I guess, it will have to be without my help."

Was the woman totally dense?

"Then I can't promise you any protection at all." I hoped Shade was having better luck with the husband. It bothered me—a lot—to know that I couldn't get what I needed from this woman. She was unreadable, in a way few people are. "Just answer me one thing—because I'm sure you know. Who's running the show now? Is it Nicky Farnsworth? Because I'm pretty sure he's in town, and he won't be happy about the latest turn of events."

She looked perplexed.

I rephrased. "Who's calling the shots? Who runs the organization? Who killed Dr. Colon and his receptionist? You can tell me that, at least."

She shook her head, then glanced just over my shoulder and smiled.

Thrown by her distraction, I turned.

"*I'm* calling the shots."

Robert Bayless stood just inside the room, holding a pistol with an enormously long barrel tight up against Ross's right temple. I realized seconds later that it had a sound suppressor attached. Ross's hands were handcuffed behind him, and he wore a look of intense pain. Although Bayless had shaved his head and grown a beard, the face was the same as the Illinois driver's license photo I'd seen earlier today.

Instinctively—stupidly—I stood. My mind shouted that I'd just made myself a bigger target. "Ross!" I said, starting toward him.

"Don't move." Bayless took a half step backward using Ross as a shield.

Against what? Me? I wasn't armed. Dear God I wish I were. Bayless was a big guy. Not ripped, but intimidating. One thing the driver's license photo didn't portray was the intense superiority that the fellow exuded. And he smelled. Like . . . Nicky.

Bayless cocked an eyebrow and jostled Ross. "This guy is safe for now. Just do what I tell you and nobody will get hurt."

Yeah. Like I believed that.

"Candy, you did great. Go on outside and pull this joker's van into the garage." He tossed her what I presumed were Ross's keys. "We'll be leaving shortly."

Candice pointed at Ross. "He gave that Shade character his backup gun."

Bayless pressed the gun up against Ross's cheek, pushing hard against the soft skin. He gave an unpleasant laugh. "That was stupid," he said. "Because that backup sure would've come in handy in the kitchen, wouldn't it?"

Ross didn't answer.

"You got your cell on you, Candy?" Bayless asked.

"Yeah."

"Give it to me. I have an important call to make."

"Don't you have yours?" she asked.

"Yeah, but I'll need yours, too. Tuck it in my pocket." She tucked it all right, and leaned up to kiss his jaw before grabbing her purse and heading out the front door. "Hurry back," he said. "I'll need you in here again, soon."

She nodded.

"Drop that camera," Bayless shouted to Hal. He complied. "Now, get over there with your reporter friend. We're going to take this real slow because we have plenty of time to get it right."

A shadow crossed behind Bayless.

My heart leaped, pounding in my ears with anticipation. Shade must have suspected something and doubled back. Thank God.

I worked to keep my eyes from giving away his position, when I heard, "Let me through."

Bayless stepped forward and the shadow came into the light.

"Nicky," I said, my voice breathless.

Not Shade. Not a rescue.

"Welcome to fabulous Las Vegas," he said with the frightening grin I remembered from childhood. "So glad you could come."

"Cut the reunion shit, Nick. Let's get these assholes in the van. Candy will follow us."

"Where are we going?" I asked.

Bayless ignored my question. He started to shove Ross out the door but halted. "Get their cell phones," he said to Nicky. "Make sure we have them all." Bayless already had Ross's Glock and now he handed it over. "Here. In case they try to get tricky."

Nicky accepted it looking like a gleeful twelve-year-old. "Okay," he said with a new air of confidence, as he put it into his own waistband, "let's see what you've got in here."

My mind raced, even as Nicky foraged through my purse, coming up with my cell phone. He then collected Hal's and confiscated the camera, as well.

When Shade realized that Bayless wasn't there, he'd know it was a hoax, and he'd head back here. There was hope, at least.

Hal's legs had apparently given out. He sat dumbfounded on the sofa I'd vacated, his head in his hands. I was forced to sit next to him, and Ross joined us on the sofa. While Bayless held the gun, Nicky wrapped my hands and Hal's with duct tape. Three bound mice, it seemed. But there was nowhere to run.

"Hurry," Bayless said. He dialed one of the cell phones as Candice returned. When someone answered, he said, "Yeah, stand by."

He handed the sound-suppressed gun to Candice. "I'm going out back. Keep them quiet and if they move, shoot them."

I worked at my duct-taped bonds while Bayless was gone. I had a little wiggle room because when Nicky had taped them together, I'd twisted my hands so that he bound me at the knuckles, where I made my fists wide. But I had small hands and narrow wrists. I used whatever leverage I could to get free.

Ross moved closer, covering my movement. I could smell Hal's fear in the sweat that slid down his face. He didn't look at either of us, he simply stared straight ahead. His lips moved, and I realized he was praying.

Candice didn't flinch, didn't budge. The bitch smiled as she watched us, her cheeks rosy and her breathing shallow, almost as if she was getting off on this.

I looked away as my hands came free. Now if there were just some chance . . .

Bayless returned about fifteen minutes later and announced we were ready to go. He retrieved his gun from Candice and sent her to the garage. "Get up, you old man," he said to Hal, whose face practically folded in on itself as he spoke.

"My wife . . ." Hal said, his voice breaking, "I gotta see my wife again. You can't kill me. Please." He started to blubber, real tears streaming from red-rimmed eyes.

Bayless backhanded him across the face with his gun, making him cry out, splitting the side of his face open. "Shit," Bayless said, stepping backward, his attention taken by the sudden appearance of blood. "That's a goddamn new couch. Candy just ordered it. Get your ass up before you drip." He looked ready to hit him again. "I said, get up, asshole."

Ross took advantage of the moment. He arched back, shouting my name as he angled himself to shoot a quick kick into Bayless's knees. The bigger man dropped to the ground. In the same second, I wrenched out of my seat and dove for his gun. I had to. There was no alternative.

My fingers grasped the cool, elongated barrel as my knees hit the floor. I tugged, but the gun didn't come out of Bayless's grip. "Let go!" I screamed as I pulled with all my might. I was vaguely aware of Nicky shouting. Ross attacked, still bound, doing his best to keep Nicky from shooting me.

Bayless leaped to his feet, gun in hand. He pointed it down at me and shouted. "Any one of you moves and she's dead. You get it, assholes?"

Hal stood, swaying. I froze in place. As did Ross.

I turned to him. "I'm sorry," I mouthed.

He shook his head in dispensation, but his eyes gave away his despair.

Bayless took a deep breath. "You see?" he shouted at Nicky. "I told you they were tricky. Why the hell did you think I gave you the goddamn gun? So you could wear it in your panty waist?" He kept the firearm trained on me even as he dusted off his slacks. He twisted his neck, the way men do when their collars are too tight. "Let's get them loaded."

He gestured for me to stand, which I did. Hal shuffled in front of me, his head bent, his shoulders shaking. Dear God, I thought. How were we ever going to get out of this alive with him as baggage? I turned to check on Ross.

Nicky had the Glock out now, like an obedient little criminal. He pushed Ross forward with it.

"Eyes front, bitch," Bayless said to me. "Move it."

We did.

The garage held only Ross's van. As we approached, Candy opened the passenger side sliding door and said, "I put our car on the street. Nobody's going to think twice about me getting in, and I wanted you to have as much room as you could in here."

Bayless beamed. "You're a treat, Candy."

The silly smile she shot back told me this was a private joke between them. Like plotting our murders was some sort of twisted foreplay.

Hal got in, still whimpering and talking about how much his wife would miss him, how much he needed to see her, just one more time. My heart broke for him, but I couldn't let my compassion cloud my thoughts. I needed to think. I needed to communicate—somehow—with Ross. He'd have ideas. A plan.

My hopes of Shade returning were fading fast. He wasn't coming back. No one was coming to save us. It was up to Ross and it was up to me.

They sat me next to Hal, our backs up against the van's surveillance equipment. Bayless again warned us not to move. He went around the front of the van and got into the driver's seat. The curtains separating the compartments were pushed aside, which allowed him to watch my every move.

Next to the wide-open side door, Nicky prodded Ross with the gun. "Move it, you asshole," Nicky said to Ross, but the power with which Bayless commanded was missing from his directive. "Get in before I belt you."

Ross started to boost himself in, but with his hands still bound behind him, he had no leverage. Nicky took that moment to shove him for emphasis, causing Ross to lose his footing. He fell backwards into Nicky, who stumbled.

The sudden explosion made me scream.

Ross's mouth twisted downward, then slackened into a blank-faced expression as he toppled sideways.

I screamed again. Ears ringing, I scuttled forward.

From the front seat, Bayless thrust his arm out, whacking me center chest. With a *whoof,* I fell, but even as I dropped to the floor, I still kept moving forward. It was do or die. Maybe . . . if Nicky had been hit . . .

Bayless grabbed the back of my collar and yanked. My throat caught, and not just because of the sudden attack.

I saw Ross.

Nicky grappled to his feet and now stood above him, gun smoking. Ross lay on the cement floor, a crimson hole burst out the front of his chest. I recognized it as an exit wound. "Please," I said, "let me check him," even though I was sure it was too late.

"Shut up," Bayless said. He swore for a full minute, calling Nicky every name in the book, before finally speaking through clenched teeth. "We weren't supposed to kill them till we got them onto the table," he said. "Are you so stupid that you can't remember simple directions?"

"It was an accident," Nicky said, with no remorse, only embarrassment. "It went off by itself."

"Guns don't go off by themselves, you stupid fool. Now go over there—there's a tarp somewhere in the corner. Go get it." He pulled his own gun out and fixed it on us, directing Nicky's efforts. "Goddamn blood."

Bayless tapped me with his gun when Nicky produced the

tarp. "You were able to get your hands free, smart-ass. You spread it out," he said.

I laid the tarp in the van's back compartment, as ordered.

"Now, load the body into the van," he told Nicky. "We can't leave him here and he'll come in handy. We can use him."

Nicky threw Ross in, facedown. When his body hit the van floor with a sickening thump, my stomach catapulted. I reached out, searching for a pulse in Ross's neck. Nothing.

"Roll him up. I don't want to have to clean up another mistake," Bayless said to me.

Biting my mouth to keep from retching, I complied.

We drove for twenty minutes, with Hal and I sitting on the van floor, Ross's body at our feet.

Hal kept his head down between his upturned knees.

I avoided looking at Bayless or Nicky. I was afraid that my fury would goad me to do something reckless, and I needed to keep my wits.

But as Ross's body shifted at a left turn, I knew I was bereft of ideas.

When we first took off I'd tried desperately to keep my bearings. I wanted to maintain a sense of where we were headed so that if the opportunity to call for help presented itself, I'd be ready. But we sat too low, and we turned too often. I couldn't see any landmarks at all. Bayless kept to mostly residential streets, and my view out the van's windows were of streetlights—and an occasional glimpse of the moon.

I knew Candy followed us because Bayless kept checking his rearview. "Atta girl," he said once.

Yeah. Some girl. Cold as ice, just like the rest of them.

When we stopped, Nicky got out of the van. Bayless kept it running, and I stretched myself to see. Nicky was opening a garage door by inputting a code in a wall-mounted unit.

I tried to see around Bayless's head. Were we at another

home? If so, this was a huge one.

A sign out front gave me the story.

Sunset Manor Funeral Home, Las Vegas.

Bayless caught me watching. His mouth twisted into a maniacal smile. "Perfect place to salvage healthy parts from unnecessary reporters. Wouldn't you agree?"

Ron Shade

Despite making a couple of minor wrong turns, I made it to Paradise and Sahara in good time. I wanted to drive around and see if I could spot Bayless, but there were a million places to hide in plain sight. I decided to stick to his instructions, for the time being, and pulled into the rear parking garage of the Arabesque. It was one of the older hotels on the Strip. I remembered photos of Elvis Presley posing by the front when he was making some movie. Still, the place had held up pretty well. Across the street was the elevated monorail station, which almost reminded my of the el back in Chi-town. Except this was way too new and not half as rickety. Maybe Bayless was up there, ready to hop on a southbound tram if he thought I was trying to double-cross him. I was more than a little worried about leaving Alex back at the house, too. With Ross there, I was sure Candice wouldn't be any trouble, but I still had that uneasy feeling as I dialed the number Bayless had given me. It rang three times before he answered.

"I'm here," I said. "Where are you at?"

"Never mind where I'm at. You come alone like I told you?"

This made me think maybe he wasn't as much on the ball as I thought. If I'd given someone specific instructions where to report to, I would have been waiting and watching.

"I'm alone."

"All right. Park your car and go down to the first level," he said. "Come outside and stop at the sidewalk. I'll stay on the line here."

"You going to meet me down there?"

I heard nothing but silence. He was either doing a good human-clam imitation, or he had his hand over the mouthpiece. I tried to listen as I drove up the winding hotel parking garage aisles. I had to go up four levels before I found an open spot. When I did, I pulled in and did a quick check of the area. I wanted to be sure of where I parked in case I had to get out of here fast. The view between the concrete floors showed me a panorama of bright lights spreading out across the cityscape. And under each one was probably a thousand suckers losing their money. I hoped that I wouldn't turn out to be one of them. I had a lot more to lose right now.

I tried speaking to Bayless again as I went down the stairwell but realized the connection was dead. I assumed he'd either call me back, since he must have had my number on his caller ID screen, or I'd redial him. I'd kept Ross's snub-nose in my right pants' pocket, but while I was still out of sight in the stairwell, I transferred it to my left hip, sticking it nose-down so the handle rested facing outward along my belt. I could easily grab it with a cross draw if I needed it in a hurry, and with my T-shirt out nobody'd be the wiser.

The night was cool and dry, and almost reminded me of Chicago. But the strangeness of the surroundings made me feel a long way from home. My cell phone rang.

"Shade?"

"I'm here. Where are you?"

"Are you on the sidewalk yet?"

That most likely meant he still couldn't see me. I scanned the area trying to spot a guy talking on a cell phone, but nothing.

"Shade?"

"I'm right where you told me to be."

"Okay, good." His voice sounded a bit more confident. "Start walking south. That's toward the Hilton. You see it?"

Directly south I saw the huge, monolithic sign with the immense block letters. "Yeah. You that far?"

"No. Stay on this side of the street, understand?"

That was all he said. I began walking, feeling more and more uneasy. The street looked almost desolate along this section. The monorail track ran parallel on the other side, and the only thing directly across was one of those high-rise condominium buildings under construction. Farther down a few blocks a quartet of completed high-rises stood across from the Hilton hotel. I was beginning not to like this arrangement very much. It looked like a great place for an ambush, but I didn't have much bargaining room until I spotted his location. Then his ass was gonna belong to me. I walked down the sidewalk. As I came to the end of the parking structure a gap appeared. To my right was a cyclone fence enclosing an unlighted field-like area. A big red-and-white *No Trespassing* sign was wired to it. I'd taken a few more steps when Bayless abruptly told me to stop. I looked around.

"You see that fence next to you?" he asked.

I reached out and brushed it. "Yeah."

"Keep walking. There's a gate about twenty feet down. It's wide enough to slip through."

I looked beyond the fence. It wasn't a field. It was a large abandoned area with sporadic sections of tall palm trees, dying scrubs, and metal railings. I could see some kind of structures . . . small, single-unit buildings from the vague outlines visible against the distant ambient lighting, as well as more trees and a few low walls . . . Remnants of an old strip mall maybe?

"What the hell is this place?" I asked.

"It's an abandoned property. Used to be a water park and a line of stores. It's got pools and bridges, so don't trip."

"Where are you at?"

"Hang on a second." More silence, then a tiny flash of light—a flashlight being switched on for an instant, shone about fifty yards inside. It was near one of the buildings in the center. I could see the silhouette against the faint glow from the rest of the Strip. An island of darkness in a sea of fluorescence. Or was it neon? "I'm over by what used to be one of the snack bars. I'm flashing my light. Do you see it?"

He wasn't flashing it anymore, but I had an idea where he was.

"I saw it. I'm on my way."

Now it was my turn to hang up. I got to the loosely affixed gate and edged through. The ground was mostly cement, covered by a layer of fine desert dust, with a sprinkling of gravel in some parts. Iron frameworks formed a lattice of barriers around deep empty cement trenches where glistening swimming pools had once entertained kids in the desert heat. Now the pits were filled with a detritus of garbage and dirt. Luckily, I had my minimag flashlight with me. I never left home without it. The little halogen bulb was powerful enough to illuminate the immediate area quite well, but wouldn't reach all the way to where he was. Plus, I didn't want him to know I had it just yet. Just like the gun. Keep 'em in reserve. I concentrated on maintaining my visual purple and cut on an angle toward him. I moved in a zigzag pattern, dodging loose cement blocks and avoiding patches of high scrubs. Mesquite, from the looks of it. Some of the palm trees were pretty big and afforded cover.

Crude gang graffiti decorated the walls of the remaining cement-block structures I went past. My phone rang and I pressed the button to answer it.

"Where are you?" he asked.

"Relax, I'm heading straight toward you. It's tricky walking in here in the dark." I ducked low and said, "Flash your light again."

"All right, just a minute." I heard the muffling sound again. At least five seconds passed. Maybe he wasn't alone. The flashlight came on. He was about thirty yards away now.

"You by yourself?" I asked.

"Of course." He sounded more indignant than surprised. "Why?"

"Just want to be sure."

I heard him breathing, then silence. "Shade, I'll tell you what. I'll keep the flashlight on and start walking. Come to meet me."

I saw the flashlight bobbing in his hand as he began moving in a straight line from the side of the building. I stayed put and watched. Nothing moved in the vicinity, which made me feel a little more secure. My best plan was to move on an oblique intercept course, scarf up this asshole, and get back to the Escalade. I could call Alex and we could meet someplace and sort this out.

"Shade, where are you?"

I let him get a few more feet before I answered. "Just keep coming. I'm almost on top of you." I saw his head swivel, but he didn't say anything.

I darted around a patch of dry bushes and almost tripped over a discarded cement block. Using my minimag would have made the trip smoother, but I didn't want to give away my position just yet. I still had about fifty feet to go before I'd be able to put the arm on Bayless.

"Shade, you there?"

"I'm here. Just keep coming."

He was moving cautiously. We were maybe twenty-five feet apart now. Twenty . . . Fifteen. He was heavier than I expected. Not formidable looking. More like an oversized pear. His feet were making little scraping sounds in the dust, and as he swung the arm with the flashlight, his face became slightly visible. Although I'd never seen the man in person, I had studied the photo that George had given me, and this guy didn't look anything like Bob Bayless. I was getting ready to rush over and deck him and figure out what exactly was going on when I heard someone from behind me say, "Don't move, Shade. I have a gun trained on your back."

And he'd said it with a Russian accent.

Chapter 22

Alex St. James

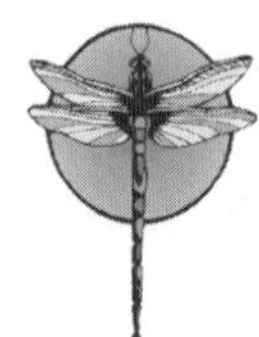

Bayless shot a sharp elbow to my head. "Get down."

I fell back, landing on top of Ross.

With a yelp, I rolled off.

I rubbed my forehead, scooting backward, as far away as possible from the tarp-covered body. Bayless's crack wasn't hard enough to knock me out, but it hurt. My eyes watered.

He pulled into a cavernous garage. Big enough for five vehicles. A limousine took up the far bay, and a hearse sat next to us. Candy pulled the BMW next to the limo, and I stared at the now-closed overhead doors trying to figure out a means of escape.

Hal sniffled.

I knew I'd have to leave him if I got any chance to run. But could I actually do that?

Head down, he shuffled behind me as we made our way through metal double doors that led into the funeral home itself. Just before we stepped in, Bayless grimaced at the van as he addressed Nicky. "When Viktor gets here, have him and his guys bring the body in. Then have them ditch the van."

"Viktor?" I said. "The same one from Chicago?"

Nicky started to say, "Yeah, as soon as he's finished taking care of your friend Sh—"

"Shut up, you idiot," Bayless said.

"Why?" Nicky sounded petulant. "What difference does it make?"

"Just keep your mind on the job. Every time you get distracted, you screw up."

Nicky had been about to say "Shade." My heart sank. They'd gotten us both. They'd divided us and they'd conquered. Shade was walking into a trap, just like I had. But . . . at least he had a gun. That gave me hope, though it was small consolation—these guys had everything orchestrated. Perfectly. They were clearly in control.

I closed my eyes for a moment, praying he wouldn't be killed. Praying *we* wouldn't be killed.

It was dark inside the building, except for meager safety lighting near the floorboards. Nicky veered away from our little parade to hit the power, and the room lit up. From the looks of it, it was a holding room, about twenty-by-twenty, empty except for some cabinets, several wheeled gurneys, and a countertop stacked with black-and-red, zippered body bags. At the far end of the room was another set of double doors. Even *I* knew where they led.

Bayless didn't waste time. "Go ahead, Candy."

She lingered near the exit to the garage. "You want me to go in there?" she said. For the first time since I'd met the woman, I detected a crack in her ice-cold façade. "I don't like it in there." Shaking her head she turned away, toward the body bag collection. When she saw them, she made a face and directed her gaze to the floor. "I'll wait in the car."

Bayless's baleful expression didn't change. "You want to hang in the same garage as the bloody guy? Be my guest."

Horrified, Candice seemed to suddenly remember Ross. "Cut it out, Bob! No. You know I hate being around dead people."

"Then get your ass inside. You can go sit in the lobby or the ladies' room or something till it's over."

She eyed the far door. "But—"

"Your ass." Bayless pointed to the doorway. "In there. Now."

Candice pulled her lips tight before twisting the knob on the right-hand door. The lights were on, and Bayless gestured Nicky and Hal through, then told me to follow them. He made sure to poke me in the back with his gun. A tangible reminder that he'd blow me away if I made a wrong move.

The room was cold.

Of course it was. We were in the embalming room—steel refrigeration units lined two walls. High-powered illumination in this windowless room gave a surreal impression of daylight. The overhead beams reflected on Bayless's shiny scalp—he squinted upward. "Nice," he said. "This'll give you enough light?"

I didn't ask. I didn't want to know what they needed the light for. Anger rolled in my chest, growing bigger and more powerful with each step I took.

This space was bigger than Nicky's embalming rooms in Chicago. Newer, too. "Business must be good," I quipped. I was tired of being afraid. Tired of waiting to see what they had planned.

Sure, I was still terrified, but now I was pissed, too. Furious that these two despicable characters would be getting away with murder—and so much more.

"Business is grand," Bayless said. "As in a hundred grand. Per week." He stared up at the ceiling for a moment then gave a soft laugh. "No. More than that."

"I'll be in the lobby." Candice couldn't get out of the room fast enough. She hit the far exit door with a flat hand, banging it open.

Nicky shouted after her. "There's a television in the lounge."

She stopped but didn't turn. It was as though she was afraid of what she'd see. "Which way?" she asked, panic making her voice wobble.

"Across the lobby, turn right. Down the corridor, last door on your left."

She kept her back to us. "What if I come across another one of these rooms?"

"You won't," he said. "I promise."

The door swung shut behind her.

Hal stared, his eyes moving about the room, taking it in. I guessed this was his first time in a room like this. I watched his Adam's apple bob, twice, as he backed up. "Watch it," I said when he nearly bumped into the embalming table.

He turned, and when he saw what was behind him, he groaned. With his hands still duct-taped behind his back he couldn't cover his eyes, but I could tell he wanted to. His legs looked ready to give out, and I moved closer. But what could I do? He had me by a hundred pounds at least. If he fell on top of me, we'd both get hurt. "Easy, Hal," I said.

But he turned again. "What's that?" he asked, pointing to a cantilevered body storage unit. I'd seen one at Sunset Manor in Chicago, where Nicky had boasted that each of the four tiers could hold a body up to 500 pounds. Right now there were four empty trays.

Nicky gave a smirk. "Your new bed, at least for—"

Bayless was unscrewing the sound suppressor from the front of the gun. "Shut up," he said. He hefted the long barrel in his hand for a moment, looking around, finally dropping it onto the adjacent countertop next to Nicky's embalming tools. "You keep to your business or I'll shoot you and sell you for parts, too."

"I have to go," Hal said. "I have to go real bad."

"Then piss yourself."

Hal hiccupped. "I . . . can't."

I tried to catch Nicky's eye. There had to be something there. Something left from the little boy that used to come over to our house with his parents. "Nicky," I said. "You can't let this happen."

He ignored me.

Bayless continued as though I hadn't spoken. "We'll do the old man first. He's easy. But . . ." He pointed the gun at me. "This one's healthy. Prime product. If we take our time and do it right, we can make a bundle on her."

Ron Shade

The guy who didn't look like Bayless moved toward me, grinning and still swinging his flashlight. In his other hand he held a cell phone. "You got us, Viktor?" he asked, holding it up by his face in walkie-talkie mode.

"Yes, now shut off the damn light," the Russian's voice said over the phone. Loud enough for me to hear. "You're too bright."

He switched it off. "Okay, I'm moving in," he said.

Too bright? That meant he must have been watching my progress all along with a starlight scope. I just hoped it wasn't attached to a rifle.

Viktor's voice came back on. "Check for a pistol on him. Bayless said he's armed."

Now how the hell would Bayless know that? Unless . . . That damn Candice. Which meant she was in on the setup, and I was lured in like a chump. Suddenly, I worried about Alex.

"Make this easy on yourself, buddy," the Bayless stand-in said. He still had a simper stretched across his mug, and I could see in the dim light that he had crooked teeth. Small consolation, but something I hoped would tear the insides of his lips real good when my fist collided with them. "Turn around and put your hands behind you." He withdrew a pair of handcuffs from the back of his belt.

I knew if he got those on me, I was as good as dead. "Hey, no problem. I'll do whatever you say." I began to turn, extending my left arm toward him, and just as he was within striking distance I sent a whistling right into his substantial gut. This bent him over and I pivoted around behind him, grabbing him with both hands to use as a shield.

The shot cracked seconds later, striking him in the chest, exiting his back with a bloody *plop,* and whizzing by me, all in heartbeat. I took us both down to our knees, his breathing coming in wet snorts. One down, how many to go?

Grabbing his flashlight with my left hand I pointed it directly toward the area where I'd seen the muzzle flash. It had been a dull popping sound. The muzzle velocity said rifle, but probably with a silencer attached. I heard an accompanying grunt and figured I had a few seconds before the shooter's vision returned. I grabbed for the cell phone and took off at a cautious, but rapid, run toward the center of the area. A low wall popped up to my right and I went for it, slowing long enough to curl over the top, since I was unsure of what was on the other side. The last thing I needed right now was to fall into one of those dusky pits and break a leg.

A Russian voice screamed something from the cell phone. They must have had it rigged for multiple communications. Then another voice came on. I recognized this one.

"Viktor, what the hell's going on there?"

Bayless.

"Everything is under control. He's temporarily escaped. Oleg and I will find him."

Oleg . . . So I was going to have to deal with two Russkies. I hoped he wasn't *Spetsnaz,* too. But, hell, I was a Ranger. A Ranger with a five-shot revolver. But still, I knew I could take these assholes if I kept my head. *No look so tough* . . . Viktor's words that Alley had told me before they'd tried back in Chicago. Yeah, I could beat them. They didn't know about my minimag. Plus, I had the other guy's flashlight as well. I took out my cell phone and was getting ready to call Alex. If I could alert her, maybe Ross could get her and Hal out of harm's way before it was too late.

Then the real Bayless came back on the phone with something that chilled my blood: "Good. Make it quick. We've got the others."

No sense in trying to warn her now. I had to beat these guys or she was dead.

"I vill call you back vhen it's done," Viktor's voice said, then silence.

If they were ex-*Spetsnaz* they'd use standard military tactics. That meant that Oleg was probably somewhere to the west, working his way toward me with another starlight scope. I could hear them chatting in Russian on the phone. Noise discipline. I adjusted the volume to the lowest position and stuck it in my right-side pants' pocket. I put my cell in the opposite pocket after turning it completely off. No sense risking getting an inopportune call. I jammed the extra flashlight in my pocket with my cell, and took out the minimag and the snubbie. Still crouched down, I weighed my options. They had at least one starlight scope. Most likely two. That meant they'd be sweeping the area looking for me, but they wouldn't fire unless they had a clear shot, with no risk of a crossfire. Letting my eyes adjust further to the darkness, I spied a section of metal piping running off to my left. Barrier around a pool, most likely. About thirty feet beyond that was a square block building. A locker room, probably. Right now it offered me shelter. If I could get inside, I'd be out of sight. I could put a call in to 9-1-1 and maybe get some Las Vegas Metro boys on the way. The sound of the sirens would probably drive Viktor and his buddy Oleg running for the hills. But they could also pick off the officers who responded like sitting ducks. I'd have to try and convince the dispatchers exactly what they were going up against. Still, I knew the drill. They'd send a patrol car, maybe two officers to check out the report. No guarantees the guys would see us. And if they tried to investigate further . . .

I took a breath and began running at as fast a clip as I could toward the locker room building. Dust skipped the ground in front of me. I dove and rolled, using the powerful minimag beam to sweep in that direction, hoping it would buy me a few minutes with some backlash night blindness. I had to keep moving. I fired off a shot in the general direction and started another run.

I used the beam to check the area in front of me. It looked fairly clear, devoid of any barriers or junk. An open doorway loomed about fifteen feet in front of me. I covered the distance in about five seconds, slamming into the solid bricks as they offered a corridor that curled back into darkness. I pressed the button on the minimag and swept the interior as I walked. They'd probably track me here, but maybe there was a hiding place where I could get the drop on them, or at least one of them. If I could get myself one of those starlights, we'd be on level footing.

The beam swept over a man huddled against the wall. I jumped back and pulled out the gun, thinking he was one of them. A second later I realized he wasn't. He was dressed in rags and smelled like a pungent roadkill. His bleary eyes stared back at me, like the proverbial deer caught in the headlights.

"Don't hurt me!" he said.

"Who are you?"

"Please," his hands raised in front of his face. He was dressed in rags, with a long, wispy beard. Homeless. "No, no, I don't mean no harm. Don't hurt me!"

"I won't. Now keep your voice down." If he kept yelling he'd lead them right to us. "Sit down over there."

"No!" His eyes widened in terror as I realized a second too late that he'd seen the gun in my hand. He bounced off the wall in a full-out run for the door. I tried to move to cut him off, but with the strength borne of desperation, he stiff-armed me out of the way.

"Don't go out there," I yelled, but it was too late. He tore around the sectioned wall and disappeared. I followed, knowing he was another walking dead man. I peered around the edge of the corner, offering as little of my body as I could, the snubbie outstretched.

He made it maybe ten feet before the shot brought him down. I saw the muzzle flash and squeezed off three rounds. I think one of them hit, but ducked back just in time to avoid another hail of bullets. One shot left, dammit. What was I thinking? The son-of-a-bitch was dead as soon as he ran out from cover.

They'd be over to check on him shortly, thinking he was me. Then, when they realized he wasn't, they'd center on this area and flush me out. Maybe I'd hit one of them with my volley. Maybe not. Panic started to wrap its fingers around my spine.

No, I had a chance, I told myself. That poor bastard had

given me one. I took out the cell phone and tried to listen. Nothing. No merry Russian voices asking if it had been good hunting. I felt the edge of the wall and found some holes broken into the cement blocks. Maybe I could get on the roof. Searchers don't often look up, which is why snipers always like the high ground. Maybe it would give me a vantage point to get off another shot. It'd been poor ammo discipline to use up one of my precious five shots before, but it had been instinctual. Slipping the minimag and the gun into my back pockets, I gripped the broken sections of the blocks and began to climb. I got about halfway up when the block I'd gripped gave way, sending me sprawling. I hit hard on my back and clipped my head on the cement wall. Shaking off the pain, I got up and jumped for the wall again, using a more cautious climbing technique. This time I made it. The roof was flat and covered with dusty gravel. The remnant of an old air-conditioning unit was in the center, its frame now empty. I did a low crawl over to the side. I didn't risk using the minimag up here, for fear of giving away my position. I scanned the area. Something moved. Maybe thirty feet away, to my right, one of them was advancing, holding his rifle up and scanning through the scope. He brought the phone up and someone whispered in Russian on my phone. Open channel. Bad noise discipline, boys. From the voice, I didn't think it was Viktor. No reply. Viktor was probably letting poor Oleg go check the body. You go, buddy. Let me know what you find.

My foot brushed against a chunk of something. It moved. Reaching and feeling, I found a section of brick about the size of a book. I reached for it and brought it in front of me. Maybe I could toss it out there for a diversion. The homeless guy's body was maybe fifteen feet from the building, which gave me a pretty clear shot if Oleg gave me his back. I had one shot left, so I had to make it count. One shot, one hit, jump down and go for his rifle. It was my only chance to level the playing field. My fingers curled around the brick fragment, then released it. Too risky to try the toss. I'd need the minimag to illuminate him if I wanted to be sure of my aim. I stretched out, holding the flashlight alongside the barrel of the snubbie. When the time came, and I had target acquisition, I'd press the button to switch it on, aim, and pull the trigger. One shot, one hit, center mass.

Then I'd have to make the drop. The roof wasn't that high. Maybe fifteen feet or so. I'd done jumps off garage roofs when I was a kid. I'd jumped out of airplanes in the army. I should be able to handle a paltry fifteen feet. I hoped.

The hulking figure advanced, still looking through his scope, alternating between the twisted corpse and the surrounding terrain, maybe about twenty-five feet away. He kept the alternating pattern. Good. Maybe he wouldn't realize that it wasn't me until he got closer. Until it was too late. But . . . too late for whom?

One shot . . . One hit.

Why didn't I take Ross's Glock instead? He hadn't offered it, but apparently it hadn't done him too much good anyway. Shit. I still had to worry about rescuing Alex. I had to make this work.

One shot, one hit.

He moved to about ten feet from the corpse, lowering his rifle as he swept over it, obviously certain that I'd either changed clothes and grown a beard in the last ten minutes or so, or he'd shot the wrong guy. He was bent over too much. I needed a better target. I made a kissing sound with my lips and he straightened. I pressed the button illuminating him and fired a half a second later, releasing the minimag button as I did so. His legs twisted under him, and he folded onto himself. Knowing hesitation was death, I rolled to the left, away from the area where I assumed Viktor was watching. Bullets clipped the section of roof on the other side of the building. He knew where I was, and he'd be coming for me. I only hoped he wouldn't expect me to go for Oleg's rifle. I jammed the minimag into my pocket and stuck the empty gun in my belt. Gripping the edge of the roof, I dropped my legs over and swung down, losing my grip from the momentum and hitting the cement in a twisted heap. Pain shot up my legs to my side, and I knew I'd ripped the stitches on my arm, but I had no time to hurt. I took out the other flashlight and struggled to the edge of the building. I knew he was watching through his scope, so maybe, just maybe he'd follow the light. I switched on the flashlight, leaned back, and gave it a hard toss, watching its arc as I started my sprint toward fallen Oleg. And his rifle.

I made about ten steps before I heard a round whiz past me and I dove forward. Landing hard on my stomach, I held the minimag in my hand and pressed the button, sweeping its powerful beam toward where I thought he might be, as I scrambled toward the rifle. It must have bought me the precious few seconds I needed, because the spray of bullets went wide. My hands gripped the gun and felt an immediate sense of relief. It was an AK-47, but a scaled down model. With a scope. Now we were on even terms, but I was still a sitting duck, and he was a lot closer to targeting me than I was him. He knew the area I was moving toward. Using Oleg's body for cover, I laid the barrel of the rifle on his side. His head was twisted toward me, a few inches from mine, his dead eyes half open and glazed over. My bullet had caught him at the base of the throat. Lucky shot. I'd been aiming at his chest but firing from above can affect your sighting.

A bullet tore through him and whizzed by me. Obviously, Viktor knew exactly where I was and wasn't lamenting the demise of his buddy. I wanted to check Oleg's magazine, search him for additional mags, but another round smacked into him. That one didn't fully penetrate for some reason, but I couldn't stay here and wait to see how many he'd stop. I had two choices. Go left, back to the building, or right toward a swatch of tall palms about twenty feet away. I opted for the right, figuring he'd think I'd head for the thicker cover. But first, I wanted to give him a little taste of his own medicine. I squeezed off a round, and another, then moved in a low crouch. I hit the dirt and scrambled the final few feet, stirring the dust and the wispy scrubs. Bullets popped in the sand too close for comfort. I rolled next to the base of one of the palms. A ribbon of thorns prickled the backs of my hands. Staying prone, I put my right eye to the scope and saw the entire scene outlined in a field of clear green and black. Viktor was running for the building. He'd made the bad mistake of being too far from cover.

I gave him a slight lead time, and squeezed off a round. His arms flailed like he'd been poleaxed, and he tumbled forward, his rifle clattering off to his side. I figured it for a good hit, or he wouldn't have dropped his gun, but I was taking no chances. I immediately changed positions by rolling to the base of another tree. I took a few deep breaths and sighted him through the starlight scope again.

No movement.

There were so many things I wanted to do. Check the magazine to see how many rounds I had left . . . scan the rest of the area to make sure I wasn't being stalked by anyone else. But one thing I didn't hesitate on. I squeezed off another round into Viktor. His body reacted with the ever-so-slight jerking motion that told me he was feeling no pain.

Not so tough, I thought.

It took me about five more minutes to satisfy myself that there were no other assailants. They must have figured three were more than enough. I left them where they were and made a beeline back the way I'd come. They could lay there until the cops came to clean up this mess. I had to get back to the car and figure out a way to find Alex. I had half a magazine of ammo left, and I grabbed the one from Viktor's rifle as well. Taking out my cell phone I pressed the button turning it on. If I tried to call her, it would alert Bayless that I'd gotten the best of Viktor and his buddies. But how could I find them?

A message signal appeared on the screen and I checked my voice mail. George's happy voice came on.

"Hey, Ron, I've got some good news for you, buddy. You're not gonna believe this. I been doing some working while you been partying in Las Vegas. Give me a call and I'll give you the scoop. Bye."

I quickly dialed his cell number.

He answered on the second ring. "About time you fucking called."

"I been busy."

"So have I. Guess where I'm at?"

"Look, I ain't got time for games."

"Ooooh," he said. Then he got serious. "You all right?"

I took a deep breath, still trying to figure out what to do. Who to call. "Yeah, sorry. You know any coppers in Vegas?"

"You in some shit?"

"Up to my knees."

"Christ, I was afraid of this. No, I don't know anybody out there I can call. What you got?"

I debated telling him, but didn't want to get into a long-winded explanation or debate. He'd just tell me to call Las Vegas Metro, and let them take over. I didn't feel like sitting in a police station answering a million questions while Bayless still had Alex. "What you got?"

He didn't answer immediately, probably figuring out the reason I was holding back. "We hit Sunset Manor Funeral Home with a search warrant."

"I thought you didn't have any PC?"

"We didn't." He laughed. "Two uniforms happened to be doing a premise check of the place and found the back door had been kicked in. Investigating what was obviously a break-in, they did a security check of the building and guess what they found?"

"Surprise me."

"The guy's got a whole morgue in this place, and it's loaded with body parts. Legs, arms, torsos. I ain't never seen nothing like it. They also found a corpse. Big guy who appeared to have been gut-shot. Sound familiar?"

It had to be the Russkie from the alley.

"So anyway," he continued, "they knew Cate and Norris had been watching the place, so they backed off, called them, and we walked through a quickie warrant."

"Sounds like good police work."

"Yeah, I just wish I could put the guy who kicked in the back door in for a citizen commendation award. If we could ever find out who he is, that is." He laughed.

"How about if I just buy him dinner when I get back."

He laughed again, and it was a good sound to hear, even if it was half a continent away.

"We found something else that might interest you," he said. "Maybe where our buddy Nicky is hiding."

"Where's that?"

"Sunset Manor Funeral Home, Las Vegas."

"What?"

"He's got another location out that way. Thought you might want to cruise by and take a look."

It had to be it. That's where they'd taken Alex. "George, what's the address of the place?"

"You going over there now?"

"Just give it to me, dammit."

"Jesus, you don't have to get your undies in an uproar." He paused, then read off the address. I took out my pen and wrote it on my hand.

"Okay, I need a big favor."

"Name it."

"Call Las Vegas Metro and tell them they've got four dead guys in an old, abandoned water park adjacent to the Arabesque Hotel on Paradise."

"What? Oh, shit."

"Tell them who I am and vouch for me."

"You're gonna wait for them there, aren't you? So you can explain everything."

"Of course," I said, doing a fast trot toward the lights of the parking garage. After I rescued Alex.

Chapter 23

Alex St. James

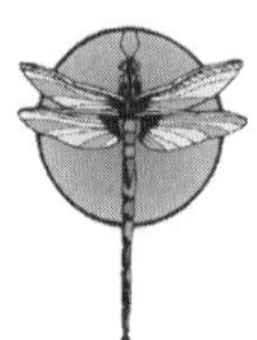

Nicky hovered close. Too close. His pupils were huge as he stared at me. No remorse—nothing resembling humanity behind those dark eyes. With uncertain movements he reached out for me. He leaned hungrily, his mouth opening for a kiss.

Repulsed, I jumped away, my backside hitting the counter. Trapped.

Nicky halted, and held his breath for a moment as he fingered my hair. "It feels just like I thought it would," he said, his voice raw. "Like silk." He moved closer. His sweet cologne coaxed bile up my throat, but there was no getting away. "I've got a place set up for us, Alex. In the residence. Just you and me."

Bayless interrupted. "Back off, Romeo. Plans have changed." He pointed to me. "You. Reporter. Free up the fat guy's hands."

I didn't move.

Nicky's jaw dropped. "What do you mean plans changed? You told me that before this was over . . ."

"That was before they tracked us to Vegas. If they told anybody what they were up to—and I'm sure they did—this place is going to come under scrutiny fast. We have to get them both done tonight and get rid of all trace before morning."

Nicky rubbed his leg. "I've done everything you told me to do . . ."

"Yeah and look where you got us."

"Come on," Nicky said. "If you keep an eye on the old fart and just give me . . ."

"I said plans changed. Now get moving." Bayless glowered at me. "And I told *you* to free the old asshole's hands."

Nicky squinted at Bayless, and for a moment I thought Nicky might push it. If he did, and if they were distracted, I might have a chance to try something. But Nicky did as he was told and reluctantly moved away from me.

Hal's lower lip trembled and tears gathered at the end of his jaw, dropping onto the tile floor. He wasn't paying attention because I had to physically turn him around in order to get at his duct-taped hands. He obeyed without looking up.

I pulled at the tape, which twisted and ripped at my tugging. Hal wobbled, and I was afraid he'd fall, so I gently pushed him forward, to lean him against the counter. Nicky kept busy next to us.

Hal pressed his forehead against the wall cabinets. The man had nothing left. His hands were limp as I worked at them. He'd given up.

Nicky was about three steps to my right, Bayless about five steps farther. The whole time I worked, I kept watch on the two of them, hoping for an opening—a chink in their armor.

"How long will this take?" Bayless asked Nicky.

Nicky shrugged. He'd returned the Glock to his waistband and was pulling out instruments from the storage above the countertop: sharp stainless steel things. Tubing. Scissors. Instead of answering Bayless, he pulled out two disposable jumpsuits, two paper face masks and two sets of goggles. "Here, put these on."

Bayless backed away, hands up. "Not a chance. This is your thing." The gun pointed toward the ceiling.

In the split second he directed the weapon away, I thought to rush him, grab the gun and hope that Nicky wouldn't react fast enough or think fast enough to pull his gun out. But I'd have to run past Nicky to reach Bayless. And I knew I'd never make it.

If it'd been Ross with me, we might have had a chance.

Hal let loose a groan so loud it startled us all. His knees began to buckle and he clenched his eyes shut.

Bayless whipped the barrel in our direction again. "What the hell is wrong with you?"

Hal's voice was rasping. "I *really* gotta go."

Ignoring Hal, Nicky shoved the protective wear at Bayless a second time. "Take these. Put them on. There's going to be a lot of blood."

Bayless shook his head. "I'm not doing the dirty work. That's what you get paid for."

"I can't do them by myself. Not if we want them both done tonight."

Bayless grimaced. "Shit."

Hal held his hands just below his stomach. "Please."

Carrying his own protective wear, Nicky moved to the near-side of the porcelain table. He turned to face us. "You," he said to Hal. "Strip."

Next to me, Hal started to retch.

I grabbed his arm. "Don't do it, Hal," I said, hoping I sounded strong, desperately trying to stall. "Make them do it for you. Don't make it easy."

Not that he could. His knees finally did give out and he dropped to the floor. "I can't," he said. "I gotta go."

"Shit," Bayless said again.

Unperturbed, Nicky kept working. He donned the white Tyvek-like garment, and pulled on heavy rubber gloves. Turning his back to us, he sprayed the porcelain table with a strong disinfectant that stung my throat and made me cough.

Hal continued to moan.

Bayless shouted, "Shut up!" He pointed his gun at Hal. "You shut up or you get one in your head right this second."

"Hal's not kidding," I said, drawing their attention to me. I needed to see the looks in their eyes. I needed to gauge them. Did they see me as a threat? Did they think they had me beat? Let them think I was helpless. Then maybe they would let their guard down, just a little. Maybe then I'd have a chance.

I cleared my throat, tried to make it sound as though I were on the verge of breaking down myself. It didn't require much acting ability—I was shaking as I spoke. "He has a problem," I continued, studying them both as I talked. "I mean, like a urologist kind of problem. He's not faking."

"Too bad," Bayless said.

Nicky twisted around. "Just take him to the damn bathroom."

Bayless made a face that told me he didn't like taking orders from Nicky. "Like hell."

"You want his parts? Then let him do his business. The minute I stop the bastard's heart he's gonna piss and shit all over the place." Nicky grimaced. "Get him out there and empty the guy out. And while you're there, make him strip. I'm not undressing a stiff if he can do it himself first." He leaned over to the shelving unit again, this time pulling out the trocar. He affixed the sharp, three-sided point to the end of the two-foot metal pole and was about to hook up the other end to a waste tube, when Bayless interrupted.

"You take him," he said. "I'll keep an eye on her."

Nicky started to protest.

"There's no way I'm trusting you alone with the girl," Bayless said. "You take the bastard to the shitter while I keep her quiet."

Nicky worked his jaw for a minute before finally giving in. "Come on, asshole," he said, grabbing Hal's arm and hoisting him up.

"You take orders from Bayless, huh?" I said, "All this time we thought you were the brains of the outfit." I shook my head as if disappointed. My stomach gave a lurch when I thought about Shade. We'd misread the structure of this organization. Badly. Where was Shade now?

I tried again. "Guess you're just a little worker bee, huh?"

Bayless came closer. "Shut up, bitch."

I kept talking. "Nicky, this guy sees you as the next weakest link. You kill me and Hal, and things will get hot. Your boss here isn't just going to skip town again. He's going to get rid of you. Just like he did Dr. Colon."

Bayless pointed the gun at my forehead. "I said 'Shut up.' "

When Nicky stopped hustling Hal to stare at me, I knew I'd struck a nerve.

C'mon, I breathed.

"The one thing I've always hated about you, Alex, is your goddamn superior attitude. Even when we were kids you were always trying to make me do the things *you* thought were right. You were a little goody-two-shoes then, and you haven't changed." The goggles and the face mask around his neck, combined with the white paper jumpsuit made him look clinical—and more sinister than ever. "I'm going to enjoy taking you apart, piece by precious piece."

He was out the door in moments, taking Hal and my last bit of hope with him.

The moment they were gone, Bayless got a terrible smile on his face. Gooseflesh popped out all over my already chilled body. We were facing one another, about five feet apart. Maybe six. My left hip skimmed the countertop where Nicky had been preparing his tools. I worked at focusing on Bayless and not allowing my gaze to waver. I had an idea. A terrifying idea. I couldn't allow myself to telegraph it.

"You know," he said, "Nick might've had a good plan after all. Why don't you strip now. Save us time later."

Bayless had relaxed his grip on the gun, he'd even dropped his hand to his side. Poor baby—was the firearm getting too heavy to hold? Please. I counted on that.

"Not a chance."

He started to bring the gun up again, so I raised my hands.

"Okay, okay."

My easy acquiescence made him smile again. He lowered the weapon and leaned his elbow on the countertop, gun pointed to the floor. I noticed his trigger finger trailed along the gun's barrel in the "safe ready" position. Someone had trained him well.

"What are you waiting for?" he asked.

I bit my lip, then leaned down to take off my left shoe, then my right. I held them by their heels in my right hand.

"Cut the shit. Get to the good stuff," he said. "Take off your top."

"Okay." Like hell, I thought.

I tossed my shoes to the far side of the room. It was a quick move and it startled Bayless. His eyes shot toward the sound and in that breathless moment, I grabbed the trocar.

It took less than two beats for Bayless to turn back, reacting to my frantic grab, but it was a two-second advantage and I didn't wait. With the memory of Nicky demonstrating the force with which a trocar needs to be shoved into the resilient skin of a human body, I thrust the deadly instrument straight into Bayless's chest.

He screamed.

The trocar chunked in with a satisfying sound. Still screaming, he dropped to the floor. Blood spurted—fast and furious. As he fell over I lost my grip on the tool.

From the ground he pulled his gun hand up—his eyes wild with the panic I'd been feeling moments before.

I kicked at his gun, but he didn't drop it.

It went off, the shot going wide, hitting something metal. The hot casing popped out and struck Bayless in the face as he struggled to get back up. I kicked again, connecting hard this time. He lost his grip on the gun for a moment, but I nearly lost my balance, and he grabbed the weapon before I could.

"You bitch." His voice was stronger than it should have been.

We were working in milliseconds here. I knew the gun was coming back and it was coming for me. Acting on instinct alone, I jammed my foot into his chest, yanked out the bloody trocar, and just as the gun went off again, I stabbed him in the throat.

The bullet grazed me. I recognized that I'd been hit with a strange sort of dispassion as heat skimmed across my left arm.

I had to ignore it. There were people coming. Running. I heard shouting—Candice. I heard Nicky telling her to shut up.

I dropped to the floor, furiously working to pry Bayless's fingers from the gun's grip, but they were frozen there. A death grip, I thought grimly.

Until he coughed.

Not a death grip.

The warning came too late. His left hand reached up and with inhuman strength he grabbed a handful of my shirt, pulling me backward. "Not so fast, bitch," he said through gritted teeth.

Although blood spurted from the gash in his throat, I must not have hit the carotid artery like I'd hoped. On my back, atop Bayless's bloody chest, I kicked, slamming my foot against his right arm, my arms too short to reach the gun as he yanked me backward. But I thought I heard it clatter to the floor.

How the hell did this guy have the strength to fight me? How was he able to talk?

I looked. I hadn't gotten his throat. I'd gotten him in the chest. Right side. Damn. The two-foot trocar, still wedged there, wiggled as we fought for control.

The door banged open. Nicky's voice was a scream. "Alex! Get away from him or I'll kill you."

In one split second I made my choice. Fight or flight.

If I flew, I'd die.

I fought.

I rolled onto my knees, and with two hands, grabbed the silver trocar and jammed it sideways as hard as I could, to the left side of Bayless's chest. Bayless howled as the sharp point encountered resistance, but I plowed through. His body spasmed.

I scuttled backwards, grabbed Bayless's gun and opened the nearest cabinet door for cover. I crouched behind it. It wouldn't do much, but—

Nicky fired one round. It went wide.

He looked stunned that he hadn't hit me.

Muscle memory took control. My firearms instructor had forced me to practice this dozens of times, and now I thanked God that she had.

Over the top of the cabinet door I aimed the semiautomatic at Nicky's center mass. I took a quick breath, let it out, and squeezed.

Nicky's legs crumbled beneath him and he dropped to the ground.

"Bob! Bob! What's going on in there?"

Candice screamed when she saw Nicky's prone form, red cascading all over the paper jumpsuit. When she spotted her husband's body, the trocar sticking up like a stake through Dracula's heart, she went white and passed out.

Thank God.

I stood, taking a long moment to catch my breath—to try to quell the shaking of my heart, my hands, my suddenly weak legs. There was blood everywhere. I closed my eyes for a precious moment and tried to focus.

Hal. I needed to find Hal.

I needed to call Shade. Maybe it wasn't too late to warn him.

I needed to dial 9-1-1.

The gun stayed in my right hand. These guys were all down for the count, but I wasn't taking chances now.

I was in my stocking feet and all the blood on the floor made it hard to walk without slipping.

Nicky was still alive, moaning in pain. Blood spurted from his side. I didn't know for sure, but it didn't look like a mortal wound. I kicked the Glock away from him, then picked it up. Two-Gun Alex. As I crouched next to Bayless, he gave a long, rattled cough and then stopped breathing entirely. He was dead. This time for sure.

And I was glad. My heart raced with disturbing elation. I'd killed him. And I was glad that I had. What was happening to me?

Candice would have to be tied up quickly, but now that the immediate danger had passed, my arm began to throb. I knew I couldn't do this myself.

As I searched the area for a phone, I called out, "Hal?"

"Alex?" his voice, coming from the next room was disbelieving, hopeful. It sounded as if he stood just outside the door held ajar by Candice's unconscious form.

Just as I was about to call out to Hal again, I heard someone coming in from the back door. I raised the pistol in a two-handed grip. Hands shaking, I was about to shout to the new intruder that I had a gun, when he burst into the room. My knees went out when I saw him. "Shade!" I said. I put the gun down. He was filthy, scratched, and bleeding. But never had I been so happy to see anyone in my life.

"Alex!" He seemed about to say more, but stopped as he took in the scene around me. "Are you . . . okay?"

Though my arm smarted something fierce, I nodded. "Better now."

Outside the door, Hal whimpered.

"Come on in," I said. "It's okay."

He shuffled through the door. Naked as a newborn.

Shade looked at Hal, then at me. He smirked. "Am I interrupting something?"

Chapter 24

Ron Shade

I watched and waited in vain for my suitcase to come through the opening and onto the carousel at Midway Airport. It felt good to be back in Chicago again after the hectic past three days in Vegas, even though the two hours we'd lost flying back eastward had robbed us of the afternoon. Each new piece of luggage that fell out initially looked promising, only to be revealed as someone else's. One of Alex's purple monstrosities came rotating around and she moved forward. With a nod to the bandage on her arm, I reached down and grabbed the suitcase, setting it on the tiled floor in front of her.

"There you go," I said with a grin.

She smiled back and nodded. It was a nice smile, too.

We'd actually been getting along better the past few days. Maybe it was the lack of time we spent together. After I'd arrived to save the day and rescue her at the funeral home, I realized she didn't need any slightly shopworn white knights. The residual toughness I'd seen flashes of in our conversations had asserted itself, and she'd taken care of business. More than that, she'd kicked ass. I locked the AK-47 in the trunk and threw myself on the mercy and understanding of the Las Vegas Metro Police when they showed up. And then I told them where to find the other bodies.

We spent the first few hours getting bandaged and stitched, then spent the next two and a half days explaining, giving statements, and talking to prosecutors. Cate and Norris arrived from CPD, as well as Lulinski, who'd somehow managed to finagle a free trip to Vegas on the department's dime. They re-interviewed Alex, Hal, and me, and then interrogated Candice and good old Nicky. He'd survived, but Alex's bullet had pierced his upper bowel. The son-of-a-bitch would be crapping in a bag for a long time to come. I figured it would make him a very popular man in whatever prison tier he ended up in. And when Clark County Nevada was finished trying him, he faced a host of charges back in Illinois. Candice was singing like a yellow canary, and Nicky's lawyer father had flown out to advise him to remain silent. I almost felt sorry for the old man, having a loser like that for a son. I hoped that Deputy MacMahan would rate a free trip to Vegas since their traffic fatality had morphed into a homicide.

Even Big Dick Mackenzie was happy. So happy, he hadn't even mentioned anything about my big recovery fee or the extensive expense report when he called to tell me that the body they'd exhumed from Robert Bayless's grave had more PVC pipe than bone in it. Looks like Nicky had cashed in on poor Howie Rybak as well. MWO stood to get back all of their money from Manus. The Attorney General was looking into that. And although I didn't ask, I figured that the first Mrs. Bayless would be able to keep a certain portion of the original payoff. After all, the prick really was dead this time. Alex had seen to that, bless her heart.

I smiled at her and grabbed the second purple suitcase coming around the bend. Hal's stuff had miraculously been among the first to be unloaded, so they were just waiting on me. But after all we'd been through, I figured they'd wait. Even though she'd spent most of what little free time we had in Vegas filming stuff for her story, we had managed a nice dinner at Binyon's the night before. Sort of a celebratory conclusion to the last leg of our Nevada adventure. In spite of Hal's presence, it had been so pleasant that I was feeling confident enough to invite her for round two now that we were back on home ground. I glanced down the carousel. Still no sign of my suitcase.

"Hey, Alex," Hal said, "watch my stuff while I run to the men's room, okay?"

She nodded. I grinned, although only partly because his departure smacked of serendipitous convenience. Time was a-wasting. Taking a deep breath, I turned to her and flashed what I hoped was my most dazzling smile.

"I sure hope he gets to that urologist tomorrow," I said.

"Don't knock him," she said. "His problem helped save my life back there."

She'd told me in detail what had happened, and I marveled again at this tough chick that I'd originally figured was a high-maintenance whiner. Man, was I wrong.

"Say," I said, making my windup, "I was wondering if you'd—"

"There you are!" a voice boomed. Both of our heads turned, and I saw the short man striding toward us like a bantam rooster. "I've been looking all over for you."

"Bass," Alex said. "What are you doing here?"

"I'm here to get you and Hal. I knew if I sent someone else they'd blow it all to hell." He was obviously ignoring me. "I saw him going to take a leak, and he told me you were over here. Come on, I got a limo waiting. We got to get busy on this story if we want to beat the competition."

"You remember Ron Shade, don't you?" she said, turning my

way and showing me that delightful smile again. "He's got a prominent place in our story."

"Yeah," Bass said, giving me the meagerest of nods. "You got your stuff? Hal said you had it all. Let's go."

"Bass," she said, "Ron and I were talking."

"We don't have time for you to talk," he said. "Come on. Let's go."

It was her boss, so I had to be polite. I grinned at him, took another deep breath, and started to place my hand on her elbow to steer her away from him for some privacy when a feminine voice sprang up next to me.

"Ron?"

I turned. A dark-haired young woman stared up at me with a lovesick expression on her face. It was a face I'd tried hard to forget. Laurie Kittermann. Her arms encircled my neck and she pressed herself to me tight enough to let everybody know we'd once been closer.

"Laurie," I managed to mutter. I glanced at Alex, hoping she'd see my expression of surprise and alarm. But all I saw was her raised right eyebrow as she studied Laurie's extended embrace. She was telling me how great it was to see me, and how it was fate, and all that. When she finally dropped her arms from my neck, I saw Alex's boss ushering her away. He'd grabbed her small suitcase, and she was wheeling the larger one.

I started to call after her, but a group of new arrivals suddenly surged in between us.

"Ron," Laurie said. "There's someone I want you to meet." She held my arm and looked around. Suddenly she flashed that beatific, I'm-in-love smile, as a blond-haired guy about her age sauntered up with a similar looking simper. "This is Dirk." Her dark eyes beamed, and she held up her left hand, showing off a ring with a huge diamond riding on it. "We're on our way to visit his parents. We're getting married next month."

Dirk shook my hand after the introduction and said that Laurie had told him all about me, and how I'd solved her sister's murder and saved her life as well.

I'll bet she had. I looked around again, trying to spot Alex, but she was nowhere to be seen.

My suitcase came around on the ramp, giving me the chance I needed to break the conversation. I wished Laurie and Dirk luck, told them to keep in touch, and beat feet out of there, claiming to have a ride waiting.

I looked around one more time to try to see Alex, but she was nowhere around. Outside, I knew there'd be a whole bunch of limos and cabs in the pick-up lane, and I had no idea where she'd gone. Finding her now would be like looking for a four-leaf clover in a field of daisies. With an air of defeat, I headed over toward the exit with my suitcase and gym bag so I could go catch the shuttle bus.

One rattled by. Just missed it.

The hell with it. With all I'd been through, I deserved a little convenience. I headed over to the line of waiting cabs and grabbed the first one. One more for the expense account.

As I rode, I realized things could have turned out worse. I'd been to Vegas and back, gone ten rounds with an ex-*Spetsnaz* and a walking dead man, and still had the title. Even though I didn't get the girl at the end, I still had a lot to be thankful for, and it sure had been one hell of an adventure.

Yeah, I could've done worse.

But, I thought as Alex's smile floated through my mind's eye, I could've done better, too. A lot better.

ALEX ST. JAMES

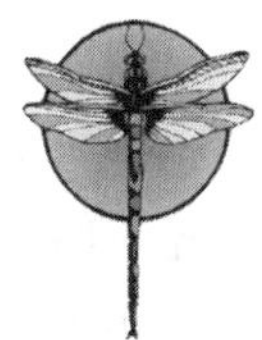

For the first time, I was truly happy to have Bass around. He'd prevented me from making a fool of myself. I was so sure I'd read Shade's signals correctly, but then out of the blue—his girlfriend zoomed in to tackle him in a bear hug. Turned out my first instincts were right, and Mr. Flirtatious was a player. I guess I shouldn't have been surprised that he had someone to meet him at the airport.

Lucky me—I had Bass.

I massaged my arm a bit—the graze still hurt—but not nearly as much as doing something stupid would have.

As we trotted around the fencing that surrounded Midway's luggage carousels I thought about how this adventure had all started with my adoption quest. Keeping pace with me, Bass blathered about not making the driver wait because he was paying by the hour, but I tuned him out. Now that Nicky was incapacitated—and incarcerated—there was little chance "Uncle" Larry would find it in his heart to help me.

At one point I'd considered telling Shade about my futile efforts. After all, he was a private investigator. But something had warned me to hold back. Now, I was glad I had.

"Over here," Bass said.

I felt my eyes widen. "You were serious. You really do have a limo."

A uniformed chauffeur held the back door open for me. I smiled and slid sideways onto the cushy leather seats.

Bass was jumping up trying to wave Hal over. He must have

spotted him because within moments Bass had climbed in next to me. "Hal's coming," he said.

This was one of those stretch limos, and I chose one of the sideways seats, leaning my back against the driver's wall, crossing my feet on the seat in front of me. "What's the occasion?" I asked, gesturing outward to indicate this surprising level of luxury.

"Nothing but the best for my ace reporter," he said.

I leaned my head back till it bumped the acrylic partition. Something was up. Right now, however, I wasn't in the mood to deal with it. I didn't ask. I decided I didn't want to know.

But Bass fidgeted. "I didn't want anything to delay our filming."

I waited. He'd spill it.

He didn't disappoint. "Gabriela's waiting for us at the station right now."

I sat up. My feet hit the floor. "Gabriela? This is my story."

"Yes, but—"

"No buts, Bass. This one is mine. I've been the good soldier, I've taken a backseat to Gabriela since I accepted this promotion. But she's got nothing to do with this story. I'm the one who nearly got killed. I'm the one who—" I stopped talking. Bass wasn't budging. I'd known the man long enough to read the rigid expression on his face.

I was alive. That was all that really mattered.

I repositioned myself, trying to relax again. I stared out the window as though I didn't care. But I did.

The chauffeur finished loading my luggage as Hal lumbered into the vehicle next to Bass. Hal groaned as he adjusted himself into a comfortable position. "Damn sciatica," he said. "Still bothers me."

I heard muffled suitcase movements and the occasional *whump* from the trunk.

"Okay, tell me," I said to Bass. "Why is Gabriela getting the story I worked so hard for?"

"This one is big," he said. "You're good, but you're not seasoned. We need Gabriela's star power on this one. And I don't know what you're so pissed about. It's not like we're cutting you out. Gabriela will be interviewing you. It's kind of like the two of you will share top billing." He framed imaginary graphics with his hands. "Heroic reporter uncovers grisly body-part black market. What do you think?" Without waiting for my answer he continued, "Anyway, we already have footage of you from Vegas. Hal overnighted his tapes to me while you and Shade were getting grilled by the Las Vegas cops."

I shook my head in disbelief.

Bass fingered his jawline. "I can see the two of you getting a Davis Award for this."

"Me and Hal?" I asked.

"Nah . . . you and Gabriela."

"Gabriela?" I sputtered. "Like she had anything to do with this story. She sat like a princess back here in Chicago, getting her nails done, while I was driving a steel stake through a murderer's heart."

Bass nodded. "Pretty much."

There was no making this guy feel guilty. I decided to stop trying.

I leaned back again and stared out the window. The trunk slammed, and the chauffeur made his way around the passenger side, checking our doors as he did so, to finally take his place behind the wheel. I sighed, and watched the crowd, ignoring the new jabber between Bass and Hal.

Just as the limo pulled away from the curb, Shade emerged from the baggage claim double doors.

He pulled his suitcase, heading toward the cab stand. Alone.

I sat up again, wondering what happened to his girlfriend.

She was nowhere to be seen.

With an unreadable expression on his face, Shade yanked open the first cab's door and got in with his gym bag, while the driver stuck the suitcase in the trunk. A moment later the cab pulled away.

Shade. All by himself. I wondered about that.

"You're forgetting something," Bass said, snapping me back to attention.

"What's that?"

"The homeless story."

"What about it?"

"This investigation—the body parts conspiracy—is great stuff. It's going to help us kill the competition." He wore a sneaky grin. "But—"

Impatient now, I asked, "But what, Bass?"

"You never actually produced the story you were assigned." The grin grew wider. "Not that I'm suggesting anything . . . mind you . . . I'm just saying—maybe you should think twice before you give me a hard time about Gabriela's involvement. I'd be happy to assign you the homeless story again." His eyes glittered. "And this time, I'll expect results."

ABOUT THE AUTHORS

Michael A. Black's first novel, *A Killing Frost* (Five Star, 2002), was recently re-released by Dorchester Publishing. Dorchester also just introduced Mike's newest series, with *Random Victim.* He's written eight novels, including two others in the Ron Shade series, *Windy City Knights* and the Lovey Award winner for Best PI Series in 2007, *A Final Judgment.* He's currently a sergeant on the Matteson, Illinois Police Department. Please visit www.michaelablack.com.

Julie Hyzy's first two novels in the Alex St. James series are *Deadly Blessings* and *Deadly Interest. Deadly Interest* won the Lovey Award for Best Traditional Mystery in 2007. Her most recent book about the first female White House chef, *State of the Onion,* came out in January from Berkley Prime Crime. Please visit www.juliehyzy.com.